The Flagon was a supersonic high-altitude interceptor. The Harrier was primarily a low-level support aircraft, and Dover was keeping it low over the water. The Flagon would have to come to him.

Anxiously, he searched the skies around and above him. Back on the stick! His 875 pounds of body weight, reflecting the 5-G pullup, pushed down into his seat pan. He had the Flagon inside his 30-degree acquisition cone, the hot exhaust of the Soviet interceptor fully exposed to his weapons. *So long, Ivan. David is about to apply the rock to the forehead of the big guy.* A Sidewinder rocketed off Dover's left wingtip, its hungry heat-seeking eye already feeling the warmth of the Flagon's fire. The Soviet jet disintegrated as the American missile entered its glowing tailpipe.

"Break right! Break right!" came an excited call from Tango Boy. Dover understood instantly. The second Flagon was on him, closing for the kill. He pulled his legs back into the seat stirrups, reached over his head and locked his fingers around the ejection pull-ring . . .

ALPHA BUG

M.E.Morris

POCKET BOOKS

New York   London   Toronto   Sydney   Tokyo

This novel is a work of fiction. Names, characters, places and incidents are either the product of the author's imagination or are used fictitiously. Any resemblance to actual events or locales or persons, living or dead, is entirely coincidental.

POCKET BOOKS, a division of Simon & Schuster, Inc.
1230 Avenue of the Americas, New York, N.Y. 10020

Copyright © 1986 by M. E. Morris
Cover artwork copyright © 1988 Ron Lesser

Published by arrangement with Presidio Press
Library of Congress Catalog Card Number: 86-8133

ISBN: 0-671-63668-5

First Pocket Books printing February 1988

10 9 8 7 6 5 4 3 2 1

POCKET and colophon are trademarks of
Simon & Schuster, Inc.

Printed in the U.S.A.

For Toogie

The story you are about to read is not science fiction.
Only the characters and plot are make-believe.
The technology, regretfully, exists today.

Chapter
1

Joe Dover stood in the warm rays of the midsummer sun and squinted in disbelief at the words typed on the single-page letter. *Letter?* Hell, the piece of paper was a set of written *orders*. He was tempted to place the Navy Department communiqué back in his roadside mailbox. But the old juices were back.

Wondering how he could make the necessary arrangements to meet the unreasonable deadline in the orders, he took his time walking back toward the main house.

Six hundred and forty acres wasn't a big ranch by anybody's standards, but it was his patch of Colorado and he was just getting the feel of it. In fact, he had owned it barely long enough to tell the bulls from the cows in his small breeding herd of Black Angus. He had hocked his soul for the thick-chested beasts after using all of his savings to buy the choice piece of valley pasture northwest of Montrose.

Besides, he was thirty-six years old and had already given the government thirteen years of his life, as well as his left eye. Subconsciously, he raised his left hand and made a minor adjustment to the black flap. The feel of the soft suede caused him to grin. An eye patch over a glass eye. What a conservative. Almost like wearing both a belt and suspenders.

For a moment he paused, idly staring across the road into the late morning purple haze cloaking the nearby mountains. The Colorado sky was tourist blue and cloudless. A thin ribbon of white condensation stretched from the western horizon to almost overhead where he stood, at its edge the faint winged silhouette of a military fighter. He knew well the magnificent view that was sliding beneath the speedy jet. But it would be flat to him now, the fine edge of the sparkling scene indiscernible with only one side of his vision triangle still intact. What the hell.

Not that he really regretted it, all things considered. After all, he had been one of the fair-haired boys, and that heady experience would carry him through plenty cold Colorado winters. No doubt about that. A towheaded jet jockey with the striking blue irises and hawk nose of the natural born fighter pilot, he had graduated at the top of his Navy test pilot class at Patuxent River, Maryland. The big boys must have had their eyes on him for he hadn't even completed his first test and evaluation project before they tapped him for the space program.

Five feet eleven, with a soccer player's lithe frame that carried 175 pounds of lean meat and muscle as if it had been chiseled on, he had been the picture-book astronaut. The boyish grin as much as his flying skill and quick grasping intellect had helped NASA pull a pile of megabucks from the halls of Congress. There were other qualifications, such as his stubborn Slavic heritage and complete dedication, that had moved him up the career ladder over the heads of more senior and longer-tenured members of the elite space community. But that had been the nature of the space game and he had reveled in it. Whether it had been a class in astrophysics, a tight formation cross country flight, or an hour on the sands of the beachside volleyball court at Canaveral, his performance was just a shade above everybody else's. Always the consummate spaceman, he had been destined for greater things.

Then, the *Columbia* accident. With his mission commander incapacitated by a freak oxygen explosion on the flight deck of the delta-winged space shuttle, he had manually brought the crippled spacecraft through reentry and to a flawless approach to the sun-seared sands at Edwards. Only a last minute glitch in the landing gear's extension system had prevented him from making a textbook landing. Even after the left main gear collapsed, he had held the *Columbia's* wing level until the wind over it died and it dropped. A violent skid twisted the forward section of the deep-throated fuselage with such force that one of the windscreen panels popped out and slivers of glass from its chipped edges flew into the cabin. A quarter-inch dart sliced into Dover's left eyeball, and his glory days were over.

Medical retirement, they had called it. That gave him a few bucks monthly pension and a disability tax credit, and with the cash he'd saved plus the extra he'd earned from the NASA fringe benefits, he had at least been able to buy his piece of Colorado high country.

There was a period of personal adjustment, but once he was over the mental shock of finding himself in the company of millions of other noncelebrities who went about their days' labors unnoticed, he began to enjoy it. Not that he didn't miss the old days. Even the casual sight of a contrail such as the one still overhead reminded him of how it once had been. Still, he considered himself to be a fortunate man. The ranch was a dream he'd just reached a little early.

Now, all that remained was to find a wife and start a family. Fortunately—for that purpose—he had settled in a state that had an abundance of eligible and desirable women, from the healthy mountain folk to the sophisticated lovelies of cosmopolitan Denver, not to mention the full breasted and tight thighed snow bunnies that were all over Ski Country, U.S.A. The hunt was on, and a pleasant hunt it was.

But now, the letter.

The damn thing was still dangling from his hand. He scanned it once more before refolding it and sliding it back inside the envelope. A thousand thoughts passed through his mind as he continued back toward the main house. His lone hired hand was ambling around the side of the single-story frame structure as Dover stepped up onto the front porch.

"You look as if you just stepped in somethin' and don't wanna look down," observed the old cowboy. He wore his leathery skin of sixty winters over a collection of oddly shaped bones that seemed to clank as he walked, and the only excess flesh on his body was a small protuberance that pushed out the front of his never-washed Levi's just below the silver belt buckle. Animal-hide cheeks hung down each side of a nose that could only be described as Greco-western, and they swung back along his skull to support a pair of large ears which featured lobes the size of quarters. Dover swore they moved in a strong wind. He had ranched and worked cattle since he had been able to sit a horse, which was probably well before he started to walk. He still didn't do it well, rocking from side to side over a stringbean pair of legs that could never be brought close enough at the knees to stop a runaway hog. In the short time they had been together—he had come with the property—Dover had learned a great deal, not just from watching the ancient wrangler work but also from picking his mind as they sat the long summer evenings on the porch and talked. The cowboy was a pretty fair cook, too, and their relationship had early on taken the flavor of partners rather than gentleman rancher and hired hand.

"Would you believe it, Carl? I've got orders to active duty."

"No, wouldn't," replied the old hand. "What they gonna do with a one-eyed soldier?"

"Navy, Carl. I was in the Navy."

"All's same to me." Carl scraped his boots on one of the untrimmed porch boards and lowered his six-foot frame into his own version of an Indian squat. "We ain't goin' t' war, are we?"

"No, nothing like that. I report to Space Command headquarters, over east of Colorado Springs."

Carl pulled his legs farther under him and scratched one ankle as if the devil were chewing on it. "How long you gonna be gone?"

"I don't know. I don't even know what they intend to do with me."

"Screwed-up government. They know you only got one eye?"

"I'd like to think so." Dover watched Carl pull himself back up on his feet and slap the dust off his jeans. He knew the cowboy could handle the place while he was gone, so his plans for the ranch could continue. "Carl, you'll have to take care of things until I get back. It may be some kind of mix-up, or a special short time project. I've got to make a call. They've got a July 31st reporting date on this thing. That's only three days away."

"We're goin' t'war."

"No, we're not, Carl." Dover went inside and sat at the kitchen table while he dialed the operator. After a few minutes explaining whom he wanted to reach, he heard the line begin to ring.

"United States Space Command Headquarters," announced a crisp female voice.

"Personnel, please," requested Dover.

"Just a moment, sir." There was a click, a short buzz, another click, and a male voice. "Personnel. Staff Sergeant Peters."

Dover explained his situation and asked to speak with the Personnel Officer. The sergeant put him on hold and then apparently transferred the call to Operations. Dover didn't know if he should feel relieved or upset that the service way of doing things had not changed.

The Operations Duty Officer confirmed the urgency of the reporting date and time specified in Dover's orders. Beyond that, everything else was classified, and no, the

Director of Operations was not in and there was nobody else who could expand on the orders.

As Dover hung up, Carl came into the kitchen and pulled out a skillet and a pair of saucepans. "If we're goin' t'war, they're being mighty goddamned quiet about it," he mumbled. "Fry bread and chili okay?"

Dover's thoughts were still on his frustrating phone call. "What?"

"Lunch. Fry bread and chili?"

"We always have fry bread and chili."

Carl had already dumped a cold bowl of thick chili from the refrigerator into one of the saucepans and was starting a doughball in the other. "Pissed?" he asked.

"Sorry, Carl. No, just a little out of sorts. Couldn't get any info on the phone." They did have fry bread and chili a lot, but Dover had to admit that Carl's fry bread was the equal of any Indian's and his chili was right off the back of a chuck wagon.

Dover hated to admit it, but he was excited. He had thought it was all over with the military. Maybe not. As long as it was something operational, not some P.R. trip around the states or back to patting the ample bottoms of Congress to keep the NASA budget viable. He'd go ahead and report in, then decide if he wanted to raise holy hell about the short notice recall.

After lunch, Dover remained at the kitchen table and penned a list of things he would have to take care of before leaving. The last item was uniforms. *Uniforms.* After his release he had had them all cleaned and hung in the wardrobe in the attic stowage space. It took a few moments to pull down the ladder and retrieve the plastic bags. Everything seemed to be presentable, although a slight musty odor had begun to make itself known. A small suitcase held his ties and accessories.

Back in his bedroom, he positioned his insignia on a set of tropical whites. He had forgotten to ask what the uniform of the day was while he was on the phone with Space Command but summer in Colorado was warm enough and he had seen whites on his occasional visits over to the Springs.

Most of his rank and ribbon insignia was replaced without any special thoughts but when he placed his gold astronaut's wings over the multicolored rows of awards and service bars he paused and thought of what had been.

Three days later, with the dash clock on his pickup reading 4:32 P.M., he slowed at the Main Gate of the Falcon Air Force Station, just east of Colorado Springs, and held his ID up for inspection by the blue-bereted Air Force sentry. Two minutes later, he swung into the parking lot in front of the impressive red brick building labeled: Headquarters, Consolidated Space Operations Center.

Before dropping out of the truck, he retrieved the suede eye patch he had carried in his bag. The medics had told him to throw it away once the eye was in place, but the patch was his security blanket. He would wean himself later, when the glass eye seemed more a part of him. Right now, he needed all the security he could muster; they didn't call a one-eyed Navy airplane driver back to active duty, even one who had held a special place within the astronaut corps, unless something desperate was in the wind. For a moment he entertained the thought that they might somehow be offering him a chance to get back into the program, but quickly dismissed such an irrational hope as foolish optimism. The crash had ended his flying career. He had to face that. This recall must be for some other reason.

An all-business first lieutenant greeted him at the entrance with an exaggerated salute and led him up the stairway and down a long corridor. At the end, under a boldly lettered ENTRANCE BY AUTHORITY OF THE COMMANDER ONLY, an armed sentry checked his orders and passed him through the door. He entered a richly paneled outer executive office.

"Joe! You one-eyed bastard, how the hell are you?" The outstretched arm led back to an enthusiastic hulk of a man, ruddy faced, and wearing the stiffly starched whites of a Navy captain.

"Brian! Brian Macfay. What are you doing here?" asked a surprised Dover.

A few years older than Dover, Macfay was every bit as fit, except for the slight bulge straining the web belt of his uniform. His skin was as deeply tanned as ever and the white teeth picture perfect. Together, they accented a physique that spelled macho-man. Two inches taller than Dover, with shoulders that stuck out several inches beyond his shoulder boards, Macfay could have been earning a fortune as the Marlboro man. All he needed was the mustache and sheep-wool coat. "Three years," replied Macfay, as if he were stating a prison sentence. "Director of Operations, Rear Admiral selected; work for a blue suiter—naturally—by the name of Chuck Samson. Ring any bells?"

"Mission commander, 41-Echo? On the *Discovery?*"

"The same. Wears a star these days."

"Good man."

"Damn good man . . . you're just under the wire. General Shyrr is expecting you at 1700."

"Listen, with only a 72-hour advance notice, he's lucky to have me here at all."

"How's the eye? I thought the patch would be gone."

Dover lifted the flap and grinned. "The color matches, but it doesn't move. Makes me look cock-eyed."

"So what else is new!" teased Macfay.

"What's this all about?"

"You don't have any idea?"

"No, just a set of orders, which came as sort of a shock."

"You've only been inactive eight months or so."

"Joe Civilian for eight months, but don't forget the twelve after the accident. I felt like a square wheel, pushing paper while you guys were still riding the thunder."

"Hey, you were a hero, Joe. Still are. We would have lost the *Columbia* if it hadn't been for you."

"Sure . . . and the Pope's Jewish."

The big astronaut grinned again and knocked on a closed door labeled, General T.W. Shyrr, United States

Air Force, Commander-in-Chief, U.S. Space Command. "We better go in."

The balding four-star rose and waved them in with a sweep of his arm. "Come in. Good to see you, Commander Dover."

Dover returned his amiable grip.

"Please, be comfortable." Shyrr led Dover to one of two chairs positioned before a lowered projection screen. As they sat, Macfay dimmed the office lights and turned on a slide projector. "Joe," he began, "this information is classified Top Secret, Ultra, Space Defense Information." As he continued, a series of slides illuminated the screen, each one timed to visually emphasize the points of his briefing.

"As you may know, we completed the final tracking station of our Ground-Based Deep-Space Surveillance System—acronym, GEODDS—in late October of last year. This system utilizes the very latest state-of-the-art technology in visual detection and computer enhancement of objects operating in the space environment. There are five tracking stations: one each at our White Sands Missile range in New Mexico; the island of Maui; Diego Garcia in the Indian Ocean; near Taegu in South Korea; and the fifth and newest station inland of Perth, Australia. Each station is equipped with two Contraves Goertz 40-inch telescopes of 86-inch focal length. These telescopes gather light from the space object under surveillance and feed the light into video sensors where it is converted into digital data. The data is then processed through a network of computer enhancement devices. The result is a video presentation of the object which features not only remarkable clarity, but superb detail and absolute color integrity. A print of the result is simultaneously produced."

Dover recognized the projection on the screen as the space shuttle, *Columbia*.

"This is, of course, your old friend on her first orbital flight. We used the Contraves Goertz to examine the extent of possible loose heat-insulating tiles on the bottom of the spacecraft."

Dover silently acknowledged the clarity. It was as if the shuttle had been snapped passing overhead at treetop level. Even the half-inch stenciled data on the underside of the fuselage was readable.

"Now, the *Columbia* was at a relatively low altitude, 130 miles. The system, itself, is quite capable of detection in deep space. The software is able to differentiate between light from stars and from man-made objects. Starlight is automatically filtered out. The characteristics—signature, if you will—of the man-made object are determined and compared against a catalogue of known objects in space. If it is a new object, the signature is added to the active surveillance list, maintained by the NORAD people in Ceyenne Mountain. Normally, the five tracking stations provide NORAD with 8,000-10,000 observations per month. I should add that should a new discovery call for any degree of urgency, the data can be passed to the Cheyenne Mountain complex in a matter of minutes . . ."

Shyrr leaned over and muttered to Dover, "Which happened this past June, and is the reason you're here."

Macfay continued, "On the twentieth of May, this year, the Soviets launched a vehicle from their space center at Baikonur which was duly tracked and appeared to be a routine *Progress* resupply of *Salyut 9*. The object continued in a progressive orbital pattern until it entered a near-polar orbit. For some reason not yet determined, our Australian station failed to pick it up, but it was reacquired shortly thereafter by the Maui telescopes. Only now, there were two objects, the second considerably smaller than the original, and by the time the White Sands tracking station had acquired them, they were rapidly growing apart. The smaller object was *changing orbit.*" Macfay paused for emphasis. "Changing orbit, Joe, not adjusting it. How's that grab you?"

"Interesting, depending upon the degree of change."

"Interesting, hell! Goddamned phenomenal!"

Shyrr put things back on track, "Go ahead, Brian."

"During the course of the next three days, the smaller object repeatedly changed orbit, not a progressive change compatible with the physical laws of the initial launch, but radical changes that differed as much as *ninety degrees with the plane of the previous orbit, and which were accomplished within the scope of a single orbit,* usually while transiting the southern hemisphere. It also changed altitudes at random intervals.''

Dover's ears had perked up when Macfay first mentioned the appearance of the second object, obviously spawned by the first. Now, his interest was riveted on Macfay's startling words, indeed. He considered the U.S. shuttles the most advanced of their kind. As far as he knew, so did everyone else within the space community. The Soviet's strong point had always been heavy payloads, not spacecraft sophistication.

''We do have some shots of the Soviet craft. Not as clear as we'd like, despite the ability of the GEODDS system. It seems they not only have achieved a quantum jump in maneuverability, but have progressed rapidly in the art of camouflage. You will note the blurred appearance of this shot. . . .''

Dover found himself enthralled in what appeared to be a winged spacecraft, generally triangular in plan view, but with six, almost wire-thin, leg-like extensions around the outline of the delta-shaped wing and fuselage. Otherwise, the object was not radically different in appearance from the U.S. shuttles. But even with the high resolution of the processed picture, it was difficult to make out any appreciable detail. Everything seemed to be diffused, with no great contrast in color and shadow.

Macfay projected three more views, all apparently of the bottom of the space vehicle, although Dover could detect some variations in the position of the six extensions.

''With careful study of these and some other shots we have from four of the five stations, it appears that the Soviets have applied some of the same radar-diminishing technology we are using on our Stealth bomber project. All surfaces and edges are rounded, with no absolute flat areas or deep crevices. This would inhibit the radar picture, of course, but we have no idea why the visual image is so

11

inconcise. The vehicle is small, about half the size of our shuttle. Consequently, we think it may be a one-man, or possibly two-man spacecraft.''

The screen went blank.

"Questions, Joe?"

Only about five trillion, thought Dover. He certainly was fascinated. "Brian, you stated that these radical maneuvers were repeatedly accomplished, which would indicate quite an on-board fuel supply.''

"It seemed able to perform multiple orbit changes almost at will. Yes to your comment on fuel. Its ability to maneuver, however, is the main mystery to the object. In pure space, free of any gravitational pull, a spacecraft could change course by the application of the proper energy vectors, provided it was a powered vehicle and not coasting. But a spacecraft in earth orbit, held there by the combination of orbital velocity and gravity, has to overcome much stronger forces to radically change the plane of its orbit. This is a very small vehicle. What is its power source? What type of maneuvering system does it have to accomplish such a feat? Our technology certainly doesn't permit it. And this stranger does it all in less than a full orbit. The obvious question follows: what means of control does it have when it is out of range of the Soviet tracking network? Preprogrammed computers? Or is it being manually flown by a cosmonaut? If so, he has one hell of a G-tolerance.''

"You feel it's manned?" asked Dover.

"Most probably, although as you know the Soviets are masters at unmanned vehicles. We're just not sure. We see no signs of a cockpit or cabin area, but we only have the underside on the visuals.''

"Or what you assume is the underside.''

"Yes.''

"Those extensions that give it the spidery look. What do you interpret those to be?''

"Most probably antennas, although a strange array.''

"You haven't detected any orbital decay or return to earth?''

"No."

"But the configuration, the wings, would indicate that capability."

"Yes, it does."

"Do the Soviets know the Australian tracking station is on the line?"

"We've kept its status classified, but I suspect they know."

Shyrr rose and led them over to his conference table. They sat around one end and a trim female sergeant entered and placed a silver tray of coffee necessities before them. It was difficult not to stare at her hip movements as she left.

"Please, help yourselves." Shyrr poured his own and took the head chair.

Dover looked first at Macfay, then spoke to Shyrr. "General, this is coming pretty fast. My orders didn't give any reason for my recall, just instructions to travel to this headquarters today and report to the Space Command Duty Officer for further orders. I don't know what I expected, but is all this leading up to my 'further orders'?"

"Yes, it is. But, first we owe you some explanation. I wanted you to see the pictures and hear Macfay before we talked about your assignment as that should put things in the proper perspective. Brian, why don't you continue?"

Macfay drained his cup and set it on the table. "Joe, I know the day you rode the *Columbia* down and crawled out of that damaged bird with one eye sliced practically in two, you figured your days with NASA were over; the Navy too, for that matter. And they were. You were one of the best. It was your skill and decisions that saved the *Columbia* from a total strike. We all remember that. But, life goes on, and while we were saddened to see you go out on a medical, we certainly didn't expect to ever see you in the space picture again. But that once-in-a-million situation has happened, all the result of that fuzzy set of slides you just saw."

"I gather that, but what does it have to do with me?"

"Let me finish. I was transferred to the Space Command right after you left active service. General Shyrr has insisted that all of his key people be ex-astronauts. Naturally, I jumped at the chance. The military is flat out in the space business, Joe, and . . .''

"You're stalling, Brian."

"Bullshit, I'm stalling! I'm just leading up to where I can wipe that perplexed look off your face. That damned Soviet UFO has us all squeezing our balls. We don't know what it is, Joe, and it's doing things we can't do."

"I noticed that."

"Let me put it as directly as I can. Four weeks ago, General Shyrr briefed the Joint Chiefs. They're pissing blue, Joe, over this thing. For one thing, it's flying right in the face of some very private conversations the Prez had with Gorbachev at the '85 summit."

"Private conversations?"

"Sure. Mano a mano type stuff. You know, where the two biggies talk eyeball to eyeball with only their translators present."

"We know what was said?"

"Well, the Joint Chiefs were privy to a presidential debriefing when Reagan came back from Geneva. He and Gorbachev had a mutual understanding that the Soviets were not developing any further space weapons and would not do so if we held back our SDI program."

"I never saw anything about that."

"Of course not. Hell, even in this society, we manage to keep a few things back from the people in the street. We have to. Especially something as sensitive as a private conversation between two heads of state. The press would have a field day."

"But we came away from Geneva with our intent to continue SDI research intact." Dover was still confused.

"That's right," interjected Shyrr. "But the public announcement was for the public. Reagan had indicated he might go along with Gorbachev's proposal."

The light came on in Dover's head. "Christ, you mean we've been deliberately dragging our feet in sort of a half-hearted SDI effort to keep the public happy and still stay within some informal agreement made by Reagan and Gorbachev?''

The General nodded. ''And now, out of the blue—no pun intended—appears a new space vehicle with all the traits of an ABM weapon.''

''The President must have been senile to agree to such a thing,'' observed Dover. ''We've been snookered.''

''In any event,'' continued Shyrr, ''the Joint Chiefs' response to our briefing was simple and to the point: find out what the hell it is. *Now.*''

Macfay leaned forward across the table, his face over his coffee cup. ''The General had us all meet him at planeside when he returned from D.C. and we spent the night hashing over the situation. Thanks to some input from NASA and the CIA, we came up with a plan. Well, not really a plan as such, but a general course of action. When we got to discussing specifics, we realized we needed a special person to carry it off, so we made a list of the skills and experience this special person would need, fed them into a computer over at personnel and out dropped only one name: little Joe Dover, one-eyed ex-astronaut.''

''Mine? All by itself? You better check your programming and updating staff.''

''I'm serious, Joe. You're the man.''

Shyrr flipped open a pale manila folder that lay before him. ''Commander, a big factor is language ability.'' He glanced down at the folder. ''Viktor and Valeska Dovarovitch, paternal grandparents. You're only one generation removed from your own Russian heritage. You speak and write the language fluently, including the technical jargon of space flight. That's why you were picked to work with the Soviets on the joint Spacelab 5 project . . .''

''Which never got off the ground—no pun intended,'' interrupted Dover.

''No, but you've worked with the cosmonauts on planning. You've seen some of their machines and been exposed to some of their techniques. Spacelab 5 wasn't a total loss. You have more practical knowledge of their systems than anyone else we know. Hell, you almost went into space with them.''

"But this sounds like an intelligence mission. With all due respect, General, why not get a Spook? The CIA boys excel at this sort of thing. Some of them are Russians in good standing.''

Shyrr held up a hand. "But this is not just an intelligence mission. It's a space intelligence mission. This is the Space Command, Commander. It's our ball, and we're going to bust a gut running with it.''

Dover was beginning to warm to the challenge. He was almost afraid to ask, "Does this mean I'm going to fly again?''

Shyrr arched his back and massaged the small of his back with his fists. At five-foot-seven, he was not exactly the John Wayne type. The harsh overhead light bounced off the large bald spot and almost gave the impression of a glowing halo. However, the possible humor of such a sight was completely overshadowed by the quite serious and much more authoritative glow of the four silver stars which sat on each of his shoulders. They were very obvious evidence that the gentleman who wore them was a very professional and seasoned senior military commander who was quite accustomed to making dramatic decisions, and at the moment was just a trifle concerned that the briefing was straying away from its primary purpose.

"We're getting a little ahead of ourselves,'' he said, "but you are right, Commander. It is primarily an intelligence mission, albeit a rather unique one, and it is your expertise with spacecraft systems that is a governing factor, here. We need that expertise, and we need it in Russian.''

Dover glanced over at Macfay. "Why not Tim Stanley? He was with me on the Spacelab 5 conferences with the Russians.''

Macfay's response was embarrassingly quiet. "He drinks. Right now he's pushing around stacks of papers as the Assistant Director of Flight Simulation at Houston. We keep him out of sight.''

Dover had to address the next point of his concern although it seemed one that should be obvious to Macfay and Shyrr. "I have only one eye. On any type of an intelligence mission, I'll stand out like a mustache on the Mona Lisa. Hell, after the *Columbia* accident my picture was on the front page of every paper from the *Times* to the *National Enquirer*. I'm a public figure, a big NASA jock."

Macfay kept his low-key tone. "The one eye was the cincher, Joe. We need a man with just one eye."

Dover could only stare incredulously at his two seniors.

Shyrr scowled at Macfay and hastily filled in the silence. "Commander, you've had a full day, travel and all—"

Dover could see that the General wasn't too pleased that Macfay had chosen the moment to hint that there was a mystery within the mystery: the need for a one-eyed agent.

"—and you've been hit with a lot. This matter is urgent, obviously, but I don't want to overload you just yet. I wanted you to have something to sleep on. Brian, you might clue him in on tomorrow's schedule."

"Flight physical at 0700. We have some film taken at White Sands that may give you another perspective of the Red bird. I'll pick you up at the dispensary. Later, one of the NORAD people will tell you what they've been able to plot on orbital data. You have an 1100 departure from Peterson Field direct to Andrews."

Dover leaned back in his chair to study the faces of Macfay and Shyrr. "You folks don't let any grass grow."

"No, we don't," replied Shyrr. "That fuzzy picture you saw could be the world's most sophisticated spacecraft. It may even be—and since it's Russian, it probably is—some sort of advanced technology, anti-ballistic missile, defense system. With the maneuvering we've observed and our knowledge of the progress of the Soviets in laser and particle-beam weapons systems, we could be looking at a Soviet weapon that will neutralize our strategic nuclear capability."

"While we've been fighting to keep our SDI money in the budget, even at a bare bones level, the bad guys have used the agreements made at the summit to mask their own moves," said Macfay. "The pissers have already made a mockery of the provisions of the SALT papers by completing the development and deployment of one hell of a capable ABM system around Moscow. I tell you we're slow learners."

"Goodbye, detente," muttered Shyrr. Then, he grinned. "Circumstances, however, are such that we have a few things going for us at the moment. You'll be briefed on those in due time." He moved away from the table and pointedly looked at the GI-issue clock on the wall behind his desk. "If it looks like we're in a hurry, we are."

Overall, Dover was elated. They needed him; though for the love of life, he couldn't see his role yet. But there were some self-doubts souring the anticipation that their discussions were generating. "I can see the urgency, General, but wouldn't an experienced intelligence type, properly trained in space technology, be a more appropriate person?"

"We don't have one. We don't have the time to train one, and we don't need one. I want an operator, not a specialist. You're an operator. Despite your hey-look-at-me days with NASA, you're a military man and you had a fine career going before you ever joined the space program. Not only that—" The General was good at pausing for effect. His lips drew back in that wide military grin that always preceded an announcement that the discussion was closed. "Your name fell out of the machine. And Macfay, here, is always telling me that when the chips are down you Navy types just salute and respond with a hearty 'aye, aye, sir.' "

Dover slowly raised his right hand and touched his forehead. "Aye, aye, sir."

Shyrr's grin broke into an audible chuckle. "By God, Macfay, you were right. Gentlemen, I think we can call it a day. My wife and I have a delegation of Colorado locals arriving for drinks, dinner, and a very boring evening of small talk. The Russians could be launching a first strike this very moment and I would still have to put on my public relations hat and preside at pre-dinner cocktails. I'm sure you could use a good night's rest, Commander. And a good meal. You best take it. You may not get another chance for a while.''

Dover and Macfay returned the General's pumping handclasp and left his office.

"Come on, Joe, I'll get you settled into the guest quarters and buy the steaks,'' volunteered Macfay.

"The General's a persuasive man.''

"Bull. You're pissing in your pants at this opportunity. Don't act so damned calm. Loosen up. You're back on the team, Joe.''

Dover couldn't resist. "Feels good—I think.''

They passed out into the long hall leading to the exit. Dover placed a restraining hand on Macfay's shoulder. "Hold it a minute, Brian. This thing's big, isn't it?''

"Very big.''

"I'm having trouble with it; figuring out my role, that is, especially since you two clammed up when I pushed the one-eye consideration.''

Macfay glanced back over his shoulder. Except for him and Dover, the corridor was empty. "Joe, we shouldn't talk too much out here. Everything's pretty highly classified. Let's get out to the car.''

They started across the parking lot.

"Let's take my pickup. My gear's inside,'' said Dover.

As they pulled out of the parking area, Macfay continued their discussion.

"Even I'm not privileged to know everything about all this. My main concern is what this all means to our deterrent posture. I can make that evaluation once someone finds out just what it is, and you're going to be part of that effort. What part, I truly don't know. When Shyrr and the NASA and CIA reps had their little pow-wow, they apparently decided that they needed you, specifically, and no one else. That bit about the personnel computer is all smoke. Once they decided upon the requirements, it didn't take personnel's wonder machine to tell them who it should be. For Christ's sake, how many Russian-speaking, one-eyed, U.S. astronauts are there? In that respect, I was in on the conference and I'm as mystified about the one-eyed requirement as you. It was specified by the CIA side of the table, and if I read the plan correctly, you'll get the full treatment once you get to D.C. Actually, until you get past tomorrow's physical, I shouldn't be telling you all this; you really don't have a need-to-know yet.''

"For God's sake, Brian. After a panic recall like this, and a preview of your slide show, I'm already deep into whatever I'll be doing. As for the physical, you and I both know that unless I've got terminal leprosy, it's just a formality. You know damned good and well I'm in. Incidentally, if everything is so hurry-up, why did they send my orders via U.S. Mail? I might not have gotten those orders until after my reporting date!''

"You won't believe this, but they figured a telegram would possibly arouse interest by someone. Everybody around that area knows who you are. It would have been picked up by someone and certainly would have been worth a mention on the nightly news.''

"And I suppose the mailman that delivered it has sealed lips? You could read the damn thing through the envelope if you looked hard enough.''

Macfay gave him an amused look as he answered, "As a matter of fact, that was Sergeant Dell from our security division. The Navy cut your orders and put them on an F-14 to Peterson Field. We just wrapped an envelope around the original and borrowed a mail jeep.''

"My hired hand knows I've been recalled.''

"That's okay. Someone talked to him after you left.''

"Sounds a little sloppy. He may already have let it slip.''

"He hasn't.'' Macfay's tone indicated he was quite sure about his cryptic comment.

"Games!'' exclaimed Dover. "As soon as the intelligence types get into the act, it's games. Someone's been watching my place ever since the mailman came. Right?''

"See? You're getting smarter, already.''

"Let's go eat.''

As they walked over to the Officer's Club, Macfay suddenly observed, "Well, at least you picked up right away on the General's code name for the Soviet spacecraft."

"I did?"

"Sure. You called it spidery. He thinks that's what it looks like, too. Some kind of menacing space-spider. He also thinks very strongly that it's a first generation anti-ballistic missile space fighter, capable of flitting all over the heavens and gobbling up our strategic missiles as fast as we can get them off."

"So? What does he call it?"

"The Alpha Bug."

Chapter
2

The four-hour flight to Andrews Air Force Base provided Dover with some needed thinking time. The past eighteen hours had been rushed and full. He wasn't too surprised to learn about a new Soviet space machine. They were good at lying dormant for a while, then coming up with a real shocker. Still, he had no hint as to his actual mission. In his briefcase were orders to report to a Doctor Anderson who would be waiting at Andrews. He could only assume that there would be more physical exam matters. The young flight surgeon back at Falcon AFB had poked in all the right places, but the examination had not been as thorough as he had expected.

The film that Macfay had shown him from White Sands didn't add much to his knowledge of the Alpha Bug, although one sequence did depict a rapid roll maneuver. The NORAD briefing had been pretty much routine.

The young captain at the controls of the T-39 Saberliner let him ride shotgun and shoot the landing at Andrews. Even with his eye gone, he managed a decent landing, although a bit solid.

They taxied up to Operations and Anderson was standing out on the parking apron.

"Commander Dover?"

"Yes, you must be Doctor Anderson."

The physician was a bear of a man, probably in his early sixties, and wore a full, grayed beard around the widest gold plated smile Dover had ever received. He was a bit stooped, and despite his bulk the beige wash-and-wear suit hung on him as if he had bought it with shrinkage in mind, and it hadn't.

"My car is right outside," he explained and led the way. They drove out the main gate and joined the late afternoon traffic on the Beltway, working their way west, then north toward Bethesda. The doctor didn't seem to want to volunteer any information on the reason for Dover's assignment to the Naval Hospital and Dover was content to go along with the game.

"When were you here last?" asked Anderson.

"Four years ago."

"Ah, after the first *Columbia* flight? I remember the press coverage."

"It was quite a thrill for me. We had lunch with the President, although I was a minor guest. I had been one of the mission controllers at Houston."

Anderson nodded outside at the passing suburban scene. "Things look different?"

"Lots more housing. This used to be a more isolated drive."

They crossed the Potomac, then left the Beltway and wound through the crowded traffic to the hospital. The doctor wheeled into his marked parking place and led Dover to the elevator set aside for service to the VIP suites. They exited on the top floor and walked to the far end of the multi-doored corridor. A starched and polished Marine sentry stood at ease outside the one they entered, recognizing the doctor with a nod as they passed.

They were in a small sitting room, made even smaller by the overstuffed furniture which almost matched the navy blue carpeting in color. The easy chair was conveniently opposite the sofa, and an apartment-sized refrigerator hummed quietly against one wall. Through the archway on the other side of the room, Dover could see a clinically clean bedroom, complete with the standard tightly-linened hospital bed and the paraphernalia usually associated with it. A high service tray, perched on a single chrome leg, peeked over the far side of the bed.

"Drink?" queried Anderson as he opened the refrigerator.

Dover glanced at his watch. "I guess it's a decent hour. Bourbon with a little water would be nice."

Anderson selected two ponies from a full shelf, jerked loose a small tray of ice from the freezer compartment, and in a moment set a pale gold bourbon-and-water on the end table next to Dover. He mixed a gin and tonic for himself.

They were just taking their first sips when a gentle knock preceded the opening of the door and a middle-aged oriental, wearing the familiar long white coat of hospital personnel, entered.

"Doctor," greeted Anderson. "Joe, this is Doctor Sam Tanaka. Sam, Joe Dover."

"A pleasure, Commander."

"Nice to meet you, Doctor." Dover's eye was drawn to the shiny black cube Tanaka placed on the table. It was about four inches on a side.

"We have a little something for you." Anderson motioned for Tanaka to open the box. He did, and lifted out a smaller, clear plastic insert. Inside it, nested in a form-fitting Styrofoam cradle, was a human eye.

At least, it looked like a human eye. Upon closer examination, Dover could see that it was actually an artificial eyeball, encased in an outer shell which was a three-quarter sphere, covering all but the front portion of the eyeball. The shell seemed to be made of a white nylon material. Tanaka lifted the assembly, still in its cradle, and set it closer to Dover.

"This is your new eye," Anderson announced. "I think you will find it rather interesting."

Tanaka carefully removed the outer shell and placed the eyeball in the palm of his hand. "I'm an optical engineer, Commander. I've been working on this with Doctor Anderson, and a third member of our team, Doctor James Fry. He's a research engineer with Kodak, and we contracted for his services. Specializes in microphotographic design and engineering. Damned good. He sends his apologies, incidentally. Regretfully, he is out of town today."

Dover looked up at Anderson. "You're not a physician?"

"Ophthalmologist—surgeon."

Tanaka continued, "Together, working under a special grant, we have developed what you see before you: an eye-camera."

The light went on in Dover's head. The need for a one-eyed agent was no longer a mystery. The eye fascinated him.

Tanaka held it closer for Dover's inspection. "This is a disc camera. The front half contains all of the functioning parts of any camera: lens, shutter, adjustable aperture, and of course, film. There are fourteen two-millimeter frames per disc. Since the compact design dictated that the center of the disc be directly behind the lens, we have installed a set of prisms which direct the incoming image to the film frames around the perimeter of the disc. The iris of the eye, which will be color matched to yours, is a light-sensitive, automatically adjusting aperture, calibrated to match the iris of your own eye as it reacts to varying degrees of light intensity."

With a slight twist, he separated the eye-camera into its two halves. "The rear hemisphere contains a power supply and the microelectronic components which operate the camera and give movement to the eye. Also, it is necessary to separate the eye to change film discs." Tanaka gingerly removed a small gray square chip from the open rear of the front half of the eye. Approximately three-quarters of an inch on a side, it contained the film disc. Dover examined it, then laid it down as Tanaka handed him the front half. *Ingenious,* thought Dover, *a complete auto-*

25

matic camera within a one-inch hemisphere. Around the edge of the open side was a series of small metallic dots.

"Electrical contacts," explained Tanaka, "which provide for the transfer of power and operating circuitry from the rear hemisphere." He handed the power half to Dover.

Inside, a maze of tiny color-coded wires connected two half-inch microchips. A silver disc-battery was implanted in the upper rear of the hemisphere and Dover traced a portion of the micro-circuitry from the battery to the chips and on to a series of six flat rectangular housings, equally spaced around the inside of the hemisphere. Each was probably a quarter-inch square by a sixteenth-inch thick.

Tanaka had followed his examination and further explained, "Without going too deeply into the technology, those are very precise electromagnetic field generators. Each is connected, through the outer shell, to one of the six eye-movement nerves which originally carried signals to the eye muscles. The faint electrical signals which accompany any eye movement are fed into the appropriate generator and change the field strength. The fields, in turn, act upon minute magnets by induction, and the resultant energy is amplified and moves the eye-camera in unison with the good eye."

"What you see is what you get," commented Dover.

"Exactly. You see, here, there are six jeweler's screwdriver adjustments, one for each field enclosure. It may take several fittings to adjust the eye and synchronize it with your good one. Once set, it won't change." He set the halves down and offered the shell for Dover's inspection before continuing.

"The three-quarter shell replaces what we call the *capsule of Tenon* in your natural eye; that's a thin membrane enveloping the eyeball from the optic nerve in back forward to the ciliary region. The membrane separates the eyeball from the orbital fat and forms a socket in which the eyeball moves. In our eye-camera, the nylon shell does that, and also provides a place for connection of the eye-movement nerves to electrical sensors on the shell. The tiny wires molded into the shell transfer these signals to the field generator modules via these small metal rub plates on the inside of the shell.''

"There would have to be lubrication between the shell and the eye,'' observèd Dover.

"Oh, yes. A non-conducting liquid is introduced to provide lubrication while the eye is being worn.''

"Non-conducting?''

"To avoid shorting out the rub plates,'' explained Tanaka.

Dover shook his head. "You've thought of everything, haven't you?''

"We hope so.''

Tanaka continued his briefing, "Doctor Anderson will surgically implant the shell, and it can only be removed by surgery.''

"The eye-camera; it can be readily removed?'' asked Dover.

"Yes, that's necessary to change the film. There's more, but perhaps that's enough technical information for now. I believe you're scheduled for surgery in the morning. Isn't that so, Doctor Anderson?''

"Bright and early. I'll have the outer shell in place by mid-morning, and we'll insert the eye the next morning.''

"No telephoto lens?'' teased Dover.

The two men chuckled, then Anderson replied, "As a matter of fact, yes. Wide-angle lens also, and a close-up lens. They're all conventional contact lenses.''

"I'll be damned. I think this calls for another bourbon.''

"Nope—I want you to get into that bed. We'll be performing some routine tests and examinations the rest of the evening. You'll be given a mild sedative to help you sleep. No reading and no TV. I want your good eye rested.''

"And no sex,'' cautioned Tanaka, grinning sheepishly at his own joke.

"Don't tell me the nurses around here are that accommodating?'' laughed Dover.

"We're assigning only virgins to your care, Joe,'' said

27

Anderson. "That way, we can tell if you've violated our rules."

Tanaka placed the eye-camera back in its double container.

"Don't forget to wash it, Doctor," lightly cautioned Dover.

"Don't worry. You'll get a brand new one. This is just the prototype." Leaving, Tanaka almost collided with a chubby white balloon who entered carrying Dover's dinner tray. The nurse was in her mid-forties, barely five feet tall, and a good 160 pounds. Her starched white uniform was strained to its limit.

"Virgin?" whispered Dover to Anderson as she set down the tray and quietly padded out.

"We figured that one didn't have to be. Eat up; you won't get anything after midnight. I'll see you in an hour or so."

Later on, after the examinations and tests, Dover obediently swallowed the pill delivered by the white balloon and slept like a baby.

He was still asleep when the male corpsman wrapped the elastic cuff around his upper arm and started pumping it for a blood pressure reading.

"'Morning," said the sailor as he checked Dover's pulse.

"Already?"

"You slept well."

It was seven o'clock. Anderson came ambling in at seven-thirty.

"How you feel?"

"Great."

"We're getting a little earlier start than scheduled, but they won't come for you for another fifteen minutes. I just wanted to pop in and make sure you were all right."

"How long will I be here?"

"Just a day or so after we get the eye fitted. The implantation is simple enough. We may have to adjust the movement a couple times. Those eye-movement nerves may be a bit atrophied and thus take a while to regain

28

their conductivity. Then, we'll have you take some pictures to check everything out. Incidentally, I should mention that all this is hush-hush. Everyone you come in contact with from now on has the necessary clearances. No visitors.''

''I doubt if anyone I know is aware I'm even here.''

''Good. Well, listen, I have to go scrub. See you in a few minutes.''

''Right.''

Dover finished brushing his teeth just as the white balloon entered. ''Lie down,'' she said.

''You get right to the point, don't you?'' Dover chided.

''Exactly.'' She held up the syringe and squeezed a drop of the contents out before slipping the needle into the inside of his elbow. ''Just a relaxant,'' she explained. ''It also turns off your sex drive.''

Dover liked her. It was actually the first chance he'd had to really look at her. She was professional but quite pretty, with delicate facial features and a rich Mediterranean complexion. While she held his wrist and counted the heartbeat, he began to experience a very pronounced euphoria. She continued holding his hand and smiled. She was very kind, thought Dover, and motherly, and pretty, and would undoubtedly take care of him forever and ever . . . and ever . . . and. . . .

When he came out of the blackness, Anderson was leaning over him, face to face, peering into his good eye. ''Well, hello,'' said the doctor, straightening up.

''That was quick.''

''Two hours. You're a good patient.''

''Everything okay?''

''Excellent. A perfect fit. It may ache a little. If so, Nurse Masconi will give you something.''

''Masconi?''

''The plump virgin with the Mafia connections. You know, we should both be ashamed. She's the best, and a very nice person.''

Dover felt guilty of making fun of the woman, even if it had only been in his head.

"I'll check on you later. Feel free to move about after lunch if it doesn't bother you, but I'd take a good afternoon rest just so you don't overwork those nerve endings too soon."

"Thanks, Doc, it doesn't feel bad at all."

Still, it felt good to rest for the remainder of the morning.

At 9:00 A.M. the next day, Tanaka and Anderson reappeared, along with Doctor Fry. Anderson slipped on surgical gloves while Tanaka removed the thick bandage covering Dover's left eye socket and dropped some clear liquid into his good eye. "This will immobilize your eye while we place the eye-camera," he explained.

Anderson opened the sterile container and lifted out the clever device. He held it under Dover's own eye, comparing the color of the iris. "Excellent match, Doctor Fry."

"Will I have to be sterile whenever I use it?"

"Oh, no. This is just a precaution since it's so soon after the surgery. It's easy to insert, just hold the lids apart like this and press straight in. There are some small alignment grooves which you will learn to feel with practice. They insure the eye-camera doesn't exceed its movement limits and also provide good contact between the eye and the shell. There, how's that feel?"

"Very natural."

Tanaka held a mirror in front of Dover's face. The color match of the irises was perfect. He did notice a slight swelling of the upper lid.

Anderson flicked on his penlight and moved it toward the eye-camera. The iris contracted. "The circuit to the iris is always activated. That way, the eye-camera reacts in concert with the real one whenever there is a light intensity change. No one will be able to tell it from the real thing."

"It's truly amazing." Dover watched the iris react to the movement of the penlight.

Doctor Fry stepped forward. "There's a pressure-sensitive switch on the outside of the shell, just under the skin of your temple. Just press the outside boney ridge of your eye socket, here, like this. That activates the camera. To take a picture, you close your eye for at least a half-second. The time delay prevents an accidental picture when your eye normally blinks. The closing of the upper lid does two things: it advances the film and cocks the shutter. When you open the lid, there's a very short delay and the shutter trips. Go ahead, try it.''

Dover closed his lids, held them for a moment, then opened them. He had felt nothing.

Fry looked pleased. "You just took my picture," he announced. "It'll take a little practice. To shut off the power, just press the temple again. Here, you try it." He lifted Dover's hand and guided his finger to the proper spot, just forward of the indentation of the temple. "There, you got it."

It took very little pressure.

Fry opened a small black leather case and explained the contents. "This vial contains your eye drops. It's an ordinary Visine squeeze bottle. Lubricate every six hours while you have the eye in. Two drops will do it. These are your accessory lenses; to anyone else they're just two pairs of contacts. Each has a nicked code on one edge. One nick is the telephoto; two, the wide-angle; three, the close-up; none, the high-intensity light filter." He removed a slim two-inch steel rod from its contoured resting place. On one end was a half-inch rubber suction cup; on the other, a small plunger.

"This assists you in removing the eye, although you can get it out as you did your old one. But the connection and fit with the shell makes it more difficult." He raised the rod and pressed in the tiny plunger. "You depress the plunger, place the rubber cup over the eye, release the plunger which creates a vacuum, and lift out the eye."

Dover felt a slight tug as Fry removed the eye-camera, and a slight pressure as the doctor replaced it.

"Questions?"

"How about focus?"

"Fixed, as is the speed: one-hundredth of a second.

We're still trying to make them variable. Meanwhile, the auxiliary lenses will compensate for those shortcomings.''

"How about light? I didn't notice a flash attachment."

Fry threw up his hands. "Mai-ya! I knew I forgot something. Ha! No, listen. The film speed is ASA 1000, with a special process to reduce the grain. You can take pictures by candlelight or in bright sun. The variable aperture will handle the light requirements."

"How can I tell the field of vision?"

Fry opened a second leather case and handed the rimless eyeglasses to Dover. "These will be fitted precisely to you. They are a special photo-gray composition which will act as a light filter, but their main purpose is to accustom you to the field of vision. Your right eye is unimpaired so the lenses are non-corrective. You will notice, in the center of the right lens, a faintly etched square. That is the eye-camera's field of vision. After some experience, the glasses will not be needed. As for their light filtering, you have contacts for that. Think of these only as a training aid. It would be too dangerous to wear them on an assignment. An astute observer could make out the etched square and might become suspicious. Besides, the glasses only show the field of vision when you're looking straight ahead, and the eye-camera can take pictures wherever your eyes are aimed."

"Color film?"

"Color film."

"I can hardly wait to enter the annual *Life* magazine photo contest."

"You may have your chance sooner than you think," remarked Anderson. "Our part in your assignment is essentially over, although we'll be with you the next couple days to follow up on the medical and technical aspects, but a very impatient gentleman from the Office of the Central Intelligence Agency has been bugging me to get with you. I told him: this afternoon."

"No grass growing . . ." muttered Dover.

"Beg your pardon?"

"Nothing, just an observation."

Anderson offered his hand. "I'll wish you luck now. One of us will look in on you tonight, and we'll be on call should you have any problems with the eye."

"Thanks, Doc. You, too, Doctor Tanaka and Doctor Fry. You folks do good work."

"Use it in good health," admonished Anderson as they started for the door.

"Hey, Doc," Dover called after him, "TV tonight?"

"Sure. Sex, too, if you can find any."

"Ha! Send in Nurse Masconi."

"Flyboys," muttered Anderson as he shook his head and closed the door.

Dover picked up the mirror and again studied his eyes. It was incredible. The swelling over the left eye was undoubtedly due to the surgery. It would pass. Slowly, he raised his hand, pressed his left outer eye-bone, and glanced around the room, searching for a suitable subject. Just as he had about decided upon a shot of the hospital grounds below his window, Nurse Masconi entered.

"Doctor Anderson said you needed me. Can I get you anything?"

Dover smiled at Anderson's joke and lowered his lids for a second. "Nothing, nurse, thank you—wait, perhaps a fresh decanter of ice water."

"I'll have the corpsman bring it."

As she closed the door, Dover pressed his eye once more. "Twelve more to go," he said, talking to himself.

Chapter
3

"Hello."

The outstretched hand and the smile beyond it were warm and friendly, the voice deep and confident, the language Russian. "Alexander Tobias. Soviet desk, Central Intelligence Agency." There was no hint of American accent.

Dover replied in kind, "Hello."

"May I sit?" The man answered his own question by plopping heavily into the easy chair opposite the sofa. The pin-striped dark blue business suit could just as easily have clothed a small-business executive from Anytown, U.S.A. Large rimless bifocals straddled a strong Roman nose and gave an additional sparkle to deep green eyes. An ample mane of thick silver hair swept back over the temples and ears in a style worthy of someone in the entertainment business and gave width to a lean face that had been exposed to a great deal of the outdoors.

He leaned forward and placed two nine-by-eleven manila envelopes on the coffee table in front of Dover. One was bulky, almost too full; the other, flat.

"Doctor Anderson told me to expect someone," said Dover.

"Yes, I talked to him yesterday, while you were still out from the surgery. I know you've been pretty much in the dark up to now—no pun intended. How's the eye?"

"Feels all right."

"Certainly looks natural. They've done a good job."

"Yes, it does. I keep standing in front of the mirror."

"Commander, we're going to ask an awful lot of you, but we honestly think you're the only man who might pull it off . . ."

"Might?" Dover would have preferred to have heard a stronger word.

Tobias chuckled. "Think positive. For the duration of this assignment, you're working for the Agency. A copy of an endorsement to your orders is in the thin envelope there. Destroy it once you've verified it. I'll be your only control; you'll be pretty much on your own after today. Anderson says he'll release you tomorrow afternoon unless something flares up. That swelling should be gone by then, I would think."

Dover examined the endorsement, then slipped it back into its envelope. "Navy to NASA to CIA. My career pattern seems to be getting more diversified and I thought it had ended."

"I understand you have been inactive for a while, due to the eye injury."

"I thought I was medically retired. I bought a small ranch in western Colorado. Was just beginning to feel at home among the cowchips."

"Well, I've looked at your record. You excel at everything you try, it seems. No reason why you shouldn't do as well in this business."

"It's a bit new to me."

Tobias studied him for a moment, as if trying to decide how well he would adapt to the task ahead. "You know, Commander, our scruples level is not quite up to the standard of everyday life. Does that bother you?"

"I don't know. Maybe I've seen too many movies. The CIA people are always stereotypes, you know."

"I know. We have an unpopular role in the overall scheme of things, but it's essential. I guess you could say it's sort of an eye-for-an-eye type thing." Tobias shook a cigarette from a crumpled pack and offered the pack to Dover.

"No, thanks."

"Do you mind?"

"No, it doesn't bother me."

Tobias touched the flame from his lighter to the end of the tobacco and deeply inhaled, cycling the smoke through his lungs before allowing it to drift lazily from his nostrils as he continued.

"I've been married to my wife for twenty-eight years; my job for thirty-one. I have a son who's a corporate lawyer and a number ten daughter who's a Sister of Saint Francis. My wife is a volunteer for the Republican Party fund raisers and works three days a week at the Veteran's Hospital. I consider myself a Christian and I sleep well. I confess monthly to an old Italian priest who's been my confessor for the last ten years and the most severe penance he's ever given me was a week in a retreat house in upstate Maryland, and that was for adultery not in the line of duty. I've cheated, stolen, lied, and killed for my country and the only thing that Father Pietro, who's been hearing confessions since Peter was Pope, has ever climbed on my ass about was humping my neighbor's wife. Does that tell you anything?"

"I get the point."

"I hope so. You're going to be working with some of my people who are not only my professional associates, but my close personal friends. I'd sure hate to see any of them die because you took an extra split-second to make a moral judgement."

He reached over and withdrew the contents of the stuffed envelope.

"I have your new identity. You are Doctor Josef Utgoff, Associate Professor of Russian Language, Georgetown

University. Here are your passport and driver's license, credit cards, social security card, triple-A auto club card, organ donor card, and paid-up membership card in the Georgetown Faculty Association.''

Dover examined the passport and driver's license. The photographs were copies of his last NASA ID picture, taken shortly before the *Columbia* accident.

"And here are your plane tickets. You leave Washington National at five tomorrow afternoon. Upon arrival at JFK, go to the Pan Am gate assigned to your flight number. There, your wife will join you. Here are your traveler's checks, cash and wallet. Also, one of my people will bring you clothes and luggage tomorrow morning. Take nothing of your own, *nothing.*''

Dover held up a hand. During the past several months, he had indeed been looking for a wife, but he wasn't sure he should be issued one. "Let's get back to my wife."

"She's one of us. You and Mrs. Utgoff—Marie Estelle Utgoff—are booked on an Intourist-approved cultural tour of Leningrad, Minsk, Moscow, and Vladivostok. It's a group tour, escorted, and you are broadening your expertise in the Russian language and knowledge of the Soviet Union. Here is a book you authored two years ago on Russian idioms. Take it with you; study it on the plane. It'll bring you up to date on some of the colloquialisms. In your wallet, incidentally, is a picture of your wife.''

The face smiling up out of the wallet photograph was a striking mixture of Negroid and Caucasian genes, with high cheekbones that gave even added length to the graceful gazelle neck. The light brown complexion provided an ideal background for dark brown eyes and sensuous, barely glossed lips. Auburn hair framed the face and rested lightly on bare shoulders. She was lovely.

"I have a black wife?''

"You're an eastern, liberal college professor, living and working in one of America's most cosmopolitan cities. What could be more natural?''

"Oh, I'm not complaining; far from it. She's enchanting.''

37

"And a professional. When she talks, you listen. Her advice and counsel could prolong your life. She's also the surviving member of a husband-wife team. He's scattered over a couple square miles of East German countryside."

"What an unlucky, once-lucky man."

"It made her a dedicated patriot."

"Aren't we all," mused Dover, intently studying the photographs.

Tobias did not appear to be amused. "When you reach Leningrad, one of our people will contact you. They will have a new identity and take you in tow."

"Underground?"

"Yes. Mrs. Utgoff will receive a telegram, a death in the family, and inform the tour leader that she and you are leaving the tour and returning home."

Tobias laid out a series of five glossy eight-by-tens. "These were taken by our *Big Bird* satellite. They're current and that complex is the Volgograd Space Center. The inked numbers on the prints correspond to the features on the identification list. That's your destination."

Dover held up one of the prints. An L-shaped complex of buildings and recognizable launch pads lay along the northeastern side of a multi-channeled lowland river. Dover pointed to the water.

"The Volga," replied Tobias to the unasked question. "The Space Center is about sixty miles downstream from the city itself."

"I thought the spacecraft was launched from Baikonur."

"It was. We have reliable information, however, which leads us to believe that the craft is assembled at Volgograd and ground tested before shipment to Baikonur, where it is mated with the launch vehicle. Volgograd is the older station, although quite updated, and primarily used for the SS-5 and SS-5 variants in their scientific Cosmos and Intercosmos programs. There is less personnel traffic at Volgograd, so tight security is more feasible there than at their main center at Baikonur."

"Oh, that's just great. Now, I know why you used the phrase 'might succeed' earlier."

Tobias didn't seem to hear the remark. "There is a special area, here on the photographs, that is a separate compound within the main compound. That is the area you must penetrate and get us some pictures with the eye-camera."

Dover studied the compound. "Suppose the spacecraft's not there."

For the first time since he had started to brief, Tobias let a smile erase some of his frown wrinkles. "Then, you will have had one hell of a training mission."

Dover leaned back and sighed. They were certainly banking on a neophyte for so critical an assignment.

"I just had a thought," he said. "Who leaves Leningrad with my wife?"

"One of our in-country people. He'll be your approximate build, but we'll have to change the photographs on the passport and driver's license."

"Sounds like a weak spot."

"It is, but we've done such a thing before. No problems up to now."

You're certainly a reassuring bastard, thought Dover.

For the next hour, Tobias discussed the photographs, pointing out each of the items on the ID sheet. The high frequency antenna farm and the radar site were easily recognizable, as were the launching pads with their overpowering gantries. The perimeter guard houses were easy enough to detect and the old V-2 monument was clearly visible. The special area appeared to be about three acres in size, just to the west of the horizontal assembly building.

"I'll leave this material for you to study tonight and tomorrow. Most of the other sheets contain information on the local area around the Center, primarily the towns of Kapustin Yar and Akhtubinsk."

"What'll I do with the material when I leave tomorrow?"

"Give it to Masconi."

"Nurse Masconi?"

"Sure . . . we're an equal opportunity employer." Tobias seemed to be loosening up now that his briefing was over. "Last chance for questions, *Josef.*"

"A minor one: how in the hell do I get back out?"

Tobias was quiet for a moment. He rubbed his chin, seemingly in debate with himself. Finally, he replied, "The same people who take you in will see that you get out. They'll get you to a coastal area on the Black Sea. We have a Company freighter on its way to the Turkish port of Samsun. It's probably passing through the Dardanelles about now. It has a false deck house forward which will accommodate a vertical-takeoff-and-landing Marine Corps Harrier, one of the two-seaters. It'll have a Soviet Navy paint scheme and markings. To the uninitiated, it'll pass for a Soviet Yak 36 Forger II. The freighter will be at sea, and the Harrier will pick you up."

"You took a long time to answer."

Tobias shrugged. "We've a few loose ends. We have to get the Harrier and pilot from the Sixth Fleet. No problem. We've got well over a week ahead of us."

"Why can't I come out the way I go in? With another tour group?"

"There aren't any appropriate ones, and we really can't project how long you'll be in-country. Of course, we don't want to leave you there any longer than necessary; you might get to liking it."

"I doubt that."

"We need the film soonest, and we need you back here."

"Jesus, don't tell me there's more?"

"Who can say, Josef . . . who can say?"

It was almost midnight by the time Dover had reached the point of saturation with his studies of the briefing sheets and pictures. His good eye ached and he was very tired. Still, he tossed and turned until almost 2:00 A.M. At last, he began to relax, perhaps because of the pill that Nurse Masconi had brought him.

He was on the near edge of sleep when the sense of a

presence caused him to stir. He opened his eye just as the shadowed outline of an arm started down, the hand at the end grasping the hilt of a scimitar-shaped knife.

Dover twisted frantically away from the plunging arm and it overshot his chest, stabbing full into the foam mattress. He drove one hand sharply at the groin of the dark hulk and swung the other wildly at where the head should be. Both connected and the shadow spat with pain as Dover rolled away and tumbled out of bed. He scrambled to his feet just as the intruder regrouped and charged, and a split second before they met, he dropped to his knees in a ball. The figure cursed and tripped forward into the metal head-frame of the hospital bed. A metallic ring clattered across the asphalt-tiled floor.

The shadow leaped across the room after his wayward blade, giving Dover time to take the offensive and dive after him. That was a mistake. As soon as he wrapped his arms around the man's waist and dug his fingers into the hard flesh, he realized that he was physically outclassed. His attacker was a mass of muscle who instantly pivoted in place and swung Dover like a hula hoop before locking him in a crushing bear hug. The astonishing grip squeezed his lungs dry and he found it impossible to inhale. In desperation, he pounded both fists into the man's face and drove his right leg forward with all of his strength. The inadvertent aim was perfect; he almost split his assailant in two. The huge hands released him as the man dropped to his knees, frantically grasping for the pain that seared up from his burning scrotum. Dover stumbled back in despair as the man rose with the knife back in his hand.

The first twinges of panic erected the hairs on the back of his neck. The dark blob staggering purposely his way was going to kill him. Dover backed to brace himself against the wall, only there was no wall. Instead, he leaned into thin air and fell through the open door of his bathroom. With a single fear-driven movement, he slammed the door, locked his right elbow through the 2-inch steel tubing which served as a support handle, and braced himself. The body on the other side hit with the force of a pair of Bronco linebackers, but the door held. Dover reached across the commode and pressed the emergency nurse-call button, prayerfully thanking the cost-conscious architect who had designed such a small bathroom. The door shook and bowed inward as the brute beyond tried to force it open. Then, again, this time shoving it inward several inches. Dover was weakening.

A shrill scream erupted from the hall outside his sitting room. The attack on the door stopped and heavy footsteps faded from his bedroom. He cracked open the bathroom door in time to see his attacker lunging through the sitting room and out into the hall. There were confused sounds of a brief struggle, then more footsteps disappearing down the corridor.

Dover ran through the open doors and almost stumbled over the Marine sentry. The young man lay face-down beside the hall wall, a thick mass of dark red saturating his lower back and oozing into the waistband of his trousers. An even darker stain above his right kidney marked the entry wound.

Nurse Masconi was struggling to her feet, a steady flow of blood enveloping her left forearm. She had been slashed just below the elbow.

"The nurse's station . . ." she stammered, ". . . dial . . . three . . . two . . . one . . . hurry!" She nodded to indicate she could control the bleeding from her arm and knelt by the Marine.

Dover ran to the phone and punched in the numbers. A sleepy voice answered on the second ring.

"Tobias."

"This is Dover . . . we just had a visitor . . . he tried to kill me. . . ."

"I'll be right there!"

Dover contacted the main switchboard and called for medical assistance before running back toward his room. Masconi was cradling the Marine's head in her arms. His unblinking eyes told the story. They were already glazed.

"He was just a kid," moaned Masconi.

"How'd that creature get past your station?"

"I was in the head, just for a minute. He must have slipped by then." She nodded toward the janitorial floor buffer which stood a few feet away. That was how the intruder had apparently caught the Marine off guard.

"We better check out the rest of the residents." Dover started for the door down from his.

"Don't bother," said Masconi, "there's no one on this floor but you."

The elevator doors at the far end slid open and a pair of uniformed civilian guards rushed toward the scene. Two nurses pushing a crash cart followed them, and bringing up the rear was Tobias and one of the duty doctors.

"What the shit happened?" yelled Tobias.

Dover took him aside and described the attack. The duty doctor shook his head over the Marine and the nurses covered him with a sheet.

"Somebody knows, Tobias," said Dover.

"No . . . he was after the eye. That's all."

"Bullshit, he was. That son of a bitch was trying to kill me."

"Just for the eye. He couldn't have known about your assignment." Tobias grabbed Dover's face and started examining the eye-camera.

Dover reassured him. "It's all right. He never hit me in the face."

The elevator doors opened again and Anderson came charging up. Doctor Tanaka had been behind him, but stopped to answer the ringing phone at the nurse's station.

"Joe, are you all right?" gasped the surgeon.

"I'm okay. Our sentry bought it, though."

"I should have had one of our own men outside the door," said Tobias. "I didn't anticipate this."

Tanaka's excited voice rang down the hall. "They've got him? The security guards spotted him running across the parking lot."

"Thank God for small favors," breathed Tobias, but his prayer was short-lived as Tanaka's next words quieted them all.

"But he's dead . . . they had to shoot him."

"Damn! . . ." cursed Tobias under his breath. "Let's go back inside," he said, preceding Dover into the sitting room. Tanaka followed, and Anderson joined them after seeing that Nurse Masconi was being attended to.

"There's no way he could have known who you are, or where you're going, or why," repeated Tobias. "The eye has been under development for over two years. Somewhere along the line, something must have slipped out. A lot of people would kill for it, but the prototype is kept too well secure. He had to go for yours."

Anderson started forward to examine the eye-camera. Dover pushed him away.

"It's all right," he said, then looked at Tobias. "So, what now?"

"No change; we go on with the operation."

Dover suddenly remembered the briefing material and his cover papers. He had placed them in the drawer of his bedside table. It took only a moment to check and see that they were undisturbed. When he returned to the sitting room, Anderson had poured them all a drink. Dover and Tanaka declined. Instead, Dover filled a glass with Coke. Tanaka still shook his head.

Tobias set his glass down after a healthy swig. "We go on as planned. I'll have one of my men here the rest of the night. I don't know how in hell you're going to get any sleep after all this, Joe, but try."

After Tobias left, Anderson and Tanaka helped Dover straighten his bedroom.

"Would you like something to help you sleep?" asked Anderson.

"Nurse Masconi brought me a pill earlier. I don't think I want anything."

As they prepared to leave, Anderson offered, "I can put you on a twenty-four-hour medical hold if you like."

"No, Doc, but thanks. We're on a tight schedule."

Anderson and Tanaka left.

Dover stood by the partially open window and filled his lungs with the moisture-laden early morning air while his eye followed the street traffic on the hospital grounds. Two military police cars pulled away from the main entrance, shutting off their emergency lights as they resumed their routine patrols. A steady but light drizzle was falling and an occasional silver streak of lightning darted among the low clouds. Far off in the distance a low rumble signaled the passing of an obscured thunderstorm. It was almost 4:00 A.M.

He mentally reviewed the events of the last twenty-four hours, particularly the attack. If only he had more time to prepare himself, but the game was started, and the bad guys might be a step ahead of the good guys.

He didn't sleep until the rising sun began to lighten things under the drifting rain scud. Then he only rested for an hour. By 6:30 A.M., he was poring over the briefing material and sipping black coffee.

His wardrobe arrived at 10:00 A.M., an ample supply of all the right things for a professor's working vacation. Some of the clothing was new, some appropriately broken in but fresh and clean. Tobias's man helped him select a representative wardrobe from those that fit best. After the Agency man left, Dover dressed and boxed his own things. The CIA guard outside his door offered to see that they were sent back to the ranch.

He set the Seiko on the third, August third, almost two years to the day when he had brought the crippled *Columbia* back,

Macfay had promised to see that his pickup got back to the ranch, but he took time to drop a note to Carl, instructing him to give his sometimes forgetful Navy friend a call if the vehicle didn't show up by the end of the month.

After lunch, he packed his bags and turned over the briefing materials to the guard. He even managed to order flowers for Nurse Masconi before his taxi arrived.

The rain had stopped and the clouds had lifted somewhat. It was still a gray day, however, as the cab carried him back across the Potomac and south on the George Washington Parkway. He arrived at Washington National at 4:15 P.M., and an hour later watched the Mall, and beyond it the Capitol, fade and finally disappear below the

45

low scud as his Eastern 727 followed the winding Potomac on its climb through the clouds before swinging northeast on its departure for JFK.

Kennedy Airport was a mass of bustling humanity, milling about in frustration and ill humor with the weather-caused delays. He had an hour between flights, but by the time he had claimed his luggage at the domestic terminal and fought the lines to check it at Pan American's overseas counter, forty minutes had elapsed. He arrived at his gate just as his flight was called.

An initial scan of the waiting passengers failed to match anyone with the picture in his wallet, but the sudden waft of subtle but very exotic perfume and the simultaneous tug at his sleeve eased his concern. Standing beside him was Mrs. Utgoff. She was even more attractive than the picture.

"Darling," she said, touching his lips with hers. "I was beginning to worry." She looped her arm in his and took his hand.

Dover assumed the play had started. "Had some last-minute details at the university . . . almost missed my Washington flight."

"We're all checked in with the tour guide, a Mr. Donovan. He's really very nice. I'm so thrilled. We've looked forward to this trip for so long."

They boarded and found their seats on the side of the coach section and Dover placed their carry-on bags in the overhead compartment. They sat and strapped in.

The Boeing 747 received its takeoff clearance and lifted into the evening sky. Marie gazed idly out the window until they leveled off over the darkening Atlantic.

"Well, Josef, we are on our way." Her voice was deliberately low, although Dover doubted that any normal conversation would penetrate the deadening whir of the cabin pressurization system and the muffled engine noises. The sound-proofing of civil aircraft cabins always seemed to dissolve conversational sound waves once they reached the aisles. But he followed her lead.

"That we are."

She shifted into Russian. "I understand you had an interesting night."

"You know?"

"I spoke with Tobias. He wanted to let me know you might be a little worried."

"You're damned right I am."

"I agree with him; the man was after the eye. That's all. Our assignment has not been compromised. I've been with the Company almost ten years. Have confidence in what I say." She leaned over and rested her head on his shoulder. "This could be our last opportunity for a private conversation for a while. Is there anything you need to talk about?"

"Yes, there is. How did someone like you get into this game?"

"Someone like me?"

"Yes. I'm new at the intelligence racket, but you don't look like a typical agent."

"That's the way it's played, Josef. We're not supposed to look the part."

"You know what I mean."

"No, I don't believe I do."

"Marie . . ." The name rolled easily through his lips, ". . . or whoever, you're a stunning woman. I thought agents were supposed to look inconspicuous. You'd stand out in a crowd of angels."

"But only as a pretty face. To answer your question, my husband brought me in. I had some special skills that were needed at the time. He'd worked for the Company since his student days in Europe."

"I didn't know husband and wife teams were allowed."

"Normally not. There were special circumstances. Anyway, it didn't last. I lost him on our second assignment."

"Sorry."

"So am I."

"Any kids?"

"You and me, or me and him?"

"Ah—I guess for both purposes."

"We don't need any for our cover. It would just be one

47

other thing we'd have to build a story around. Another thing we could get tripped up on. Ted and I had none, either." It was the first time she had said her husband's name and it caused the smile generated by her previous facetious question to abruptly fade.

"I didn't mean to pry."

"Hey, no problem. We had some good years together. For a while, before I knew what he really did for a living, we were white-picket-fence folks. Very much in love, both good in bed, lots of plans."

"Anybody since then?"

"Never again. It's been too much hurt. I'm okay, but I think about the last day. We were all through and Tobias had promised us a soft one for the next go around. New Zealand, of all places. Nice safe assignment where we could enjoy each other."

"You don't have to talk about it."

"No, I don't have to. But I need to. With someone like you, Josef. My husband for the next few days. You're entitled to know the reason I may do some things." She lifted her head as if in some posture of defiance to an unseen listener. "We were all through. Mission accomplished. We'd made our contact, passed on some—some things, and managed to evade some clever East Germans who had made us at the last moment. Clever? I should say goddamned clever. They worked us north through the lake country to a spot on the border near a little place called Ratziburg. We had it made, Josef. Across the border and a short run to Hamburg and home. Lowlands off the Baltic Sea.

"They worked us right up to the last half mile and then watched us. There wasn't even a fence. We ran and then Ted tripped. 'Keep going!' he yelled. He wasn't hurt. Got right up and was about 20 yards behind me and off to the left when it happened. He just blew up. My husband was shredded. When I looked back he was gone. I stopped, maybe feet from West Germany, in the middle of a mine field. Across the field, the East German militiamen came out of the trees and stood watching. I'll never forget the look on their faces. They were getting their kicks right there. They could have had us any time they wanted us but they had deliberately worked us onto that mined field. I didn't care. Ted was gone. I just turned and walked straight out of their goddamned country. Didn't step on a thing. I hope to hell I ruined their whole blessed day.''

Dover couldn't think of anything to say.

Her eyes were moist, but she sat for a full minute and Dover could see that she was determined that no tear would come. Instead, her face softened.

''Your turn,'' she said.

Dover's mouth was lined with an ill-tasting fur. He glanced back down the aisle but the drink cart was just being positioned. ''My life's been pretty routine.''

''A fly boy, test jock, and astronaut? Hardly routine.''

Her obvious attempt to lighten the conversation relaxed him. He was relieved to talk about himself. ''Really. Pretty normal childhood. Always wanted to fly. Navy after college. Flight school and a couple tours flying off Pacific Fleet birdfarms. Lucked into test pilot school and made the astronaut program.''

''Boy, you are a genius at understatement. Married?''

Dover was surprised her briefing hadn't covered such things about him. ''No.''

''Looking?''

Dover nodded.

The 747 was leveling off.

''Perhaps we should get some rest,'' she ventured.

''Perhaps.'' Dover was eager to agree. The conversation was uncomfortable. ''I didn't get much sleep last night.''

''From what Tobias told me, you didn't get any. Close your eyes, my Josef. I won't let the boogie man get you again.''

''Funny, Mrs. Utgoff. Funny.''

She squeezed his hand. ''You can relax. Now's a good time. We're stuck up here, isolated and with no demands upon us. It won't be this way for long. We go to work soon enough.''

She was warm against him, and soft.

"With my luck," murmured Dover, "a wing will probably fall off this thing over mid-Atlantic."

She giggled and closed her eyes.

Dover sat and enjoyed her closeness. She woke for dinner, after which the cabin attendants turned down the lights and they slept together.

Chapter
4

The India ink darkness that enveloped Dover's and Marie's smooth-riding 747 lightened to the east, becoming a rich blue-black over the far reaches of the North Atlantic. Beyond that, in a general northeastern direction it faded even more until at the edge of the Arctic Circle it bled first into the vibrant lighter blue of pre-dawn and then began to display the first orange-yellow fringe of sunrise.

The far north city of Arkhangelsk was still asleep, but a mere 250 kilometers to the south the premier Soviet spaceport, the Northern Cosmodrome by designation, home of military space research and development, was alive with pre-launch activities—and had been so throughout the short mid-summer night.

The heavy night air bathing the space center was alive with an ocean of microscopic ice crystals. The tiny bits of solid water swirled and mixed together in a random dance of incredible beauty as they caught the light of the stars before settling to lay a paper-thin coating of silver frost over the entire area. The skies were clear and there was no wind, an ideal condition for the clandestine business at hand on the spaceport.

One dark object dominated the launch pads west of the village of Kochmas. Like some giant symbol of phallicism, the sinister, dark green and silver rocket projected its erect form over 70 meters into the still pre-dawn air, its lower one-third dominated by six slim teardrop-shaped boosters strapped around its perimeter. Shadowy wisps of liquid oxygen boiled off and drifted lazily around the base of the rocket before losing themselves among the four steel arms holding the upright cylinder firmly onto its launching pad. An advanced development of the reliable SL-13 heavy booster that had put the Salyut space stations into orbit, it held on its upraised tip a strange winged nose cone. Thick aluminum sides enclosed a massive load of fuel, liquid oxygen mixed with kerosene, and its engines waited patiently for their first spark of life. At the proper time, an instantaneous flow of electrons would surge through their ignition systems and start the hell fire that would lift the rocket and send it on its path from earth.

This was a different death machine.

The steel labyrinth of service towers were in their retracted position, silent witnesses to the approaching dramatic event. Four ground-mounted searchlights, each with a glaring eye that shone with the brilliance of one million candlepower, slowly played their bright beams along the height of the rocket, illuminating every square inch so that those who were responsible for such things could insure that all was well.

Overhead, spider web strands of high altitude cirrus began to drift across the eastern horizon of the pre-dawn heavens, forerunners of one of the fast developing storm cells that regularly spun away from the polar regions to bring frigid blobs of arctic air into northern Russia, even in these days of summer.

"Get me an update on the weather." The speaker wore the fern green working uniform of a colonel in the Soviet Strategic Rocket Forces. He was not concerned about the weather. High thin cirrus presented no problem. But he was responsible for the launch, and procedure called for an update on the weather at this point. Far be it for him to overlook even the tiniest detail, for should some avoidable factor prevent this critical operation from being an unqualified success, he would find himself supervising political prisoners in some remote archipelago in the East Siberian Sea, definitely not a wise career move.

He stood before a flickering bank of television and computer monitors, methodically scanning each and satisfying himself with the display on one before moving to the next. It was a responsibility he had carried many times before. The battery of screens gave him not only every detail of the bowels of the gigantic rocket but also those of the human being who lay strapped atop the booster. Always of particular interest were the vital signs of the cosmonaut during such a launch. For the moment, they were quite stable, the cosmonaut's heart rate and blood pressure actually below those of the colonel. For all the glory of the Motherland he would never ride such a thing. Those that did were a breed beyond his understanding. He had seen too many launches terminate in a blinding fireball that in an instant carried the rocket and its occupants into eternity. But he was an unshakable launch director.

A white-coated technician handed him the weather clipboard and he gave it a cursory glance before handing it back. For the record, he had done his duty. This was an operational launch, not a scientific one. Weather was of little consequence unless there were gale force winds or lightning. Previous launchings of this particular space vehicle had been conducted at the Baikonur Cosmodrome half a continent away and well down in the temperate latitudes of the Soviet Union. They worked in shirtsleeves there and knew nothing of the hardships facing the most routine tasks at the Northern Cosmodrome. But he preferred such duty. He was a member of the operating forces, not some eight-to-five research officer with a desk full of technical papers and a trip home every evening to endure a poorly cooked meal and a nagging wife. He had controlled launches for every operational test from the first surface-to-surface SS-2—a terribly primitive adaption of a German design—to the sophisticated SSX-25, a fifth generation long range missile with multiple warheads, each of which carried more destructive power than all of the bombs of World War II and could be placed within yards of their individual targets. It was only logical that he be selected to head the launch team for this most important task.

"Resume countdown," he ordered. The large digital display on the front wall of the underground launch control center once more began flickering off the seconds.

Six minutes to launch.

The Colonel sensed a presence at his elbow. That would be the First Deputy Commander in Chief for Special Space Operations, General Colonel Leon P. Koidunov. He was always present at important launches and liked to peer over the launch director's shoulder at the most inopportune times. There was plenty to do in the last minutes without having a high ranking observer to consider.

"It is good. Right on schedule," softly spoke Koidunov.

The launch director nodded. When he was in charge, it was always on schedule.

"How does it feel, comrade?" asked Koidunov. "This last one."

"Ten more days, comrade General Colonel, and we will have a fully operational system."

"It is a great step." Koidunov studied the monitors for several minutes.

Five minutes to launch.

Koidunov moved back to one of the rows of supplemental controllers, each of whom had a specific aspect of the launch under his supervision. He took a relaxed stance behind one individual and would stay there for the remainder of the launch. He felt much more comfortable at that favorite spot than beside the launch director who was as cold a fish as he had ever encountered in the military. This controller, on the other hand, was a vibrant, outgoing, heroic cosmonaut in his own right—and also the General Colonel's son. He leaned over to see if he could hear any of the exchange taking place between the controller and the man atop the rocket.

"The umbilical is pulled. You are on internal power," advised the controller. He, too, wore the sharply pressed uniform of the Soviet Air Force's elite cosmonaut corps, his special wings prominent on his breast over the five rows of service and award ribbons. The shiny insignia gave off a perceptible sparkle even in the dimly lit launch control center. Colonel Vladimir M. Koidunov—Koidunov the Younger, he was known as among his peers—was a senior cosmonaut, especially well suited by background and experience for his duties as the primary communicator with his fellow cosmonaut waiting resolutely at the top of the rocket.

At the moment, Vladimir was too busy to acknowledge the presence of his father with other than a friendly nod. His thoughts were on the launching pad, identical to the one at Baikonur where he had ridden the winged demon through the first five test missions. Now, it was time for the final prototype flight and a younger man was called for. This would be the most punishing test of all and even he had to concede that a youthful 35 was less of a risk than a mature 43. He was unaware, however, that his father had a hand in the crew selection for this ride. The General Colonel was looking forward to having his son on his staff where he could guide the remainder of his career, perhaps into his very own boots.

Four minutes to launch.

General Colonel Koidunov let his thoughts drift to the significance of this occasion. He had been a military man for over 50 years. A veteran of the war that had cost the lives of 20,000,000 of his countrymen, he had no delusions about his profession. It was a vital part of the Revolution, more so now than at the beginning. The military was the third prong of the Revolution pitchfork, a necessary complement to the political and economic warfare systems. If those two failed, as they had in times past in Czechoslovakia, Hungary, Angola, Afghanistan, Nicaragua, and so many other places, it was the troops that would solidify the social order. An old Bolshevik in his communist philosophy, he tempered his idealism with the lessons of his life. World revolution might be inevitable, but if it could lead to world annihilation, some adjustments must be made. If those fools in the Kremlin became impatient, the new social order would disappear along with everything else on the face of the earth. He had made a career of laying his life on the line for his beloved country, and would unhesitantly do so again, but unless the current project was successful such a sacrifice would be a futile demonstration of patriotism. There would be no one left to recognize the act.

Perhaps he was finally witnessing the end of that terrible dilemma. Until now, the Americans had the advantage. After this final test, the Soviet Union would have the supreme defensive weapon. American intercontinental ballistic missiles would never reach the soil of his native land. Soon, he could retire to his summer home on the shore of the Black Sea and soak his aching bones in the sunshine.

Three minutes to launch.

Koidunov the Younger made a routine communications check with the rocket-mounted cosmonaut. The countdown was proceeding smoothly and the man inside the winged nose cone was performing his many tasks with the confidence instilled by thorough training and years of background experience in space station programs. If anything, he was merely impatient for the adventure to begin.

Two minutes to launch.

Time would accelerate, now. Most of the routine leading up to the launch had been accomplished. The next 120 seconds would fly by, propelled by an increased level of apprehension and excitement. Two rows ahead of Colonel Koidunov and his father, the launch director was nodding in recognition of the anticipated increase in heart rate and blood pressure displayed by the monitors. But they weren't coming. The man waiting for the fire was ice. Only a very slight rise. Nothing exceptional. Surely the man's adrenal gland would trigger some type of measurable response.

One minute to launch.

* * *

Comrade Major Andrian E. Bykovsky lay on his back, firmly strapped into his seat and generally comfortable in the air-conditioned suit that surrounded him with its own unique atmosphere until the dangerous launch phase of his mission was over and he could enjoy the less confining cabin atmosphere. Everything was in readiness. All he need do now was provide the on-board monitoring of the launch. The hundreds of individual evolutions necessary to blast him off his steel perch would be infallibly handled by the bank of computers which shared his compartment. Their displays were constantly changing, noiselessly informing him of each event as the countdown progressed. It would be a flawless launch, to be sure.

Wait! There it was again! That slight light-headed feeling he had first experienced riding up the elevator to the entrance platform. Excitement? Probably. But he was a veteran test pilot and cosmonaut with several thousand hours in the latest of fighters. He had pioneered the tactical development of the MiG-25 Foxbat, an airplane that exposed him to a nerve-wracking surprise on almost every flight, not to mention his previous space time aboard *Salyut*. Not once had there ever been any sign of unusual stress. Yet, twice now in the past two hours, for a fleeting moment in each instance, he had felt the dizzy detachment of his senses from the events taking place around him. It concerned him but there was no way that he was going to sacrifice this opportunity by mentioning it at this late time.

"Andrian? Everything all right?" The launch director must have picked up something on the monitors.

"Everything is fine."

"We just recorded a transient peak in your pulse and blood pressure."

"I am 30 seconds away from launch, comrade. How is *your* pulse and blood pressure?"

"Ha! I understand. All is normal, now."

Ten seconds . . . nine . . . eight . . . seven . . . six . . . five . . . four . . . three . . . two . . . one . . .

Andrian felt the massive vibration of ignition and the

first "G's" of liftoff. The rocket rose rapidly and within seconds passed through the speed of sound as it started its programmed arc toward the speed and altitude window of its insertion into orbit. Andrian was in his own world, a lone rider of the fiercest fire ever kindled by man.

Already he was passing over the frozen edges of the arctic ice cap and nearing his orbital altitude.

"Prepare for insertion."

Andrian checked the readouts on his primary control computer. "I concur. Insertion—now."

The "G" forces, almost intolerable at the point of maximum acceleration, had gradually slackened and now he experienced the neutral gravitational forces of weightlessness. His booster, almost a hollow shell with practically all of its fuel expended, fell behind, and in reaction to the separation force began to drop on its inevitable fall toward a fiery death in the outer layers of the earth's atmosphere.

Andrian flipped up the visor of his helmet and loosened the straps which had held him rigid in his liftoff posture. For the coming days, he would merely be a rider as the automatic functions of the spaceplane were tested and re-tested by various control facilities across the surface of the planet which now appeared to be bright blue. The glimmering hue was eye-shattering. He was arcing southeastward across the Bering Sea, heading for the North Pacific Ocean, his path over the face of the earth a function of the physics of his launch and the spinning of the earth around its axis within his orbit in space. His initial southern swing would take him to where he would pass across the South Pacific very near Antarctica and then northeastward toward Africa.

His main concern now would be to make himself comfortable. His cabin was roomy and there would be opportunities for daily exercise in between his duties of monitoring the ground-controlled programs and his own testing of the various components of his on-board weapons systems. His main contribution to this, the last evaluation launch of a series of six, would come in the final days of his mission when he would check out the manual mode of operation. Until then, except for certain periods of unique maneuvering, he could forget that this was a machine of war and enjoy his return to the peacefulness and detachment of space. The spaceplane was positioned with its topside facing the earth and through the large window in the top entrance hatch he could enjoy his passage over the surface of the planet.

Andrian would accomplish one important "first" on this mission. He would be the first man in space to see every point on the face of the earth during a single flight. Until now, such an ability had been beyond the most sophisticated of the previous space vehicles.

His first task would be to confirm a communications link with the Soviet Antarctic Station, Leningradskaya. The scientific research station lay on the side of the ice-covered continent closest to Australia and New Zealand in an area known as Victoria Land. The abandoned joint U.S./New Zealand research station, Hallett, was close by and the main U.S. station, McMurdo, was only a scant 900 kilometers southeast of Leningradskaya.

By treaty, the countries engaged in antarctic research were forbidden to use the area for military operations. However, weather and communications satellites were regularly monitored from almost all of the various national stations. Leningradskaya was no different. Still, the communications check must be discreet. Actually, an antarctic contact was not critical to the proposed mission of the spaceplane. The southern hemisphere was not a vital factor in the aerospace defense of the Soviet Union. But Leningradskaya could be a vital emergency source of communications and even search and rescue once the spaceplane system was fully deployed.

Andrian retrieved the communications packet from its stowage drawer. He would be using a standard open frequency and by prearrangement the nuclear icebreaker, *Lenin*, would be at the edge of the winter pack ice off Leningradskaya, conducting routine communications with the scientists of the station. Andrian would merely follow the prescripted communication dialogue and interject his own transmission at the proper place.

He was still 15 minutes from the southernmost swing of his first orbit. He watched the waters of the Pacific Ocean slide by, the subtle deep-blue, blue, and blue-green of the various depths shining in the mid-afternoon sun. He had already sped across ten time zones and was south of the Tropic of Capricorn. The portion of the South Pacific under him now was the most isolated of all the earth's waters. From his present position south to Antarctica, and from Chatham Island off New Zealand eastward clear across to the Pacific coast of South America, there was nothing but water. There was no other area like it on earth. But it made for poor sightseeing. A chance to reflect upon one's good fortune was rare for an inflight cosmonaut but for the next few minutes he found himself reliving his youth in the profound quiet of his solitary space voyage.

This had always been his destiny. Born practically within the confines of what was to become the Northern Cosmodrome, in the Russian town of Plesetsk, he was of the first space-age generation. Andrian even remembered the excitement of his family, although he was only five years old at the time, when man's first orbital object, *Sputnik*, beeped its message of Soviet space prowess to the world. He was nine when Yuri Gargarin made his epic 1961 orbit around the planet. Andrian had written his first comprehensive school essay on his feeling about that achievement and so intense was the excellence of the paper he was marked for advanced scientific studies. Two years later, when comrade Valentina Tereshkova became the first woman in space, Andrian wrote a second paper on the destiny of the Soviet Union among the stars. It earned him a trip to the town of Kaluga, just to the southwest of Moscow, where he visited the National Museum home of a Russian schoolmaster, Konstantin Eduardovitch Tscolkovsky, whose turn-of-the-century theories on rocketry and space travel marked him as an eccentric dreamer who was out of touch with reality. Yet his pronouncements, including a sketch of a proposed spaceship, were remarkably accurate. It was during that visit to the home of the first disciple of the Space Age that Andrian realized what his own destiny would be. His subsequent university graduation with a degree in astrophysics, entrance into the Soviet Air Force, duties as a premier test pilot, and selection for the cosmonaut program had been as natural for him as his feeling of accomplishment and joy at this very moment in space.

It was time, and he heard the *Lenin* commence the communications check.

"Leningradskaya, this is *Lenin.*"

"Your communication is clear, *Lenin*. How are the seas?" That was Andrian's cue.

He keyed his mike and read off his coded response, "The seas are running from the northwest with only a slight ground swell." The message told all concerned that his orbit was exactly as programmed and communications were loud and clear.

Leningradskaya's next transmission was a double check. "Understand slight swell. Is there any cloud cover in your area?"

"No. Skies are clear." Again, the communications were perfect.

"Copy, *Lenin*. We have a strong bearing on your signal." Leningradskaya was telling him that they held the small spiked blip of his radar echo on their special "weather" scope.

The *Lenin* came back with a concluding response. Andrian's participation was over and he listened to the routine chatter as the ship and station exchanged weather and news comments. He was on a northern swing now and heading across the South Atlantic Ocean.

General Colonel Koidunov leaned down and patted his son on the shoulders. "It all went very well."

The younger Koidunov smiled broadly in agreement. He had no communications responsibilities for a while. The spaceplane had left his control 45 minutes ago and was on the far side of the earth by now. "I would like to sit in on your briefing, Father, but I have some duties and Andrian will be switching back over to me in a half hour or so.''

''You already know more than will be covered, Vladimir. When you next speak to Andrian, tell him of my pleasure at observing such a professional performance.'' The old warrior turned and walked from the control center. The special conference room was only a short distance along a wide tunnel which farther on sloped upward and led to the ground level office spaces.

He entered and shut the door behind him, then flipped a nearby wall switch. It activated a red warning light outside the door which would alert passers-by that a classified conference was in session. It also activated an electrical door lock and turned on the room recorder. He took his seat at the head of the long table, a three man briefing team to his left. They had been working on the final plan for the deployment of the spaceplane.

To his right sat the Deputy Commander in Chief for Combat Training, General Colonel Aviation P.S. Mikoyan. There was a delicate relationship between him and Mikoyan. Both were equal deputies of the Commander in Chief of the Soviet Air Force. But Koidunov's background was in rocketry and he was a non-flyer. Mikoyan, on the other hand, was one of the Air Force's senior aviators, a relative of the famous aircraft designer who had engineered the Mikoyan/Gurevich series of high performance jet fighters, and had assumed he would be placed in charge of the spaceplane program, but the powers that be had tapped Koidunov and Mikoyan was left in his combat training staff position. The two men were polite and proper to one another but that was the extent of their relationship.

Before each of the five lay a red folder labeled: Kosmolyot II Deployment Plan.

Koidunov opened his folder and nodded for the senior member of the briefing team to commence.

The young Air Force lieutenant colonel began, ''Comrade General Colonels, we have made the final adjustments to the deployment plan, an earlier version of which you have had for some months now. The plan now reflects the results of the past five prototype missions and it is not anticipated that today's launch will result in any further modifications. Please refer to diagram A.''

Koidunov and Mikoyan both flipped to the appropriate plate. It showed an outline of the earth with the northern hemisphere tinted red. A series of blue-line orbital paths were arranged around the globe, each oriented on a different plane of orbit.

''Using the data obtained from the operational testing program, we have adjusted our original plan and determined the optimum variety of orbits the spaceplane can achieve. Needless to say, it is even more capable than our plans call for. However, to go on, the versatility of the craft allows us to arrive at an effective deployment well within our planned deployment strength.

''As you know, we are primarily concerned with the northern hemisphere, specifically the ICBM launch sites within the continental United States and the operating areas of the U.S Trident submarines. The third strategic threat, the B-1 bomber force, can be dealt with by conventional air defenses and is not considered a suitable target for the Kosmolyot II.

''By placing the force into elliptical orbits not unlike those of our surveillance satellites, we can position the apogee—the highest point of the orbit—over the center of our target area. The elliptical orbits will cause the spaceplanes to have maximum time on station, that is, over the northern hemisphere. The advantage of using an orbital weapon of course, despite the present threat orientation being the northern hemisphere, is the bonus of a no-cost coverage of the entire world should the United States decide to redeploy its submarine fleet or base its ICBM's at some other location. Obviously, the time when the deployed force is in the southern half of its orbit affords us also the opportunity to demonstrate our complete domination of the space around our planet, a by-product which may be of some value in future years.

''Nevertheless, the elliptical orbit plan will provide the

required anti-ICBM coverage by the employment, initially, of only six 20-spacecraft squadrons. At any one time, three squadrons will be on station; that is, there will be 60 spaceplanes within the target envelope over the northern hemisphere.

"Air time for U.S.-based ICBM's is 30 minutes in all but a few cases. For the submarine missiles, the time is reduced to an average of 20 minutes. Each Kosmolyot II has a fire rate of one beam per ten seconds. Therefore, each spaceplane can realistically engage 150 missiles, allowing a few seconds delay in initial acquisition and five minutes at the end when the multiple warheads may already be deployed. One hundred and fifty shots times 60 spaceplanes, considering a 95 percent kill rate, is 8,850 kills."

"And the rest of the United States missiles continue on," interjected Mikoyan. If he could not run the program he could at least take some particular delight in arguing its shortcomings.

The young briefer was undisturbed. "The Americans have a theoretical launch efficiency of 98%. *Theoretical.* But they have very little history of actual missile launches and our own experience tells us that the actual rate of successful launches will be less than that. But, let us consider the 98% figure as accurate. Another 5% will have guidance problems. An additional 5% will have faulty warheads. Our point ABM defenses around Moscow and our other strategic areas have a proven 98% reliability. Very few—very few—American missiles will ever reach their targets. Certainly not enough to stop our massive retaliation or affect our continued viability as a nation.

"I should add," said Koidunov, "that further down the line we will have 120 spaceplanes on station at any one time. The kill capability doubles—and that wipes out all threat of an American attack."

"What is our target date for deployment?" asked Mikoyan, apparently unable to locate it in the pages he had been slowly turning while the briefing officer talked.

Koidunov answered him. "Production indicates the first

squadron can be launched within six months. It is the cosmonaut training that concerns me.'' He had put the ball back in Mikoyan's court.

"The first squadron offers no problem,'' replied Mikoyan. "We have enough experienced people for it and most of the second squadron as well. After that, it may become tight unless we can accelerate the turnover in the Salyut program.''

"We can do that,'' decided Koidunov.

The briefing officer raised a question. "One of the factors that concerns us is the availability of launch vehicles.''

"That, also, has been taken care of,'' said Koidunov. "We have eleven SL-13's ready now and anticipate one every four days.''

"Then it is only a matter of cosmonaut training,'' suggested the briefing officer.

"That is *also* under control, comrade,'' announced Mikoyan, obviously irritated by the junior officer's implication that he might not be on top of his responsibilities.

"Yes, comrade General Colonel,'' quickly responded the briefing officer. He had not meant to infer anything. It just seemed like a logical question to address at this time. Belatedly, he realized the delicate area he had entered. That was all he needed, disfavor with one of the most senior officers in the Air Force.

"All right,'' announced Koidunov, recognizing the officer's plight. "I am sure the deployment plan is in order.'' He was not concerned about the details. He had a staff for that. He would study the highlights of the plan and be ready to brief the Members of the Military Council of Command and Staff of the Soviet Air Force on schedule. His boss could brief Gorbachev and the heads of the other branches of the services. "I will read it tonight,'' he added, picking up the report and standing.

The briefing team also stood at his cue and saluted with their heels. Mikoyan nodded in recognition that Koidunov was leaving and busied himself with thumbing through the annexes to the deployment plan.

Koidunov decided to step outside and enjoy the sun before returning to the control center. He did not like being cooped up in a windowless enclosure like some fox in a snowhole. He walked up the tunnel incline, passed through the office wing, and accepted the smart salute of the outside sentry with an amiable grunt. It was still early morning and a light haze transformed the rising sun into a muted orange glow around which a ghostly halo shimmered. If he looked directly overhead he could see blue sky. Shaking off the fatigue of the past few early morning hours, he tapped a cigarette from its pack and inhaled deeply while holding the flame of his lighter against the tip. The logo on the package caught his eye, a familiar logo but one with perhaps some symbolic meaning on this historic morning. The blue and white package sported an illustration of a dog. A heroic pose of a white-faced terrier with black ears that were raised in alert position against the blue field of night sky. A very special dog. There were stars and a nose cone hurling through the darkened heavens, also a golden sphere and a crescent moon.

Laika, the space dog, rider of the second Sputnik.

Laika brand cigarettes. He chuckled even as he winced at the strong bitter taste of his first full draw. He had been smoking them for over 30 years and they still tasted like the dog had raised his leg to the tobacco.

Inside he felt a warming satisfaction. Ironically, he had fought long and hard for the Kosmolyot II against his Air Force contemporaries whose common sense should have dictated enthusiasm for the program. But now, in a few short months, the first squadron would be ready.

The world's first space squadron. A Soviet space squadron. The Americans would surely lose control of their bowels when they walked out next December and found the heavens over their land controlled by the Soviet Union. They had triggered the Strategic Defense Initiative race with their paranoia about a Soviet first strike. Why they could believe that the Soviet Union, which had seen so much war on its own soil and lost so many sons and daughters, would ever have initiated a nuclear exchange, he could not understand. The Americans were the ones for the world to worry about with their constant buildup of military bases around the Soviet Union and their incessant agitation of the European community and the rearming of Japan. He had a great deal of admiration for the American people and their willingness to stand up to their imperialistic government. Sometimes, he wished his own people would take to the streets and show more backbone in their displeasure with the slow advance of the socialist order in their own country. But the Revolution was still in its middle stages and setbacks must be expected.

Progress would be faster now with the Kosmolyot II. Any fears of further American expansionism and their reckless nuclear attitude would be put to rest now that the citizen workers of the Soviet Union had outpaced the Wall Street cartel. An umbrella of space technology was about to be raised over Mother Russia, and no matter how dark the cloud of American militarism became, not one drop of nuclear rain would ever fall on the sacred soil of his native land.

He dropped his Laika butt and ground it in the dirt with his boot. Before stepping back inside, he raised his face once more to drink in the emerging warmth of the sun. The sky was even bluer and the haze seemed to be thinning. Andrian should be somewhere up there, starting his second orbit.

Chapter
5

The morning light probed through the pressure cabin's oval window and flickered across Dover's eye, waking him. Marie was quietly reading, and the flight attendants were starting down the aisles with the breakfast carts. They were still three hours out of Frankfurt.

"We should come up with a common marital background, in case the subject comes up while we're with the group in Leningrad," Marie suggested.

"That's a good idea. Married six years?"

"Okay. No children. I'm from upper New York State; Lake Placid."

"Sounds good."

"It should. I am from there. How about you?"

"Let's leave it Colorado; Montrose on the western slope."

"Never heard of it."

"It's where God goes for his vacations. You'd like it."

"I've never been with God on one of his vacations— I'm a housewife and a part-time model. That way, I have a serious and a frivolous side."

"What else?"

"You've been with Georgetown three years; you wrote your idiom book the first year."

"That was in my briefing material. I'm surprised that you're aware of it."

"I read a copy. We're first team, Josef."

"Do I play around?"

"Absolutely not. We're devoted to each other."

"I like that. It means we're sexually compatible."

The corners of Marie's mouth turned up. "I suspect that we would be. Buy me a drink, sailor?" The beverage cart had stopped beside them.

"Before breakfast?"

"Bloody Mary. I love juice."

Dover asked for the same and Marie held hers over for a toast. He tapped her glass with his and waited.

"To our vacation, Josef. It is time we enjoyed ourselves." Her lips puckered mischievously as she lifted her drink.

"I can hardly wait," he responded and they each took hearty swallows. "Tell me, did you get to meet any of our group while you were waiting back at Kennedy?"

"A few. Pretty much the standard crowd. A couple advanced students, several widows, older couples."

"Any plants, you think?"

"Just us, I think. Sorry, didn't mean to be facetious. I think they're all legit. We'll be closely supervised, of course. We'll see only what they want us to see."

"The glory of the new socialism?"

"Yes, but don't be too hasty with prejudgement. They have some things going for them. The man in the street feels strongly about his country. He may be impatient with their economic progress but opportunities are increasing."

"You have pretty eyes."

"One drink and you're making a move?"

"I mean it."

"Thank you. Didn't you notice them before we were married?"

Dover picked up immediately on her subtle inflection to

prompt him that perhaps they should stay in character. They were only an aisle away from an older woman who kept glancing their way to see if she couldn't stir up a conversation. Marie raised the arm rest between them and pulled her legs under her to lean closer. Ten minutes later, breakfast arrived.

The big Boeing droned on, its passage marked by only an occasional jolt as it passed through spots of clear air turbulence.

Marie excused herself. "Time to go put on my face."

Dover held her tray as she unstrapped and left for the washroom, then handed both it and his to the alert flight attendant who materialized from the rear of the cabin. It was too early for breakfast, but the Bloody Mary had refreshed him and he stood for a few minutes to stretch. The cabin had a slight musty smell even with the efficient pressurization and air conditioning system. No wonder. There were no empty seats. The jumbo jet was crammed with armpits and groins. Such high density seating would tax the most carefully engineered air recovery systems.

He casually scanned the passengers around him, returning a smile or nod when his eyes met others. Surprisingly, most were wide awake, picking at their breakfasts and engaged in low chatter prompted by their sharing of the night with their fellow passengers. The travel group he and Marie were with were probably all seated in the same section. They all looked innocent enough. Still, there were sufficient interesting faces to make him wonder if among them there was a member of the other team, put there for the express purpose of ferreting out imposters such as he and Marie.

She returned and they took their seats.

"My, you do look better," teased Dover. "Everything in order?"

"What you see is what you get." The lips puckered again.

The next 90 minutes passed routinely. Dover found himself fantasizing about his relationship with his CIA-provided wife. There was that certain intangible quality about her personality that had immediately indicated they were attuned to each other as if they had a prior relationship. Curiously, the feeling brought back a long-forgotten conversation he had once had with a colleague concerning reincarnation. No believer himself, he had nevertheless listened intently to the man's argument for the turnaround of one's soul.

"Haven't you ever met someone for the first time and immediately felt a certain familiarity, as if you were actually friends, already?" his friend had offered.

"Yes, of course. Everyone has," he had replied.

"That's because you had known each other in a previous life. The soul never forgets, even though it only hints at its vast stowage of prior knowledge."

Dover had smiled tolerantly, content in his own mind that such a phenomenon was merely the result of similarly inclined personalities, accidents of birth rather than the reassociation of souls. Still, it pleased him to speculate that his instant rapport with Marie was more than that. It gave him an excuse for imagining all sorts of possibilities for them down the line.

What if they *had* known each other in some prior life? Maybe as mother and son? Or father and daughter? Or perhaps brother and sister? Or lovers? That would be more to his liking. Of course, she need not have been black then. Perhaps, he had been; or Oriental, or Spanish, or whatever. Reincarnation must, by nature, be color-blind. In that respect, he was all for it.

His reverie amused him and ended only when the 747 started its smooth descent into Frankfurt. A slight haze lay over the city as the big Boeing passed over the vibrant center of the financial capital of West Germany.

Almost completely destroyed by the massive bombings of World War II, the city had lost a great deal of its old world charm. In its place had erupted the glass-walled skyscraper look of a German Houston, with the towering offices of the great banking cartels of Deutsche, and Dresden, and Commerzbank dominating the modern skyline, all but overpowering the reminders of old Frankfurt such as the rebuilt medieval city hall. In its day, the multifaced beige structure with the stepped and gabled rooftop had housed coronation balls for German emperors, and, today, provided a gingerbread contrast to the sleek, sterile exteriors of the postwar high-rises.

The airport, as anticipated, was a frenzy of activity and Dover and Marie felt quite fortunate to find an available porter to assist them in their transfer from the ultramodern Pan Am gate to the more restrained boarding area for Aeroflot.

As through passengers, they had no business with German customs and were able to amuse themselves during their waiting time by picking over the items in the abundance of shops in the terminal and sampling the delicious pastries offered by bakery alcoves. They were tourists, doing tourist things, as were the other members of their tour group.

And like tourists all over the world, they found their waiting time exasperatingly longer than planned.

The layover and airline exchange was prolonged by several mechanical difficulties which plagued their Aeroflot Tupolev transport. The DC-9 look-alike left the line twice, each time only to return while the captain apologized for the inconvenience in a lackluster tone that indicated such an event was all part of the flying game. The third attempt was the proverbial charm, and after an uneventful two hours they broke out of the damp overcast over Leningrad at 3:37 P.M. local time.

As the pilot rolled into a steep turn to commence his approach to the airport, Dover and Marie peered out the small window at one of the world's showplace metropolitan areas, the City of Peter, the birthplace of the October Revolution. Dover spotted the old Russian naval cruiser, *Aurora,* permanently enshrined at anchor in the Neva River just off the southeastern tip of Aptekorsky Island. It was from the deck of the now lifeless warship that a single blank shot rang out in 1917 to signal the start of the Bolsheviks' bloody overthrow of the Tsar and his opulent court.

Below the rapidly descending jet sprawled the gateway city, its uncountable pastel palaces and public buildings shimmering in the summer rainfall and casting pearly reflections skyward. In addition to the Neva and its wide winding branches, all slicing the northern section of the city into five major islands before pouring their waters into the adjoining Gulf of Finland, numerous canals ran hodgepodge through the city. They wound underneath hundreds of streets, giving the metropolis its flavor as the Venice of the North, and spawning a myriad of gracefully arched stone bridges, over which moved a steady stream of antlike pedestrians and a smattering of vehicles, forerunners of the approaching rush-hour traffic.

Everywhere they looked, the gilded domes and brightly painted steeples of picture-book cathedrals and churches dotted the city with colorful elegance. Originally the tallest structures, they had been the only buildings allowed, by Tsarist decree, to exceed the 92-foot height of his Winter Palace. Even now, there were few taller buildings; however, the 1050-foot television tower on the Petrogradskaya Storona was the most notable exception as its tip reached for the base of the clouds.

As the Tupolev swung wide around the city, Dover pointed out the massive bowl of Kirov Stadium, and a minute later the magnificently domed Peter and Paul Cathedral and Fortress which sat on a mini-island of its own only a few yards downstream from the sullen *Aurora*. Directly across the Neva from the Cathedral, the large complex of the State Hermitage Museum, the Admiralty, and the Peter the Great Monument faced southeast along the angled main thoroughfare, Nevsky Prospekt—Neva Avenue. His briefing sheets had been very thorough.

The many islands of Leningrad, along with the asiatic mainland of the city, were heavy with the weight of over five million people. If Dover were to go underground in Mother Russia, this looked like the proper place. The sheer logistics of maintaining surveillance over those teeming masses below must be mind-boggling. The largest port and the second largest people-place in the Soviet Union, despite its spectacular baroque and neoclassical architecture, undoubtedly had its seamy side, like all great cities. It was within those environs that Dover figured he would vanish.

The transport touched down on the long concrete with only a whisper of wheel contact, and after disembarking, the tour group was herded into the customs area. Their luggage was waiting. Dover and Marie claimed their two large bags from the cart-train and a pleasant, elderly official directed them to a long table tended by three customs agents, all female. A male overseer stood conspicuously nearby, supervising his area with a nonchalance only a yawn away from boredom.

The real attitude was apparent to Dover, however, as he glanced around the barn-like room. It was clear that not all of the officials were in uniform. A number of dark suits mingled with the passengers, taking careful note of faces, dress, and demeanor. Dover had a brief whimsical urge to press his temple and take a picture, but that would be a reckless use of precious film.

Despite his natural nervousness at being in such a situation, he felt confident of the eye-camera's appearance. A glance at the mirror in the aircraft's washroom had confirmed that all swelling had left his eyelid and the device was as normal as his own eye.

"May I see your passports, and would you open your bags, please?" He and Marie had drawn the oldest and squattiest of the three inspectors. She spoke in heavily accented English.

"Certainly," Dover replied in Russian. "These two are ours."

With an appreciative smile, the woman reverted to her native tongue. "May I also see your carry-ons?"

Dover laid them on the table, along with the 35-millimeter camera Marie carried.

The woman ignored the camera and made a meticulous search of all four bags, taking care to minimize her disturbance of Marie's careful packing system, but exercising considerably less concern with Dover's jumbled possessions. She paid particular attention to their toilet articles, opening and sniffing the bottles and feeling the toothpaste tubes. Her experienced fingers deftly ran along all of the corners and crevices of the bags.

"You may close them, thank you." She opened the passports and glanced up to verify the photographs. "Professor Utgoff, you have a fine old Byelorussian name. I, too, am a Byelo. Do you have relatives here?"

"Possibly. My ancestors emigrated in the late eighteen hundreds."

"Ah, you have hordes of distant cousins, I suspect. You will enjoy Minsk. That is my home. As you undoubtedly know, it is the center of our culture and the capital of the Byelorussian Soviet Socialist Republic. A magnificent city. There are some Utgoffs there."

The woman's blond hair and fair complexion supported her claim to be a White Russian, and her comments made Dover realize how and why Tobias had come up with his cover identity. Dover, also, was fair of skin and light-haired, although a shade darker than the inspector's, but his paternal grandparents had come from the Ukraine rather than the northern republic of the Byelorussians. He had heard that the CIA troops liked to walk a narrow edge in their cover identities for the sake of authenticity. Still, such a ruse as his might be counterproductive if his imagined heritage created unusual interest by the customs people. He wasn't too sure he enjoyed performing on the delicate balance beam of international espionage, and these were the simple maneuvers. The tricky jumps and flips would come later—and the difficult dismount.

Her voice interrupted his mental analogy. "Do you correspond with anyone?"

"No, I'm three generations removed. My family lost contact years ago."

"Of course. Your Russian is excellent, almost native. I compliment you.

"I teach it at an American university in Washington, D.C."

"Ah, your capital city. I have seen pictures. It is a beautiful place."

"Thank you."

"I must apologize, professor. Our regulations require a random selection of passports for visitor survey statistical purposes. I will be gone only a moment."

Oh, God, here it comes.

She retired through a small door near the supervisor, who nodded apologetically to Dover and Marie. In less than a minute, she returned and handed over the passports to Dover.

"Thank you. I regret the inconvenience. We have the bureaucrats here, too, I am afraid. They must write regulations to appear useful." Her uplifted hands emphasized the remark as did her raised-eyebrow smile of resignation.

"We understand," responded Dover.

"Have a pleasant stay, Professor and Mrs. Utgoff. Please return again."

The other members of the tour group were climbing aboard the bus as Dover and Marie handed their bags to the driver.

Mr. Donovan had been superseded by a young woman and the ride into the city was highlighted by her enthusiastic commentary on local history. Long blond braids hanging over her sheer peasant blouse and multicolored overdress added flavor to her animated remarks.

Their hotel was just off Moscow Street and the massive stone structure featured an ornately chandeliered and richly furnished lobby. Dover signed the register and collected their Intourist meal vouchers. After checking their passports, the desk clerk handed them their key.

"Welcome to Leningrad. Our services are listed on the door in your room. I'll have your baggage sent up."

They joined some of the others in the grillwork elevator and were lifted to the fourth floor.

Their room was bright, with gauze-thin drapes over the tall windows. The aged, but well cared for, bedroom furniture rested on an exquisite oriental rug.

Once inside, Marie turned and hugged Dover. "Oh,

Josef, this is such a lovely place. I'm so glad we could come.'' She had placed her mouth close to his ear and her next words were whispered. ''The room is alive with microphones, of course. Everything we say and do here must be very natural.''

Dover was enjoying the embrace. Their bodies fit together well. ''In that case, I shall look forward to this evening,'' he whispered in return.

''I assume you are an exhibitionist,'' she muttered, and nibbled his earlobe.

''I beg your pardon.''

''The mirror over the dresser. It is most probably one-way and some dirty old man will be taping us whenever we're in here.''

''That shoots down my plans.''

''Perhaps not. Making love could strengthen our cover. It is expected.''

''By you?'' Dover tried to hide his surprise at her frankness.

''Of course not. By the dirty old man.''

''I don't know. I have a feeling that mirror may bring on a devastating headache.''

''That's my line.'' She nibbled his ear again.

Dover let his hands roam her back and settle on the soft mounds of her upper buttocks. She kissed him lightly, then pulled away at the sharp sound of a knock on the door.

Dover reluctantly opened it. Their bags were sitting in the hall, but the hotel boy was nowhere to be seen. He brought them in and placed them on the bed.

''Let's see, where were we?'' he asked, turning and reaching out.

Marie touched a finger to her lips and placed it across his. ''Let's unpack, darling,'' she said, pushing away.

Dinner included an attempt at good food, endless toasts, and a review of their next five days in Leningrad. Dover and Marie used the remainder of the free evening to stroll along the banks of the Fontanka River which cut through their section of the city. They held hands and blended with the evening pedestrian traffic.

"They won't contact you tonight. Too soon," commented Marie.

"I figured as much. I wonder why the switch wasn't delayed until we got to . . ."

Marie stopped him in mid-sentence. "Don't, Josef. I don't want to know any more about your assignment. It might not be wise."

For the first time, Dover thought of the consequences should something go wrong when she and his replacement left Leningrad. Her eyes told him that if it did, she wanted to know nothing more than her part in the dangerous charade. The Soviets would break her.

They turned back just short of reaching Neva Avenue, and by 9:00 P.M. reentered their hotel. A leisurely nightcap in the bar off the lobby and an early surrender to the jet lag ended their day.

That night they played their roles well. At first, Dover found it difficult to perform enthusiastically with the cold reflection of the mirror only a few feet from the foot of the bed, but the unexpected expertise of Marie blotted out all awareness except the erotic feel and movements of her supple body. After their initial lovemaking, she aggressively took over the active role, playing his body as a maestro would stroke and pluck the strings of an average violin, producing reactions and sensations far beyond the usual scope of the instrument. She moved with the measured frenzy of some primeval love-animal, taking him with her to dizzying heights of nerve-shattering ecstasy, then allowing him a brief respite in the deep valley of sexual exhaustion before arousing him once more, always with a different and innovative technique. She was insatiable, and aside from her obvious self-gratification, she seemed to be shouting defiance, even anger, at the unseen person behind the mirror, determined to frustrate him with the sight of a thousand pleasures he would never know.

Afterward, they lay together, he sprawled on his back, she sideways tightly against him with one leg pulled up to rest on his abdomen. There was no desire to talk. Their mutual need and performance had given a new depth to their relationship. Dover suspected she had known that it would and that it had been a necessary ploy on her part to give them a real intimacy to support their illusion of man and wife. Talk about method acting! He couldn't help feeling, however, that hers was a lousy profession. True, he had detected a sense of to-hell-with-it when she had talked about her husband's death. But it was still hard for him to imagine a person so cold and calculating that she had no hesitation about using her body as she would use any other instrument of deception. Of course, there was always the chance she had been sincerely attracted to him. From his viewpoint she was certainly desirable. But casual sex, if what had just happened could fit into that category, had never had a strong appeal for him. He could only surmise that she was of a different world, one in which all of the normal standards of human relations were subservient to the task at hand. Perhaps there was even some morality to it. Espionage was a form of war and killing was justified in the name of war. Why not sex?

"You're very quiet," mused Marie.

"Lost in thought," replied Dover.

"I'm in bed with a thinking man?"

"And a man of action," responded Dover, pulling her closer.

"Just a minute." She reached over and turned on the bedside radio, adjusting the volume just enough that it would mask their whispers. "Want to talk?"

"I don't know."

"It wasn't all for show, you know."

"I'd like to believe that."

"You can. Listen, I won't hesitate to do anything to get back at these bastards. Not after what they did to Ted and me. But tonight was more than that. I need a security blanket—Josef—and for tonight, you're it. I won't pretend to be anything other than what I am to you. I'm lonely and I'm pissed. But I'm a professional and my job will always be the number one thing on my mind. Maybe, when this is over, we can get back together for a real evening and you can buy me flowers, take me out to dinner, and we can go dancing and to my place for breakfast. Then, if you want to take me to bed, it can be different."

Dover kissed her forehead. "Are you asking me for a date?"

"I'm a liberated woman."

"You're a beautiful woman."

"At this particular moment, I feel like one." She ran her lips lightly across his chest.

"My God, don't start me up again," cautioned Dover. "Even us macho astronauts have our limitations."

"Ha, ha! I win!"

"This has been a contest?"

"No, silly. Just a display of feminine superiority. We are sexually superior, you know."

"I concede."

She placed her cheek against his. "I could learn to like this. Maybe we should carry our charade back to Colorado and lose ourselves in the high country as you call it."

"There would be something to say for that."

"But I would probably kill you with my sexual enthusiasm."

"At least it would take the undertaker two weeks to get the smile off my face."

She punched him in the stomach. "Oh! You're terrible."

They rolled over to the side of the bed together. It was good to lie there, very close and very fatigued.

"Do you remember when you were a little boy in school and the first thing in the morning you all stood and recited the Pledge of Allegiance to the Flag?"

Dover laughed. "What a strange change of subject."

"No. Answer me. I want to make a point."

"Well, yes. I remember."

"What did you feel?"

"Feel? I felt proud I was born in America although I didn't really know why, then. It was all part of that childhood innocence."

"You aren't proud now?"

"I didn't mean that. Certainly, I am. But not in that same naive way. It means more now. What's your point?"

"That is. That feeling we have that makes us do the things we're doing. I don't want you to misunderstand me. I love my country—this is my way of showing it. I don't want to be ashamed. This is my Pledge of Allegiance."

Dover kissed her eyes and tasted the salt of her tears.

The next two days were humdrum tourism. They ran through a series of guided visits to all the right places; engaged in lively discussions with faculty and students at Leningrad State University; and shopped along the bustling Nevsky Prospekt. They nourished themselves with an unbroken sequence of filling but uninspiring meals; listened to several cultural lectures each day; and paid private visits to a great many of the beautifully preserved cathedrals and churches.

On the third evening, they were driven to the Kirov Opera and Ballet Theater for a special performance of the Moiseyev State Academic Folk Dance Ensemble, out of Moscow.

Upon arriving at the impressive artifact of imperial Russia, they were ushered into the great hall and led to their individual chairs, each upholstered in rich sapphire velvet and arranged in curved rows which stretched the width and depth of the orchestra. Along each side, five tiers of gilded box seats led from the edge of the stage back to the multileveled and equally gilded loges and balcony. Except for a few discreet Soviet emblems where the imperial double eagles must have once flourished, Dover and Marie could have been in early Petersburg, preparing to enjoy the tsar's favorite performers.

The theater rapidly filled with the chattering classless society of Leningrad. As anticipated, the tour group had been seated together, in chairs identified by numbers on their tickets. Dover found himself at one end of the group with the seats on his other side occupied by an older and very friendly Russian couple. The woman, plainly dressed in a cotton smock, oversize imitation pearls, and with a nondescript sweater draped across her shoulders, took obvious pride in pointing out the features of the theater.

"Over 900 pounds of gold went into the finish of the walls and facades," she stated.

"It's magnificent," responded Marie, leaning in front of Dover to acknowledge the woman's descriptions.

"Yes, and it belongs to all the people, now. Alexander II had it built to honor his wife, the Tsaritsa Maria. It was called the *Mariinsky Teatr* in the old imperial days." With a faraway look in her eyes, she continued, "The great Pavlova once floated through the air across that very stage."

"What a sight that must have been," observed Dover.

"Oh, yes."

He was still marveling at the ambiance of gold and ivory that surrounded them, illuminated by the incredible brilliance of the immense multi-faceted chandeliers hanging from the high vaulted ceilings when the lights dimmed and the curtain rose. Soon, he was lost in the spirited music and the skilled dancing of the swirling, foot-stomping troupe. An hour passed, though seemingly only a few minutes. The men and women of the folk group had danced with boundless energy and fired the audience who rewarded their performance with thunderous applause as the curtain descended for intermission.

"Would you care to join us for some refreshments?" invited the woman.

"We would love to," replied Marie, and the four made their way back to the crowded foyer.

It took a while to get their lemonade and they had only a few minutes to exchange small talk about their respective countries when muted chimes called them back to their seats. In the happy confusion, Dover felt the woman's husband slip something into his jacket pocket, and as soon as they returned to their seats, he casually straightened his coat and felt a folded piece of paper.

The performance ended at ten and the tour group gathered at the hotel bar for drinks and discussions of the next day's activities. Dover took Marie aside.

"I think we just made contact."

"Here?"

"No, at the theater. The couple we joined at intermission. On the way back to our seats, he put something in my coat pocket."

"What's it say?"

"I haven't read it yet. I'll be right back."

He passed through the lobby and into the men's room. In the privacy of one of the stalls, he unfolded the paper:

At eleven tonight, walk where you walked the first night. Leave your passport at the hotel. There is a fascinating view of the Kazansky Cathedral from the intersection of the river and Dzerzhinskogo Street.

He and Marie reached the intersection at 11:15. Only by standing on the southeast corner could they see the dome of the cathedral outlined in the evening sky. They had been standing there for almost ten minutes, arms entwined in the manner of lovers and romantically watching the easy flow of the water, when a loud screech erupted from the next intersection to the north. It was immediately followed by a heavy metallic crunch. A taxi had failed to negotiate the turn and had struck an empty flatbed truck.

Dover and Marie whirled toward the sound just as two men who had been approaching them from their blind side drew beside them. They also turned toward the noise, and as all four watched, most of the late evening strollers started toward the scene. Dover felt a slight tug at his sleeve, then heard, "Come, Professor," as one of the men covertly grabbed his arm and led him on. The other stranger remained beside Marie and placed his arm around her waist.

It was all very subtle and quick, and Dover realized that if the switch were to go unnoticed he must resist the maddening urge to turn for one last look at Marie. The man walked him over to the scene of the accident where they melded into the crowd. Neither driver was injured and a policeman was talking to them.

"Well, comrade," said Dover's escort, "we have had at least some excitement this evening, yes? I could use something to prepare myself for the wrath of my wife who takes strong exception to me being out at this hour."

It took only ten minutes for them to walk a block south, then west on Zagorody Street to the Vitebsky Metro Station. They boarded a southbound car and a half-hour later entered a darkened Intourist automobile-rental garage, somewhere in the southwest section of Leningrad.

The stranger led Dover into a cluttered office, pulled the light string, and put a pot of water on the small electric burner.

"Sometimes, even in our summer, the evening calls for some internal warmth, does it not?"

Dover sat silently as the man busied himself with finding his tin of tea and rinsing some well used cups in the sink. There was always the chance he was not in the company of whom he assumed, but his doubts vanished when the man poured two steaming cups, held his up for a toast, and said with a mischievous grin, "Now, my friend, we go to see the Alpha Bug."

After a satisfying sip, he set down the cup.

"For you, my name is Yuri. I have some new identity papers, also some hair coloring and glasses. You will need a trim to match your identification photograph. We will do that tonight. Tomorrow, you and I, two trusted and long-time employees of this office, will fly to Volgograd to pick up two badly needed vehicles which were left there as one-way rentals. Even in this wretched business, we sometimes fall short of the essentials. However, the situation is to our advantage at the moment, or at least yours. I will return with them, while obviously you will not. Your contact in Volgograd is waiting for you."

After their tea, Yuri armed himself with a pair of oversized scissors from a tool box and hacked at Dover's hair until it agreed with the tousled look of his Intourist ID picture. A glance at the broken mirror on the wall confirmed Dover's suspicions that the man would starve as a barber, even a state-employed one.

"There is a sleeping loft up the stairs, also some clothes. I will be back at dawn. We have a morning flight." He tossed a small liquid-filled bottle to Dover. "Here, wash your hair with this in the garage sink, and put the clothes you are wearing in the bottom of the used-rag bin."

Dover walked into the garage and fumbled around for the light. There was no wall switch and even in the dim light from the window in the far wall he could detect no pull string for the overhead bulb. He was about to reenter the office when he heard the outside door burst open and a scramble of feet preceded a noisy struggle. He recognized Yuri's voice.

"Please, you are breaking my arm . . ."

"Yes, comrade, I am. I am going to break it off. You have not been to your house this evening. Instead, you play games down by the river. That clumsy switch. Who is the man? Where is he? I lost you in the Metro—perhaps I am getting old. But I find you here. Alone, comrade?"

Yuri screamed.

"What have you done with him?"

Dover's eye had adjusted to the darkness. Only a foot away, leaning against the wall, was a length of pipe. He carefully wrapped his hand around the foot-long lead cylinder and reached for the door latch.

The voice of death itself stopped him. He felt the man's breath as the words were spoken against the back of his neck, "Go ahead, go on in." There was no mistaking the hard object jammed into the small of his back.

Yuri was face down on the floor, blood oozing from a smashed nose. Sitting astride him, twisting his left arm upward to where the blood-starved hand rested against the base of his skull, was an original Neanderthal man, wearing a white turtleneck sweater. The attacker's eyes gleamed with sadistic satisfaction as he looked up at Dover, then leaned over to speak into Yuri's ear. "Your worthless life is spared, comrade-manager." As the sarcasm slipped between his clenched teeth, he lunged forward, throwing his full weight on the arm. A loud crack accompanied its separation from the shoulder socket. Yuri jerked, then lay still.

The replica of early man stood and faced Dover. "And who have we here?" His breath not only carried his words full into Dover's face, but also the putrid odor of neglected teeth and a recent meal of fish and herbs. When Dover didn't reply, he rubbed his right fist into the palm of his other hand. "A quiet one, aren't you? Perhaps, all you need is some encouragement."

The blow to Dover's midsection forced his head forward, but the gorilla had telegraphed it, giving Dover a split second to set his abdominal muscles. Still, the force of the gloved fist dropped him to his knees. The brute then turned to gloat over the fallen Yuri.

"You see? I have him!"

Despite his pain, Dover recognized the moment of opportunity. The man behind him had turned to close the garage door, so both were turned away from him and neither had paid any attention to the fact that he still held the pipe in his hand. Springing up and painfully twisting at the same time, he swung the weapon with all of his strength at the head of the armed man behind him. The pipe cracked open the back of the skull and drove the man through the door.

The Neanderthal grunted his surprise and lunged forward, but Yuri managed to grab his calf with his uninjured arm and threw him off balance. The half-second delay allowed Dover to spin around and bring the pipe forward, butt-end first. He drove it past the groping hands and into the man's sternum. The breastbone split and the turtleneck toppled backward. Dover adjusted his grip and fiercely laid the pipe across the man's forehead. He was dead before he hit the floor.

"Jesus! You're a mean bastard when you get riled, aren't you?" murmured Yuri. The language was pure American.

Dover dropped to his knees beside him. "I'm a quick learner."

"Don't move me, yet. I've got to stay conscious. This sort of changes things. You just wasted two KGB-ers."

"We've got to get you out of here."

"No . . ." Yuri paused to gasp for more air, his eyes moist from the pain. "Chances are their control doesn't know they're here. These locals aren't the most coordinated . . . but they'll be missed at morning check-in. All the terminals will be swarming with security people."

"I can fly out alone."

"No, you can't. We have to report all travel in advance, in order to get the permits and the tickets. They're expecting two people. You won't get on the plane unless they know why you're alone. It won't work . . . but we do have to get you out of here." Yuri stopped to breathe again. "Take them . . . take them into the garage . . . put 'em anywhere out of sight."

Dover dragged the bodies out of the office. The only hiding place was a small spare parts and tool closet. He grabbed a handful of rags, wiped up the blood, and stuffed the rags under the greasy ones in the used-rag bin.

When he returned to the office, Yuri had dragged himself to the wall and was sitting against it, his left arm hanging at an impossible angle.

"I could use something to drink," he said. "There's a bottle in the desk."

Dover unscrewed the cap and handed him the vodka.

"That helps. I'm getting too old for this. When you get back, tell that bastard, Tobias, to get me the hell outta here."

The clear grain-liquid seemed to give him strength. His eyes regained their shine and his breathing was less pained. He braced himself against the wall and Dover helped him stand.

"There's some cloth in the washroom. We've got to immobilize my arm."

Dover tore the worn towels into strips and strapped Yuri's arm to his side. The man was tough.

"There's one way. Risky as hell, but not as risky as you staying in the city. With a little luck, you might pull it off." He had Dover hand him a folder from a rack over a set of keys. "Early tomorrow morning, we are to have a car at the Astoria Hotel to pick up a Colonel and Mrs. Smythe-Whitehall. He's retired British Army, and they're on an Intourist approved independent tour of Leningrad and Moscow. You will be their driver to Moscow. Here are maps and their tourist papers. You can study them tonight. It's an approved tourist route, all prearranged and cleared with the authorities. The bastards will be much more interested in the colonel than in his driver. Our records here already show you as an employee if anyone should check. I like it. It'll get you out of town.''

''And out into the open.''

''What better place to be than right under their noses? Provided, of course, you become familiar with the traffic laws by morning. They're strict as shit, but we drive on the right side. Under no circumstances let the old colonel talk you into any side trips. They'll be on your ass before your turn signal blinks. You'll be watched, anyhow, but such surveillance is routine.''

''I can't drive around Moscow. I've never been there.''

''No need to. You just drop them off at their hotel. One of our Moscow drivers will take it from there.''

Dover thought for a long moment, trying to foresee the weak spots of the plan. ''Don't they already have the name of your driver?''

''Yes, but they give us some leeway on that. Occasionally, it changes. As long as you have your papers, you'll be okay. I figure it'll take a good twenty-four hours before they can trace those two to this garage. By then, you'll be in Moscow and I'll be somewhere. We're a small office. I'll leave it locked and put a note on the door for the regular driver that the trip is cancelled. It happens from time to time.''

Dover studied the roadmap. It was roughly 930 kilometers to Moscow. Considering the 90-kilometer-per-hour speed limit and necessary stops, it would be a good 12-hour drive. If they could get away on time—the schedule called for 6:00 A.M.—they could reach Moscow well before dark, which was almost a prerequisite in a country that didn't actually forbid night driving but seriously discouraged it. It looked like a simple route: the Leningrad Highway into the outskirts of Moscow, then onto the Leningrad Prospekt into the city and the Minsk Hotel on Gorky Street.

"You go to the loft and study the maps. Also the traffic regulation booklet. The highway traffic inspectors are strict, and use both cars and motorcycles. The slightest infraction and you'll be stopped. Memorize the route to the hotel. Once you're in Moscow, you'll have little time to consult your maps."

"Isn't there any way I can get some help for you?"

"Don't worry about me. I've been in this country for over twenty years, right here in Leningrad mostly. I have friends who ask no questions. I will disappear for a while. Go on upstairs; there are no windows. I need to get these lights out. I have some phone calls to make; that'll take me most of the night. The damned phone system is impossible."

"One question: what do I do once I get to Moscow?"

"I don't know yet. If I can get a call through, we have some people there, just go to Moscow. Every day at noon, read the posters at the Bolshoi. There's money in the desk. I'll see you off in the morning. Go on, now."

After an edgy sleep, Dover checked on the black four-door Zhiguli and placed the papers in the glove compartment. Yuri was in the office, perspiring heavily and obviously very weak. He had his chair tilted all the way back and his feet were resting on a wooden box. He managed a goodbye. "I'll be all right . . . someone will contact you . . . go . . ."

"I can't leave you like this."

"I have someone coming. Go on."

Dover pulled up in front of the Astoria at six. The colonel and his lady were waiting in the lobby, resplendent in beautifully preserved pink skin and white hair. They were right out of the movies. The old gentleman even grasped a baton and wore a pith helmet. Unbelievable.

Dover greeted them in his best Russian-accented English. It wouldn't fool the natives, but he reasoned the English couple would think it quite authentic.

"Good morning, Colonel and Mrs. Smythe-Whitehall, I take your bags and we are on way."

"Thank you. It's a smashing day, isn't it . . . ah . . ."

" Viktor, sir."

"Isn't it, Victor?"

"Yes, the drive will be most pleasant. You will enjoy, I am sure."

He assisted the ancient couple into the rear seat. There was hardly any early morning traffic and he followed Yuri's recommended route out of the city. By the time they reached the outskirts, he had a good feel for the Zhiguli and its handling on the road. Very little traffic was eastbound, just a few trucks and vans and an occasional Army vehicle. The road was dry and in good repair. Dover let the needle creep up on the speedometer and steadied it at 90 kilometers per hour. He figured he should sound something like a guide.

"This is all collective farm country, although not best growing land; mostly a few beets and some cabbage. We are too far north for hot summers, but much moisture." He had no idea whether what he said was authentic, banking on the probability that the English couple wouldn't know either, and they were passing several farm communities, set back from the highway.

He pulled out to pass a slow-moving transport and searched ahead to clear himself.

"What's that, up there?" asked the Englishman.

Dover's heart started a slow climb up his throat. Ahead were several traffic-inspector vehicles, positioned across the highway in a manner that left only a single-lane passage through the center opening. A nest of motorcycles sat off to one side on the shoulder, next to a khaki personnel carrier, and twenty or so militiamen and soldiers were stopping and inspecting eastbound traffic.

He eased up on the accelerator pedal and let the small sedan glide back into position behind the transport. They slowed and finally stopped.

"They will want to see your passports," Dover said over his shoulder.

"Yes, yes, of course."

Don't get nervous, Colonel, I'm the one they're after.

Dover tried to appear properly agitated as the militiaman approached.

"Your papers, comrade."

Dover handed him the travel packet, along with his personal papers. The man thumbed through them, checking the car's registration against the rental identification. Keeping the papers, he asked for the English couple's passports. After a moment, he walked away and returned with a stern-faced civilian who glowered at Dover and re-checked his papers.

"You are not the driver on the travel permit," said the civilian.

"That is correct, comrade. The man listed fell ill. I was routed out of my wife's bed at four this morning for this trip and told the necessary changes would be submitted at the opening of the business. A radio call will confirm what I say." Dover nodded toward the personnel carrier which bristled with antennas.

The civilian studied the papers and passports, glanced back and saw that traffic was piling up, nodded his head, then returned them to the militiaman. "I see no reason to detain our English guests. The two men we seek bear no resemblance to this driver."

The militiaman returned the papers and passports and saluted smartly toward the English couple. "My apologies for the delay, sir. You may be on your way."

As Dover threaded the Zhiguli through the narrow opening between the police cars, the Englishman leaned forward.

"That was a bloody thrill. They must be looking for someone, eh?"

"Yes, Colonel. I heard that two government employees failed to report for their shift last night."

"All this for two missing workers? They must have been flaming important!"

"I would not know, sir." Dover smiled and pegged the speedometer on ninety.

It was 7:15 P.M. when they reached the intersection of the Leningrad Highway and the Leningradski Prospekt. A bend to the left placed them on the thoroughfare and they joined the sparse evening traffic flowing smoothly toward the central city. The Prospekt carried them to Gorky Street and it was only two blocks to the Minsk Hotel which sat opposite the theater complex of Pushkin Square.

Dover carried the luggage inside and asked the desk clerk for directions to the nearest Intourist car-rental office.

As he turned to leave, the old colonel approached him and offered his hand. "Thank you, Victor," he said, "that was a most pleasant journey. Mrs. Smythe-Whitehall and I enjoyed it and your informative comments."

Dover felt the folded bills being pressed into his palm. He returned them. "That's not necessary, sir. It was my pleasure to serve you. Goodbye. Enjoy Moscow."

He dropped off the Zhiguli, and one of the workers directed him to a small inexpensive hotel which was also conveniently located near a Metro station.

The next day, he took the underground to Red Square and walked the block down Karl Marx Prospekt to stand in front of the posters outside the Bolshoi. The street was crowded with Moscovites and tourists enjoying the spectacular scenery of the many theaters, government buildings, and patriotic statues and banners that filled the main governmental area of the capital city. Over 7,500,000 people lived within its limits and it seemed to Dover that all of them were strolling along in front of the renowned ballet theater, but no one gave him a second glance. He waited until after 2:00 P.M. before deciding there would be no contact. After picking up some food and magazines, he caught the Metro back to his hotel and remained in his room for the rest of the day.

The following noon found him back reading the posters. He had been standing for ten minutes before a young woman joined him in front of the theater and studied several of the coming attractions. She was a little on the plump side, but not overly so, and her cheeks glowed with the rosy tint of a healthy Soviet citizen. She dressed well, her beige sweater complementing a dark sand skirt. Her hair was bobbed, and she had the sleeves of the sweater pushed up to her elbows in the way of Western women. A brown leather shoulder bag matched her low-heeled street shoes and a colorful scarf was arranged loosely around her shoulders to give the otherwise unicolor outfit some brightness.

He could tell she was keeping him within her peripheral vision as she pretended to read the posters, all the while inching closer to him.

"I love the ballet, don't you?" she commented, her softly spoken words more of a decision than a question.

"Yes, I do."

"Do you have a favorite?"

"Swan Lake." Ballet was not one of Dover's strong suits. Swan Lake was the only ballet he had ever heard of.

"Yes, it is a beautiful story. Are you alone in the city?"

"For the moment."

"I, also. There's a very comfortable cafe just a few minutes' walk from here. Perhaps you would like to join me."

Dover knew it was logical for a metropolis the size of Moscow to have practitioners of the world's oldest art form, but he hadn't given the matter any thought. She was certainly attractive enough, but her timing was atrocious.

"I'm waiting for someone."

"Perhaps it is me. I'm clean. You won't catch any-thing—except perhaps the Alpha Bug."

Her impish smile reached out at the same time as her hand. Dover took it.

"Let's go," he said.

She led him west along Karl Marx Prospekt and turned left onto Gorky Street.

"Were you there yesterday?" asked Dover.

"Yes, I watched you for a while."

"Oh?"

"We have to make sure of these things. The description Yuri gave us was quite accurate but there is always the chance of a mistake. We can't afford that, so we are very cautious. You understand."

"And agree wholeheartedly."

"Did you have any trouble coming in?"

"No. We ran into a roadblock just outside Leningrad but they weren't looking for me yet."

"They are now."

"They found the bodies?"

"Yes. I talked to Yuri this morning."

"He is here?"

"No, he is in a safe place."

"How's his arm?"

"Very painful but repaired."

The young woman did not use any unnecessary words. They had walked two blocks north and made another right onto a side street. Several doors down, she led him into a small but practically empty stand-up tearoom. Only one other couple stood at a tall round table near the front of the room, young people. A cheap portable radio sat on the table before them and Dover was surprised to hear a subdued form of rock music pulsating from the speaker.

The woman led Dover to a back counter. At her indication, he waited while she went to the service counter and brought back two glasses of hot tea. "Forgive me, my name is Tania," she announced.

"What else?" kidded Dover.

"Our transport will be here shortly," she announced, lowering her voice to avoid compromise and smiling broadly. To anyone who might be interested she and Dover were another casual Soviet pair making small talk. "When do you have to be at your destination?" she asked.

"As soon as possible. I have a pickup deadline although I'm not sure what it is yet."

"That's normal. It will take us only a day or so to get you out of here. Do not worry."

Dover sipped his tea. It was strong and very hot. He did not notice the tall young militiaman enter. He just suddenly appeared at their side. The girl talked on, ignoring him.

"May I see your papers, comrade?" he interrupted, placing one hand lightly on Tania's shoulder.

She looked over her shoulder at him, annoyed, and searched through her bag, finally fishing out her identification card.

He glanced at it for a moment before placing it in the upper right-hand pocket of his tunic. He addressed his next question to Dover. "Do you know this woman?"

"Of course," lied Dover. "We are old friends." He was amazed at the youthfulness of the militiaman. His cheeks still puffed with baby fat and there was absolutely no sign of whiskers, not even fuzz.

"Then you must know the place of her work as listed on her card?"

So, test time.

"No, I do not. We are social friends. We do not work together."

"May I see *your* papers, please?"

Dover handed over his Intourist identity and his driver's permit.

"You are a long way from the Leningrad facility."

"I drove an English tourist couple here. It is an approved trip. You can check if you want. The verification number is on the card."

"I am interested in the woman." He handed Dover back his papers and addressed Tania, "You were in front of the theater yesterday, also."

"Is that some sort of new crime? Two days on the same street?" she questioned angrily.

"It is if you are seeking male companionship and accepting money for it."

"Give me my papers! How dare you insult me! Give me my papers!"

The couple at the front of the tearoom hastily downed the last of their drinks and hurried out.

"Listen, this lady is my friend," stated Dover, leaning toward the militiaman. "If you wish to accuse her or me, take us to your superior. This is stupid. Is this the way a militiaman of the Soviet Union earns his pay? Standing around on the street waiting to harass his fellow workers?''

The young man suddenly looked unsure of himself in the face of Dover's bluff. He was determined to do his duty, but it would not go well with him if he were mistaken. There had been complaints lately that some of his comrades had taken their authority to ridiculous extremes. He did not want to be lumped in with them. Apparently deciding that his services could be more productive elsewhere, he pulled Tania's identification from his tunic and handed it back. As she jerked it from him, he searched for a verbal way out of his dilemma.

Dover began to feel his heart rate slow back down toward normal. The youthful official would never make it as a New York cop.

''I will take your word, comrade. I am sure you realize we cannot tolerate any such conduct, especially in such a revered place in the season of tourists.'' He was on the verge of an apology but that went against the grain of his training. He must retire with dignity and his authority intact. Turning back to Tania, he issued a warning just in case his evaluation were correct. ''I am sure I will not see you there tomorrow.''

''Then you will be patrolling somewhere else,'' snapped Tania.

Don't push it, Tania. Quit while we're ahead.

Outclassed, the militiaman turned and walked back out and onto the street.

Tania buried her face in her hands and giggled like a little girl.

''I'm glad you enjoyed that,'' muttered Dover. ''My legs are without bones.''

''He is a young one,'' she stammered, wiping her eyes and making a heroic effort to stop her giggle attack. ''It is probably his first patrol duty, poor ass. I could hardly keep a sober face.''

''Forgive me. I was somewhat more concerned.''

"You handled yourself well. I believe you intimidated him more than I. You think fast, comrade."

"Especially when I am panic-stricken."

His remark triggered her giggles again. She took several deep breaths to gain control. Abruptly, she pointed out the door. "Our transport is here. Let us leave before my sides burst with amusement."

The driver was another young woman who waved and motioned for them to hurry. As they pulled away from the curb they passed the young militiaman. The driver tooted her horn and both females waved vigorously at him. He looked the other way.

Dover could not have felt more conspicuous had he been naked and painted bright orange as he sat in the back seat, exposed to all the world by the large windows of the small car. This was not exactly the kind of scene he had ever expected to be involved in within the Soviet Union.

He had no idea where they were taking him and could not keep up with the frequent direction changes as they wound their way towards the outskirts of the city. Actually, his watch indicated they only drove for five or six minutes before the driver swung over to the curb in front of one of a series of seedy hotels and small shops.

They entered the compact lobby and the driver went over to the desk cage and handed some bills to the ancient clerk. He didn't bother to look up from his magazine.

The lift took them to the top floor and they entered the room at the far end of the hall. Once inside, Dover immediately recognized that the young militiaman was not such a fool after all. He was actually in a suite. A rundown suite, but certainly well suited to its purpose. Obviously, the hotel was not on the approved Intourist list.

One couple was sitting on a large cushioned sofa, pressed closely together as they waited their turn for one of the rooms. There were apparently two more and he was led into one. Only Tania accompanied him.

"We will keep you here tonight. My brother will be by shortly and tell you of the arrangements."

Dover had difficulty in keeping his mind on her words.

The noises of movement and grunts from the adjoining room were poorly masked by the thin walls.

Tania recognized his mild surprise and amusement. "It may be a bit noisy for you to sleep well. Russian men have needs also, you know."

"I'm just a little taken aback. You *are* a hooker."

"A what? Houker?"

Dover did not know the Russian word so he had spoken the term in English. "American slang," he explained.

"Ah, you are surprised that we have so much in common with the capitalist societies, are you not?"

"I should have known."

She laughed. "You will not be bothered. The room is yours. Do not leave it. Be certain no one is in the toilet when you must relieve yourself. There are doors from both rooms. I will bring you food. Here are refreshments." She waved toward the heavy oak dresser. A bottle of vodka and a glass sat on a metal tray. Beside it was a plate of smoked salmon and several lemon wedges. "If you need anything else, except the obvious, knock on the door. Someone will be in the outer room all night."

Giving a teasing wave, she backed out the door. "Bye, bye," she said in English, "I go to work, now."

Dover sat on the bed. It was the only piece of furniture in the room except for the dresser. The narrow window was heavily curtained and there was only one other door on the opposite wall. It must be for the toilet. The room was clean. He had to admit that, although he suspected he would lie on the bed linen with some trepidation.

The smoked salmon was delicious, moist and fresh and firm. The vodka served as a good catalyst but he would have preferred water. That from the tap in the bathroom would undoubtedly have catastrophic effects on his digestive system. No time for that. The noise from the adjoining room had stopped. Time for the next shift. It was still early in the afternoon and he suspected he would be treated to a long evening of world class entertainment if the antics of the previous couple were any example.

There was nothing in the room to read. No radio.

Strictly stripped for its purpose, it offered no diversion. Dover pulled back the curtain but let it fall back into place after seeing that the narrow street would offer no entertainment. Besides, a drawn curtain would be out of place.

Oh, well. Why not look at the humorous side. He lay down on the bed just as the door to the next room opened, followed by the muffled thumps of bodies falling on the unseen bed and a resumption of the grunts and groans. Shaking his head in surrender to the inevitable background noises, he at least reasoned that somewhere in the future he could sit on the front porch of his Montrose spread and tell Carl about the night he spent in a Russian whorehouse.

Chapter
6

Comrade Engineer Grigori Solovyov placed his papers and pen back in his briefcase, closed it, and stood to stretch. His back and legs were very stiff from the inordinate delay. Perhaps he should get some tea. That would refresh him. However, the tabs on the flight schedule board flickered into life. Opposite his destination, Volgograd, a new departure time appeared. It was only fifteen minutes away. First, the long delay which scattered the passengers, and now such a short notice. He would stay right where he was. The comrade executives that ran Aeroflot were as unpredictable as any bureaucrats he had ever encountered. It would seem that domestic air routes could maintain some degree of consistency. With a tone of disgust, Solovyov remarked as much to the old woman who still sat on the hard bench.

He took his place in line and offered his papers to the official as they started to board. He was waved on and quickly sought a window seat near the rear of the cabin. That was always the safest area; in the event of an accident, the tail section seemed to be the only part that sometimes survived intact. It was a habit with him, and he gladly paid the penalty of a rougher ride for the infinitesimally slight increase in personal safety.

The soft seat felt much better than the hard waiting bench had, but the cabin was too hot. He should have removed his coat and tie. Perhaps when the engines started, the cabin would cool. His beard itched and it felt good to scratch around it.

A slightly bewildered man approached the empty seat on the aisle. "Is this seat taken?" he asked.

Of course the seat wasn't taken. Did the man see anyone sitting in it? "No," replied Solovyov in a tone more of resignation than of invitation.

The man looked to be a laborer, tanned from outdoor work and lean of body. His clothes were well used, but clean and neat. He placed a loosely tied bundle in the overhead stowage before he sat.

"It is a fine flying day, yes?" asked the man, his expression indicating some concern as if he were asking for reassurance. Perhaps this was his first flight.

"I suppose so. This time of year one can expect a few bumps from the summer clouds, however."

"Do you take this flight often?"

"Often enough, perhaps three or four times a year." Solovyov didn't relish the idea of prolonged conversation. You never could be quite certain who your traveling companion might be. The KGB certainly had an interest in this route since it terminated near the space center. Inconspicuously, he studied the man's face. He was in his late thirties, perhaps near forty, with features that were rather common and there seemed to be some sort of irregularity with the set of his eyes. There was the faint odor of animals about him, as if he were a farmer.

The heavy Ilyushin lifted into the air.

The flight attendant passed down the aisle, offering magazines. Solovyov declined, electing instead to retrieve his briefcase and continue with the notes he had been preparing back in the waiting area. His seat-partner selected an agricultural magazine. The man must be a farmer; who else could wade through such material?

There was welcome quiet for the next half-hour. Solovyov punched the buttons on his hand-held calculator and pursed his lips in approval as the figures confirmed preliminary calculations. The farmer placed his magazine in the seat pocket in front of him and gazed idly about the cabin. Solovyov had a feeling that his peace and quiet were about to end. He was right. The man leaned over and studied his computations.

"Are you a mathematician?" he asked.

"No."

"You seem to be very handy with figures. Those equations look very complicated."

What would a farmer know about complex equations?

"I am an engineer, an astrodynamics engineer."

"Oh, I see. You work with the large rockets at Volgograd?"

"Not actually. I teach theory and design at Lomonosov University."

"Moscow?"

"Yes."

"You are not going to the space center, then?"

"I am, but my purpose there is to see old friends and consult with them."

"We Soviets can be very proud of our space accomplishments. I feel very honored to be sitting here next to so important a person."

"Thank you, but I do very little that is useful in a practical way. My work is mostly with students, as I mentioned."

"Yes, you did say that. Ah! Here comes some food."

Solovyov was not hungry, but the man made him irritable. Perhaps a snack would help. He nodded and accepted the small plastic tray offered by the flight attendant. A second attendant handed him a glass of hot tea.

The cold fish and black bread were quite palatable, especially after he spread an insulating layer of butter between them. The cold vegetable, on the other hand, was a bland potato-like irregular ball with the taste of a turnip, but mushy. He could not identify it. The farmer smacked his lips loudly as he wolfed down what he seemed to consider a feast. "That was very good," he announced, disregarding the folded paper napkin for the more intimate taste of his fingers.

Solovyov continued sipping his tea.

The farmer shrugged, perhaps miffed by Solovyov's silence, and reclaimed his agricultural magazine.

Solovyov was napping when the big jet started its descent. The change in engine rhythm waked him and he sleepily peered out the window at the terrain below. He must have slept some time as they were quite low, perhaps only 3,000 meters or so, and crossing a swampy area crisscrossed by several branches of a lowland river. That would be the Volga. As the aircraft commenced a sweeping turn to the right, Solovyov pushed the button to erect the back of his seat and tightened his seat belt, then realized he would be on the wrong side of the aircraft to see the space center.

Within minutes they were on the ground and the huge cabin became a confusion of noises and movement as the passengers reclaimed their belongings and disembarked. The farmer was apparently talked out. He grabbed his bundle from the overhead compartment, hurried ahead of Solovyov, and disappeared into the crowd fanning out into the terminal.

"Grigori! Over here!"

Solovyov spotted the caller and waved. They embraced and patted each other's back.

"Come, my car is just outside."

As they traveled east toward Kapustin Yar, Solovyov thought back to the farmer on the plane. He had asked lots of questions. What a strange one. Of course, even with their considerable security skills, some of the KGB operatives were incredibly naive when it came to cover identities. Perhaps that was who the farmer really was, but Solovyov had trouble forgetting the odd cast to the man's eyes.

"Here we are, comrade." The driver parked beside a modest farm house and escorted him inside. The place was homey and clean. His host led him to a small bedroom off the living area. "Put your briefcase in here. I will dispose of it. There is hot water on the stove. While you get rid of your facial hair, I will get your clothes and papers. We have much to talk about."

Solovyov poured some of the water into a large clay bowl and splashed it on his face. The small academic beard came off with a little tugging as did the eyebrows and mustache. His host returned and handed him a fresh towel.

"I am Mikhail. Welcome to my humble house. Here is your new identity."

Dover looked at the face in the mirror, still flecked with bits of adhesive. The people in Moscow had been very talented. Now, he wondered who he would be this time. He was beginning to feel like a chameleon.

Chapter

7

"Here is a layout of the space center," said Mikhail, unfolding a large chart. On the pale blueprint paper, black outlines depicted buildings, launch facilities, roads, and all of the other features which made up the large complex. Someone had penciled in amplifying information, including distances from buildings to fences. "There is much in-and-out pedestrian traffic during the day, but it is closely monitored. Most of the scientific personnel live on the center, but the vast majority of the workers, like myself, live in either Kapustin Yar or Akhtubinsk. We commute daily."

"You work on the center?"

Mikhail answered in English, "I am a comrade garbageman."

Dover matched his grin.

"All of the maintenance equipment is kept on the center. I pick my truck up at Transportation, here, and make my rounds. At the end of my shift, I dump everything here, in the dump area." Mikhail pointed to a spot well removed from the operational and administrative areas.

"What's your shift?"

"Eight P.M. until six in the morning."

"That sounds opportune."

"It has been in the past. But security doesn't slack off during the night; there's just less activity. The administrative people are gone. That's about all."

"I have to get into here, this area by the horizontal assembly building."

"That's the special projects complex. It has its own security. I've been studying it for days, looking for an opening."

"Do you go in there?"

"No, I pick up their trash at this guard position."

"Inside or outside the gate?"

"Outside. The guard brings it out. No one goes in without a special pass and positive visual identification."

"This railroad—it looks like it runs inside."

"It does. It serves both the horizontal assembly building and the special projects area."

"Have you seen the spaceship?"

"No, but we've observed shipments of crates, big bastards, three to a shipping unit."

"How many shipments?"

"Three, so far. There's a fourth ready to load."

"Where did they go?"

"The first two were taken to Baikonur. Our man there confirmed their arrival. The third went to their Northern Cosmodrome, near Plesetsk."

"That's the military launch center."

"Right."

"For God's sake, I was just in Leningrad. That's only about 400 miles from Plesetsk."

Mikhail shook his head. "You would never have gotten near it. We haven't been able to get a man even close."

Dover's brow wrinkled. "If the last shipment went to the Northern Cosmodrome, they're close to being operational."

"Exactly," agreed Mikhail.

"Any idea as to what kind of spacecraft it is?"

"Shit, we don't even know for sure it's a spacecraft. All

we've been able to report is the increased activity in the special projects compound, the presence of some pretty high-priced scientific help, and the shipments. The crates could house canned borscht for all we know."

"I doubt that."

"Look, we don't even know who you are, or what are your qualifications. We were just given the assignment to get you here, and if possible to get you onto the center," said Mikhail.

"You keep saying 'we.' "

"Our people in Leningrad and Moscow."

"You the only operative here?"

"There's one more."

Dover could read Mikhail's face. That particular subject was not open for discussion.

Mikhail continued, "This is a no-error fun and games assignment, damned dangerous. If they make you, forget about that one call to your lawyer."

"I'm aware of that. Do you have an assistant on the truck?"

"No, it's a one-man operation. An Army guard rides with me at random intervals. Doesn't do a goddamned thing but look bored and smoke that dog dung that passes for Russian tobacco. It's a security measure. Keeps me honest."

Dover studied the chart. "There has to be a way," he muttered. "How about the train track? Where it passes through the gate into the special projects area?"

"It's a manually operated double gate. There are two guards assigned whenever it's open."

"How closely do they check the train?"

"Like a gynecologist with a whore—they don't miss a thing. It's a slow mover, nothing but flat cars, and there's a mirror set between the rails."

"Suspicious bastards, aren't they?"

Mikhail laughed. "I can get you onto the center. It's a bit complicated, but relatively risk free. That way, you can familiarize yourself with the layout before you try to penetrate the special projects area. I'll help you all I can, but

I'd prefer not to blow my cover. It's taken us six years to get me established as a routine figure on the center."

"How complicated?"

"As I said, the guard rides with me at random intervals. But he's never ridden two days in a row, and he rode with me yesterday. I'd say we've got two to four days before he shows up again."

"Tomorrow. Let's shoot for tomorrow."

"Good enough." Mikhail picked up a pencil and placed the point on a road leading northeast from Kapustin Yar. "This road passes through an old abandoned range area and leads to Saykhin, a small village about eighty kilometers away. At this point, here, it is actually a perimeter road around the center." His pencil rested on the indicated spot. Just below it was the space center. "The road is seldom patrolled except when there's a launch. It coincidentally parallels the general direction of the launch axis. You drop me off at the main gate tonight when I go in, take my car and follow the road to this point. If, by chance, you run into a patrol car, your papers are in order. Just say you're headed for Zhitkur—that's another small village farther north. They'll just assume you're lost and turn you back toward Kapustin Yar."

"Aren't they pretty suspicious of night drivers?"

"Not if you have a good excuse and it's early. Tell them it's a woman. That, they'll understand. Drive with your lights off. If you see headlights coming from either direction, pull off the road and be studying your map with a flashlight when they reach you. Actually, I doubt you'll run into anyone."

"Okay, so I follow the road to this point?"

"Right. There's an abandoned service road leading off to the north. It's no longer used at all. Go a kilometer or so and park off the road in the brush, where no one can see the car from the road. You'll have about a four kilometer walk to this spot, outside the fence opposite the dump. Wait there. I'll show up around four-thirty. Simple enough?"

"How'll I get through the fence?"

"You won't. You'll go over it."

"It's that easy?"

"I'm afraid I wouldn't use the word 'easy.' There's a bunch of good old Russian alternating current running through the mesh. Touch it and you not only become a fried pie, but every alarm on the center sounds. But, trust me. I'll get you over it."

"Sounds like fun."

"I haven't lost anyone yet."

"How many have you taken over it?"

"You're the first."

"Jesus."

Dover dropped Mikhail at the main entrance to the center and by 8:40 P.M. was creeping along the back road toward Saykhin. He kept his headlights off as advised, but the visibility wasn't bad. The dirt road was certainly at the bottom of the list when it came to upkeep. Rain-washed gullies challenged the suspension of Mikhail's car and attacked Dover's kidneys with equal ferocity. It took over an hour to reach the old service road, then almost another half-hour to negotiate the last mile of what was essentially open terrain. There was plenty of thick vegetation and he hid the car several hundred feet off the road remnant.

Despite the cool evening, it felt good to walk. That was one activity he had enjoyed back at his small spread in western Colorado; walking the fenceline in the early evening and planning improvements to his land. He certainly hadn't had time to do other than plan.

This countryside had much the same feel as that around his ranch. The Russian latitude was higher, about the same as that of the U.S./Canadian border, so the air was a bit frosty for August, but it had that same clean, crisp smell. But not nearly as thin. His high country land sat over a mile above sea level. The ground softly passing under his feet was lowland. But the stars that sparkled in the Russian night had the same intense brightness as those that shone in the western skies of the United States. There were no mountains, of course, but with the darkness around him it wasn't difficult to imagine he was back walking his fence line. Here, there were Russian peers, most probably with similar patches of land to work, but hopefully none in his immediate vicinity. The security of the spaceport mandated that.

One of Dover's most precious pleasures was time to himself. Perhaps that is why space flight was such a personal experience, particularly those rare times when he had a few minutes with no duties and could take the opportunity to drink in the beauty of the earth below. The Apollo astronauts had often remarked about the fragile appearance of the blue planet as they viewed it from the great distances of their moon flights. It was not nearly that small when viewed from the *Columbia*. Still, at just 170 miles it took on a whole new personality without any indications of national borders or ills brought about by the human species that dominated it. And the overwhelming peacefulness of it all. What a fantastic future awaited the world if the various peoples could stop thinking about using space to blow themselves into extinction. As much as he disliked the thought of expansion of the arms race into space, he had to face reality. If the Alpha Bug was indeed what Macfay and General Shyrr thought it was, he would *have* to get his pictures and make it back. The history of warfare since man's first ancestor discovered the advantage of a well-thrown rock over the club was one of weapon and counterweapon. The Alpha Bug might be the weapon to give the Soviets space supremacy. If so, the first step in countering it would be to find out what it was.

He thought of Marie. It had been eight days since the switch on the banks of the Fontanka River. It pleased him that his fondest thought of her was the warmth of her hand and the glow of her smile as they walked by the river that night. Her passion during their first night, on the other hand, had not seemed the real woman but more the erotic playing out of some sinister fantasy. Women were a complex sex, always a continual challenge to his understanding, and Marie was the most extreme example he had ever encountered. A mixture of tenderness that had enabled her to guide him gently through the first steps of his mission with genuine concern and a steely toughness that was an exquisite mixture of hatred and revenge, she was someone he would like to know well. There was a chemistry between them, a certain emotional link that hinted at the possibility of a deeper commitment. She would be back in the States by now, badgering Tobias for another assignment. And if Dover were not such a romantic he would admit to himself that their relationship was over.

Farewell, Marie. I owe you.

He reached the spot opposite the dump shortly after midnight and settled in to wait for Mikhail. At 2:30 A.M., a patrol car passed along the road to Saykhin. Otherwise, he had the starlit night to himself.

It was 5:00 A.M. before he heard the first heavy rumblings of the garbage truck. Mikhail drove the massive vehicle head-on toward the fence, stopping just a few feet short, and switched off the headlights. With the disappearance of their blinding beam, Dover could see the huge steel lever arms of the fork used to dump the contents of the large trash containers into the open box of the truck. The rig was in its uppermost position. Mikhail engaged a lever in the cab and the arms started down, arcing the wide fork over the fence. He stopped its descent with the lever arms a scant foot above the top wire. The two parallel probes of the fork were about eight feet off the ground outside the fence.

Mikhail leaned out of the cab. "How's it look?"

"Don't lower it any more. I can make it." Dover wasn't at all anxious to inadvertently test the conductivity of his body. He leaped and grabbed one of the fork probes, swung himself up, and climbed into a crouched position. "Okay, take it up."

The arms jerked, causing him a split second of serious concern that bordered on panic, then started upward. As soon as he was clear of the top of the fence, they stopped and Mikhail backed the truck. Another jerk, and the fork lowered Dover to the ground.

"Piece of cake," Mikhail said, smiling. "Climb in."

He turned the truck around and they lumbered over to

an abandoned equipment shack some fifty yards from the dump.

"Your hotel," said Mikhail, stopping beside it. He opened his door and dropped out of the cab. Dover did likewise. Mikhail opened a small door in the side of the trash compartment of the truck and pulled out a plastic-wrapped bundle. "Food and water, also an Army uniform. There's an AK-47 behind the seat in the cab. We'll leave it there. You'll be safe here. I'll pick you up tomorrow night, provided the guard doesn't show. If he does, the night after. You'll ride shotgun and I'll give you the grand tour. There may be a woman here during the day bulldozing the trash. Don't let it concern you. Just stay out of sight. There'll be no one else. The stench keeps away the routine patrol."

Dover had every confidence in that. The food seemed superfluous at the moment. He wasn't too certain that he could keep down what was already inside him.

Mikhail led him around the shack and pried loose one of the wide boards that walled the structure. A large gray rat shot out and scampered toward the dump.

"And they say we government employees get the best of everything," dryly observed Mikhail.

Dover slipped through the opening and Mikhail pounded the board back in place. The truck rumbled off.

There was an old worktable against the far wall. Dover shoved the debris off the top and climbed on. He felt better with his feet off the floor. He had spent some interesting times in many places, from the compact two-man state-rooms aboard Navy aircraft carriers to seedy hotel rooms with fellow astronauts on NASA publicity tours, and on to the cramped cabins of vehicles in weightless space. He had even shared a room in a curry-contaminated family inn near the Indian spaceport at Vikram Sarabhai, his roommate on that occasion a dark-skinned native who was a prince of a fellow but must have considered water much too holy for such a mundane use as bathing. But, in all his travels, he quite literally and figuratively had never spent the day with a rat, particularly a Russian rat whose constantly quivering mouth would have looked more appropriate on a great white shark. The filthy creature returned in late morning and rustled around the floor of the old shack, alternately burrowing under a pile of discarded boxes and boards in one corner and sniffing around the legs of the table as if weighing the chances of consuming the man crouched on top against the effort required to reach him. The animal was apparently fearless, or deaf. Dover's sharp shouts and hand waving were regally ignored.

After several hours of enduring the intimidating stares of the creature's beady little black eyes, Dover ended the confrontation with a well-aimed blow of a broken pick handle. Kicking open the loose board, he tossed the limp carcass outside. By late afternoon his hunger had overcome his disgust and he downed some of the food.

Mikhail returned shortly after nine and Dover joined him in the truck.

"I'm curious. Why didn't we do this last night?"

Mikhail kept his eyes on the dark road. "Wrong section of the center. On odd days, I hit the administrative and support areas; even days, it's the operational sites. Today's the twelfth."

Dover still couldn't fathom the reason he had to spend the sixteen hours with the rat.

Their route took them by the Vertikal probe sounding rocket facilities; range headquarters; the high frequency antenna farm; the sounding rocket area; several radar sites; the C-1 pads, two of which held giant green Cosmos launch rockets in the firm grip of tall steel gantries; and, finally, the horizontal assembly building. After it, Mikhail wheeled the truck over to the gate of the special projects compound. He climbed down and emptied the trash containers handed him by the guard. Afterward, they engaged in easy conversation and shared a smoke together. Dover remained in the truck looking appropriately bored but covertly studying the compound.

Except for the personnel gate, the area was protected by a double row of steel mesh fencing, the rows approximately eight feet apart and each row topped with three triangularly strung strands of barbed wire. Coal-coated guard dogs padded restlessly back and forth between the fences, panting and slobbering on the ground as they swung nervously around in their anxious wait for intruders. The large heavy dogs, some sort of Doberman mix, kept their heads pointed toward Dover and the truck even as they paced. The main building, a hangar-like structure, was fifty feet beyond the gate. There was no personnel traffic, but Dover could see slits of light seeping out of the cracks around the sliding doors in the near end. The single railway track ran between the security fences and the building, all the way to the far end where three garage-sized crates sat on the loading dock, bathed in the glow of a single overhead floodlight.

The small upright guardhouse at the gate was most probably only a weather shelter. The gate was apparently kept locked; there was a steel latch which could only be opened from the inside. At the moment, it was open while the guard and Mikhail talked and enjoyed their cigarettes.

They remained for almost ten minutes and Dover saw no movement whatsoever within the compound.

"Well, goodnight, comrade." Mikhail ground out his cigarette with his boot and climbed into the cab. The guard closed the gate and slid the latch.

"Any way to get around to the other side?" asked Dover.

"Not with the truck, but on foot. However, the fences run all the way around, with a divider every two hundred feet. There are two dogs in each segment, and in case you're wondering, they won't eat anything thrown over the fence. The only raw meat they have a fancy for must be wrapped around living bone, such as your trunk and extremities."

Dover tilted his head in respect for the well-trained animals. As they pulled away, he glanced back at the point of entry of the railroad. The double gate, ten feet tall by thirty wide, was a break in the double-fenced security enclosure. Regretfully, it was also in plain view of the guard.

By 5:00 A.M., they were back at the dump, and Mikhail lifted Dover back over the fence. He jogged to the car and arrived at the main entrance at seven. Mikhail was waiting.

"I've been thinking," Mikhail said as he took the driver's seat and started for his house. "I can get you into the compound, but there's no way I can get you out without killing the guard or blowing my cover. Either one would alert the security people and we'd have one hell of a time getting out of the local area."

"How would you do it?"

"Let's eat, and let me sleep on it a few hours. I'll need to go into town and get some things. We'll go over the plan before I go to work tonight. I suspect my Army friend will show up and make my rounds with me. If so, and you can come up with a way to get back out, we can shoot for the second night."

After breakfast, Dover closed the curtains in his sleeping area and flopped onto the bed. Once in the afternoon, between rat dreams, he woke and heard Mikhail driving off in the car.

Chapter

8

Marie pulled herself to her feet and felt her way to a wall. She could see nothing, but the wall at least provided an invisible reference in the black void. She was in some sort of windowless cell, but she could not remember being brought there, or how long she had been unconscious. Her last memory was of the twisted face of the KGB brute, who after questioning her for three days in the room off the terminal of the Leningrad airport, had finally let his black-gloved fist express his frustration. She became aware of a tightening and severe aching in her face, and when she raised a hand to examine it, the touch made her wince. The left side was extremely sensitive and swollen.

The room smelled strongly of stale urine and fermented fecal matter. There was absolutely no light and although she knew her pupils must be fully dilated, when she lifted her hand to her face she could see no movement or shape in the darkness. For a moment, the chilling prospect of blindness panicked her, but her eyes felt normal and the blow had landed lower.

There was no way she could measure the passage of time. She may have stood pressed against the wall for an hour or a minute. All she knew for sure was that the searing stench of the human waste was making her nauseated. Spurts of sour mucus kept rising in her throat, causing her to belch and gag, and she could taste the unmistakable signs that it was only a matter of time before the churning mass in her stomach would surge upward like the exploding extracta of a volcano and erupt all over the cell. She began to feel her way along the wall, searching for a corner. That way, when the vomitus came, she would know where she had deposited it.

As she crept cautiously through the black void, her right foot suddenly slid and fell part way through a small circular opening in the concrete floor. As it was, her stumble ripped the shoe from her foot and she stubbed it on the edge of the hole. She recoiled in disgust; her panty-hosed toes had broken through the thin crust of a slimy, soft mass. She had stepped onto the toilet hole, the source of the foul odors.

She could hold back no longer. She retched and tried to position her head over the opening as the stomach contents burst upward and spilled out of her stretched mouth. Again and again, the spasms came, each more violent than the last, until her throat became raw and her mouth hot with the strain from the dry heaves. She backed hastily away, crying furiously at the futility of her situation, and feeling her way back along the wall.

She reached a corner, turned it, and walked her hands along the cold damp concrete. When she reached the second corner, she knew she was as far from the toilet hole as she could get. Sobs of despair shook her body and she sank into a crouch on the floor. Her stomach and chest repeated the awful series of muscular contractions but there was nothing left inside her. No liquids, no solids. After a while, the chills came, and after them, the relative calm of fatigue.

If only she could see. She had transited two walls. The toilet hole must be near the rear of the cell. That meant the door was most probably in the wall to her immediate right. She managed to stand and felt along it, and there was the outline of the door, midway down, but no handle or knob, and no visible cracks of light. She returned to her corner and sank back down.

She should have known that when the Byelorussian customs woman had taken their passports into the room off the arrival area for "visitor survey statistical purposes" that they had been photocopied. What a simple thing it had been for the KGB, in their routine check of departing passengers, to compare the photographs with the passports once more, and the substituted picture of Josef's replacement had been an instant giveaway. She wondered what they had done with the man. She had hardly known him, just during the brief time in the hotel and the journey to the airport. He had sort of looked like Josef. At least she had completed her assignment. Josef was underground somewhere and she would be unable to compromise him even if she wanted to. Her thoughts returned to the hotel room and their embraces. There had been pleasant moments, despite the mirror.

The sudden sound of the key in the lock startled her and the brilliant light that stabbed into the room when the door swung outward caused her to shield her eyes with her hands.

"Come, come," said a female voice. Marie squinted toward the sound and could see the outline of a uniformed matron take on a third dimension as her eyes adjusted to the light. The woman took her by the arm and led her out into the hall.

"You poor dear," she said when she could see the pitiful state of Marie's body and dress. Gentle hands guided her down the hall and into a spartan but clean bedroom, off of which was a most beautiful sight: a plain tiled bathroom.

"This has all been so unnecessary," the woman said. "When the comrade-colonel heard of your treatment, he flew into a rage. The men responsible have been disciplined." She opened a cabinet in the wall of the room and removed several fluffy white towels and a bar of yellow soap. "I know you wish to cleanse yourself. I will bring food. There are clothes in the wardrobe. I will return in a moment.''

Marie gazed in anticipation at the ancient four-legged cast iron bathtub against the far wall of the bathroom. Impatiently, she dropped her clothes where she stood, and walked almost reverently to it. She twisted the molded glass handles and watched in fascination as the clear water rushed into the tub. She adjusted the mix to give a stimulating hot flow, and while the tub filled she poured cool water from the china pitcher on the washstand into an adjoining glass and sipped the refreshing liquid. It soothed her raw throat and washed away the bitter taste that had stayed with her after she had retched herself dry.

The deep steaming bath warmed and caressed her sore muscles and she paddled her hands along the sides of the tub to create a current that swished up between her legs and around her hips. By sliding down and humping, she could sit neck deep in the soothing heat. The soap had a not unpleasant odor and she glided it across her stomach and up over her breasts in a sensual cleansing that was ritual as well as practical. The nightmare in the hell-hole down the hall had temporarily destroyed her femininity; the crude bar of Russian soap restored it. She vigorously soaped her hands and scrubbed her face and neck, then her legs and feet. There was no shower, but by letting some of the water drain from the tub, she could place her head under the common faucet and lathered her hair for several minutes before rinsing it.

A brisk rubdown with the deep-piled bath towel and a luxurious dusting with the plain body powder she found in the cabinet under the sink completed her renewal. Underwear, a slip, dress, and slippers were on the bed, but her own clothes had been removed. A plate of cheeses and fruit was on the side table, next to a hemispheric loaf of dark bread and a deep dish of butter. She still had no appetite, but nibbled some of the cheese for strength as she stretched out on the bed.

She was weak and very tired and her basic needs had been reduced to only one: sleep.

A soft persistent knock at the door awakened her and she pulled the still-moist bath towel over her nakedness as the matron stuck her head around the opened door.

"You look much better. The comrade-colonel would like to see you if it is convenient. He wishes to apologize and make the necessary arrangements for your return to your country. May I help you dress?"

"No, I can manage. Do you have something for my hair?"

"There is a comb and brush in the drawer. I am afraid we lack some of the more sophisticated conveniences you are accustomed to having."

"They will do nicely, thank you. Please tell the colonel that I shall be ready shortly."

For Christ's sake, what kind of naive baboon do they take me for?

"Please, come in." The speaker came from behind his desk and greeted Marie with an outstretched arm. She ignored it and seated herself in the chair indicated. The colonel smiled understandingly and resumed his seat.

"I regret what has happened. I am sure you can understand the concern of my comrades when they discovered your ruse; however, they overreacted, of course. I offer you the apologies of the Soviet State for the mistreatment. They have been disciplined." His attempt at cordiality was forced and as typical of the KGB's lack of such emotion as was his stoic face and hollow voice.

Marie remained silent.

"I am Colonel Timonkin. May I offer you something to drink? Some wine, perhaps, or vodka? Surely, two professionals such as we can understand the awkwardness of this situation. I wish to make amends." He motioned toward the corner of his desk which supported a half-full bottle of clear vodka and several wines.

"Nothing. Thank you."

"Ah, that's better. We must talk together. You are a brave woman, and loyal. I like that. I can understand that. It is part of our profession, is it not? I think we can put aside the matter of Professor Utgoff for the moment. It is you I am interested in. Very interested. You are obviously a person of some breeding and education, and I am certain you are quite good at your work. The situation you now find yourself in is most serious, of course, but can be turned to your advantage. I wish to make you a proposition.''

I bet you do.

"Do you mind?" He poured himself a small vodka and raised the glass in silent toast before downing it. "You and I are in a special and sometimes difficult occupation, one which has certain hazards, but one which sometimes provides us with unanticipated opportunities. Our loyalties are often misunderstood by those outside the business.'' He studied her before continuing.

"You are a Negro."

"I am an American."

"Yes, yes, of course. I meant no disrespect. Here in the Soviet Union we have many ethnic groups: Estonians, Slavics, Oriental Tuvans, Armenians, many groups—just as in your America. But we have no prejudices, unlike the vicious social system in your country which subjected your people to two hundred years of slavery, and even today denies them the dignity of their skin. Surely, somewhere in your loyalty there is regret for such a situation. Even as you sit here, you are being used."

Marie sat silently, her eyes locked onto his, waiting for the point of the game.

He poured himself another vodka and downed it. "Let us talk as equals. I am a member of the Soviet intelligence service. You are a member of yours. But, while I am legitimate at this moment, you are illegitimate. You have entered this land illegally, with forged documents, and introduced one of your countrymen into our society. His purpose is incidental to the argument; the point is that I have every right to have you carried off to prison as an alien enemy of the Soviet people. You know that I am prepared to do that, but I would rather come to some accommodation. There was an American whose name escapes me at the moment who said 'My country, right or wrong,' or something to that effect. But is not such blind loyalty an insult to the Negro people of today? Are not we much more enlightened? You are in a position to do us a service. All I ask is that you return to your country, resume your duties, and when we ask, accommodate us. In return, I am offering not only your life, which I hold here in my hands, but generous payment. You can have the best of both worlds, American and Soviet.''

''I am an American citizen, illegally detained. I demand access to the American consulate.''

Timonkin laughed as if he had just heard the funniest of stories. *''Demand?* You *demand?''* He shook his head in amazement. ''You are an illegal alien engaged in espionage activities!'' He slammed his empty glass onto the desk. ''You dare sit here and make demands as if you are some pissy-assed tourist who has been charged with a minor infraction of our traffic laws? I have been giving you some credit for being intelligent. Do you think your country gives a shit about you, a compromised agent who is worthless to them from this point on? They will let you die before admitting any connection.''

His solicitous attitude had vanished. The heavily browed eyes, which had failed miserably in expressing concern and consideration for Marie's predicament, began to glow with his true nature. The blood vessels of his face had been brought close to the surface by his constant reliance on vodka to get him through his difficult days, and now they filled with his flow of anger and reddened his skin. He placed his hands on the edges of the desk and stiffened his arms to force himself into a more erect position.

''If you wish, I can break you. You know we have our ways, as you have yours. I am trying to help you. Take my offer! Give your black people some dignity. Rise above servitude—it is no better than slavery.''

Marie could see that he was trying to control his anger. He allowed himself a pause, then walked from behind his desk. His eyes softened, his manner became less agitated. ''You are a lovely woman. You can do many things for us.

I would consider you my protégé. Look at the reality. I can do many things for you. I am not an ungrateful person.'' He leaned forward to see if his words were having any visual effect. His benevolent smile once more slipped toward its sinister side. ''Or . . .'' he said much more slowly, ''. . . to use a fine old American term, I can have you terminated.''

''I am an American citizen and wish to see the American consul.''

Timonkin stood over her, his breath coming in slow, deliberate cycles. ''I can break you,'' he said.

''I know nothing.''

His hands lashed out, grabbed her shoulders, and jerked her to her feet. ''Who is he? Where is he going? My patience is at an end!''

Marie's mouth dropped open from the pain of his grip. ''Honest to God, I don't know.''

The open hand landed on the already injured side of her face, knocking her backward and across the chair. It tilted and she tumbled onto the floor. Timonkin gave her no time to rise, instead he drove the point of his shoe viciously into her side. She heard the crack of the rib and felt the sharpness of the bone as it penetrated her lung and forced the air outward. She gasped to regain it.

''You pig! You fucking pig!'' she hissed, rolling over onto her knees and elbows.

Timonkin filled his fingers with her hair and slung her across the room against the wall. She bounced off it and her legs collapsed. Totally out of control, he pounced on top of her, ripped open the front of her dress and slip, and forced her brassiere up and off her breasts. Sitting astride her hips, he produced a knife and laid the razor edge into the crease under the mound of flesh on her right side. Fury danced in his eyes and he tilted his head back to glare down across his cheekbones.

''So help me, Christ, I will make you as flat-chested as a child unless you tell me where he is headed. *What is his assignment?*'' He drew the blade just enough to slice the outer skin and release a thin ribbon of blood.

Marie could no longer make out his face. Tears filled her eyes and obscured the details of the form pressing down on her. She was afraid, but the tears had their origin in a futile anger that was vibrating her body with a hate she had never known. She could not answer his question and thanked God that such was the case. The blade under her breast pressed harder. She was determined not to waste her waning energy on an ineffective scream. Instead, she spat at the glob that should be his face. Even with her breasts gone, she would be more of a woman than he had ever had.

The room weaved and pulsated with ever-changing undulations, while Timonkin's silhouette swelled and contracted in surrealistic patterns as her consciousness began to fade. He was heavy on her abdomen and her broken rib stabbed deeper each time he shifted his weight. Again and again, she felt him moving against her. *Oh, God!* He was forcing her legs apart and slipping between her thighs, his movements taking on an unmistakable rhythm. She knew he was inside her, but could feel nothing. Each violent thrust cut off her wind and she was forced to gulp for air each time he withdrew. His pace quickened, causing her to gasp more rapidly, and she felt the first dizzying signs of hyperventilation. His rage had turned into sadistic passion and he ignored the metal blade of the knife for the more penetrating one of hard flesh that he was slicing deep into her body. His rhythm peaked, and with the final surges of his pelvis, all of the angry lust in him spurted from his loins into hers.

A series of exhausted grunts signaled his finish and the movements stopped. Syrupy spittle dripped from his mouth and wet her breasts as he pushed away from her. Instinctively, her hands sought the disarrayed brassiere and she fumbled with it until she could pull it down and over her. The bottom edge of the right cup began blotting the slow flow of blood oozing from the cut under her breast.

Timonkin closed his trousers and straightened his clothing before speaking into his intercom. The matron returned, her face expressionless as she helped Marie stand.

"Put the nigger back in her cell," snarled Timonkin. "Let her rot."

He watched the matron take her from the office, then lifted the vodka bottle to his lips. The rape had satisfied him physically, but it had been like mounting a corpse, and inside he seethed at the realization that the woman had not responded.

But, it was time to go back to work. She had known nothing. That was their way. Her task had been to provide cover for the American agent's entry into the country. The man arrested with her was even more ignorant of the operation. That might make his job harder, but that was all. He already had a start.

He walked over to a covered chalkboard and flipped back the plastic flap. Two rectangular boxes had been drawn on the upper left side. Inside the top enclosure was the name: Josef Utgoff. Inside the second were two names: the identities of the two KGB men found murdered in the Intourist rental-car garage. Utgoff had disappeared on the seventh. The bodies had been discovered on the eighth, but had been dead for almost 24 hours. The manager of the Intourist facility had disappeared on the eighth. That was Timonkin's starting point.

The records of the murdered KGB team indicated a long-held suspicion of the manager and they had him under surveillance for several months before their fatal encounter. Their daily log for the seventh indicated that their task on the last day of their lives was observation of his activities.

There had to be a connection. Timonkin drew a chalked line between the two boxes. Assuming that the missing manager had assisted Utgoff in slipping away from the tour group, it was logical to further assume that the KGB pair discovered what he was up to and confronted him in his office where they were murdered. Timonkin reasoned that the manager and Utgoff would have left Leningrad, but not necessarily together. His first task would be to find some indication of where either, or both, had gone.

He spoke over the intercom, "Andrei, get me the computer printout of the results of our terminal security checks on August eighth and ninth.''

His aide entered and laid the folded sheets on his desk. There were the usual discrepancies in citizen travel permits at the rail and air terminals, and a few minor criminals had been apprehended. The highway roadblocks appeared to have uncovered nothing indicative, except for one item which caught his eye. At 7:15 A.M., 72 kilometers out of Leningrad on the highway to Moscow, a comrade-Major had noted in his report sheet a discrepancy in the passage of an Intourist rental automobile. The Zhiguli had an unlisted driver, because the assigned driver became ill. The passengers were legitimate, and the substitute driver's papers were in order. In addition, his name was on file with the Intourist office, *but the same one,* Timonkin recognized, *as where the two murdered men had been found!*

He took the chalk and drew in a third box below the original two. Inside it he scratched: Unknown driver to Moscow. It was logical, but was the driver the American or the office manager? He must assume the worst-case situation. It was the American.

Now, was Moscow his original destination? If so, why did not he wait until the tour group arrived there? The answer was simple. If he went underground at Leningrad, his replacement would be subjected to only one travel security check. So Moscow could be his destination, or it might be the only place he had to run after killing the two Soviets.

Timonkin triggered his intercom again. ''Andrei, contact comrade Colonel Vasilotova in Moscow. Have him transmit his security logs for August ninth through twelfth.''

The logs came within the hour and he labored over them into the night. In the early morning he had his lead.

On August tenth, a member of the Moscow Airport Security Group had conducted a routine passenger list verification on Flight 12 to Volgograd. One name was worthy of a precautionary mention: Grigori Solovyov, an aerospace engineer on the faculty of Lomonosov University. A routine follow-up call to the university had confirmed that such a person was on their staff, but it was understood that he was on holiday in Crimea. The university spokesman had no idea why Solovyov may have changed his plans. The Moscow agent had booked himself on the flight and had procured a seat next to the engineer. The man had seemed legitimate, had no suspicious characteristics, and was well versed in space mathematics. The report ended with the notation: no follow-up required.

No follow-up, indeed! Timonkin drew a fourth box and inside chalked the name: Solovyov. He had been with the KGB for thirty years, and when a sequence of unexplained but possibly related events surfaced, his instincts cried out for further investigation.

He backed up to study the board, then chalked in dates and times. Everything correlated. Conclusion: An American agent, familiar with space technology, was in Volgograd, only sixty miles from the space center.

Last question: what was his mission?

The Volgograd center was primarily a scientific launch area for the Cosmos and Intercosmos programs—except for the Special Project. *That* was the American's task: infiltration and collection of data relative to the Special Project spacecraft!

Timonkin called his aide one more time. "Andrei, book me to Volgograd on the next available flight."

He sat, weary but immensely pleased with himself. The remainder of the vodka brought a finish to a fruitful day. How incredibly stupid the Americans were. By way of contrast, his own experience and expertise had overcome the stubbornness and ignorance of the black bitch slowly dying in the cell down the hall.

Wait! There could be another purpose for her. He leaned forward and pushed his intercom button.

"Yes, comrade Colonel?"

"Andrei, tell the matron to clean up the woman and see that she gets medical attention. Also a good meal, and put her in the room with the decent bed. I want her well rested.''

"I will do that immediately."

"One other thing. Get me a military airplane for the trip."

"Yes, comrade Colonel."

That would be much better. Timonkin was beginning to feel like his old self. He needed the American. His career had not gone well the past few years. It was hard to sit in his dismal office and interrogate common criminals and irresponsible citizens. That was work for a Major or even less. He needed to return to the field where he could match wits with the likes of the woman down the hall. True, she had told him nothing but that was because she knew nothing. However, she didn't need to know anything to be of further use. One thing about capitalists. In addition to their relentless pursuit for the almighty dollar, they valued their personal relationships beyond reason. With the Americans, the easiest way to break one of them was with another, a sentimental weakness that was not at all characteristic of the KGB.

He was almost shaking with anticipation. The successful foiling of an American attempt to penetrate the Northern Cosmodrome would give him the leverage to ask for reassignment. And he would catch the man, make no mistake about that. The pieces fit too well. There was too much conformity for them to be merely coincidental.

There was a problem, however. The detaining and interrogation of Marie and her accomplice were well within his authority and responsibility, as well as any subsequent disposition he might feel appropriate. But going to Volgograd and taking the part of a field agent, even temporarily, was for the moment outside of his purview. For that, it was time to call in one of his markers. He picked up his private line and dialed a number he held only in his head.

"Yes?" Good. The General was in.

"This is Vasily, comrade General," began Timonkin, "may I have a moment?"

"Of course."

Timonkin expected such a reply. He might be in the autumn of a sagging career with respect to most of his superiors but he and the General had shared some special times together in the early days and the deep voice on the other end of the line was there only because of a deep and personal sacrifice once made by Timonkin. "I need a special authorization," he said.

It took only a few minutes to brief the General on his theory concerning the insertion and mission of the American agent.

"I want this acquisition, myself. I need it. I am asking you to arrange my entry into the spaceport on a 'special assignment' and authority to take whatever steps necessary to apprehend the American."

"You are asking for a lot."

"I know that."

There was a long silence, then again the deep voice.

"I will arrange it. But use some tact, Vasily. The people in that section are very protective of their responsibilities."

"I recognize that. I'm sure you understand what this could mean for me."

"Yes, of course. But you, in turn, must understand that I have only so much influence with the director of that sector."

"Do you have transportation access?"

"That is no problem. My authority allows such trips for liaison purposes."

The deep voice chuckled. "This is something more than liaison, old friend."

Timonkin realized the General was stretching the authority of his office to give the assistance he asked. "I know, comrade. And I recognize the magnitude of your intercession on my behalf. But, we were good in the old days. I still have the ability."

"And the temper, and the impatience."

Timonkin winced at the General's reminder of the traits of his personality that had finally taken him out of the field and placed him in a less critical assignment. "I have learned during the months of boredom in this damned perfunctory office. It is a lesson I can respect,'' he offered in his defense.

''Vasily, I am doing this for you because of our times together in the old days—and I feel you may have indeed recognized your shortcomings. We paid for them, once or twice, you will remember. So, go to Volgograd and bring back the American. It will be an achievement and I hope it provides you with a further opportunity. I have another call.'' The receiver clicked.

Timonkin leaned back in his chair, pleased with the General's response, and restudied the chalkboard. The squares and connecting lines led him once more to his conclusion. He *had* to be right. But there was nothing more he could do tonight. Grabbing his coat off the back of his chair, he slipped it on while tidying up in front of the bathroom mirror.

Andrei was sitting at his desk as Timonkin passed through the anteroom. ''I have your aircraft schedule, comrade Colonel.''

Timonkin glanced at the note and nodded concurrence. ''Seven o'clock departure—good. I will eat breakfast on the aircraft. The American woman will be going with me. Have her there.''

''Yes, comrade Colonel.''

His car and driver were waiting but he waved the man off. ''I will walk some,'' he said. The more he thought about his cleverness in following up the fruitless encounter with the woman with his professional analysis of facts on hand, the more he was determined to press for a field assignment when he returned with the American agent.

He would have another strong argument in his favor for by that time he would have convinced the woman that her only future lay in the role of a double agent for the Soviet Union. She was strong but the nature of their profession was such that she, like all, could be approached for such a thing. What a coup he was about to carry off! The capture of the man and the turning around of the woman.

Perhaps there would even be a promotion.

* * *

Timonkin's driver pulled up alongside the waiting Ilyushin IL-14 medium transport a few minutes before seven. His aide, Andrei, met his car and held the door for him.

"The woman is on board, comrade Colonel," reported the aide.

Timonkin nodded and tried not to show his disappointment at the sight of the aging aircraft provided for his use by the Military Transport Command. Not only was the twin-engined transport 40 years old, the pilots assigned were normally just the opposite: brand new aviators who required more seasoning for a significant assignment in the Soviet Air Force. Too often they were only a step above the near washouts that wound up in Aeroflot cockpits. Today, there were two grinning idiots peering out of the cockpit windows to watch him board, neither apparently old enough to shave. At least, they knew something of protocol; the big radial engine on the opposite side to his boarding ladder was already started, its irregular concert of staccato engine noises shaking the aircraft as an old dog would shake a dusty rag. The outdated engine would be spurting oil back over the wing and emitting periodic puffs of black smoke.

Well, this would be his last ride in such a relic. When he came back with his task accomplished he could look forward to air transport more suitable to his station, perhaps even a modern jet like the brand new Antonov AN-72 assigned to the General. As he entered the cabin, returning the lukewarm greeting of the cabin crewman with a disapproving grunt, he had no trouble understanding the rationale of the NATO code name assigned to the IL-14: Crate. The interior was suitable for his purposes, however, outfitted as it was for a working staff with pairs of seats arranged on each side of rows of small conference tables. The woman was already strapped in a window seat and he sat opposite her. They were the only passengers.

Conversation was difficult until the transport had taken off and climbed through the morning haze to its cruising altitude. The engines were retarded to their cruise settings for the four-hour flight to Volgograd and Timonkin sat impatiently while the two little-boy pilots up front fiddled with the propeller RPM levers until there was some semblance of synchronization and the noise and vibration settled into a tolerable hum.

Marie had also remained silent during the climb out but Timonkin could easily see the rage in her eyes.

It even masked the pain he knew was present in her rib cage. The matron had covered the face bruise well with heavy makeup, but that would be removed when they reached Volgograd. It would be better for the man to see her suffer. He would come around quicker. She was a professional, Timonkin would grant her that. For the moment she sat staring at him as if she were the one in control—calm, confident, even arrogant. If only he could penetrate those eyes and read her thoughts.

She should consider herself fortunate that he had decided to place her in the comfortable bedroom rather than back in the hole. She might have reason for her anger, but he could handle that, and this was the perfect place for their discussion. Even an old aircraft such as this one presented him with a certain psychological advantage. Flying smoothly along, far above the earth, he and the woman were a captive audience for the muffled sounds within the pressurized cabin. They were in a different element and events that had occurred on the ground could be viewed more objectively. The impact of his assault on her would fade a bit. And a bit was all he needed.

The cabin crewman brought hot tea and flavored biscuits. Both he and Marie took one. Good. She was hungry.

"We have some more time together," he announced.

"Where are we going?"

Even better. She was talking.

"You will see. We have several hours to share. I think you will find the conversation interesting, even rewarding."

"Why didn't you kill me?" The brown eyes flashed with the fire of hate.

"I had to use whatever means I had to assure myself that you truly did not know the identity or details of the mission of your Professor Utgoff. I am convinced you were merely used with no regard as to the actual importance of your task. It is typical of the CIA. Come now, you used your body for your own purposes—in the hotel. I used it for mine. We are no different."

Marie cursed inside. They were practically alone in the cabin but there was no realistic way she could expect to kill him. She had already tasted his strength.

"Conversation is not easy here so I shall speak plainly, with candor. I intend for you to become my protégé, a fellow agent in my service. You will be of great value."

Marie could hardly believe the audacity of the man. Less than 12 hours earlier he had assaulted her, cut her, and raped her. Now, he was proposing to enlist her services as a double agent with all of the nonchalance of a personnel manager interviewing a job applicant. "You must be fucking mad," she hissed, switching to English for the obscenity.

Timonkin appeared amused but certainly not deterred. "You Americans have a sort of inbred affinity for that particularly crude Anglo-Saxon word. Someday, I must teach you some of our unique Russian expressions."

"I'm sitting across from one."

Excellent: She still had spirit. He could convert spirit.

"You will work with me. It is compatible with the realities of your situation."

"Which are?"

"You do or you die."

Marie did not underestimate the significance of his statement. He was undoubtedly quite sincere, but she was not being taken somewhere to be killed. KGB colonels had flunkies for such mundane tasks. There was another thought that disturbed her. Even if death were not her destiny should she resist his proposal, the alternative was more likely a long ride in a bare boxcar heading north, an equally unwelcome alternative.

133

"It is all part of the risks of my profession," she replied.

"No, my sweet thing. Bravado is for screenplays. You may like to think that such resignation is part of your conditioning but when the time comes—as it has now—and you are offered an out, the more primitive instinct of survival wins out. You are a survivor. You also realize that there is absolutely no other course open to you. So, you will work for me."

"Do you have some kind of instant pill for loyalty?"

"Ha! I like that. May I remind you that loyalty may be negotiated."

"You feel no undying loyalty to the Soviet Union?"

"Oh, I do, I do. But loyalty without dedication can be said to be the prostitute of the intelligence profession. It can be bought."

"You work for money? A socialist official? My, my."

"A typical American interpretation of such a remark. Rubles, even dollars, mean nothing to me. It is the reality of the Revolution that buys my services, the inevitable progress of the restructuring of world order."

"Jesus. Kill me if you want to but spare me the idealistic bullshit."

"I am through preaching. I do not have the time or the motivation to convert you politically. It is not necessary. As I just implied, we work for the highest bidder and while the United States offers you dollars, I offer you your life which is at this moment in my hands."

You have a point there, bastard.

"As a matter of fact, you are even now on your first assignment."

Marie let her eyes ask the question.

"You wonder what it is? A simple test to see if my proposal interests you. In a short time we shall be at Volgograd. That is where your professor is. It is my intention to apprehend him and you will assist me as required in his identification and interrogation."

"You think I will switch that easily?"

"I am certain of it. There is a direct rail line from there

to a quaint little gulag on a very small arctic island off our northernmost coast." He leaned forward, the evil that had stared down at Marie when he had pressed her to the office floor returning to his eyes. "A woman ages fast there, alone, the constant object of male inmates and guards alike. The attention I gave you last evening will seem the love of a prince by comparison. And you will endure such an existence until you are as dry as an old hag and finally wither away to vanish from a world you will not have seen for twenty years, perhaps even longer for such a strong one as yourself. So, you do as I say or you step off this aircraft onto a train." Timonkin leaned back and motioned for the cabin crewman. "Vodka," he ordered. "The lady and I have just come to an understanding."

Marie could not doubt the awful truth of his words. The pain of them stabbed into her as sharply as had the toe of his boot the night before. She had a decision to make.

The continuous drone of the aircraft as it passed south across eastern Russia did have a hypnotic effect as if she were not actually present in her body, only in spirit. It was as if her ethereal self were looking down at the two lone passengers seated at the table and listening to their bizarre conversation. There was an awful, disturbed feeling within that spirit, one that could not deny a certain logic in Timonkin's proposal. Her life had not gone exceptionally well but it had been life with occasional pleasures to offset the anguish and disappointments. She would like to be able to live up to what she thought were her ideals and spit in the arrogant KGB officer's face again, then march defiantly off the plane onto the train. But, in the overall scheme of things, what purpose would that serve? Better to pretend to serve the KGB until such time as she could return to the States. But the man was not stupid; she would be closely monitored even there. Still, why not a triple agent, serving the KGB with the full consent and knowledge of the CIA?

Then again, why should she? Timonkin had triggered some unpleasant memories. She was a black woman in a white woman's skin. If she had the broad nose and thick

135

lips and ebony body that were rightfully hers, would she be as accepted as she was now? Would she have won Ted as her husband? With all of her intense feelings of patriotism and pride in her country was she still less than equal? If so, where should her first loyalty be? To the country of her birth or the blood of her ancestors? Was there a conflict? Would there be any resolution by serving the Soviets? Should she take the offer and the great deal of money that she knew went with it, and to hell with everything else? She had already lost the only one she had ever truly loved.

As her mind seemed to hover above her own body in the stuffy cabin of the Ilyushin transport, she wrestled with the conflict inside her. It was only when the aircraft abruptly nosed over for its descent into Volgograd that flesh and soul were reunited and she knew what she must do.

Chapter
9

"Worked out a plan yet?" queried Mikhail.

"Nothing foolproof," replied Dover.

"You won't come up with anything that's a sure thing. I've got a couple hours before I go to work. Let's kick around a few ideas. Tea?"

"Thanks." Dover reached up with his cup and Mikhail filled it with dark hot liquid. Dover set it next to his plate and twisted off a chunk of the heavy bread, lathered it with butter, and laid it next to his vegetables and fish. "You live well for a peasant."

"I know a few people. We do favors for one another. The butter is sometimes hard to come by, but I manage."

"What's your plan for getting me into the compound?"

Mikhail leisurely finished chewing and swallowed before replying, "I figure we can use the same method of entry to the center as before. When we reach the special projects guardhouse, I'll distract the sentry and you slip by him. Let me show you." He rose and returned with a small bundle which he emptied onto the table. There were two packages of Marlboro Light 100's and three small pellets not much larger than quarter-inch lengths of pencil lead. There was also a syringe and a five-centimeter pharmaceutical bottle of cloudy liquid. Mikhail tore open one of the packs of Marlboros and withdrew a cigarette. Into the unfiltered end, he inserted one of the pellets, using the tine of his fork to tamp it a half-inch into the tobacco.

"The guard and I usually share a smoke and some conversation. It's become almost a ritual. He gets lonely and I'm ready for a break about then. I'll give him one of these. The Russian hasn't been born who'd turn down an American cigarette. It'll take him about five minutes to smoke down to the pellet. When he does, he'll get a headache and become disoriented. In fact, he'll be out on his feet. We could drive the truck through the gate and he wouldn't notice. I'll give you the high sign and you get your ass through the gate and into the building pronto. As soon as you're out of sight, I'll give him a shot of the antidote and he'll snap right out of it."

"He won't suspect anything?"

"I doubt it. He'll just have had a brief dizzy spell, and it'll only last for a few seconds—that's why you have to haul ass. I give him the needle behind the earlobe. He won't be conscious of it, and when he comes around there won't be any visible mark. It may itch a little, but that won't clue him in.

"Beautiful—why can't we use the same method to get me back out?"

"Listen, these guys may be slow, but they aren't stupid. Two fainting spells while smoking an American cigarette with the comrade garbageman will start him thinking. Besides, I can't stay and wait for you like a damn taxi. My schedule is somewhat flexible, but the roving patrols wouldn't let me get away with a longer stay without investigation. It would be too risky to wait anywhere else for the length of time you need. You'll have to come out a separate way. I have some things which will help." He rose a second time and placed a pair of coveralls and a plastic badge on the chair beside Dover.

"These coveralls aren't exactly identical, but close enough to what the personnel in the building wear. I'm also working on an outer garment; the technicians wear a sort of gray lab coat. This badge is a reproduction of the special badge they use within the compound, but it won't get you in because the guard has a visual identification plate and your face and its face won't match. There's no way we can substitute anything on the plate, but once inside you can go around as if you belong there with the badge pinned on your coat. Now, here's the tricky part. I've never been able to find out what security measures are in force inside the building, other than the badges, and I don't have any idea how many personnel work that shift, but reason says there's a few. Whether they're technicians, or scientists, or janitors, or what, I don't know. How's your knowledge of space technology?''

"I know enough to get by."

Mikhail studied him for a moment. "I bet you do," he said. His instincts told him that Dover had the special knowledge needed, otherwise he would have drawn the assignment, which didn't bother him at all. "Do you need a camera?''

"No."

"Photographic memory?"

"Something like that."

"Okay. So, how do you get back out?"

"I've been thinking. The railroad gate is the only possibility. Is it electrified?''

"No, I don't think so. It might be too dangerous for the dogs or the people who have to open it. Also, it's in full view of the sentry."

"We need a diversion."

"The weed is out. I can't pull the same routine twice, like I said."

"No . . . something else. How about an accident, or an explosion?''

"Or a fire?'' interjected Mikhail.

"Yes, anything that will draw the guard's attention away from the gate.''

"The shipping dock. It's in the opposite direction. You'll have to set it." Mikhail drummed his fingers on the table.

"You'll need a rope and grapple hook to get over the gate; I can get those."

"Let's look at your layout map again."

Mikhail spread the blue paper over the table. Dover started tracing the railroad line. It entered the range just south of Kapustin Yar, extended northeast 32 kilometers, then bent around to the south, entered the Center fence, and five kilometers later reached the horizontal assembly building. There it passed through the double gate into the special project compound. The road to Saykhin intercepted it near the dump.

"Wait." Dover tapped his finger on the dashed line that paralleled the railroad. "That looks like the main powerline."

"It is, but they've got auxiliary power which automatically cuts in should the main line fail."

"Everywhere? It must be a restricted-access auxiliary line."

"What do you have in mind?"

"The perimeter fence, is it on the emergency line?"

"I don't know."

"If I can get over the railroad gate, it's a five-kilometer jog to the perimeter fence. If you can blow the power, I can get over the fence north of the dump, hide beside the Saykhin road, and you pick me up."

"Possible. I'll have to blow the line somewhere in the south, near Akhtubinsk maybe. That'll draw the security forces away from the Sayhkin road."

"Exactly," said Dover, warming to the challenge. Mikhail could see that he had better try to bring him down to earth.

"Look, it's a good plan, but don't overlook its demands. We better dry-run the times involved. We not only have to get you into the special compound by way of a wide-open area—and by the way, there are randomly roving security patrols all over the center—you have to gain entrance to the building and masquerade as a Soviet spacetechnician. Then, you're going to have to crawl all over one of the machines, slip out to the loading dock and start a fire, evade the guard, and get over the railroad gate. Assuming you haven't been hauled away to join a Siberian tour group by that time, you have a five-kilometer run to the perimeter fence, one hell of a problem if it's still hot, and an undetermined wait for me to pull your ass out of the fire. I don't know—but I don't have a better plan, either.''

"I can pull boards off the old shack and use them to get over the fence. It'll work.''

Mikhail sat and considered all the factors. "All right, you're the pigeon. I'll have everything you need by tomorrow night.''

The lift over the fence went as before. Dover already had on the coveralls and slipped the Army tunic over them, donned the cap, and rested the AK-47 beside him. The folded lab coat lay on the seat.

Mikhail guided the truck away from the dump and started his rounds. They reached the special projects compound at 4:00 A.M. and Mikhail parked so that Dover would have a view of the gate in the rear view mirror. The guard handed him two loaded trash containers, and after they were dumped the men stood by the open gate.

"I have a treat for us tonight, comrade.'' Mikhail plucked the Marlboros from his shirt pocket and tapped one out into his hand. He offered it to the guard.

"American! You have been slumming with the American tourists in Volgograd again, Mikhail.''

"Yes, I made a connection yesterday. Please, keep the pack. I have more.''

"Thank you, I shall.'' He leaned over for a light. "Ahhh . . . that's very good. I am afraid the capitalists excel in one area, at least.'' He inhaled deeply and laughed at his little joke.

"It seems to be very quiet tonight,'' observed Mikhail.

"It's always quiet on this duty. I hate it, but only eight more days and I have some time off for holiday. I may just go to my woman's house and sleep the whole time.''

"Sleep, my friend! Ha! I think you will do other things, also."

"You are correct . . . she is a mink."

The guard had been sucking hungrily on the cigarette, letting each draw linger in his lungs before reluctantly allowing it to filter up through his nostrils and pass into the night air. Now, he looked puzzled and shook his head as if to rid himself of a sudden weariness. "I feel funny," he said.

"Here, sit for a moment." Mikhail guided him backward to the stool in the guardhouse. "Is that better?"

"I am dizzy . . . I must call my officer." The guard fumbled for the telephone on the inside of the back wall. Mikhail gently restrained his arm.

"Perhaps you ate something. . . .

The guard sat staring straight ahead, supported by Mikhail who anxiously looked around the area. Dover had been watching the drama unfold and made himself ready by slipping out of the Army tunic and grabbing the lab coat. At Mikhail's nod, he dropped from the cab and dashed through the gate. There was a personnel door in the near side of the building.

Mikhail quickly pulled the syringe from his back pants pocket and deftly inserted the tip of the needle into the soft fold of skin behind the guard's left earlobe. Almost immediately, the man stirred and blinked his eyes.

"I almost passed out," he murmured.

"You look ill. Have you been feeling all right lately?"

"A bit tired, maybe. It just came on so sudden. I am feeling better, now." He stood and felt his face.

"Yes, the color is returning to your cheeks. You gave me a scare, there. Do you want me to stay with you until you can call for a relief?"

"No, I must not do that. My officer would be very angry. It is passing." He had walked out into the open and was refreshing himself with deep breaths. "Maybe the American cigarettes are too strong for us, eh, comrade?"

Mikhail was relieved to see that the remark was made in jest.

"You had better have a medical checkup before you try your holiday with your mink," suggested Mikhail, grinning broadly.

The guard was fully recovered. "Ah, yes. She will either cure me or kill me! Either way, I will be a happy man. Thank you for being with me. I am fine, now." He closed and latched the gate as Mikhail climbed into the cab and slipped the big machine into gear.

Dover found himself in a small anteroom to the main space within the hangar. Several tables and chairs were about in casual disarray and there were scattered magazines and loaded ashtrays all over the room. A few crumpled paper bags were in the trash can. It was some sort of utility room, probably a place for the workers to take their breaks and eat their meals. He crossed over to the inside wall and cracked open the door.

There is a unique feeling of horror that comes over one when encountering a situation which suddenly reveals some sort of dreaded truth, and from which there is no retreat, such as a disturbing nightmare wherein the dreamer faces an impossible and horrible dilemma. In the dream, one positively believes that he is not dreaming at all. In fact, the realism of the images formed by his subconscious is so vivid that the dreamer falls into a deep depression, so very life-like that even as he wakes he lies terror stricken, convinced beyond a doubt that the evil of the dream is still with him. It is a feeling of hopelessness, of utter surrender to dark forces.

Such was the sensation that chilled Dover as he peered into the vast interior of the special projects hangar.

It was crammed with Alpha Bugs, some in the final stages of assembly, some apparently completed but with inspection plates open for final checks and connected by arm-thick electrical conduits to computerized analysis and test instruments. Several had collapsible dish mirrors opened and raised from compartments in the tops of the fuselages. A few were sitting at the far end of the building, surrounded by bulk shipping materials, waiting to be crated. All were dark blue-green and wore on their tall tails the white-outlined Red Star insignia of Soviet space forces.

Dover had expected to find the Alpha Bug, but the number before him was devastating when he considered the impact they would have on the military balance of power between the Soviet Union and his country. His eye wanted to stay on the raised mirrors. They meant that the spacecraft carried a laser weapon; possibly even a particle-beam gun. Only a few had their spider-like legs extended. He pressed his eye-camera and took his first picture.

There were only a few people scattered about the hangar, most wearing the gray lab coat. Mikhail had provided him with a clipboard stuffed with assorted documents he had gleaned from the trash during his rounds, and Dover was surprised to see that his tense grip on it had turned his knuckles white. Hardly normal for a member of the night shift. He relaxed his hold and entered the assembly area, walking easily but purposely toward one of the unattended spacecraft. He positioned himself so that he faced away from the nearest workers and studied the impressive machine.

It was, indeed, a miniature of the U.S. space shuttle in overall configuration but a completely different machine in concept. The bottom was not covered with heat tiles, but instead was composed of a dark ceramic skin, an unbroken heat shield that appeared much smoother and more sophisticated than that on the *Columbia.* The skin encased the sharply pointed nose and covered the leading edges of the wing and vertical stabilizer as well as the forward parts of a pair of teardrop bulges which sat to the rear and on the upper sides of the fuselage. The spacecraft was canard configured with the horizontal stabilizer forward of its wing. It, also, was protected on the leading edge and bottom by the hard ceramic material. The upper part of the spacecraft was protected with some sort of pliable plastic-impregnated tiles, molded where required in compound curved form. It appeared to be a true *kosmolyot,* the Russian term for spaceplane, and an evolution of an earlier spaceplane they had tested back in the early '80's.

The wing itself was a near delta with a broad sweeping leading edge and a straight trailing edge along which were positioned a pair of flaperons, the control surfaces which gave the spaceplane its ability to roll and slow whenever it was within the atmosphere. Farther out along its span, the wing curved sharply downward, the last foot or so nearly vertical. A long, slim airspeed probe jutted forward from the left wingtip as if the sky warrior carried an ancient silver spear. The overall effect of the design was that of a giant insect with its wings frozen in a downbeat.

There was only one engine exhaust in the rear of the fuselage, a massive metal tunnel with an adjustable mouth of blue-black heat resistant steel panels. The single orifice was a radical departure from the multifunnels normally found on both Soviet and American space vehicles. Directly underneath the edge of the exhaust lay a horizontal row of much smaller outlets. Dover counted nine and they appeared to be solid rocket exhaust ports.

For maneuvering in space, attitude thrusters were installed around the nose cone and the after fuselage section, four to each set, 90 degrees apart. Roll thrusters were at the ends of the wing just inboard of the downward turn of the airfoil.

There was no cockpit bulge but instead a flat entry hatch, flush with the top of the fuselage when closed. But as Dover could see on a number of what appeared to be completed spaceplanes, the hatch could be raised forward to nearly a right angle for easy access by a spacesuited cosmonaut.

The Alpha Bug was a manned spacecraft, as suspected.

Dover winked off four more pictures: front, back, and each of the two sides, making sure that all printed fuselage data were included. Dropping to one knee, he began his examination of the underside. Puzzled, he realized that there was no landing gear. Quickly glancing around at the other spaceplanes, he confirmed what appeared to be a serious omission! Instead, each nested in individual ground handling cradles. Why would they be building winged space vehicles without landing gears? He stood and reexamined the fuselage. Those teardrop humps on each side of the vertical tail must be parachute housings. The Russians had always favored chute recoveries just as the Americans did—until the space shuttle. Weight was undoubtedly a critical consideration in the design of the Alpha Bug and a parachute recovery system would carry very little weight penalty when compared to the heavy and complicated hydraulic and air pressure tricycle landing gear systems. It was still confusing. Why have a space vehicle with such obvious aerodynamic characteristics and not provide a set of wheels? That was the whole purpose of a reusable spacecraft: launch it, fly it, and recover it for reuse. The intelligence photographs Tobias had shown him back at Bethesda had even revealed an unusually long runway at the Northern Cosmodrome, although he didn't recall seeing any such facility on the Volgograd and Baikonur pictures.

The light came on! Dover suddenly realized that the answer was so simple it bordered on the ingenious. The aerodynamic feature was not primarily for recovery in the normal sense, it was for escape and evasion. During launch and when in orbit, the shape of the spaceplane was really immaterial. But it was a military weapon, and a highly sophisticated one at that, with maneuvering and armament features that had been developed with the utmost secrecy. The Soviets had never been ultra precise when it came to hitting their landing targets and a premature deorbit burn due to a faulty insertion or in-orbit emergency could force the spaceplane down over other than Soviet territory. That thin Concorde-like wing was to allow the cosmonaut to glide—perhaps even fly with power from that huge rear exhaust nozzle—away from unfriendly territory. That ability would give them considerable flexibility in their deorbit points which, in turn, would open up many new recovery and service areas in the Soviet Union.

There was, perhaps, another reason. Dover recalled that one of the Soviet three-man capsules had wound up splashing down in a remote Russian lake. Like all others, it was designed for a hard landing on Soviet soil. But some miscalculation in the deorbit burn put the cosmonauts in dire danger of drowning should they open their escape hatch so they remained imprisoned for several days before a rescue party could reach them. He had also heard stories about capsules that simply were never found. Winged flight capability would go a long way toward minimizing that hazard. Nevertheless, Dover had to wonder about the wisdom of such a typical Soviet solution to a compound problem: build a winged reentry vehicle then have its final descent controlled by what appeared at first glance to be an outmoded landing system. But one didn't argue with success. The Alpha Bug could perform some remarkable feats and it would be premature to consider its lack of runway capability a design flaw.

Overall, it was a thing of awesome beauty, about one-half the size of the *Columbia*, and apparently a devastating jump ahead in technology. The pure pilot's side of Dover's personality was falling in love at first sight.

That is, until the full impact of what was before him began to surface. Since the early '80's, the term "Star Wars" had been picked up by the media and bantered about in almost every article about the development of space weapons, an acknowledged exaggeration-for-the-sake-of-emphasis syndrome. The science fiction technology of the popular series of space movies had always been well beyond the realistic state of the art—until now. The Alpha Bug had every appearance of being the first step toward manned-vehicle combat in space. It represented not one, but at least two quantum jumps: it apparently carried an advanced weapons system and its observed ability to change orbital planes was unbelievable.

Dover moved over to one that had its spidery legs extended. They weren't actual legs, but flexible coiled-steel rods that were expandable as they projected outward from their narrow wing and fuselage housings. Probably some kind of detection or aiming antennas, their purpose was beyond Dover's expertise at the moment. He reasoned them to be part of the overall weapons system, however. Perhaps the requirement for such elaborate antennas was another factor in eliminating the landing gear. The antenna housings took up much of the space that would have been required to house retractable wheels. Maybe the designer was not quite as goofy as Dover had at first imagined. He took several shots, including close-ups.

Studiously making notes on his clipboard, he walked casually around the spaceplane. He was surprised at the small number of night shift workers. Certainly, the program was of the highest priority or was there a shortage of qualified skills? He doubted that. A shortage of parts? Just as unlikely. Trouble with development that had placed the program on hold? Hardly. There were at least four toward the back end of the hangar that appeared to be in a final test and check stage. One of them would be the best object for his in-depth examination.

Off to one side of the hangar were offices and in the hangar proper several long tables upon which were stacks and stacks of drawings and specification charts. Such information would be invaluable to an analysis of the machine but the tables were too much in the open and several of the workers were busy in the areas near them. He would have to rely on the spaceplane itself for photographs first, then if the opportunity presented itself later—well, he would see.

He had been inside for almost 15 minutes and was beginning to feel more confident. Everyone seemingly had his own duties to attend to but there was always the possibility he would be approached and with such a small work force they all probably knew each other. Certainly, the man in charge would know all his shift. Dover must stay in the shadows.

Keeping his clipboard busy and his face diverted, he worked his way toward the completed vehicles and selected one which had its entry hatch open and a boarding ladder attached to its side. Waiting until he was sure that all of the others were busy with their own tasks, he stepped onto the ladder and climbed into the cockpit.

He had made a good choice. From what he could initially observe, the spaceplane was completed with all of its weapons systems installed. It sat well. With all of the design consideration in building an airplane, or a spaceplane in this case, the engineers could make all of the scientific measurements and computations they desired. They could design a seat for the average man, whoever that was, and configure the cockpit for its computed efficiency, but the real test came when the pilot climbed on board and felt how it sat.

Much roomier than he had envisioned, it was still not large enough for two cosmonauts but rigged for only a pilot. The extra space was packed with sanitary facilities, several isometric exercise devices, and a stack of food stowage and preparation units. The spaceplane was designed for extended space missions with no crew relief required.

The pilot's seat was not ejectable but consisted of an ingenious G-couch which seemed to be automatically positioned for the conditions of flight and allowed the cosmonaut to have all of his essential controls at his fingertips. Dover settled into it and studied the instrument panels. Before him were all of the computerized attitude, orbital, and navigational screens and indicators. Overhead were the electrical system schematics and controls, as well as six rows of systems-status lights. Along the left side were the power controls and along the right the avionics and life support system connections.

In the center, below the flight instrument panel and between the cosmonaut's legs, was the weapons control console.

Dover marveled at the technology, easily the equal of that found in the OV-104 Atlantis, the latest U.S. shuttle, and all within the reach of a single crew member. It was something of a sobering shock for him to realize that he was sitting in a one-man, orbital, recoverable space fighter. The world's first. He studied the weapons console. From the display of electrical and chemical-mixture instrumentation, he felt certain that the main weapon was a laser gun. The acquisition and fire-control radar were miniaturized beyond anything he had ever seen and he located a spare parts compartment behind the console with racks for several black-box repair components. As for the machine's anti-ballistic missile capabilities, he could only speculate, but it had all of the right things. His mind flashed back to the days he had read about when the valiant pilots of the Royal Air Force had raced their stripped-down Spitfires in desperate pursuit of the German V-1's in the skies over Britain. Aerial warfare had certainly progressed since those days, or had it? He used his final pictures on the weapons console and removed the eye-camera.

Carefully, he peeled back the bloodstained band-aid from the back of his left hand and removed one of the square film chips from inside the pad. He replaced it with the exposed disc, reloaded the eye-camera, and used the small plunger to reinsert it.

With the second disc, he recorded the various system control panels, making sure that he had several copies of the engine instruments and gauges. It had to be radical in some respect to provide sufficient thrust for the extreme orbital changes, but the fuel quantity gauges indicated a partial use of the older, Russian-favored, liquid oxygen and kerosene mix with a series of solid rocket augmentation firings for maximum thrust. There wasn't an unlimited capability; the rocket selector switch stopped at number nine. Dover still couldn't believe the amount of fuel carried. Every unused nook and cranny in the spacecraft must house fuel. Considering the volatility of the Russian mix, the pilot certainly would have no worries about a slow death should the system malfunction.

He used the rest of the film to shoot the bank of computers and display hardware that lined the far right side of the cockpit. He was not surprised to see that should all else fail, the cosmonaut-pilot could manually override all remote control and automatic systems and execute an unassisted reentry as well as required space maneuvers to keep the Alpha Bug operational. As for recovery, after reentering the earth's atmosphere, the spacecraft would glide to a predetermined area and use the recovery chutes for final descent. Considering the probable weight of the vehicle and its limited wing size, plus the fact that it didn't need to slow for a wheeled touchdown, the gliding speeds were probably well above those of the *Columbia.* The stall red line on the airspeed indicator confirmed his estimate. It bisected the 392 kilometers per hour mark—approximately 215 knots.

Once more, he pulled loose the band-aid and loaded the final film square.

A series of overall interior shots, with the balance of the film aimed at the test equipment, exhausted his film supply.

As a pilot-astronaut, he could have sat in the Alpha Bug and played airplane-driver the rest of the night, but he had the pictures and had been in the building for forty-five minutes. Every minute longer would increase the possibility of detection. Also, it was very near dawn, and the darkness was a vital factor in his escape plan.

The double doors that led to the loading dock were only a few yards away, but as he started for them he almost collided head-on with a technician who suddenly appeared from around a nearby support cradle.

"Excuse me, comrade," apologized the man, "have you seen the comrade-inspector?" Penetrating eyes searched Dover's face. "No, no I haven't," stammered Dover.

The man looked quizzically at him. "Have we met? My name is Yuris . . . Yuris Popantov." He held out his hand.

"Andrei Gretorovitch," responded Dover, using the name on his identity badge. "I just started last week; transferred from Baikonur."

"I hope your inspectors there were more conscientious than the dumb bastard we have on this shift. He is never around when you need him. I should have his position. Certainly, anyone could be more responsive than such a person." He hurried on toward the other workers.

Dover walked out onto the loading platform and casually smoked a cigarette, wishing it were one of Mikhail's Marlboros instead of a Russian brand. It seemed that no one else had an interest in the area. Good. The gate guard was in his cubicle, absorbed in some sort of manual. Dover took the fountain pen from his upper coat pocket, twisted the top one-half turn, and laid it next to one of the crates. He had five minutes to reach the far end of the building.

The long walk on a random path through the array of Alpha Bugs ended when he reentered the utility room. Two minutes later he heard the first cry.

"Fire! Fire on the loading dock!"

Dover cautiously opened the outside door. The guard was frantically spinning the numbered dial on his telephone. Dover sprinted for the double gate across the railroad track, pulled the coiled nylon cord from under his coat, and slung the grapple for the top crosspipe of the gate. He pulled the line taut to test its hold and leaped off the ground.

"That is far enough, comrade." The menacing baritone was followed by a flurry of metallic clicks, unmistakably the ominous sounds of rifles being readied for firing. Dover released his grip and dropped to the slag between the tracks.

"Slowly, with your hands high please, turn around."

The barrels of the AK-47's were small round eyes of death, staring at him from a cluster of Army Khaki. Out of the glare of the gate floodlight emerged a sinister civilian, wearing a Cheshire cat grin of satisfaction and pointing his automatic at Dover's chest. It was the technician he had met earlier.

"Stupid," said the approaching figure. "The oldest diversionary trick in the book. Hardly worthy of a professional."

The soldiers escorted him through the gate and led him to a waiting 4-door Volga. He sat sandwiched between one of the soldiers and Timonkin as they were driven to the security and detention building. There, he was hustled inside to a holding room and left with another white-coated soldier.

"Remove your clothes."

The strip search was thorough. The soldier donned

medical gloves and probed all his body openings, thankfully the mouth, nose, and ears first.

"You may dress. The comrade colonel will speak with you."

He was left alone for several minutes and as he dressed he silently thanked the team back at Bethesda for the incredible eye-camera. The soldier had not given his eyes a second look.

Timonkin entered and took the second of the two chairs while Dover remained seated in the other and they faced across the bare table.

"Professor Utgoff," mused Timonkin, pronouncing the name with the same seriousness he would use to address Dover as Mickey Mouse.

"Colonel."

Timonkin seemed amused at Dover's formal reply. "You have excellent manners for an American intelligence agent."

"Superb for a language professor at Georgetown University in Washington, D.C."

"A college professor does not murder two of my men, enter a restricted military area, and damage valuable defensive weapons by such a clumsy fire. Hardly; wouldn't you agree?"

"So, I've got a mean streak."

"And a CIA personality: arrogant." Timonkin loosened his tie. "What were you doing in the special compound area?"

"Sightseeing."

"Oh, the Agency has added humor to its training curricula. That's good. Our profession is so devoid of it. Perhaps it is not such a bad idea. We tend to treat our profession with such seriousness, do we not?"

Dover did not reply.

"The flippant tongue seems to hesitate. Forgive me if I seem to repeat myself. What were you doing in the building?"

"You know damned well what I was doing."

"Yes, but I wanted to hear it from you. A matter of

153

personal pride. Did you find our little surprise interesting?''

"I tip my hat.''

"Hmmm. What is your name?''

"Josef Utgoff.''

"And Grigori Solovyov, and Andrei Gretorovitch, and so on—I suspect Joe Smith or Bob Jones would be closer.''

You'd be surprised to know how close, thought Dover.

Timonkin had been studying Dover's face as if trying to place it in his mental catalogue of seen-before countenances. He directed his attention to the band-aid. "What did you do to your hand?''

"Scraped it on a concrete wall.'' Dover was telling the truth. He had needed a genuine wound to give the bandage authenticity.

"I must apologize for the insensitivity of my Army associate. He should have removed it and provided you with a clean one.''

"It's okay.''

"Perhaps I should take a look at it. May I?''

Dover peeled back the band-aid and exposed the moist injury.

Timonkin reached over and ripped the strip off. "My, my,'' he said, feigning sympathy. Carefully, he fingered the pad. A triumphant smile curled his lips and he glared over his glasses at Dover. It took only a second to separate the pad and reveal the two film squares. He removed them and turned them over slowly with his fingers before holding each up to the light for a closer examination.

"Where is the camera?''

"In the fire. I had no further use for it.''

Timonkin nodded. "Very interesting.'' He pried open one of the small enclosures and held the film disc to the light. "I hope I haven't ruined any snapshots of the wife and children.''

Dover shrugged.

"I should like to know more about this.'' He walked to the door, opened it, and spoke in a low voice to the soldier outside. Then he sat back down.

"Incidentally, I had occasion to meet with your lovely wife, Marie, back in Leningrad. She seemed to be involved in some type of subterfuge. A fake message about a family illness. An attempt to leave with a companion who held—imagine this—your passport. I am afraid he was not quite as handsome as you. Really, it was a very clumsy switch. Actually, I got to know Marie quite well."

The cat had taken the mouse into its mouth and was starting the game. Dover resisted the urge to respond. It would be better not to express any concern.

"Tell me, how does a white man satisfy such a woman? My own ardor seemed to leave her quite unfulfilled, but then the tapes revealed she has a very demanding passion as well as an exquisite feminine skill. I must say, however, your performance was somewhat lacking."

"Is that what KGB colonels now do for a living? Watch people have sex? Things must be slow for paper pushers." Unknowingly, he touched a nerve.

Timonkin bristled. "I saw only the tapes."

So, there had been someone behind the mirror. Despite his chagrin at the moment, Timonkin looked like the type that would have enjoyed the tapes. In any event, Dover decided he would not rise to the bait. Instead, he cursed to himself for not being more emphatic when he told Tobias that the departure of Marie would be a weak spot in the plan.

"I am somewhat surprised. You don't seem to have the husbandly concern for your wife that I would have expected."

"She gets paid well for what she does well." *Forgive me, Marie.*

"Ah! Perhaps it is that Mrs. Utgoff is not actually Mrs. Utgoff, but rather an employee of the CIA, as yourself?"

"You are a shrewd man, Colonel. Did you figure that out all by yourself? If so, you are mistaken. My wife and I are on holiday."

Timonkin clapped his hands and roared with laughter. "Incredible! I catch you in our special projects compound, trying to vault a fence with exposed film strapped to your hand; I find your wife trying to exit the country with an imposter; and now you tell me you are on holiday! This is good!''

Dover never saw the blow coming, just felt the impact of Timonkin's gloved fist against his jaw and the sharp jar against his side as the punch lifted him off the chair and onto the floor. Instinctively, he sprung to his feet, fists clenched. Timonkin was too fast for him and already had an ugly little automatic out and pointed at his chest.

''Please, retake your seat.'' The cat prepared to chew the mouse.

Dover sat back down.

''Your wife is in my custody. Does that lend a bit more severity to our discussion here?''

Dover noted the use of the present tense. Marie must still be alive and if they were reunited there was always a chance—

Timonkin returned to the business at hand. ''Who helped you get into the center?''

''No one. I work alone.''

''I will concede you may have entered the center unassisted but someone had to help you get into the special projects area. I want the identity of that person—or persons.''

''Mikhail Gorbachev.''

The mouse was beginning to have an unpleasant flavor. ''You Americans watch too many of your own movies. John Wayne can answer such a serious question with such bravado. You may not.'' For emphasis, he moved his automatic closer to Dover's chest.

''I walked through the gate with the morning shift. The guard was distracted for a moment by the ringing telephone.''

''And all day and during most of the night you hid until this morning?''

''Yes.''

''You are lying.'' Timonkin removed his glasses and rubbed his eyes as if they were very tired. Half smiling, he returned his automatic to under his coat. ''I have been in this business for over three decades and never have I encountered such an awkward liar.''

"Did you expect me to do otherwise?''

"Perhaps not just yet. We are just beginning this relationship. Are you surprised I use American idioms? Relationship. I like that concept. We are forming a relationship here, comrade. Isn't that right?''

Dover gauged the distance between himself and his interrogator. Three, maybe three-and-a-half feet. An easy distance to cross if he could catch the colonel off guard. But even if he succeeded in grabbing the gun, then what? Undoubtedly, there were guards outside the door. He would not get far, even with the colonel as a hostage. And the crafty colonel probably knew that or may even be baiting him with an unloaded gun.

"You are in an impossible position. At the very best, you will be executed *unless* you spare me a difficult and trying task. I will know who your accomplices have been. That you may be certain of. And you are going to tell me.'' He reached again inside his coat, unholstered his automatic, and pointed it across the table at Dover's face.

Was the cat tiring of the game? Was he ready to let his sharp teeth put an end to the mouse's insubordinate existence?

"I have been up all night waiting for you. My patience is wearing quite thin, in fact you might say it has just worn out. You will give me the name of your accomplice, or you die here, now.''

Dover studied the man's face. Deep lines curved down the sides of his mouth in testimony to the years of stress in the demanding requirements of his profession. The crow's feet around his eyes, at the same time, projected a certain weariness that took the edge off his words. He would not kill him, yet. That would destroy any chance of identifying the accomplice, and that was what he wanted. He already had Dover and knew that whatever Dover had seen and retained inside the special projects building would die with the American in Siberia if nowhere else. Dover tried not to appear concerned as he made a decision to bluff and laid his life on his conviction.

"Go ahead, kill me."

Timonkin's expression was locked in granite. Deliberately, he leaned forward and placed the gun's barrel against Dover's forehead and tightened his hand muscles. The world stopped. All matter in the universe condensed and then ceased to exist except for that which made up the blue steel of the weapon in Timonkin's clenched hand and the flesh and bone which lay adjacent to its deadly exit hole. Dover's confidence faded into a fervent prayer and he waited for that terrible instant of time that would be his last. He wanted to cry out and plead for his life and tell the colonel of Mikhail but forced himself to say within, "This is my last moment, wait for the next, this is my last moment, wait for the next—" It was a silly last thought, but if he could control each moment, each tiny bit of time, in the next it would be over. His life didn't race before his eyes but he did feel a deep sorrow that he would never see the ranch again, or Marie, or his hired-hand partner, or—.

Timonkin lowered his gun. "There is no satisfaction in killing a fool. It is much better to see him disintegrate under the hell of slow pain. Never fear, you will tell me what I want. I have only to reunite you with your wife. I have yet to see an American hold up in the face of a proper interrogation. So let us begin it now. Let us see how much pain you can truly withstand. I suspect your body can withstand the fiercest of assaults. But the mind, that is another matter. Pain in the mind is a thousand more times intense as that of the body."

Timonkin stood. "So we begin with a reunion. I am a sentimental person. Nothing pleases me like seeing the joy of reunited lovers."

He pulled open the door and motioned with his hand.

The woman that appeared, supported by a soldier on each side, was gaunt and pale, her eyes moist. Yet her head was held erect and there was the defiance of the damned radiating from the dark brown eyes behind the tears. A third soldier carried in a chair and they seated the woman beside Dover. The colonel followed them out the door.

"Josef . . ." As they embraced, Marie pulled his ear closely to her lips. "Whisper only or they will hear us."

"My God, what have they done to you?" murmured Dover.

Marie managed a tired smile. "Your friend there, Josef, is an animal. Tell him what he wants."

"I can't."

"No. *I* can't. You can." She placed her hands over his.

"Why this way? Surely, he knows that a syringe of sodium pentothal will save him time and effort."

Marie's eyes thinned and drew into twin lines of hate. "He likes this, Josef. This is the way he gets his jollies. We're dead, Josef. And I don't give a damn. But there's no sense in letting him do this to you. Tell him and it'll be over quickly. But when you do—" She squeezed his hands. "We kill him before the guards kill us."

"We could never do it before they came in, even if I can get his gun." *Why was she telling him to betray Mikhail?*

"He is so cocksure of himself, he is careless. Go along with him. Tell him what you can. It won't make any difference.

"Marie, there's always hope."

"No, not now. And before I go, I want to settle accounts." With great difficulty, she unbuttoned the top of her frock. Elastic bandages ran from below her breasts to her waist. Clotted blood from where Timonkin had cut her stained the upper right side of her wrappings. She pressed his ear back to her lips.

"He's right out of the old school. That's why they put him in a Leningrad desk job. He's out of control in the field."

Dover stared at the battered human before him. The left side of her face was a blue bruise from her temple to the bottom of her jaw, her blackened and puffed lower lip swollen almost to the bursting point. She had no color and little energy. Yet, she was determined to reach beneath the elastic wrappings. He tried to keep his eyes off the cut below her right breast. He could see she hadn't the strength to do whatever it was she was trying.

"Under the tape, a rod. Get it for me," she directed.

"Marie—"

"Look, that bastard in the other room busted a rib in his enthusiasm for a two-way conversation, then decided to give me a radical mastectomy but changed his mind when he decided he needed something to chew on while he went for the big 'O.' "

"He raped you."

"He had me, all right, but he didn't have *me*. Now, I want him. We don't have anything to lose."

As gently as he could, Dover retrieved the rod from under her wrappings. It was chromed hospital steel, about the size of a pencil, and had one blunt point.

"They left me alone for a while after they bandaged the ribs. I pulled it out of some kind of respiratory machine. It's a tightening rod of some sort."

"This is too light, Marie. We can't do any damage to him with this."

"You grab him, Josef, and hold his fucking head and I'll ram this rod up his nose clear into his brain. Believe me, it'll do the job."

Until this moment, Dover had not realized the fierceness of her determination to kill the KGB colonel. He could only wonder if she had ever done such a thing before. They could never pull it off. The colonel was certainly not a young athlete but he was still man enough to put up a struggle that would prevent Dover from holding him still enough for Marie to use the rod. The soldiers outside would intervene.

He held her lightly to him and kissed her hair. She trembled all over, in pain and anger and despair. He placed the rod up his coverall sleeve. Perhaps it would come to some use later. Marie sobbed, realizing also that Timonkin was going to get everything he wanted.

As if on cue, Timonkin walked back into the room and

stood across from them. "The rod, please," he said, holding out his hand.

How did he know? thought Dover. Had he heard even their whispers?

"Well, now," he continued, "the woman gives you good advice. But I am not as bad as she would have you believe. I admire determination. And even hate. One has to feel very deeply to hate. And deep feelings reflect deep determination. So, I will make an agreement with you. You will tell me the name of your accomplice or accomplices and I will spare your lives. You cannot be together, of course, but you can live useful lives in our north country."

The bastard was clever. He had taken them through physical punishment and mental stress to the point where they figured they were lost. Now, just to add the right ingredient to tip the scales, he offered a reprieve, aiming it primarily at Dover. "Come now, a simple statement and the two of you will know at least that the other lives. Is that so difficult?"

Dover did not see how he could stall much longer. Marie was in obvious distress.

Suddenly, there was an audible click and the room was plunged into darkness. *Mikhail! You old bastard, you've blown the power!* Dover lunged forward in the blackness and felt the colonel's body collapse under the force of his charge. The automatic went off in his ear as he groped for the outstretched arm and they fell together. The door to the windowless room flew open, flooding it with light from the outer room, and Dover found himself with a death grip on the KGB man's weapon but helpless under the guns of the soldiers. Dover looked for Marie. Confused, he had only an instant to see her standing by the open door, her face expressionless. Why had she not helped? An even more disturbing thought briefly surfaced. Had *she* opened the door?

"Don't shoot! I want him! I want him!" screamed Timonkin.

Instead of bullets, for which Dover had steeled his body,

there was an instant of excruciating pain as the stock of an AK-47 smashed into the left side of his face. Sight, feel, taste, smell, and finally sound disappeared altogether; and then there was nothing.

The first thing to return was the pain, searing the side of his face with the whitehot feel of a branding iron. Dover opened his eyes and blurred sight began to return. He could not focus and for several moments he tasted the fear of never being able to see clearly again. But the dancing blobs and waving lines steadied into recognizable objects as his vision cleared. He touched the area around the eye-camera. The rifle butt had struck just below it. He was lying on a cot in a bare room, one smaller than the interrogation space, and he could hear muffled voices beyond the walls. Only taste and smell seemed to be lagging behind as his brain struggled to regain its sensory functions. It was still daytime. That was apparent from the small wedge of sunlight that was spilling through a slit window near the ceiling.

He sat up and a thousand jackhammers pounded the inside of his skull. The faint odor of dust and mold told him that his nose had rejoined in his precarious return to consciousness. He tried but could not move his jaw without intense pain.

Marie? His last vision of her returned. He should not have lunged for Timonkin when the lights went out but it had been an instinctive reaction. In sad retrospect, it had also been a serious mistake. Timonkin's bullet could have struck either of them. Or had he really tried? Marie's actions after the lights went out troubled him. She had been so vengeful just a moment before.

He sat lost in thought for a long time, maybe the better part of an hour, before the door opened and a soldier pulled him to his feet. Timonkin strode in.

"That was foolish," he said.

"Where's Marie?"

"She will no longer be joining us."

"What have you done with her?"

"Ah, the valiant champion of the fair maiden. You and I are going to Leningrad where I will break you before my superiors." His next words were spoken over his shoulder, "I need a car and driver."

A white-coated amazon entered and started to examine Dover's face. She was surprisingly gentle, feeling his jaw carefully and making clucking noises while examining the swelling. From her physician's bag she took a small penlight and raised it toward his face. He jerked away.

"It's all right," he said. "Leave it be. Get away."

She glanced at Timonkin.

"That's enough. He can travel," decided the colonel.

The woman poured two white pills from a brown bottle and handed them to Dover. "Take these. They will help the pain."

He swallowed them dry as she placed several more in the breast pocket of his coveralls.

They left him alone for another few minutes, then the soldier returned and cuffed his hands behind his back. The car was waiting out front and Timonkin joined him in the back seat. Dover still wasn't thinking and hearing clearly but he heard Timonkin's directions to the driver and the door slam. He was conscious of the car passing out of the space center and turning to the right. That would be the way toward Kapustin Yar. The driver's window was partially open and the flow of cool air revived him to the point where he was aware of the passing scenery and he started to mentally explore the ramifications of his predicament.

Timonkin raised a metal flask to Dover's lips. "Here, drink some of this. I don't want to have to carry you."

The vodka jarred him fully awake. They were speeding down the highway toward Volgograd and were already passing through the outskirts of Kapustin Yar. Dover let his gaze wander to the east. Somewhere out there, Mikhail was probably bouncing along the rutted Saykhin road, trying to carry out the last item of their plan.

They passed out of Kapustin Yar and drove along a lonely stretch of highway. Timonkin sipped on the flask.

Dover watched the passing countryside, forced to sit uncomfortably upright with his hands cuffed behind him.

The driver slowed the car. "I must apologize, comrade Colonel, but I must stop and relieve myself." He searched the shoulder for an appropriate place to pull off.

"You will continue on. You can go at the airport."

The driver turned, his face contorted with distress. "It is the *runs,* comrade. I must stop."

Timonkin did not wish to take the consequences of a further refusal. "Great Peter!" he complained. "Why must these things be visited upon me. Take the road to the left, ahead. I don't want to sit out here in the open while you drop your pants and pollute all of southern Russia."

The car skidded onto the road and they careened over the uneven surface as the man hurriedly headed for a grove of trees off to their right. As the car slid to a stop, the driver swung open his door and turned again. "Thank you, comrade Colonel, I will only be a moment."

Timonkin sneered and turned his face away to look back toward the highway. He didn't see the driver's other arm raise and swing stiffly over the back of the front seat. Nor was he aware of the snub-nosed revolver until it went off and sent bits of his skull and brain back in an obscene splatter that sprayed upon the gray felt of the car's interior.

The driver smiled at Dover. "There are times, comrade, when the day is not a total loss."

Chapter
10

Dover sat staring at the dead Timonkin. Only a trickle of blood oozed from the black dot of the entry wound, but the exit side of his head had shattered and released a gelatinous glob of brain and bone onto the back of the seat.

The driver replaced his gun, restarted the car, and drove deeper into the grove. He opened Dover's door and removed the handcuffs before hurrying around to the other side and jerking Timonkin's body out and onto the ground.

"There's probably some rags in the trunk. Clean up as well as you can. I'll take care of him."

Dover reached over the back of the front seat and pulled the keys from the ignition. There were only two oil-stained rags next to the spare, but he managed to wipe up the bulk of the bloody residue and clean off most of the blood.

The lining around the rear window and the top of the back seat remained dark with blood stain. Just as Dover stepped from the car, the air rang as five muffled shots sounded from the low area where the driver had dragged Timonkin. Dover disposed of the bloody rags by scooping out a hole in the soft ground with the jack handle and throwing the dirt back over them before hurrying to help the driver.

The man had unfolded a large pocket knife and was cutting off the end joints of Timonkin's fingers. The dead man's face had been mutilated beyond recognition, primarily by the five shots, and he was sprawled naked before the kneeling driver. "Go through his clothes; remove everything. Keep his identity papers and wallet. Bury everything else and spread some of the ground cover around."

Dover slipped the watch over his wrist, dropped the loose change into his pocket, and examined the wallet. He left the identity cards in their plastic holders and searched the main compartment. The two eye-camera film squares were stuck deep into the bottom crease and almost hidden by three hundred and thirty rubles in paper currency. The film Timonkin had exposed was worthless; nevertheless, he took both of the squares and wrapped them in his handkerchief before stuffing it into his back pocket. After turning all of Timonkin's pockets inside out and feeling the seams, he scooped out another hole and placed the garments in the bottom. The driver joined him and together they replaced the dirt and spread loose leaves and brush over the site. A day or so of neglect and winds would return it to its natural state.

It took a while longer to bury the remains of the KGB veteran, but the shallow grave covered well. If no one stumbled onto the slight ground bulge within the next month, the dirt would settle and Timonkin should be able to enjoy that particular piece of Mother Russia for a very long time.

The driver picked up Timonkin's hat, which still held the fingertips, and nodded in satisfaction as he surveyed the scene, looking for loose ends. "Well, we've done it now. It sure as Hades better be for a worthy cause . . . name's Charlie Kiger." He offered his free hand to Dover.

"My pleasure, Charlie . . . I think."

"Oh, don't let this business get to you. He would have done a lot worse to you once you got to Leningrad. I work with Mikhail, or I guess I should say I used to work with Mikhail. This blows my cover, but if we're lucky it'll be a while before some animal comes along and digs the useless bastard up. It'll take a day before they figure he's missing, anyhow.''

"How'd you know they had me?''

"Easy. Mikhail couldn't find you on the back road. I knew they had somebody in interrogation—I work at the transport pool—so, when they called for a car for the colonel, I made sure I was assigned as driver. After a while in this business, you get so you can smell what's going on . . . I didn't catch your name.''

"Just call me Josef.''

"Okay, Josef. My identity papers don't say Charlie Kiger either, but I might as well revert back to C.K. with you. After we get you on your way, I'll be heading for Turkey and a new assignment.'' He started back toward the car and Dover followed. "I'll drive. You sit in the back and look important. We've got a KGB tag so we won't be stopped.''

They were fifteen minutes on the road to Kapustin Yar when they started across a clear stream leading west toward the Volga. Charlie Kiger stopped in the middle of the bridge and dumped the fingertips into the swiftly flowing water. They raced away with the current, tiny flesh balls that some ocean carp would eventually eye as potential hors d'oeuvres but refuse when he was close enough to smell the decay.

Another fifteen minutes and they pulled up at Mikhail's house. He was waiting and anxiously opened the door.

"I was worried,'' he said.

"So was I,'' conceded Dover.

"Some shit of a Leningrad investigator had him. We planted the late colonel north of town, about thirty miles back.'' Kiger was obviously at home at Mikhail's; he unerringly walked to the cupboard that housed the vodka and settled at the table with the bottle.

Mikhail sat beside him and motioned Dover into the third chair. "How'd you do?'' he asked.

"Got three sets of pictures . . . the comrade-colonel ruined one set. I still have the other two."

"You had a camera?"

Dover realized his faux pas, but there was no reason to reveal the eye-camera. "They took it when they searched me."

"Spacecraft?"

"Oh, it's there, in spades. Probably twenty of them; I didn't stop to count. They've got a big jump on us inside that hangar. My guess is it's some kind of anti-ballistic missile weapons platform."

"By God, I knew it! I started sending reports two years ago. You just couldn't get in there and there were too many high-priced experts coming and going. Then, the shipments started. We may have earned our pay on this one." Mikhail squinted as he examined Dover's cheek. "Your face looks like lumpy borscht. What'd they do, use a club?"

"Rifle butt . . . have you got anything?"

"Yes, come into the bathroom."

Dover held a soaked cloth on his cheek and let the cool water fight the throbbing pain. It hurt like hell, but he could move his jaw. Mikhail took a medicine tube from the drawer in the cabinet under the washbowl and squeezed a translucent salve onto his fingers. After Dover had patted his cheek dry, Mikhail gently spread the salve over it.

"Antibiotic . . . it'll keep the infection down and speed the healing. Damn good stuff. I've got some pain pills."

"They gave me something about two hours ago, before we left."

"In that case, it's just as well you don't take any more right now. Put these in your pocket. We need to get you on your way, but there's nothing we can do until I make some necessary arrangements. Charlie's cover's blown, so he'll see you to the coast. He'll be going on to Turkey."

Dover could use the time to get off his feet, but first he taped the two film squares together and placed them back in the wallet. He added another strip of tape to hold them in place.

It felt good to get out of the coveralls. Marie had bled slightly on him during their final embrace, and there was a rip in one arm seam where he had torn it trying to ward off the rifle blow.

He still had the clothes he had worn from Moscow. The shirt and pants would do nicely and Mikhail had thoughtfully provided a light coat. He didn't know what escape plans had been formulated but obviously Mikhail was on top of the situation. What manner of man would devote his life to living such a clandestine life? Living a lie, putting his cover to the test each time he entered the space center and climbed up into the garbage truck? It was easy to criticize the CIA. Dover had done it, himself, in days past. But there was no more urgent need for such a hard, professional, intelligence organization than there was in the case of the Alpha Bug. Marie. Yuri back at the Leningrad car rental agency. Tania, the Moscow prostitute. Mikhail. Charlie Kiger. All of them waging a daily war against an enemy known for its skill in counterintelligence and all of them deep inside the bear's lair where capture would not even elicit a sign of recognition by American authorities. Dover wondered at the size and scope of such an organization that had time and time again during the past few days jerked him from the jaws of mission failure and kept him on his way. No one had better bad-mouth the Spooks again in his presence.

He could hear Charlie Kiger moving around in the other room. Glancing through the open door, he could see his latest benefactor settling down with his bottle for some serious drinking.

Mikhail left Dover to his rest and Charlie Kiger to his vodka, and drove east of Kapustin Yar. The sun was low behind him and the fading colors ahead cast the long shadows of early dusk across the barren terrain leading toward Saykhin. He passed through the village and out onto a lowland desert which the approaching night rendered colorless. The dirt and gravel road disintegrated into a barely perceptible path across the sand and eventually led him to a long-abandoned range telemetry shack.

He lifted a heavy-duty truck battery from the trunk and carried it across the soft sand into the shack. It took considerable effort to pry up the floor boards and he made a vow not to secure them so tightly this time. The crawl space was deep enough for him to move around on his hands and knees, but he still managed to strike his head against the floor joists and curse several times before he managed to drag the battery into position and connect the leads. A push of the starter button coaxed the gasoline-powered engine into life and he threw the switch, activating the generator. After the ammeter steadied, he switched on the inverter and checked the alternating current before flipping the master switch on the low-frequency radio.

While it warmed, he struggled back out of the crawl space and strung the wire antenna from the roof of the shack to a weathered fence post, adjusting a shorting device to give him the optimum antenna length for the frequency he would be using.

Two more head konks with the accompanying profanity found him back at the radio. He fitted the earphones, triggered the hand-mike to check the power output, and made his first call.

"Hello, Tango Boy, this is Dancer. Over."

His fingers held the tuning knob with a light touch and he gently fooled with it until he caught the tail end of a reply.

". . . this is Tango Boy. Go ahead."

"Roger, I need date-time and coordinates for delivery, reference Alpha Bug. Make it plus nineteen."

"This is Tango Boy . . . date-time follows . . . break . . . two-zero-zero-five-zero-zero local . . . coordinates foxtrot charlie . . . break . . . point-three-two . . . break . . . one-seven-point-four-four . . . do you copy?"

Mikhail read back the message verbatim, received a "Roger," and shut off the transmitter. The total exchange had taken forty seconds. He secured the engine-generator, lifted the battery back through the floor, and replaced the boards. After dismantling the antenna and stowing it under the shack, he tackled the soft sand path back toward Saykhin and Kapustin Yar.

"Here's your pickup point." Mikhail had a map of the area along the north coast of the Black Sea spread on the table and placed the tip of his pencil on the intersection of the two lines he had drawn using the coded coordinates he had received from Tango Boy. The dot marked the tip of a tiny point of land on the southern edge of the Kerch Peninsula which reached out east of Crimea in the southern Ukraine. "Charlie will drive you in the KGB car to Rostov na Donu, here, where the Don River leads into the Azovshoye More—the Sea of Azov. It's a good five-hundred-kilometer drive. We have a fishing boat there. It's about a day's sail, maybe a bit more, south to the peninsula. This is the peak holiday season and the crowds will be unbelievable, which is good. The local militia there just throw up their hands and go through the motions, so it should be easy to land you during the night. I've marked your path across the peninsula. It's a twenty-kilometer hike, but it's barren and too rough for the fun hikers so you shouldn't run into anyone. Once you hit the southern beaches, head east to this point of land. It's the only place along the coast where the terrain is too rough for the sun worshipers. There's a large flat concrete pad, the foundation slab of an old lighthouse. Your pickup will be at dawn on the morning of the twentieth."

Dover reviewed the route. "Where's the nearest fighter or interceptor base?"

"Krasnodar, two hundred fifty kilometers east. Mostly older SU-15 Flagons. Not much priority in the air defense picture. Most of the new stuff is over at Odessa."

Dover recalled the Flagon as a Mach-2 interceptor at altitude, but a well-tuned Harrier should be able to outrun it at sea level. "How do the Soviets feel about hot pursuit?" he asked.

"Ha! They'll shoot down anything that penetrates their air space, and follow you all the way to New Jersey if they have to, to do it. They consider the Black Sea a Soviet lake. The Harrier will come in on the deck, of course, and has a good chance of avoiding the radar coverage.''

"Dawn, on the twentieth . . . and today's the seventeenth.''

"Right. That gives you about fifty-seven hours. Not a lot of time, but enough. You want to be there early, at least a half-hour before dawn. The Harrier will stay on the deck for a maximum of ten minutes. Absolutely, no longer.''

Charlie Kiger had been busy packing provisions while Mikhail briefed Dover. "We leave as soon as you're ready,'' he said. '' Until they miss you and the colonel, we'll be home free. After that, it's a real Soviet fox hunt with us as the main course.''

"I'm ready.''

Mikhail and Charlie Riger embraced and Kiger hurried out to the car. Mikhail placed his hands on Dover's shoulders. "You're good stuff, whoever you are. Maybe we'll run into each other again sometime.''

"Nothing personal, Mikhail, but I hope not! I'm indebted. Take care . . . comrade.''

Mikhail yelled after him as he ran to the car, "You need a piece?''

"I've got Timonkin's automatic.'' Dover jumped into the back seat and Charlie Kiger gunned the black sedan out of the yard.

The road to Rostov na Donu was almost void of traffic, reflecting the Soviet attitude against travel after dark, but a few commercial vehicles still headed toward late deliveries. Charlie Kiger certainly had faith in the KGB tag; he kept the car rolling along at 100-110 kilometers-per-hour. They passed several oncoming traffic-inspector patrol cars and once a uniformed militiaman pulled around them on his motorcycle, but kept going after a backward glance at the illuminated front tag. It was 1:20 A.M. when they reached the resort city at the exit of the Don River and the start of the canal to the Azovshoye More.

After passing through the sleeping town and its southern outskirts, it was another 40 kilometers to the narrow tip of the porkchop-shaped Sea of Azov. Three hundred and twenty kilometers south across its waters lay the Kerch Peninsula. Charlie Kiger eased the car to a stop.

"That's our boat, the *Zaliv Azov,* out there swinging on the hook."

Dover could clearly make out the bobbing fishing ketch as it rested on the calm waters under the moonlit sky.

"You stay here," directed Charlie Kiger. "That's the skiff, tied to the pier. Take the provisions. I'll get rid of the car."

He returned after a short absence and they rowed to the *Zaliv Azov,* secured the skiff on the forward deck, and Charlie Kiger quietly motored the thirty-five-footer into open water.

He checked Dover out on the mainsail and jib rigging, and handled the mizzen, himself, as they switched to sail and ran smoothly before a light night breeze.

"I'll take the first watch. You get some rest and I'll wake you in a couple hours so you can spell me. The weather looks good. I doubt if we'll get anything beyond a few afternoon thunderstorms. We'll sail right down the middle as long as it's good like this."

Dover went below but the pulsing right side of his face wouldn't let him sleep, despite his reluctant concession to two of the pills Mikhail had given him. He had more jaw movement, which was a good sign. He had felt sure the bone was fractured, but perhaps not.

When he went back on deck, they were far out from land, sliding noiselessly through the night, which like an ebony blanket was pulled high over their heads. Millions of tiny pinpoints sparkled silver with starlight eons old, and the half-crescent moon sat low on the southern horizon, seemingly right on top of a cluster of red, green, and white running lights. The local fishermen were getting an early morning start on their day's labors, their ghostly forms pulling slowly away from the black sliver of land between sea and sky.

Charlie Kiger gave him the helm. "Keep her on two-five-oh. The sea's almost due west through the narrows here. We've a good quartering breeze and should make some time.'' He sat with Dover for a while, enjoying the taste of his cigarette and assuring himself that Dover could handle the boat. A long, rolling ground swell lifted them periodically and eased them over its crest with a rhythm as ancient as the sea itself.

The breeze had freshened and sporadic patches of white caps tipped the wind-born chop of the water.

The ketch rode solidly in its element, whispering through the night air and lulling its two occupants into an appreciative silence until Charlie Kiger stood and stretched his back muscles. ''Beautiful water,'' he observed.

''Beautiful night,'' added Dover. ''How long you been in-country?''

'Shit, I came here in seventy-two . . . God, that's thirteen years, now. The company hired me out of college; I was a Russian Literature major with a minor in the language. They sent me to the Farm, and after I finished the course they put me in administration for a year. An opening came up at the Soviet camp in the West Virginia hills. I learned fast and was quick on the uptake. They posted me here along with two other new agents.''

''Sounds like you were relatively inexperienced.''

''Hell, I was green as owl shit. But they planted me in the outskirts of Petrozavodsk, that's in the Karelian Republic a hundred miles north of Leningrad. It was a sleepy little place at the time; I lived there three years, working as an auto mechanic, of all things. No assignments, just living Russian and acquiring the cultural subtleties that make a good agent. Actually enjoyed it. I was all full of piss and vinegar and none of the natives were any the wiser.''

''All by yourself?''

''Basically. The other two guys went south. Oh, I had a control officer who checked on me every few months. After the first year, he even took me around a bit, you know, routine stuff. I was just getting seasoned. Even married a Karelian girl and we had a kid.'' Charlie Kiger abruptly stopped talking and turned his face away. Again, they sailed in silence.

After a while, Dover ventured, "Where are they now?"

Charlie Kiger didn't answer right away. First, he checked the rigging of the mainsail and jib before trimming the mizzen to better catch the wind which had shifted almost dead astern. Then he stood back by the helm, resting one hand on the mast stay and looking out to seaward. When he spoke, there was a quiet bitterness in his words.

"She's dead . . . the fuckers killed her."

Dover wanted to say something, but he didn't know what would be appropriate. Instead, he regretted bringing the subject up. Tears ran down Charlie Kiger's cheeks and dripped onto his shirt. "I'm sorry, Charlie; I'm sorry," said Dover softly.

"That's okay. It's been a while now." He rubbed his free hand over his face and wiped it on his trousers. "We'd been married two years. The boy was just starting to walk. A couple of local Party officials let their drinking get out of hand and caught her one night when she was walking home from her friend's house. Hell, it was only a hundred yards down the road. They raped her, drank some more, raped her again and forced her to do some other things. They finally passed out, thinking she had fainted. She used a rock—pounded one of the bastards' heads into a flat disc and ran home, out of her head. The next morning, the survivor showed up with a pair of KGB goons. She panicked and ran." He paused and ran his tongue across his lower lip. "They put seventeen fucking rounds into her back—she was nineteen." He wiped his eyes and blew his nose into the water. "They took the kid and made him a ward of the State. I told my control I was ready to operate . . . I hate the fuckers."

He walked forward and straddled the bow, letting his feet dangle in the spray, and rested his arms and head on the bowsprit. After a while, he stretched out on the forward deck and slept.

They alternated four-hour watches until noon when Charlie Kiger shot a sunline. They had covered a straight-line distance of 148 kilometers, thanks to an ever-increasing wind which had them cutting through the chop like a racing sloop. "How about some chow?" he called as he started down below to stow the sextant.

"Sounds great." Dover fed in a touch of right rudder to hold his tack.

Charlie Kiger returned triumphantly holding aloft a soup-filled liter jar, two cups, and a plastic sack of fried rolls. "I cleaned out our comrade, Mikhail, of his choicest leftovers. We have *akroshka* and *pirozhky,* a feast fit for the tsars themselves, or at least for a couple of down-on-their-luck *Americanskys.*"

He had warmed the soup on the small galley stove. Thick with vegetables and bits of meat, and strong with the heavy stock of yeast-fermented dark bread, the hearty soup found a welcome receptacle in Dover's stomach. It had been a while since he had ingested any solid food, and also his sore jaw had suppressed any desire to eat until now. The delicious flavor and filling substance made up for the pain of chewing and the chicken-filled rolls went down equally well, although they would have been better hot from the grease. To wash everything down, Charlie Kiger produced a bottle of vodka. "Zubrovka," he announced. Dover recognized the name as a flavored brand that carried the delicate taste of a sweet Russian grass. Afterward, Dover applied a new layer of Mikhail's salve.

The afternoon was spent making equally good time, slicing across the heaving bosom of the Azov, tacking southwest and southeast to sail the strong wind which had swung around to the west. Charlie Kiger had the helm and Dover leisurely scanned the horizon. They were beyond the sight of land. As he watched, an intermittent irregularity in the line dividing sea and sky caught his attention. The flickering spot steadied, then began to grow. There was something out there, growing in size and taking on a shape. Before long, he could see an aura of sea spray around it. The shape became a hull, bow-on. Dover pointed and Charlie Kiger broke out his binoculars.

He had barely raised them to his eyes when his words

sounded the alarm: ''Patrol boat . . . Soviet Inland Sea Forces . . . and the son of a bitch is headed right for us.''

''Do you think they found Timonkin?''

''I doubt it. If so, we should have stayed in bed. I don't see how they could this soon. It's probably just a routine patrol, out checking on small craft. I wouldn't imagine the Transport people even miss me yet. They'd check out all the traffic accidents first.''

''He's coming fast,'' said Dover.

''Shit, we don't have any papers for you.''

''I've got Timonkin's wallet.''

''Jesus, I forgot. Throw it over the side. That's all we need, a dead KGB agent's wallet.''

Dover retrieved the taped film packet and kept the rubles. Crossing over to the side opposite to the approaching boat, he dropped the wallet and watched it disappear beneath the waves.

Charlie Kiger had altered course to run with the wind but it was obvious to both him and Dover that they would be no match for the patrol boat. About all they could gain was some time.

''It's probably a routine patrol. We may have a chance of bluffing our way through,'' said Charlie Kiger. He didn't sound too convincing. He raised his binoculars again and studied the approaching craft.

A few minutes later, Dover could make out figures in the pilot house with his unaided eye.

''Take the helm and keep her steady.'' Charlie Kiger gave the wheel to Dover and hurriedly went below only to return a moment later with a thick-stocked assault rifle cradled in his arm. Its tubular shoulder extension was folded forward and a wicked-looking semicircular magazine curled from under the firing chamber just forward of the pistol grip and trigger. He placed it on the deck, under a canvas near the base of the helm. He was bare-chested. ''Get your weapon—and leave your shirt below,'' he ordered.

Dover leaped down the ladder into the forward cabin and ripped off his shirt. If things didn't go well, the crew

177

of the patrol boat might want to board. Was Charlie Kiger planning to resist that with force? In any event, was there anything in the cabin that might give them away? He foraged through the few lockers and around the bunks. All appeared to be standard fishermen's gear.

"Get your ass back up here! They're almost on us!"

Where was Timonkin's automatic? Oh, yes, he had stowed it in the galley cutlery drawer. The clip was full.

When he returned back on deck, Charlie Kiger pointed toward the patrol boat. It was less than a kilometer away and its approach had a certain seriousness that did not bode well.

"They'll be on us in a minute," said Charlie Kiger.

"Can you see how many are on board?"

"Looks like four or five. There may be a couple below deck."

Great. At least two-to-one odds, maybe worse. Dover placed the automatic inside his back waistband.

Charlie Kiger retrieved the vodka bottle and splashed some on his chest before handing it over to Dover. "Take a healthy swallow and pour some on your pants. Lie on the fo'c'sle like you're taking the sun and let me do the talking. Keep your weapon ready, and follow my lead if we have to use it."

Five minutes later, the blue-hulled patrol boat was within hailing distance, its sharply pointed bow aimed at the *Zaliv Azov.*

"You there! On the *Zaliv Azov!* Where are you out of?"

Charlie Kiger looked back and cheerfully waved. "Comrades! We sail from Rostov!"

"What's your destination?"

"The sun on the beaches of Crimea! My mate and I are on holiday after a most profitable season of catching the elusive fat fish of these magnificent waters." He waved his arm in a grand gesture of exaggerated happiness.

"You are too far out! This is open sea! That wretched boat is no match for the wind and waves of a hot summer afternoon storm."

"There are no clouds, comrade. We make good time out here in the stronger winds."

Dover tilted the bottle up to his lips and waved happily at the crew of the Soviet craft. A naval officer and two armed sailors stood in the afterdeck well and a third sailor manned the helm in the pilothouse. The fifty-footer carried a forward gun, but it was unmanned.

"Are you the only two on board?" the officer asked through the bullhorn.

"Yes, comrade!"

"Heave to! We're coming on board." The patrol boat was closing on the starboard side of the *Zaliv Azov,* the officer and the two sailors preparing to jump aboard.

Charlie Kiger grinned widely and continued waving his arm. "Yes, join us! We have plenty vodka for all!" Then, he directed Dover, "Drop the mainsail, Josef."

Dover released the stay and let the canvas flutter across the boom. The jib remained filled as Charlie Kiger dropped the mizzen and the *Zaliv Azov* slowed.

The Soviet helmsman brought his craft close aboard, port side to the ketch, and gave his engines a burst of reverse to match its speed. The two sailors shook their heads in amusement, enjoying the encounter. Running across a pair of half-drunken carefree fishermen was a welcome break in their monotonous patrol. Perhaps their officer would allow them to share a drink from the fishermen's bottle.

Charlie Kiger lowered his voice. "You take the helmsman." Still wearing his ludicrous grin, he turned from the helm, stumbled, and reached his arms out in front of him to break the fall. His hands landed beside the canvas.

The three Soviets crouched to jump and Charlie Kiger came back up with an armload of chattering death. The Israeli Galil sprayed a lethal stream of 5.56 millimeter projectiles at the rate of ten per second, exhausting its thirty-five-round clip in two short bursts, the first tearing the officer almost in half as Charlie Kiger swung the barrel point-blank across his midsection. The second volley of steel poured into the two sailors.

Dover had a brief glimpse of the startled helmsman's wide-open eyes before he pumped two rounds into the man's chest.

He ran aft. Charlie Kiger lay sprawled at the base of the helm support, desperately clawing at his throat in a futile effort to stem the spurting rush of blood rapidly draining his life. The last sailor to die had squeezed off a reflex round from his AK-47 as he dropped.

Dover leaped on board the patrol boat and dashed for the open hatch to the engine compartment. He met the engineman coming up the ladder and stopped him with three rounds from the automatic. There were no other crewmembers. Quickly, he grabbed a deck line and wrapped it around one of the gunwale cleats of the *Zaliv Azov* to hold the boats together.

Jumping back aboard the ketch, he knelt beside Charlie Kiger whose lips were silently mouthing his favorite profanity. The words were silent but easy for Dover to read: I hate the fuckers. He died with his mouth still open.

The Soviet officer lay with his upper body on the ketch, his booted legs upright against the taller hull of the patrol boat in a macabre imitation of a dropped marionette, his shredded belly draining blood and body fluids into the water lapping between the two hulls. One of the sailors was crumpled in the steering well of the ketch, only a few feet from Charlie Kiger. The other was on his back in the patrol boat with both hands still locked around his AK-47.

The helmsman was swinging back and forth in a swaying death dance, his jumper caught on one of the wheel handles, as the rudder was moved by the swells of the sea.

Everything had happened so fast that Dover had acted spontaneously. Only now did the carnage cause him to grimace. He had not been unduly disturbed by the necessity to kill the two men back in Leningrad. Nor had Timonkin's sudden death bothered him. They were all evil men. But the young crew of the patrol boat, and their handsome officer, so conscientious in their duties—he couldn't see how they had deserved to die in such an improbable place on such a beautiful afternoon.

And Charlie Kiger. Tobias's words of caution came back to him. "I'd sure hate to see any of them die because you took an extra half-second to make a moral judgement." Had he hesitated when his eyes met those of the young helmsman? No. Even if he had, it was the sailor aft who had shot Charlie Kiger.

He wanted to blame the CIA man, but he had wielded the automatic. The dead helmsman and engineman were his doing, and he had wasted no instant of time. Still, the enlisted crew were just kids, eighteen to twenty, he judged. He was still on the adrenaline high from the brief combat, but guilt was slowly creeping into his soul. The depression deepened as he mentally replayed the action of the last few minutes. Why did it have to happen? It was all so unrelated to the dirty business of his mission. He could feel the tears welling in his eye, and he was unable to stop the sob that jerked up through his throat. He tried, but he was unable to control his chest and stomach muscles as they reacted to the reality around him. He rocked in despair and cried in his hands. The Alpha Bug was no longer important, nor the film, nor his pickup rendezvous, nor honor and duty, nor anything. He just wanted to go back in time, to the clear Colorado day he walked the long path to his mailbox and found the envelope with the tell-tale return address of the Navy Department. He wanted to tear it up and scatter the pieces to the wind that curled down from the high Rockies.

Too late, he tasted it coming and hung his head over the side as the *akroshka* and *pirozhky* he had shared with Charlie Kiger surged up through his throat and onto the blood-flecked waters of the Sea of Azov.

Slowly, reason returned. He couldn't sail the ketch to the Kerch Peninsula alone and still make his pickup time. He dragged Charlie Kiger below and placed him on one of the bunks. On the other, he laid the dead naval officer. The four sailors, he lashed to the top of the cabin. The fire ax was on the forward side of the aft cabin bulkhead. He unlatched it and chopped a ragged hole in the hull just below the waterline.

As the sea water rushed into the cabin, he threw down the ax and scrambled topside. He cast off the line holding the ketch and climbed on board the patrol boat. From the pilothouse, he watched the *Zaliv Azov* fall behind and slowly sink below the waves. There were still no other craft in sight as he pushed the twin throttles forward and resumed his course toward the Kerch Peninsula. He backed off the dogs that held the movable portion of the windshield closed and pushed open the panel of glass to let the rushing air flow across his face and upper body, as if the sea air could ease his nagging sadness.

The fuel tanks were only down a third, and apparently the PC was a long-legged craft. Uncertain as to just how long-legged, he would watch his fuel consumption and as soon as he had a feel for his range, he would make whatever decisions were necessary.

He had little worry. With the 25-knot cruising speed of the sleek Soviet PC, he ran the remaining 170 kilometers in a few minutes over four hours. It was 9:00 P.M. when he turned parallel to the north shore of the peninsula, about a half-mile out, and let the boat idle just fast enough to maintain steerageway. His fuel tanks were still almost a quarter full.

He would lay offshore until after midnight. The area should be sparsely settled, but on the dark strip which he assumed to be a bathing beach, several red-orange bonfires burned with such ferocity that he could almost hear them crackle. When he shut down the engines and drifted, and the wind was right, he could hear the excited voices and happy laughter of young Russians on holiday. Occasionally, a pair of headlights would wind down from the higher ground inland, blinking intermittently as they passed behind one of the isolated beach cottages or the scattered clumps of low foliage. Most of them eventually wound up at one of the fires.

Dover figured he must be a good 600 nautical miles

south of Leningrad's latitude, and the warm air was balmy, almost sticky, in contrast to that of the cool evenings when he and Marie had walked along the banks of the Fontanka River. He'd had little opportunity to mix with the Soviet people on this assignment, just during the few times he'd observed the passing scene. But as he stood on the rolling deck of the PC and heard the happy sounds from the beach wafting through the warm air, he could just as well been off Martha's Vineyard, or Avalon, or any number of places off America's beaches. He had no doubt that across the water, lying on the sand in the seclusion of the night, some young Russian lad was trying to put the make on his girl without getting her mad, just as she cuddled close to him and wondered if she really wanted him to stop. That blacked-out strip of sand was probably America of the fifties, peppered with young bodies who for one night were forgetting their labors and problems. Too bad, he thought, they couldn't party with their contemporaries from Kansas, and California, and Maine, and talk about the promise the future could hold for them and their children. Instead, they would probably someday blow each other to hell and back. At that moment, Dover finally overcame the anguish he had developed back in the middle of the Sea of Azov and realized how critically important the small discs of film in his pocket really were. His hand unconsciously felt along the reassuring small bulge.

While he waited, he found a plastic bag and stripped. He rolled up his clothes inside, and added a few items of food he found on the boat and some water flasks. He had Timonkin's rubles, but wondered if he should have taken Charlie Kiger's. Yet, he doubted he'd need more than the three hundred and thirty he had.

He had only one final item to attend to. In that respect, the water should be plenty deep at this distance offshore.

The activity on the beach continued with enthusiasm until after 2:00 A.M. He waited through the next hour of quiet, then opened the sea cocks in the bilges of the engine compartment and slipped into the water.

Chapter
11

At first, the night chill made the water a bit too invigorating, but after a few minutes, Dover's body adjusted to its temperature and he settled into a relaxed sidestroke, towing the plastic bag of clothes and provisions with his trailing arm. As he reached the midpoint in his swim to the beach, he glanced back at the slowly settling patrol boat. Only a few inches of freeboard remained and that disappeared as the weight of the water pouring through the open sea cocks carried the craft to the bottom of the small bay. A bubbling cauliflower of air-filled froth marked the passage of the superstructure and the thin mast was last to slip beneath the shadowy surface of the sea, leaving only a slight swirl to temporarily mark its final resting place.

He resumed his steady stroking, and as he neared the beach the light surf lifted him and he rode the lapping waves until his body began to drag bottom. The sand shone clearly in the bright night and he scanned it for occupants. Fifty yards off to his left, two huddled bodies lay with arms and legs entwined, the absence of any movement suggesting they were asleep. Nevertheless, he decided to give himself an additional thirty yards and slipped to the right, half-swimming and half-crawling in the shallow surf. Rather than arouse the curiosity of any unseen all-nighters by running, he stood and nonchalantly strolled across the open beach to where the ground cover began. It was mostly scrub grass and prickly low foliage. He took a few minutes to dry off in the sea breeze and dress.

He was fairly sure of his location. Mikhail's detailed map had shown his dropoff point to be a small bay near the base of the Kerch Peninsula. All the landmarks indicated he had scuttled the PC in the middle of that bay. The prominent beach lights inland to his left should come from the village of Lenino. If so, the narrowest portion of the peninsula lay dead ahead. With that in mind, he started inland and before long crossed a twin-tracked dirt road which wound back toward the beach, and about a kilometer farther crossed a two-lane highway. That checked. Kerch should be 50 kilometers to his left, and the Black Sea only 20 kilometers ahead. If he kept slightly to the left of south, he should make seafall on the eastern half of a much larger bay which was his southern shore landmark.

The terrain began to rise and fall with the first humps of the low hills running lengthwise out the peninsula. He had plenty of time, over 24 hours, so he decided to stick to the back country and give wide berth to any roads or dwellings he might come upon.

He hiked until sunrise, refreshing himself periodically with sips from one of his water flasks, and figured he had covered seven or eight kilometers. Still climbing the north side of the hills, he could see behind him the awakening surface of the Azov stretching and blinking under the glare of the first rays of the rising sun. The expanding light erased the dark profiles of night and colored his surroundings with stimulating greens and browns. The lush hill vegetation thickened even more, but it provided excellent cover, an easy tradeoff for a slightly reduced pace.

A level stretch appeared and he rested, deciding that since he was not yet pressed for time, it would be advantageous to sleep. A cluster of fat oaks on the far side of the clearing provided him with privacy and shaded him from the climbing sun. He bedded down on the bunched-up ground cover, feeling safe and secure.

The KGB watch read 8:13 when a breeze-disturbed branch allowed a streak of sunlight to flicker across his eyelid and awaken him. The three-hour sleep had been very sound, and he felt rested and anxious to be on his way. After rinsing his face, he rubbed the last of Mikhail's salve into his cheek, then noticed the water flask was down to its last quarter. Despite the second full one in his plastic sack, he satisfied his morning thirst with measured swallows.

Only two additional stops interrupted his morning progress and he was able to maintain a steady pace despite the irregular undulations of the hill country. At noon, he topped a ridge and was rewarded with his first view of the vast waters of the Black Sea. Beyond the ridge, perhaps two kilometers, he could see another east-west paved road which he figured to be the Feodosiya-Kerch highway. Another hour to the next ridge and his eye feasted on the wide crescent of Feodosiya Bay, with its namesake resort town cluttering the western bow. He had made good time, still felt fresh, and was in excellent position. All that remained was to continue south to the edge of the hills and hole up until nightfall. After that, he should have no problem reaching his pickup point well before dawn.

When he stopped in the late afternoon, the horizon before him lay at the far edge of the magnificent body of dark water. Offshore, sparkling white pleasure boats shared the white-capped waters with fat fishing craft, while farther out several freighters plowed through the deep water, leaving behind a spiderweb of black boiler residue. Their tell-tale funnel smoke thinned as it rose, eventually dissolving into the nothingness of clear air. Dover wished he could see beyond the horizon to confirm that somewhere on that invisible extension of the Black Sea, a Turkish freighter with a false deck house and an anxious aviator was steaming leisurely back and forth.

He had traveled far enough since swimming ashore and his eagerness in setting a hard pace had taken its toll on his leg muscles. It felt good to sit on the sweet-smelling grass and conserve himself for the remainder of the day. After removing his shirt, he stretched out in the late afternoon sun and let the familiar rays ease the fatigue. The pleasant warmth reminded him that even with their highly restricted life style the people of the Soviet Union still enjoyed a chunk of the good life along the Riviera of the Black Sea, where the water and the air and the sun were free, and every bit as therapeutic as those of other countries.

As he idly watched the skies, puffy white cumulus clouds drifted overhead, changing shapes and direction with the whims of the upper winds; sometimes, they were chubby cotton clowns performing daring feats by balancing each other on twisting bodies, then thinning and tearing into clumps of odd faces and strange animals in an endless display of the imagination of nature. Profiled against the rich blue of the Asiatic heavens, they provided an ever-changing backdrop for the gray and white seabirds which caught and soared the thermals rising from the hot beach sands, their tapered wings flexing as they rode the lift. Masters of aerodynamics, they milked even the barest currents to spiral tirelessly over the water, their downcast eyes ever watchful for the fleeting dark shadows below the surface that heralded another meal.

The night came slowly, the sun reluctantly disappearing behind the thickly populated hills of Crimea. With its last peek over the horizon, it winked goodnight and Dover struck out around the east curve of the bay, staying far enough inland to skirt any possible beach activity. As he hiked once more toward his rendezvous, the ground became more uneven and walking much more difficult. He tried moving closer to the water, but travel was little better there and the short brush afforded less cover. He hated to admit it, but the ordeals of the last three days had lowered his overall stamina and his pace slowed below the standard he had set by his first day's walk. As a consequence, the thirty kilometers from his last resting place to the point of land where the old lighthouse had stood took an exhausting eleven hours. Fortunately, he had provided himself with an ample supply of tinned sea rations from the patrol boat and carefully managed his water to keep his thirst down and his strength up. When he finally stood on the broken concrete remnant of the lighthouse base, he audibly thanked his God and began to savor the first strong hope that his mission was at last almost over. It was 4:30 A.M.

For the first time since he had reported to Falcon Air Force Base, he had time to wonder how Carl and the ranch were doing. This last taste of the realities of international intrigue made him appreciate the advantages of his past life with NASA, and made his future on the ranch all the more attractive. The next time some idiot put an official envelope in his mailbox, he would return it "Address unknown."

Twenty minutes later, the first lightening of the eastern sky prompted him to commence a search to seaward.

As it had since the beginning of its time, the earth continued to rotate and whirl his tiny corner of the Black Sea coastline toward the dawn. The sky bled robin's egg blue, then almost white before the faraway concentration of dust particles tinted it with a radiant apricot, which in turn gave way to the first real light of the day. The sun tarried for just a moment below the dark peaks of the Caucasus Mountains, then sprang over the horizon.

With the sun came a barely perceptible movement from the south, at first a flickering reflection on the horizon, then an indistinct object closing across the sea. Dover's heart tripped into an extra beat as his eye watched it grow and become the unmistakable head-on profile of a Harrier speeding so low over the water that it flew within a mist of transparent sea spray kicked up by the powerful thrust of its thundering turbojet exhaust.

He ran to the center of the concrete and wildly waved his arms. The Harrier dipped its wings in recognition and began to slow. It actually had to climb to reach the slab, and as it did so he could see the Red Star of the Soviet Navy emblazoned on its vertical stabilizer in brilliant contrast to the dull blue-green overall color. On the side of the fuselage, just behind the large rectangular air intakes, the blue and white flag of the Soviet sea forces added to the authenticity of the camouflage which was completed by a boldly painted squadron identification number, a three-foot-high yellow ''27.'' Indeed, unless one looked very closely and had an intimate knowledge of Red Navy aircraft, the machine preparing to descend was a Yak-36 Forger-II. The illusion was so complete that the pilot even wore the oversize Russian hardhat with the red ''CCCP'' across the eyeshield cover!

Dover backed away and shielded his face with his arms as the Harrier descended vertically onto the concrete amid its self-generated jetwash of swirling dust and debris.

The wheels touched and he started forward, ignorant of the drama taking place behind him. An old road ended a hundred yards short of the lighthouse site, and although he had noticed it when he first arrived, he had given it little thought since it appeared to be in poor repair and only led east to the small village of Cornomorskoje. But at the moment, a speeding military car was skidding to a rocking stop at the end of the road. Two figures jumped out and ran toward the lighthouse base. He didn't even hear the gunfire, but suddenly felt the awful tear of a bullet as it passed through the flesh of his right thigh. The shock collapsed his leg and he pitched forward. Instinctively, he rolled and managed to pull Timonkin's automatic from his waistband. Surprised, and shocked with pain, he emptied it wildly in the direction of the runners who dropped to the ground, uncertain as to the amount of firepower they faced.

He struggled to his feet, holding the flesh wound, and tried to wave the pilot back, but the Marine had jumped from the cockpit and was racing toward him with a spare flight harness. He had also unholstered his service revolver and was firing at the prone figures hugging the grassy sand a good seventy yards away. He rushed up to Dover.

''Get this on! What the shit's going on?''

''Hell, I don't know.'' Dover struggled into the garment, leaving it unzipped. He could do that after he got in the Harrier. "Let's get out of here!"

The pilot helped him hobble to the lowered boarding ladder and Dover pulled himself up. He was on the second rung when an awful premonition made him look back to check on the pilot. He was on one knee, emptying his revolver, but even as Dover called to him, his hardhat jerked and he fell forward on his face.

The two men were up and running.

Dover had only an instant to act. Like most of the other astronauts, he had flown the Harrier when it was being evaluated as a training platform for an advanced version of the lunar-landing module, but that had been over three years back. The renewed lunar program had been scrubbed, but he had accumulated almost a hundred hours in the bird.

There was really no other choice.

Painfully, he lifted his leg over the side of the front cockpit and dropped into the seat, grabbing the control stick and jamming the throttle forward as he did so. The fore and aft pairs of jet exhaust nozzles were still pointing downward in their vertical-landing mode and the Harrier responded immediately by leaping off the pad. He pushed left rudder, which also activated the maneuvering thrusters, and swung the nose of the aircraft at the pair of strangers charging toward him. Holding his hover, he flicked on the master arming switch, selected the pair of 30-millimeter Aden gun pods on the Harrier's belly and squeezed the trigger on the control stick. Twin lightning bolts erupted from underneath the fuselage and streaked toward the two men. He walked the rudders, swinging the nose back and forth, and watched the two endless streamers of bright tracers rip the runners into shredded rag dolls that collapsed in an instant.

He immediately set the Harrier back on the pad, pulled the throttle into idle, and crawled out to aid the pilot. The Marine was still alive, but the severity of the head wound made his survival tenuous at best. Regardless, Dover could not leave him. The discovery of a U.S. Marine officer along with the two shattered Soviet bodies would set off a crisis which could give the State Department a long series of eight-day weeks. Not to mention the President and DOD.

His thigh wound was still bleeding, but it seemed to be only a muscle puncture. With the Marine's flight scarf packed tightly over it, and held securely by the form-fitting G-suit, he could at least retrieve the Marine. Getting him up the ladder and into the rear seat was another matter, and it took him an agonizing five minutes before he was able to belt in the unconscious aviator and strap himself into the front cockpit. The area back along the road was clear, and since no one was approaching, he took a few minutes to familiarize himself with the cockpit. The two-seater was a later model, but basically the arrangement was unchanged. He was also dismayed to find that his depth perception wasn't worth a shit with just one eye. His first takeoff and attack on the two assailants had been the result of a rush of adrenaline, and a fair measure of luck. Now that he was faced with a more deliberate action, he had to deal with his shortcomings. But at the same time, he knew what he must do and the flight back to the freighter would give him some valuable learning time. He closed the canopy, lifted off, transitioned to forward flight, and sped south low over the waves.

In his initial briefing, Tobias had indicated that the freighter would be located 160 miles due south of his pickup point. How accurate that was now, he could only speculate, but he did note that the navigational radio was on and preset, most probably to the freighter's homer. He wouldn't know for sure as long as he skimmed along at wavetop level for the signal was line-of-sight and the CIA ship was somewhere beyond his visible horizon. For the time being, then, he would fly due south. A quick check of his airspeed indicator gave 650 knots, right at Mach 1. He could ignore the light surface wind. If the freighter was where it should be, he'd be over it in fifteen minutes. Inexplicably, a wave of nausea hit him and then passed.

He jettisoned the empty wing tanks and used his fuel

flow and fuel quantity gauges to compute his endurance. Normally, the Harrier's range was extremely short. But that was with a 3,000 pound combat load, although it did consider vertical operations. But he was much lighter, and the wing tanks that he had just dropped had provided most of the enroute fuel. His only external weight was the ammo in the Aden gun pods and the two Sidewinder missiles on his wingtips. Still, his endurance at this fuel-guzzling low level would allow him only another 20 minutes.

Ten minutes into his escape he zoomed skyward to see if he could pick up the freighter's homer. At 12,000 feet he had a steady signal indicating the ship lay 20 degrees port and the distance meter read 54 miles. The communication radio must be on the proper frequency, also. He had no idea of either his call sign or the ship's, so he used the aircraft serial number stamped on the instrument panel.

"Hello . . . hello, this is Marine 39166 . . . over."

He received an immediate reply. "Roger, this is Tango Boy . . . we hold you bearing zero-two-three, five-zero miles . . . advise you have two bogies, six o'clock, angels three-five-zero, closing fast."

Dover dove for the deck. That could very well be a flight of Flagons out of Krasnodar, balls to the wall at 35,000 feet. High-altitude interceptors, they probably had little if any look-down radar capability, but he had no idea how efficient the shore-based air defense system was. Certainly, the Flagons were on their supersonic dash for some reason—and it could be him.

He could see the freighter! She was steaming at about 12 knots and as he closed he reduced his power and slowed the Harrier. The ship was turning to give him an advantageous relative wind for his landing and the crewmen were dropping the sides of the false deckhouse.

"Tango Boy, where are the bogies now?" he called.

"They've separated . . . one is descending and slowing at your eight o'clock position . . . ten miles . . . the other is overhead."

Balls! They either had him or one was dropping down to look over the freighter; in either case a Flagon was closing off his port quarter. A buzzing in his earphones confirmed his analysis. His rear-warning radar receiver was picking up the rapid signals of a fire-control radar beam. It had to be the Soviet jet. He triggered the chaff release and thousands of the tiny tinfoil-strip radar deceptors sprayed from their fuselage containers. Simultaneously, he twisted around in the cockpit and his eye picked up a long descending arc of black jet exhaust curving down from the sky behind him. At its origin sped the ugly wide-bodied snout of a SU-15 Flagon. A tiny orange spurt of flame glowed for an instant under its left wing and a black needle pulled rapidly in front of the onrushing jet and zeroed in on the Harrier.

Dover max-rolled to his right, gasping from the pain which shot through his leg as he jammed the rudder, and shoved his thrust-vectoring lever to the full down position. The combination of the tight turn and the full engine thrust directed toward the outside of the turn shoved the Harrier into a butt-crushing, multiple-G maneuver that arced it around in an ever-tightening semicircle beyond the match of any purely aerodynamic vehicle. Even the supersonic air-to-air missile which had sprung into life from under the Flagon's wing lagged well outside the Harrier's unbelievably tight spiral until it passed beyond and the infrared sensor in its nose lost the scent of Dover's roaring exhaust flame. The 12-foot rocket arced aimlessly down toward the sea.

The Flagon was right behind it and the Soviet pilot had it tight in a 90-degree bank in his attempt to stay with the Harrier.

Dover matched the Flagon's turn for almost half a circle then laid in full aileron and rolled away from the direction of turn. He held it through two complete rolls before recovering in a 90-degree bank opposite to the original. Straining against the "G's" of his tight turn, he looked back over his inside shoulder.

The Soviet pilot was good. He had matched Dover roll for roll and was trying valiantly to pull his nose around sharply enough to allow his fire-control radar to lock on the Harrier. It was a classic Lufbery Circle, a World War I combat maneuver that pitted two opponents on each side of a continuous turn, each trying to tighten his aircraft without overpulling it into a high-speed stall.

Once more Dover deflected his thrusters down and the agile Harrier tightened its side of the circle. The Flagon was no match for the agile VTOL fighter and broke off his attack.

Dover rolled out and headed for the last direction of the freighter but knew that the Soviet pilot was only pulling away temporarily and would set himself up for another run. Searching the skies, Dover kept the Harrier on any given course for only a few seconds at a time.

Once more the buzzing in his earphones confirmed that the Flagon had closed within acquisition range. Dover immediately pulled up into a thrust-augmented loop. The buzzing stopped! The Flagon had lost him! Arcing sharply across the top of his loop and down the backside he could see the Soviet plane directly over the top of his canopy, about two miles away, rolling smartly into a vertical climb. Dover pulled through until he was above and slightly to the rear of the Flagon. The Soviet pilot rolled left. Dover matched his roll but overshot as the Soviet executed a perfect reversal and dove away to Dover's right. He was *damned* good! Straining against his shoulder straps, Dover tried to pull over and after the diving Flagon.

He could not match the Soviet's speed and watched helplessly as the Flagon leveled off just above the waves and opened to the north. For the moment, they were disengaged and Dover searched once more for the freighter. All of the turns and sweeping climbs and dives had moved him somewhere relative to the ship, but where? He was low but didn't want to climb, preferring to use his speed to open the distance between him and the Flagon. The buzzing in his earphones told him that it was futile to consider such a thought.

Roll ninety degrees. Full down thrusters. Pull back on the stick. Pull, pull, pull! He didn't see anything but his fighter pilot's instinct told him that the Flagon's second missile had left the security of the underside of the wing of its carrier aircraft and was on its way. He released his remaining chaff. Abruptly, the buzzing stopped again. Twice, he had lucked out! But it was about time for Lady Luck to desert him; she had been too faithful back at Volgograd and on the Sea of Azov to see him through much more of this. The Flagon wouldn't disengage. The pilot was undoubtedly under orders to stop the bogus Yak-36. But Dover had one advantage. The Flagon was a supersonic high-altitude interceptor. The Harrier was primarily a low-level air support aircraft and Dover was keeping it low over the water. The Flagon would have to come to him and fight in his environment.

Anxiously, he searched the skies around and above him. Incredibly, the Flagon was directly overhead at about 5,000 feet, on a parallel course! The blue disguise paint on Dover's Harrier must be blended completely with the dark sea and the Flagon's radar lacked the look-down capability of the more modern interceptors. Dover licked his lips. This was a classic textbook position for him: behind and below his adversary. Back on the stick! His 875 pounds of body weight, reflecting the 5-G pullup, pushed down into his seat pan. He had the Flagon inside his 30-degree acquisition cone, the hot exhaust of the Soviet interceptor fully exposed to his weapons. *So long, Ivan. David is about to apply the rock to the forehead of the big guy.* Dover pressed his missile-release button. A Sidewinder rocketed off his left wingtip, its hungry heat-seeking eye already feeling the warmth of the Flagon's fire. The Soviet jet disintegrated as the American missile entered its glowing tailpipe.

One down. One to go? Dover laid the Harrier back on its side and commenced another tight circle. The skies appeared to be clear although the thinning fluff of a long contrail was drifting high to the southwest. He switched his search seaward and reversed his turn. Where in hell was the freighter?

"Tango Boy, do you still have me?" he radioed.

"Roger—come out of your turn heading north—I'll be dead ahead 12 miles."

Dover rolled his wings level as directed and within 30 seconds caught the sunlit glimmer of the ship's wake. Still high from the excitement of his aerial death-dance with the Flagon, he allowed himself to think that he was going to make it. Nevertheless, he was very uneasy about the whereabouts of the second interceptor. The first had undoubtedly reported his attack on their tactical frequency. As he once more closed on the freighter, rapidly working his head around to catch any visual indication of another attack and listening for the buzz in his earphones, he suddenly experienced a drastic change in his focusing ability. The ship blurred, then cleared, then blurred again. He shook his head. No change. It must be from the leg. His flight suit was soaked with blood from the wound. In the heat of combat he had forgotten it. Now, he realized that the series of high "G" maneuvers had drained his precious body fluid toward his lower extremities and reinforced the bleeding despite the tight grip of his anti-G suit. His eye cleared too late for him to start his approach and he passed over the freighter in a wobbly turn downwind. Maybe, the real fun was still ahead of him. Weak from loss of blood and without the depth perception capability of the normal pilot, a vertical touchdown on the freighter's tiny recovery platform was going to reveal the cruelty of the real world. If he screwed it up, he could prang himself on the small deck and end up as a very charred hors d'oeuvre for the local fish population or roll off the side of the ship into the sea for an underwater ejection.

"Break right! Break right!" came an excited call from Tango Boy.

Dover understood instantly the urgency of the warning. The second Flagon was on him and had either fired a missile or was closing for the kill with its guns. Which form his impending death was to take was strictly dealer's choice at the moment. He was on the verge of going under and there was little strength left in his body, certainly not enough to withstand another radical turn like the ones he used to thwart the first attack. Besides, his squinting eye would never get him on board that freighter; he could barely make out his instruments. As if that weren't enough, the needle on his last fuel-quantity indicator was only a hair's width from the big red "E."

It was time to let discretion replace his flagging valor. He pulled his legs back into the seat stirrups, reached over his head and locked his fingers around the ejection pull-ring. With his last vestige of strength, he yanked the curtain across his face.

He didn't seem to feel the canopy separation or the fierce blast of wind he expected, but he did feel the welcome thunk of the rear seat shooting up and out of the fuselage, followed immediately by the explosive kick into his own rear. He was rocketed high above the Harrier just as a violent orange fireball erupted below him, the result of the impacting Soviet missile.

Dover rode his ejection seat in a dream world, neither unconscious nor fully aware of his surroundings. He did retain the impression of tumbling through space, then felt the push in the small of his back as the automatic sequencing of his escape mechanism inflated the separation bladder and simultaneously released his seat harness. The seat fell away and his chute deployed, its opening shock jarring him momentarily awake. Again, he settled into peaceful ignorance as his body swung gently below the billowed canopy. Contact with the cold water roused him one final time and he had enough presence of mind to release his parachute fittings. But that was all. He didn't feel his plunge and then his return to the surface of the Black Sea as the sensing devices of his life vest tasted the sea water and reacted by filling it with a buoyant expanse of CO_2.

Dover slipped into the nether world of unconsciousness, his last thoughts a montage of Flagons overhead, spitting missiles in all directions, and below him open-mouthed sharks rising from the dark depths, drooling at the scent of his bloody leg.

Chapter

12

"Away the motor whale boat!"

The crew of the *Marmara Denizi* had watched the sky battle and the ejection of the two occupants of the Harrier with more than considerable interest and now they concerned themselves with their rescue task. For a moment, they were delayed as the victorious Flagon passed low over the ship, forcing them to take cover. But the aircraft fired no weapons, content possibly with scoring the aerial kill.

The two parachutes had splashed into the water a few hundred yards off the starboard bow and the captain had immediately ordered his engines stopped.

"Twenty degrees right rudder," he ordered before stepping outside on the starboard wing of the bridge to observe the lowering of the motor whale boat. As soon as the boat crew felt the boat wet its keel with the surging waters along the freighter's hull, they released the fall lines and the coxswain swung away from the ship. At full speed they passed ahead of the freighter and steered for the bodies bobbing in the swells.

The near one was dead, entangled in his parachute and with an ugly head wound.

* * *

Overhead, well beyond the perception of the participants in the drama unfolding on the heaving waters of the Black Sea, Andrian Bykovsky was sleeping soundly within the weightless environs of his spaceplane, having earned a few hours' rest after a series of demanding tests. Several had taken longer than programmed and it had been almost 4:00 A.M. on his body clock before he had been told to eat and try to get some rest. Since that time, he had been orbiting around his home planet under the constant control and monitoring of his controllers back at the Northern Cosmodrome.

"Comrade Major, awake! It is another day!"

The words crackled in Andrian's ears simultaneously with a short series of high-pitched whistles. It was a normal wake up. Had there been any urgency, the voice would have played against a background of irritating claxons.

"The nights are getting shorter, comrades," responded Andrian, a wide yawn in the middle of his reply betraying his attempt to hide his fatigue. This was his 15th day since liftoff and he was beginning to think that for purposes of alertness an operational pilot should be limited to three weeks before relief. Of course, his schedule had not been typical, having been considerably more demanding than if he had been merely riding on station. True, the first five days had been almost boring as the various ground control and communications stations had exercised their facilities. The middle five had been somewhat more interesting as he had been put through several ground controlled orbital plane changes, a bit rough from the "G" standpoint, but all had been executed flawlessly. Finally, the past five days had been a simulated mission stretch and conducted just as would actual operations. His insertion into polar orbit had been accomplished in two steps, each changing the declination of his circle around the earth by more than 15 degrees until the 90 degree angle with the equator had been accomplished. Next, he had been accelerated into an elliptical orbit with its apogee 1,600 kilometers over the North Pole. The elongation had enabled him to remain within his northern hemispheric target envelope for over 70% of his orbital flight time. It was a practical evaluation of one of the actual tracks the weapons system would use when fully deployed. And the bonus for maintaining a path in alignment with both the earth's poles had been an opportunity to observe the entire surface of the planet as it rotated within his orbit.

The isometric exercise devices were readily available and he felt he had kept his muscle tone close to that he normally maintained on earth. The food was certainly nourishing although some of the meals were somewhat tasteless, in those cases being identifiable only if he read the labels. But that was a minor inconvenience when he considered what his contemporaries in the ground forces had to eat in their battle environment. There was no dirt or mud up here nor was there any summer heat or winter cold to sap his energy. If one were to fight a war, Andrian could think of no better way than flat on one's back in a custom tailored couch with everything one needed at an arm's reach. And the warrior that rode the Kosmolyot II would be fighting an impersonal battle against machines, not men. The emotion of combat that so often affected the performance of the soldier would not be present in space. Out here, it was cold deliberation and uninhibited judgement, if anything. The multi-brained computer bank within his craft would make decisions without any nonessential inputs such as doubt or concern or shame or regret or any other human characteristic that could adversely influence a military decision. Much more efficient.

He was passing over the Black Sea on a southward track. Below him was the irregular bulge of the Crimean peninsula and while he could make out the kidney-shaped sea that separated the Soviet Union from Turkey to the south, his altitude was too great to visually pick up the beaches of Sevastopol and Yalta. The latter city had a special place in the memories of his last summer holiday, a year ago almost to the day. Somewhere down there, on the edge of that green blob, was the narrow Promenade, one of Yalta's walking streets, closed to motor traffic, where he had encountered and been completely captivated by the terrific body topped with flowing yellow hair and a pair of sparkling blue eyes. The Latvian beauty was also on holiday. At times like that, it was no disadvantage to be one of the Soviet Union's hero cosmonauts. He could recall every moment of their brief encounter: the quiet getting-familiar walks in Nagornyi Park, their bodies touching, her perfume mingling with that of the flowers; the pausing to stand close and enjoy the magnificent view of Yalta and the sea. At this very moment, detached as he was from the earth, he could still feel the tingle in his blood that had stiffened his body as they enjoyed their first embrace in the chilly water off the beach at Mishkov. It was easy for his mind to relive that final night at the Chekhov Theater, the late dinner, and afterwards the unbelievable pleasure as they lay together on the balcony off their small resort suite and heard the surf and felt the sea breeze as they made love. It was a passing thing and they had never met again but he could feel with some assurance that she was down there again, this year, making a new conquest. His vantage point seemed most appropriate for such memories.

The earth was slowly spinning from his left to his right as he lay stomach down to it, his head to the north. The Kosmolyot II was riding nose first, upside down, in effect making a gigantic inside loop around the moving planet. It was an ideal position for him to observe the ever-changing panorama of blue seas, purple mountains, green and brown foliage and soil, and white ice. Due to the earth's rotation, his path would take him next over central Africa and across the vast South Pacific to Antarctica. The combination of orbital-plane changes he had undergone during the past two weeks had resulted in a direction opposite to that of his initial launch, a dynamic achievement in itself. He had little to do on his southern hemispheric swings but he could enjoy the advantage of having his perigee—his closest point to earth—over the South Pole. On previous passes, before he had slept, he had taken particular pleasure in studying the ice-covered continent with its mantle of pure white. It might be the coldest, highest, windiest, and most remote continent on earth but it was a continent of peace, the only place of its kind. What a shame the countries of the world could not do in space what they had somehow managed to accomplish with respect to that 5,500,000-square-mile land. There, their differences did not exist, and all the peoples of Antarctica worked in harmony and peace.

He reviewed the list of scheduled activities for the next few hours with some eagerness. This would be his time, when he could get to control the spaceplane in a series of manual operations that would duplicate many of the automatic-mode tests that had already been conducted. On his northern swing he would be making a deceleration burn to convert his orbit back to a circular path, then 45 minutes after that he would be executing the most radical maneuver of all, a single rocket firing that would place him in an orbit identical to that the Americans used for their Kennedy launches. The final two days would be set aside for some routine reconnaissance for the purpose of updating the photographic files on the southern United States and Australia. Then he would ride the fire one last time to reenter the envelope of air around the earth and glide for hundreds of kilometers in a simulated emergency deorbit flight path. Finally, he would slow the returning spaceplane, deploy the parachute recovery system, and drop to the soil of Mother Russia near Baikonur.

It was time for his contact check with the *Kosmonaut Yuri Gargarin*, the space-tracking ship assigned to the South Pacific for the Kosmolyot II tests. The four huge dish antennas that gave the *Gargarin* such a pronounced top-heavy appearance would undoubtedly be following his path across the heavens. There was no other ship like the *Gargarin*, just as there was no other space craft like the Kosmolyot II, and the unique pair was a powerful symbol of the preeminence of the Soviet space program. This day, they were coupled in a deadly display of military capability as well.

"Hello, *Gargarin*. Verify Operation 27-Y."

"Operation 27-Y verified. No adjustments." The *Gargarin* confirmed his orbital track and his programmed time to reenter circular orbit.

Thirty minutes later, Andrian began making his preparations, talking now to the brand new Soviet communications relay station on the southern tip of Vietnam. For the remainder of his mission, he would return to the scramble communications radio and use coded call signs.

"Kochmas Control, I am ready for manual operation."

"Kosmolyot II, you are cleared for manual."

Andrian smiled as he recognized the voice of his mentor, Vladimir Koidunov. He could not resist a friendly dig. "Ah, Koidunov—the Younger, are you envious of your star pupil?"

"Andrian, at this moment you are the pride of my misspent life. What a glorious achiever you are!" Koidunov's voice came across loud and clear as it was relayed through the southeast Asia transmitter. So did the somber voice of the circuit monitor.

"Communications on this net are restricted to necessary command and control."

Andrian knew that Vladimir was laughing just as hard as he at the pompous announcement. The voice was thick with a heavy Ukrainian emphasis and probably came from the deep jowled throat of some political supervisor who could not imagine the exhilaration of space flight nor understand the special affection and camaraderie that existed among the men who rode the fire.

Now that he was cleared, the clock would be his only supervisor. He placed his computer bank readout control to MONITOR and made a final check of all his navigation readings. Everything was in order. Reaching over to his left sub-console, he raised the red safety cover and turned the black plastic switch from REMOTE AUTOMATIC to MANUAL—at least, he turned it there in his mind Actually, his fingers positioned the switch one click beyond that, to the MANUAL OVERRIDE combat position, which would prevent any signal, friendly or foreign, from interfering with the operation of the spaceplane. A simple mistake, but he had unknowingly removed himself from the back-up control of his ground support network. Ordinarily, the error would be picked up by his onboard monitoring circuits and telemetered to the control room back at the Northern Cosmodrome, but the same gremlins that plagued the U.S. space program by giving false fuel valve settings and faulty APU readings played no favorites. On the one console in the control center which carried the warning light for that particular setting, the gremlins had burnt out the filament of the two-kopeks light bulb under the red lens.

His return to circular orbit was achieved routinely. Andrian checked his attitude instruments to insure that his burn axis was opposite to his direction of travel and offset the necessary pitch and azimuth. His timing of the liquid-fuel rocket-engine burn was accurate to the microsecond and the decrease in orbital speed reacted with the gravitational pull of the earth to adjust his path in space, once more demonstrating the infallibility of the laws of physics and the validity of vector solutions.

His next maneuver would be much more critical.

During the time it took him to travel northward to the equator, he completed most of his pre-burn items on his check list. He was almost ready. He pressurized his modified spacesuit. An orbital plane-change burn would severely tax the cabin integrity with the instantaneous stress of high "G's." Unlike a straight acceleration or deceleration burn, there could also be massive side forces if his alignment were off even the slightest. Using his attitude thrusters, he aligned his axes with the orientation called for by his computer display.

The dark blue-green, delta-winged spaceplane was in position. He felt the contour couch adjust in response to the input signals it received from the change-plane program.

Of the bank of nine solid rockets nested under the tail, he selected number eight, the first seven having previously been used and the ninth remaining as a safety back-up should he need it. The earlier rocket firings had demonstrated to him their terrific thrust components, far above the capability of his liquid fueled maneuvering engine. The composition of the solid rocket propellant was the real secret to the spaceplane's remarkable capability and was the most highly classified aspect of the vehicle. Even the manufacturing of the rocket motors was carried on in such a way that no one worker or group of workers knew the composition of the fuel cylinder and the only statement made at his briefings had been that a simple ingredient had been added to a standard chemical composition, the first time by accident. So uncomplicated was the secret formula that it could easily be ascertained should one of the rocket motors fall into the wrong hands.

All was in readiness. Now he must watch the time readout on his main panel. One minute to ignition, then seconds. Five . . . four . . . three . . . two . . . one . . . now!

He pressed the firing button and felt the dynamic kick of the engine. It would be a three-minute burn and he would have to change his attitude three times during that period to adjust to the resultant forces of the maneuver. One, gravity, he could do nothing about. The second, the dynamic energy of his hypersonic speed in orbit, would be changing in response to the third force, the unbelievable thrust of the rocket engine. His prime responsibility, now that ignition had occurred, would be to aim the thrust during the three phases of orbital change. First, he must closely monitor the deceleration; second, he must realign the spaceplane for its new orbital plane; and third, he must monitor his acceleration as he reestablished speed.

The inside bladder of his spacesuit was fully inflated, squeezing his body with the force of a hundred hands to insure that the awesome "G" forces did not pull blood away from his brain. His arms were astonishingly heavy on the armrests but all of the controls were at his fingertips and he had full authority over those. The Kosmolyot II was in expert hands.

The devastating deceleration pressed him tightly onto his couch. With the concentration born of thousands of flight hours in the testing of high performance jet fighters

205

and riding the space rockets, he monitored his rapidly decreasing velocity through space.

There!

He activated his maneuvering thrusters and swung the spaceplane simultaneously around two of its axes to establish his new attitude. The forces on his body increased even more and he was almost immobilized by the unfamiliar side forces. The Kosmolyot II was feeling the same stress and the instrument panels began to vibrate with an intensity that made the readings almost indistinguishable. The spaceplane was actually veering in orbit, fighting two sets of force vectors at the same time, those of the old orbit and those of the new thrust direction.

He was two minutes and 20 seconds into his burn.

Gradually, his body confirmed the G-meter's readings that the fire blasting from his tail had him established in his new direction. Only one adjustment remained: a minor realignment of his longitudinal axis to use the remainder of his rocket time for pure acceleration back to orbital speed.

He activated his thrusters a final time and just as the alignment marks on his master attitude indicator merged with the target marks, he experienced for a brief moment that loss of sensory perception he had felt just before lift-off. He tried again to clear it by shaking his head, unaware that the already weakened wall of a small artery serving his primitive brain area was expanding under the forces of the artificially increased weight and pressure of the blood within. The tiny balloon had sat in Andrian's head since before his mother had pressed him from her womb, a cocked gun that even the most sophisticated examinations of Soviet space medicine had failed to discover. Now, weary from flexing, the 35-year-old aneurism burst and released the deep scarlet fluid into the surrounding tissue, fatally detouring it away from the vital portion of the brain it normally nourished.

The massive pain bulged Andrian's eyes from their sockets as if a pair of sharp knives were trying to carve them out of his skull. Frantically, he tried to lift his arms, to tear off his helmet and grip his head in a panic-stricken attempt to stop the hurt, but the "G" forces were still enough to prevent him from doing more than just barely breaking the helmet's seal with the spacesuit. No matter, for the lack of blood began to starve his brain of life-sustaining oxygen and his motor skills ceased as he slipped into a deep coma.

The rocket engine stopped. And so did the electrical impulses to Andrian's muscles. His most vital muscle, beating against his chest wall in a fury of protest, convulsed to a stop.

Chapter
13

Dover's nose gave him the first indication that he was returning to the land of the living. The faint rubbing-alcohol odor could originate only in the sanitized environment of a hospital room, but he had never known a hospital to slowly roll from side to side or surge up and down with some vaguely familiar rhythm. Not quite ready to open his eye, he first analyzed the quiet noises picked up by his ears. There was the unmistakable ka-chug ka-chug of ship's screws cavitating in deep water, accompanied by the heavy vibrations of their rotating shafts. Then there was the low background whisper of a ventilation system and he could feel the cool air.

A voice spoke to him. "Dover . . . Joe . . . can you hear me? It's Tobias . . . Alexander Tobias."

Dover cracked open his eye and there before him was the anxious face of the occupant of the Soviet desk at the Central Intelligence Agency.

"Welcome back," said Tobias. "How do you feel?"

"Bushed."

Tobias nodded in understanding. "You did one hell of a job, Joe." Dover wondered how the man measured success. Three agents and a Marine pilot dead, a twenty-million-dollar aircraft scattered along the bottom of the Black Sea, and two out of three film discs ruined, assuming the salt water had penetrated the tape wrapped around the second disc. It had.

"We got one good set of pictures, Joe. Invaluable."

Dover felt his left eye socket. The eye-camera was missing. Tobias put him at his ease.

"It's still down in the photo lab; we'll have it back to you later today."

Dover allowed his good eye to wander beyond the figure in front of him and recognized the white-painted bulkheads and exposed overhead piping of a ship's sick bay. An inverted bottle of colorless liquid hung from a chrome arm over his head, dripping its contents down and into a vein in the back of his left hand by way of a needle held in place with white surgical tape. His leg pained him and he inadvertently touched the fresh bandage. It was bulky but dry.

"You're lucky," said Tobias. "It's a flesh wound, but you lost a lot of blood. We'll fill you full of glucose and steak for a couple days and you'll be good as new."

"How'd you get here?" asked Dover.

"Air Force ride to Ankara, caught the ship at Samsun before she sailed. We've been out here since the fourteenth, waiting for Mikhail's call."

It was difficult to talk while prone. "Raise the bed, will you?"

Tobias cranked the handle at the foot of the bed until Dover stopped him with a raised hand.

"Charlie Kiger bought it getting me to the Kerch Peninsula."

Dover's announcement caught Tobias off guard. His cheerful attitude disappeared. " How'd it happen?"

Dover filled him in on the incident with the patrol boat.

Tobias nodded. "Maybe just as well. He's had a hell of a time. I almost pulled him several times. Too anxious to kill. Goes back to his wife . . . "

"He told me"

"I've never known a man, particularly an agent, to carry such hate for so long. Well, what's done, is done."

"I owe my life to the Marine, too. We paid a high price for this one."

"Yes. He'd worked with us before."

"They have Marie."

"I know. We got word from Yuri. It's all part of the game."

"Shitty game."

"Joe, the pictures you managed to bring back will tell us a lot. I've already seen the proofs. They cost us three—maybe four—valuable and precious lives. Marie is special to me, too. Just be thankful you made it out. That's quite an accomplishment in itself."

"I was lucky."

"No, you were good, and you were working with good people."

Dover knew he agreed with the latter part of that statement at least. Still, even good people are lost at times. "Masconi?" he suddenly asked. "How is she?"

"Fine. She'll be flattered you remembered."

"Hell, she saved my life with that scream. I told you that gorilla in the hospital knew about all this."

"No, Joe, he didn't. We got a make on him later. He was an East German agent. They got wind of the eye-camera when word leaked out of the Kodak lab about the film discs. They were able to trace the operation to Bethesda and made a play to get the one we gave you. They had no idea what you were being assigned to do."

"Then, how come that bastard caught up with me at Volgograd?"

"He was smart at addition. You know, two plus two equals four. Yuri alerted us to the fact that Marie had been taken into custody, so we knew they would realize the man she came in with was not the man she was leaving with. All it took was some good deductive reasoning to follow you to Moscow. I don't know how they figured you from there, but they're thorough when an operation concerns such a sensitive issue as the Alpha Bug."

"I still say they got wind of it back at Bethesda. I've seen better security in my day."

"No. We're sure you were not compromised there. Look,

all of the medical team were cleared for Top Secret. Masconi and her relief nurse were both our people. We had a single Marine on guard only because a greater show of security might have aroused questions among the regular hospital personnel. We kept all other patients off your floor. The leak was back at Kodak. You were just the body with the eye in it.''

"I don't know. They seemed ready for me. I barely made it out of Leningrad. The KGB puke showed up hot on my heels at Volgograd. Someone knew about the Harrier pickup. Otherwise, how come we were fired on and lost the Marine jock?"

"My guess it was another innocent happenstance. I suspect air defense radar picked up the Harrier enroute and it was a simple matter to correlate it with their own airborne traffic. Alert a coastal defense unit and they were johnny-on-the-spot. If—*if*—they had advance knowledge of the rendezvous point, they would have been waiting for you, not arrived too late.''

"I suppose that's a possibility, but the Harrier came in right on the deck, below their radar.''

"Did it? How do we know their specific capabilities in that area? Maybe they've got some look-down stuff? Maybe they have visual observers at sea—in fishing boats, for example. We're beating a dead horse, Joe.'' Tobias's face was very sober.

Dover had to agree. It was of no consequence now, in any event. He was safe. "I guess I'm paranoid. This has been a first for me. I'm not sure I'm cut out for this kind of work.''

"Hey, listen, I'll say it again. You did great. Leave the security questions to us. We'll review the whole operation in due time. You've got your own areas of expertise, Joe.'' His grin returned. "You're quite a one-eyed fighter jock, still. We watched you nail the Flagon.''

"Just shows what stark terror can do.''

"I know the feeling. Look, I should leave you alone for a while. Get some rest. One of the corpsmen will bring you some chow. You need to get your strength back.''

"Corpsmen? Aren't we on the freighter?''

"Yes, but we contract for an undercover Navy crew to man it. Incidentally, this sick bay's five levels down, under a false hold deck. We have a whole operations complex down here."

Five levels down. No wonder the shaft vibrations shook the bed.

Tobias poured himself water from the bedside table and pulled up a chair. "I better make arrangements to get Yuri out. He got word to us about what happened. The KGB has too good a dossier on him, especially after you wasted those two in his office."

"He's ready, I'm sure."

"What do you think about the Alpha Bug?"

"Shit, it's everything General Shyrr thinks it is—and maybe more."

Tobias drained his glass and poured another. "Eight a day—keeps the system flushed. Do you think we could get another man in, maybe to foul up a few birds?"

"No way, in my opinion. After my penetrating their assembly area, I suspect they've increased their security even more. They may put two and two together and come up with Mikhail also."

"I've been thinking about that. He's been getting us some good stuff. In fact, he was our first agent to pick up on this thing. Damn, I'd hate to lose him, too. He's native born."

"Well, he's good."

"So was Charlie Kiger. And Marie. Listen, don't feel too badly about Marie. She knew the risks."

Dover could hardly believe Tobias's apparently detached attitude. "For Christ's sake, we made love, maybe real love. Things might have worked out with us. They raped her and they still have her and I'm not supposed to feel too badly?"

Tobias stood. "I'm sorry. Truly. Get some rest."

Dover ate and slept, waking only when they changed the intravenous bottle. A full day passed before he felt strong enough to walk around the compartment. His leg supported him with some discomfort but he helped it with a makeshift cane. Tobias dropped in and returned the eye-camera. Dover had become accustomed to its feel and immediately replaced it. Tobias also left a set of the Alpha Bug prints. They were much clearer than Dover imagined they would be, particularly when he considered the magnification from two-millimeter square negatives to seven-inch prints. The instrument dials were all readable and the markings on the panels clearly legible. Even the console switches and knobs were identifiable.

In the late afternoon, Tobias returned. "We'll be in the Med by the day after tomorrow and you and I will be leaving the ship that morning. We're rendezvousing with a Sixth Fleet battle group and they'll send over a chopper for us. It'll take us to the carrier and from there we'll grab a COD flight to Naples. Commercial back to D.C., and you'll continue on to Colorado Springs. Here's your passport."

He laid it on the bed and Dover was relieved to see that it was in his own name. "I take it my services are no longer required."

"Not by us. You report back to the Joint Space Command. They'll want to debrief you and go over the pictures with you at least. I'm having copies run off. After that, who knows? Maybe by the end of the week you'll be back on the western slope of the Rockies shoveling cowshit or whatever you gentlemen-ranchers do."

"It sure beats hell out of what you people do for a living."

Tobias laughed. "I guess so." He turned to leave.

"Alex . . . I'm really sorry about Marie and Charlie Kiger. I wish to hell I could have done something to prevent it."

Tobias looked back. "It's on my shoulders, Joe. Don't let it climb onto yours. We may yet see Marie. It's not over."

The next day, Dover felt strong enough to go up on deck and talked one of the corpsmen into helping him up the five decks of ladders. By the time they'd reached the last one, he had developed an ingenious hop that enabled him to climb by himself. The *Marmara Denizi* was passing through the Bosphorus and he leaned on the lifeline and watched the busy port activities as they passed close aboard Istanbul. With a delicious sense of deception, he even waved at the Soviet seamen manning the main deck of a passing cruiser. One of the *Kara*-class guided missile ships, it rode low and swiftly through the water, its twin gas-turbines capable of accelerating it quickly to 34 knots should the need arise. The towering superstructure, reminiscent of the World War II Japanese combatants, ran almost two-thirds of the length of the hull and bristled with scores of antennas to direct its formidable weapons toward an enemy, even if he lay beyond the horizon. Two sets of surface and air search radars topped the electronic masts, identical in their configuration. Backup for battle damage, or redundancy for equipment failure? Whatever the case, the deadly cruiser represented the latest in Soviet naval thought. Dover couldn't help but compare it to its American counterparts, which with their sanitized box-like superstructures and economical sets of weapons, seemed to sail nude in contrast to the awesome Soviet ships. But as he watched the warship fall astern, he thought of it with respect to the Alpha Bug: the sea surface combatant was a swimming dinosaur, doomed to extinction by some future catastrophe just as its reptilian predecessors had been, and the Alpha Bug could very well play the key role in that final conflagration.

His thoughts were sharply shattered by the blare of the freighter's deck speakers, "Commander Dover . . . dial 143 . . . Commander Dover . . . dial 143."

The nearest hatch was only a few feet away and he hobbled through it. The short passageway led to several staterooms, and after knocking he entered the nearest. It was empty but he surmised the occupant wouldn't begrudge him the use of the phone. He dialed the number and immediately it was answered.

"Joe?"

"Yes."

"Tobias. Where are you?"

"On the 02 level, aft. Stateroom 203."

"Wait there. I'll be right up."

If Tobias had been seven levels down, he must have been catapulted upward for he appeared in less than two minutes.

"We just received this from the Kennedy Space Center," he said, stooping to enter the compartment and holding out a flimsy dispatch copy.

Dover took it and read:

ACTION CMDR DOVER X PROCEED KENNEDY SPACE CENTER UPON
ARRIVAL DULLES X STAFF T-39 WILL BE STANDING BY AT MIL-
ITARY GATE X MACFAY SENDS BT

Dover glanced up at Tobias. "What's this all about?"

"Haven't the slightest."

"Is this the first contact you've had with the center?"

"Yes. We did send word to Space Command that you had
been recovered."

"Maybe Shyrr is at the Cape and wants to see the pictures
soonest . . ."

"Maybe."

Dover made his way back out on deck with Tobias tagging
his rear. They stood by the lifeline watching the passing sea
traffic.

"You know," muttered Dover, "I'm really not cut out for
all this. If they've got another assignment for me . . . I don't
know."

"Well, we have no call on you. I would suspect it's just a
debrief of some kind. You can expect that, certainly."

"But you said I'm on my way back to the Springs."

"That was the word I left with. Obviously, there's been a
change."

"Obviously."

The next day, the Sikorsky SH-3D arrived on schedule
and transported Dover and Tobias to the USS *Carl Vinson*.
The gigantic nuclear powered carrier had a twin-engined
Grumman Greyhound turning up on its flight deck and
the sleek turboprop delivered them to Naples within two
hours.

At 9:00 P.M., they stepped off their Pan American flight
to Dulles after a long day chasing the sun westward across
Europe and the Atlantic.

Dr. Anderson met them at the airport.

"This is a surprise," observed Dover as Tobias and the
doctor led him aside.

"You won't need the eye-camera, Joe," said Tobias. "Doc
Anderson has a replacement for it."

215

The ever-rumpled Anderson produced an artificial eye matching the eye-camera in iris color and with an identical rear hemisphere full of power components. "At least you get something out of all this: the most sophisticated eye prosthesis in existence. You can change here in the men's room if you like."

Dover entered an empty stall and switched the eyes, pausing to examine the new one in the mirror over the wash basins before rejoining the others. It matched, had the same synchronized movement, and the iris moved with his own.

As he rejoined the others, Tobias was handing his baggage tags to a uniformed Air Force sergeant who hurried off.

"He'll get your bags and see they get on the T-39. Come on, we'll walk you to your gate." said Tobias.

As they walked, Dover felt he had to ask, "Alex, am I going to get a call every time you folks get an itch for a one-eyed agent?"

Tobias shook his head. "You're off the hook. We'll punch out an eye of one of our people." He grinned broadly before becoming serious. "We just didn't have the space expertise this time. That's all."

When they reached the military gate, they silently shook hands and Dover hurried out to the waiting Saberliner. They blasted off into the night and Dover was asleep before the pilot had the wheels tucked in their wells. He had already been in transit for over 14 hours and he had an uneasy feeling that his day was far from being over. He didn't move until the less-than-perfect landing jarred him awake as they touched down at Patrick Air Force Base.

The Operations Duty Officer was waiting with a sedan and driver. Within minutes, Dover was back in the familiar environment of the space center as they entered adjacent to the huge Industrial Area and crossed over the Banana River.

Far off to the left, in the darkness on the edge of the Atlantic Ocean, sat launch complexes 39-Alpha and 39-Bravo, the latter his departure point on the ill-fated *Columbia* mission. Despite his agitation at being diverted to the Center for some as yet unknown purpose, he felt welcome and at home amid the cluster of modern space-oriented buildings and distant rows of launch pads stretching for 25 miles along the adjacent beaches. Here he had departed planet Earth and whirled around the spinning globe in the infinitely larger world of space, enjoying the special camaraderie of the men who rode the thunder and traveled in the infallible grip of irrevocable laws of gravitation and energy. As they had circled the fragile blue and white planet of their birth, Dover had secretly found his spiritual self, and there had been times as he hung above Creation when he had almost touched the hand of his creator. But, from the day of his medical release until this moment, he had temporarily forgotten how precious those days had been. The sedan reached the east bank of the river and turned south amid the support buildings. The sight of the moonlit lowland sand and the great expanse of concrete that all but covered the seaward strip of land known as the Cape Canaveral Air Force Station, along with the recall of his flights into space, brought a swell of moisture from his tear duct. Embarrassed, he wiped the droplet away.

Five minutes later, they made another right turn and stopped in front of the Command control building. Brian Macfay was waiting.

"By God, Joe, you did it! Where are the pictures?"

Dover handed him the sealed envelope and followed him inside. They commandeered an empty office and sat on the couch. Macfay continued to talk while he opened the envelope and spread the prints before them on the coffee table.

He studied each one, laying it aside as he went to the next. "Fantastic . . . clear as a bell. These answer a lot of questions." He finished his examinations, and leaned back on the couch. "Joe, this is the goddamnedest thing I've ever been involved in. I thought sending you into Russia with that eye-camera was an incredible gamble. It paid off, obviously. But—and you may hate me for saying this—it may have been only part of your mission, maybe even the easiest part."

Dover didn't want to believe what he was hearing. "You're leading up to something I'm not sure I'm going to like, aren't you?"

"I don't know how you're going to like it. You weren't too enthused before." Macfay seemed to be searching for just

217

the right words. "Joe, we may have a better source of information about the Alpha Bug than your pictures."

"What do you mean?"

"The spacecraft, itself. How would you like to fly the son of a bitch?"

Dover was not certain he had heard correctly. "Fly?"

Macfay nodded. "Yes, bring it back to earth. Do you think you could do it?"

Dover slowly realized that Macfay was quite serious, and in his office as key operations authority in the United States Space Command was not asking a question, but making a proposal, one so fantastic in its implications that Dover could see no possibility as to how it might happen.

"I don't know," he answered.

Macfay thumbed through the prints one more time. "You sat in it. You studied the layout. You must have imagined how it would be to fly it."

"Certainly. But that was a bit of fantasy. Obviously, I compared it to the *Columbia*. That was part of the mission."

Macfay again nodded, as if reassuring himself of some previous decision.

"Joe, on the fourth the Soviets launched another Kosmolyot II, that's their designation of the Alpha Bug—and apparently recovered the other one. This latest one duplicated the first's orbital flight program, until the nineteenth. We're not sure what, but something went wrong on one of their burns. The Kosmolyot II entered an orbital plane-change maneuver and wound up in an orbit identical to our Kennedy launches. That's well beyond the limitations imposed by their launch area at their Northern Cosmodrome which is 2,000 miles farther north. But, somehow, they did it. That's one of the mysteries of the power and control capabilities of the vehicle. However, something went wrong. The Kosmolyot II has remained in that orbit ever since. There have been no communications and no telemetry that we've been able to detect, and we can't figure out any reason for them remaining in that orbit for this length of time, unless there's some operational requirement we don't know about. That's a possibility, but we have concluded something else. We think they may have a dead bird, or an incapacitated cosmonaut.''

Dover sat stunned. Macfay's proposal was based on a very real situation. ''That's possible. A complete power loss would keep them from bringing it back, but that's very unlikely.''

''Right. We operate within a technology whose second name is backup systems. Losing everything at once would be almost inconceivable,'' said Macfay.

'' But not impossible.''

''No.''

''Still, if they've lost control, it has to be one of two things: complete power loss or the cosmonaut has done something he can't reverse.''

''There's a third if you consider those two as separate. He may be unconscious, or dead,'' said Macfay.

''How would that happen?''

''Hell, I don't know, but we have every indication that no one has any control over the damn thing.''

''They could have lost their remote control mode,'' suggested Dover.

''Then, why doesn't the pilot bring it back?''

Dover had to admit that it was a perplexing situation. ''Are you sure you're not just reaching, Brian? The pilot may still bring it back.''

''Unless he's actually incapacitated, like I said at the beginning. He's not talking to anyone, and the black boxes aren't sending any information back.''

''Maybe we just aren't getting the transmissions.''

''Bullshit! We'd be picking up something.''

''All right, I'll concede for the moment. How's that going to put me back in space? And I already don't like the answer I think you're going to give. You've already started something rolling, haven't you?''

''We had to, Joe. If we're going to act, it has to be now. General Shyrr is in D.C., conferring with the Joint Chiefs. We think the problem is with the cosmonaut. Something's happened to him while he was in manual override . . . ''

''*What* happened to him, Brian? Hell, if he were incapacitated, the machine would still be sending back life-support monitoring data. If there is anything wrong, it'd have to be a complete power failure for everything to stop. And if that's the case, there's no way anyone can bring it back.''

''Hold on. You forget that the Kosmolyot II is a military spacecraft. The luxuries we're accustomed to in development vehicles, even the shuttles, such as life-monitoring equipment, could be waived for more operational capability. That's a logical assumption, wouldn't you say?''

''That's all it is—an assumption.''

''Let me finish. Shyrr is briefing the Joint Chiefs. If he can convince them, they'll go to the President; for obvious reasons they'll have to on this. If we get his go-ahead—and the old bastard jumps at every chance he gets to pull the Soviet's short hairs—we go get it.''

Dover's reaction was a mixed bag of enthusiasm and trepidation. It would be an ultimate challenge for him, but the big unknown in his mind was the Soviet reaction. For the moment, that was a very overriding concern. ''That's a Soviet military space machine. You think they're going to stand by and even let us approach it without raising holy hell, or worse? And that's assuming we have a ghost of a chance in reaching it, and I go out of my frigging mind and join you crazies in all this.''

''The Kosmolyot II is in free space, like international waters. The Space Treaty says as much. If it were one of their nuclear submarines adrift on the open sea, with a dead crew, don't you think we'd be going for it? The Russians can't recover it, because they can't reach that orbit—we barely can out of Canaveral. Unless, of course, they send up another Alpha Bug, but they won't risk that until they know what's wrong with this one. Joe, we can launch into that orbit, and there's a window coming up at dawn the day after tomorrow.''

''All right, for the sake of placating a madman, I'll accept your premise. How do you get me to it?''

''The *Valley Forge* is sitting on 39-Alpha. It's dedicated to the military program and we've had it there, evaluating readiness requirements for some time. It has an experienced crew and we can set the remainder of the countdown in motion as soon as we get the President's okay.''

"The remainder of the countdown?"

"Well, we've already done a few things, just in case."

"So, we blast off and effect a rendezvous. What then?"

"You strap on a manned maneuvering unit and take a look-see."

"And our comrade cosmonaut takes a dim view of our big nose and puts a laser through the *Valley Forge*. The United States and the Soviet Union go to DEFCON I, and I become the first human in free orbit . . . which under those circumstances might make me the last surviving earthperson. But, frankly, I'm not sure my flight pay obligates me to all this."

"No, if the cosmonaut's on board, and still has control, he'll move away. Far away, rather than risk compromise of the spacecraft."

"My God, it's already compromised, and we've got the pictures to prove it, and the Soviets have three dead KGB operators and one less small boat crew to remind them of it."

"A picture's worth a thousand words, Joe, but the real thing's worth a thousand pictures. We need to study that propulsion and weapons technology. The pictures just give us— excuse me, give you—an idea of how to operate them. From what I can see, the Kosmolyot II is exactly what we thought it was, an anti-ballistic missile weapons platform. Unless we can match it, or negate it, the edge goes to the Soviets, and the ball game could be over."

"Am I going to be ordered to do this?"

"Will you have to be?"

Dover knew he wouldn't. He was becoming as enthused about the possibilities as Macfay. "No, not if the President goes along with it. But it looks to me like we'll be pulling the bear's tail on this for sure."

"No doubt about that. He'll rear up and growl like we've got him by the balls, which is more the case. But we claim our motives are humanitarian. They couldn't rescue their cosmonaut, so we tried. After we examine the Kosmolyot II, we give it back."

"Jesus, Brian, they'll never buy that fairy tale."

Macfay shrugged. "Neither would Shyrr. I mentioned it as a cover and he said that if we do it, we call it what it is: a military hijack. The Russians will know it, and we know it. If the President wants to call it something else, that's his prerogative."

"All right, let's get back to basics. I'll need to study the pictures. I got some good hands-on experience sitting in it, but I didn't in my wildest imagination figure on flying it. My lack of depth perception won't be a problem since it comes down by chute, and everything else I do by watching the gauges. But, I'll need some deorbit data. The computers are programmed in Russian and I wouldn't have the faintest idea of how to take advantage of them. I could wind up on my way out of the galaxy with the power that thing must have."

"We're already on it. I have a crew preparing reentry figures. The cosmonaut undoubtedly has his own manual check list. All you'll have to do is adjust it for a landing in the Pacific. It has flotation bags, doesn't it?"

"It has ground cushion bags and it's certainly watertight. I don't know if it'll float upright or not, but there's a decent chance it will. I would think they would have given it that emergency capability since it's a military machine."

"Too bad it doesn't have a landing gear. We could shoot for Edwards."

"Not with me on board. A one-eyed four-hundred-knot touchdown is not my style, and the sink rate of that thing would make the *Columbia* look like a high performance sailplane."

Macfay placed the pictures back in the envelope. "I'll have some blow-ups made for you right away. We've got plenty to do. How's the leg?"

"Stiff, but it'll be okay."

"I'll alert the therapy people and have someone standing by whenever you can work in a session."

"I'll need an update on the MMU. Any changes?"

"No, it'll be the same type you had along on 41-Mike.

222

The training harness will be available whenever you want it."

"The *Valley Forge;* any differences I should be aware of?"

"No. For the insertion and rendezvous, you'll be a passenger. Besides, it's practically identical to the other five shuttles. There are some military avionics and sensing devices, but they'll be of no concern to you. We've an empty cargo bay so your egress won't be any problem. You'll ride the mission specialist's seat."

"You seem to have this thing pretty well thought out."

"Hell, Shyrr came up with the first thought. It seemed like a natural to me so I started kicking a few asses to get a head start. We knew that you'd been picked up and weren't in too bad a shape. Everything just seemed to fall into place. It's kismet, Joe."

"Suicide is the word that comes to mind."

"Hey, you're bubbling inside about this, just like I am. We've been hitting the space program twenty-five hours a day for most of our careers. Admit it, this could be the coup of all coups. And it's been dropped right into our laps by that same fickle finger of fate that's massaged our rectums for these many years. God, I wish it could be me."

"So do I . . . but right now I need some sleep. Okay?"

At nine the next morning, Dover was soaking his leg in the whirlpool at the Space Medicine therapy room, letting the swirling hot water combat the stiffness.

Macfay came through the door at a fast walk, and after checking to insure that the therapist was out of earshot, gleefully announced, "It's a go. Shyrr just called. The President says it's a go. We launch at dawn tomorrow."

Dover knew that he should feel good and wondered why he didn't. It had taken him most of the sleepless night to convince himself that the Alpha Bug could be reached and boarded, and probably brought back. He had even recognized that if it could, he was the logical choice to do it. Yet, when he heard Macfay's words, he suffered a letdown. Once before he had experienced such a depression, on the evening before his first shuttle flight. All the hoopla was over, and he and the other crewmen had trained until they had peaked. Then the thrill just died. They ate dinner like other mortals, turned in for a few hours rest, and walked out to the spacecraft almost ignored by the busy groundcrew. As on that night, the fun was over. The ride was about to begin.

"We'll brief at seven this evening, Joe. The crew will get their final briefing an hour later; no use putting you through all of the flight profile data. Breakfast at 0230. I've had the photolab boys make you up some poster-sized reproduction of the Alpha Bug pictures and you can use what time you need to study the panels. What say we get together late this afternoon in the event you come up with any new ideas? General Shyrr will arrive here at 1400 and I'll fill him in; he may want to attend the briefing. In fact, he probably will. Anything we've left undone?"

Dover removed his leg from the stainless steel tub and tested his weight on it. "No, I'll get in one more session on the MMU trainer after I leave here."

"Okay, I'll see you at seven, if not before. We'll brief right in your room so you can get comfortable early."

Dover spent the next half-hour in the manned-maneuvering-unit trainer, readjusting to the sensitivities of the delicate jet thrusters he would use to approach the Kosmolyot II. Macfay had arranged for lunch to be brought to his room and he ate while studying the enlargements pinned to the wall. He had made mental dry-runs of the probable deorbit procedures for over two hours when Macfay stuck his head in the door.

"Everything's on schedule. The bird will be ready. You want to get together with the crew after the briefing?"

"I think the rest would be more beneficial. Who's the mission commander?"

"Major Bob Ortega. He's got two *Valley Forge* flights under his belt, one from Vandenberg and one from here."

"I remember meeting him; don't know him well."

"You know the payload specialist . . . "

"Who's that?"

Macfay's grin reached for his ears. "Me!"

Dover shook his head. "No wonder you've been on a two-dollar high. I thought we weren't going to have a payload."

"You don't. That's why I could talk Shyrr into letting me ride the empty seat. Besides, in a manner of speaking, you're the payload, and who knows your bad habits better than I? Actually, since this thing could get a bit sticky, the General feels it might not hurt to have a member of his staff on board. See you at seven?"

"I'll be right here."

After Macfay left, one of the NASA team dropped by and left the orbital data they had compiled on the Kosmolyot II. They had some preliminary deorbit figures, but pointed out that they had to use the *Valley Forge's* specifics to make the calculations. Dover needed the thrust and weight figures for the Alpha Bug, but was fairly confident the cosmonaut would have the data on a cue card, otherwise he wouldn't have had full manual capability for deorbit and landing. If they weren't on board, Dover could use the *Valley Forge* computations as a basis for a by-guess-and-by-God deorbit burn, but he'd have little if any control over where he'd touch down.

He showered and shaved after dinner and Macfay ushered in the General at seven.

"Good to see you, Joe," greeted Shyrr. "You've been a busy man since we last talked."

"Yes, sir, I have, and I guess I still have a ways to go."

"That you do. The President asked me to remember him to you. He's quite enthused about this mission. I hope you don't mind my sending Brian along. We're treading on thin political ice, you know."

"I would suspect the military ice is a bit thin, also," commented Dover.

"Let's hope not. We've given this a lot of thought, and feel the risk is manageable. Any other overriding concerns?"

"I have a philosophy, General. I have my misgivings before the decisions are made. Afterward, I just concern myself with carrying them out. Of course, if I were wearing your hat, I suspect it wouldn't be so simple.''

"I'm glad you recognize that. Brian?''

Macfay opened a folder and briefed from its contents. "Lift-off is set for 0515. Initial orbital altitude is 200 miles. It'll take you eleven orbits to get into position and be on the daylight side—that's about 17 hours and 16 minutes. The *Valley Forge* will burn up to 250 miles just before the rendezvous; the Kosmolyot II should be about 10 miles ahead, and Major Ortega will put you next to it. You'll have a spacewalk of 30-40 yards in the MMU, and your first task will be to ascertain the condition of the cosmonaut. If he's incapacitated, regardless of the condition of the spacecraft, see if you can get him out and bring him back to the *Valley Forge.*''

"I may not be able to reach him while strapped into the MMU.''

"We've equipped it with a couple of magnetic tethers; had them put on for this flight. Just be sure they're solid against the spacecraft before you start fooling with the hatch.''

"You can put money down on that.''

"You've got a six-hour limitation in your time to determine the condition of the spacecraft and deorbit down to the atmosphere. That's been taken into consideration when we planned the flight profile, and you have a three-hour safety margin. Your present burn goal for out-of-orbit is three hours after you leave the *Valley Forge,* if you're right on schedule. Now, we're assuming your spacesuit life-support system is not compatible with that on the Kosmolyot II, but we're giving you one of the umbilical adapters we developed for Spacelab 5. If it does happen to fit, it'll eliminate one of the pucker factors. Of course, if you can pressurize, you can go off your suit supply until you deorbit.''

"Where am I coming down?''

"In the Pacific, 1,650 miles south of Oahu, just north of the equator. We've got the nuclear guided-missile cruiser, *Virgina,* with two *Kidd*-class destroyers returning from a joint exercise off New Zealand. We've diverted them to your splashdown area."

"Have they ever participated in recovery before?" asked Dover.

"No, not the ships. They may have some experienced personnel on board from the old Apollo days, but that would be unlikely. It really makes little difference; their main job will be to keep the Kosmolyot II afloat until we can salvage it. They can do a good job and they have the radar capability to pick you up almost out of blackout."

"What if the Kosmolyot II is a dead bird?" asked Dover.

"Get as many pictures as you can, spend as much time as you can looking it over. Then, come on back to the *Valley Forge.*"

"You know, I'm going to feel silly as hell if I knock on that hatch and there's nothing wrong."

"No danger of that. If we start getting too close, we'll be warned away if the cosmonaut's okay. I would think he could communicate with us on the international distress frequency. And, like I said, if everything's okay, he'll not let us get close."

Dover still had some reservations. "I wish we knew how uptight the Soviets are going to get over this."

Shyrr spoke up, "As soon as you're in orbit, the President is going to inform them that we've started a rescue mission. He's taken personal responsibility and anytime he thinks we're getting in too deep, he'll call it off. But, he has some pretty reliable information that something definitely went wrong on that last burn, and they can't bring it back."

"You know," said Dover thoughtfully, "since it is a military vehicle, there's a chance it may have a destruct system to keep it from falling into the wrong hands."

"I doubt it," replied Macfay. "Of course, we may not know until you crack open that hatch, so it's worth further thought. Did you see any indication of one?"

"No, but then I wasn't looking. I'd hate to find out the

hard way. Incidentally, has anyone been able to come up with a more definitive analysis of the weapon system?''

''Yes,'' responded Macfay, ''we believe it carries a five-megawatt chemical laser. Your comments about the collapsible mirror on the ones at Volgograd support that; plus, the weapons console instrumentation is pretty indicative. A five-megawatt beam would require a 13-foot dish mirror and could have a range of 4,000 miles in space—perfect for standoff ICBM use. The Kosmolyot II may carry enough chemical fuel for its laser to destroy several hundred targets.''

''My God, are we that far behind?''

''Well, we have weapons on the drawing board—satellites—that can do that as far as fuel capacity and load requirements go. But we don't have the beam technology yet. They've always expended more effort on lasers and particle-beam weapons than we have. It's apparently paid off. It looks like they've pulled another Sputnik on us,'' observed Macfay.

Shyrr rocked back in his chair. ''We all three know what the Kosmolyot II may mean, although it could be just a test vehicle. I personally feel they are either operational, however, or damned close. There were too many of them in that hangar. And I'm sure we all know the risks we are taking, including your personal risk, Joe. If it weren't for the fact that we have someone like you—call it fate if you will—who's almost a native with the language and has some working knowledge of Soviet space technology, we couldn't even begin to think about bringing that spacecraft back. Even so, we may be extending ourselves beyond our capabilities. And I think we have to very seriously consider that possibility. The President stressed that in the final analysis it's actually up to you, Joe. That's why I came with Brian this evening. I'm ready to assume the responsibility of ordering you to do this, knowing full well that in a day's time you may be a very dead man. That's the nature of our profession. But, I want you to tell me if you think the odds are too stacked against us. You're the only one who can put together all of the unknowns in this.''

"I'm not much on odds, General. But I'll tell you this: I think that if it can be done, I can do it. I'll admit that at first I thought you folks were out of your gourds, but as I've looked at it, and reasoned with the possibilities, I say we go. If there's power in that thing, and its flight integrity is intact, I'll bring it down. I don't like the political aspects, but as a military mission, I can't fault it. I think Brian put it best a bit earlier when he said that everything was just falling into place. Maybe the gods are with us; I just hope they aren't the gods of war.''

"That's what the President gets paid for—to decide the overall risk,'' said Shyrr.

Macfay started for the door. "The final countdown starts at midnight, Joe. The handover/egress crew will board at that time and have everything ready for the flight crew when you board at 0325. Any questions?''

"No. This is a long way since we were riding the steam off the old *Enterprise*, eh, Brian?''

Dover's question brought back their days together when Lt. Macfay was leading Lt. (j.g.) Dover around by the hand as they flew F-4's off the Navy's first nuke birdfarm.

"We were hot shit in those days, Joe.''

"Well, we're about to see if we've still got it, Brian.'' Macfay held out his hand. "Navy all the way.''

"You better believe it, flyboy.''

"See you at breakfast.''

229

Chapter
14

General Colonel Koidunov studied each of the five main consoles responsible for the overall monitoring of the Kosmolyot II. The life support systems and the power systems indications were all normal. The onboard computer banks were continuing to track the spaceplane in orbit. But for five hours there had been no change in attitude nor had there been any communications from Major Bykovsky. There were absolutely no signals coming from the cabin that reflected a conscientious human input. At the moment, the spaceplane was on a northeasterly course across the North Atlantic.

He spoke to his son at the main communications console. "What was his last transmission?"

"When he spoke to me just after I cleared him to go to manual control."

"What did he say?"

The younger Koidunov looked up at his father. "It was a personal message. He asked me if I were envious of him."

"Nothing operational?"

"No."

"We've checked all of our stations for any communications?"

"Yes. Nothing."

"Was there anything irregular about his last orbital-plane change?"

"No, Father. It was executed flawlessly as has been every aspect of the flight."

"I don't see how all of his communications could have failed."

"I do not think it could be that. All power systems indicate normal. His main electrical supply shows the proper power."

"Then, we must take over. Whatever is wrong may be affecting his ability to deorbit. Have we tried to rotate the spaceplane around any to check and see if we can use our remote override system?"

"Several times. Nothing responds and we get no indication that we are overriding his manual mode."

"That's impossible. We have used the system continually throughout all of the previous tests."

The son could only shrug. "I don't understand it at all."

"Could he be in manual override?"

"He shouldn't be. There is no light. See?" The son pointed to a system of condition lights aligned across the top of the control console to his right. The one marked MANUAL OVERRIDE was dark. *Wait! All of the indicator lights were dark.* Andrian had to be using *some* mode. The younger Koidunov vigorously shook his finger at the row of indicator lights and called to the controller, "Sergei! Test your indicator lights immediately!"

The major manning the console replied with a startled look and a rapid pushing of the lens covers of each light. As he did so, each individual light momentarily came on until he came to the one over the MANUAL OVERRIDE decal. It remained dark. Quickly he lifted the lens and inserted a replacement bulb. It immediately lit up bright red.

"Stupid!" roared the General. "Have you been sleeping? Have not you been monitoring your panel? An idiot

231

should recognize that all lights out indicate that *something* is wrong. Leave the console. You are relieved of any further responsibility and will confine yourself to the rest lounge. I will speak with you later.''

"But comrade General Colonel, everything else was normal. It must have just gone out while I was checking my other readings.''

"Normal? Everything is normal? Everything except that we can't talk to our cosmonaut—is that normal?'' Koidunov's hair bristled as he impatiently waved the hapless officer away from the panel.

"Why in the name of Peter would he be in manual override? That is his combat position,'' wondered the younger Koidunov aloud.

"But even that fails to explain the lack of communications.''

"He has not instituted his lost communications procedure, either. All that requires is an input to his master computer and we can use telemetry to communicate. I tried querying the system earlier with no reply.''

"Something is seriously wrong, Vladimir. Andrian is too good a technician not to be able to react to such a situation and come up with something. Turn your station over to a relief and come with me. We need to have a conference with the Mission Director. Where is he?''

"He is already in the conference room going over the situation with Chibovitch and Mironenko. They are the duty power system technicians.''

It took only a moment for Vladimir to summon and brief his relief. He had to trot in order to catch up with his father who was stalking toward the conference room practically breathing fire and smoke. They entered the conference room and sat at the table with the other three key personnel. General Koidunov wasted no time in taking charge. "I should have been called several hours ago. What have you decided?''

"We think the problem may be with Bykovsky. All of the spacecraft monitors indicate normal operations,'' replied the Mission Director.

"Except he is in manual override rather than in manual," spat out the General.

"That was not reported to me," exclaimed the Mission Director.

The elder Koidunov knew the Mission Director was not at fault for the oversight. Like his son, the man was a qualified cosmonaut and a very capable colonel. "I sent the idiot out of the control center. He had been sitting at his station with no mode indicator light showing."

"Then, the problem does appear to be with Andrian. Why would he be in that position of control and not communicate with us? I can only guess that he is ill although even that does not explain everything," offered Chibovitch.

"Could it be anything political?" asked Mironenko.

General Koidunov's eyebrows raised until they threatened to disappear across the top of his bald head. "Political? What kind of a remark is that?"

"He has always been something of a radical thinker. Even today he used vital communications time for a personal conversation with your—with Colonel Koidunov," continued Mironenko.

"You are an ass," stated General Koidunov, leaning across the table, his face flashing red and his teeth bared as if he were going to bite Mironenko on his red-veined nose. "Andrian is a professional military officer and a Party member. He is also a free spirit, like all our cosmonauts. Occasional levity is a way for them to disperse their anxieties. What do you think he intends to do? Refuse to come down?"

"It is only a thought. If only we had continued to provide the spaceplane with cosmonaut vital signs monitoring beyond the launch phase, we may have had some indication if there is a physical problem. That is the only other possibility."

The General stared at Mironenko. The man was babbling.

"All right," interjected his son, "let us suppose he is ill. What courses of action do we have?"

"We can wait and see if he recovers sufficiently to resume communications," offered Mironenko.

"No," disagreed Chibovitch. "If he is this ill, we must not wait. We must consider recovery."

"How?" asked Mironenko. "He is in manual override. We have no control over him."

Koidunov the Younger had already picked up on Chibovitch's suggestion. "We will go get him!"

The remarks caused several jaws to drop, but not the General's. "Of course," he agreed. "We have the first operational vehicle here, already mated to its booster and sitting on the pad."

"But we have no cosmonauts trained yet," complained Mironenko.

General Koidunov fumed. First, he had endured the stupidity of the controller who had let the crisis develop undetected, and now an unthinking statement from one of the key people who one would think would be aware of the obvious. "What is my son? An orange? Who else will ever be better qualified for just this type of thing?"

Mironenko squirmed. Certainly, he was aware that the rescue cosmonaut was sitting only two feet away. Flustered, he tried to cover his hasty remark with another, equally as ill thought out. "It will take a full day to get the launch team ready."

General Koidunov wanted to break something. He was surrounded by asses. He silenced any further comment with his eyes and a single sentence, "You have five hours."

"I can go immediately," added the younger Koidunov.

The Mission Director held up a hand in caution. "First, we must make certain we do not overlook anything. We not only must strive to get Andrian back, but salvage our Kosmolyot II."

General Koidunov liked the young Tatar Colonel. He was a rarity in the Soviet military, an Islamic descendant of the Mongol horde that had galloped across Russia in the thirteenth century and a highly thought of officer who had overcome many obstacles to gain his present position. He didn't let Koidunov's harsh manner intimidate him, either. A cool thinker. The General also had him marked for better things.

His son was radiating enthusiasm, perhaps from his anticipation of another space flight but more probably an anxiety reflex from his concern for his comrade, Andrian. "Even if he is helpless, Father, I can reset his primary control mode back to the remote position once I reach him. We can bring him back with no difficulty. If only his condition is such that he can survive reentry and recovery." The second thought sobered the lines of his mouth and eyes.

The elder Koidunov nodded. "There is no way for us to know his condition until you rendezvous with him. Even in the worse case, we must recover the spaceplane."

Chibovitch spoke up. "What if the difficulty is with the spaceplane and not Andrian? There is no room for Vladimir to bring him back with him."

"There must be," exclaimed the younger Koidunov, his concern for his friend trying to override what he knew was the truth in Chibovitch's statement. The cabin of the spaceplane might be considered roomy for a single cosmonaut, but much too small for another body, even one without a bulky spacesuit. Every other available square millimeter of space was crammed with irremovable equipment and cells for fuel and chemicals.

"We will do what we have to do," decided the elder Koidunov. His son understood, as did the others. If the difficulty was with the spaceplane and it could not be recovered, it must be destroyed to avoid eventual compromise.

"The ready spaceplane has its weapons system, does it not?" queried General Koidunov.

"Yes, Father. It is a concept weapon with somewhat limited range compared to the operational model, but it is ready and is to be tested when the next launch occurs."

"God keep us from testing it on Andrian," muttered General Koidunov. It was the first time his son had ever heard him invoke divine intervention.

"We must get to him, then," said the Mission Director. "I will alert launch control."

The two subordinates followed the Mission Director out the door. Vladimir rose to leave but was restrained by the hand of his father.

"Wait, Vladimir, we have to talk."

Vladimir retook his seat.

"When you get to Andrian, the difficulty must be with him, not the spaceplane. Understand?"

"Father?"

"We can not afford any type of failure on this final test. We are too close to going operational. If there is something wrong with the spaceplane, it must be a one-of-a-kind thing. Find out what it is; we can correct it on subsequent models. Our tests have been going well. I intend that they remain that way."

"But any problem will be revealed when we recover it."

"No, we are not going to recover it—unless the problem is with Andrian. If we allow any further delays in going operational, both you and I as well as half the personnel in this building will serve the rest of our careers in the very far north."

"Do I understand that if the spacecraft is faulty I am to destroy it?"

"That is correct."

"But I can not do that without killing Andrian."

"One life, Vladimir, even if that life belongs to a treasured friend, is a small price to pay to stop the American plot to attack us."

"We can not stop them with a faulty system."

"The Kosmolyot II has no faults except perhaps a unique one in this individual case."

The younger Koidunov shook his head. "I can not do such a thing."

General Koidunov slumped in his chair and his son became aware that his father had aged appreciably during the past months. Now, with the weight of a terrible decision on his mind, he looked beyond his 68 actual years.

His voice was very soft when he next spoke, like that Vladimir remembered from the days when as a child he sat on his father's lap and listened to delicious stories of gypsies and fairies. "I must tell you a story. Perhaps I should have told you long ago, but I have not wanted to. Forty-five years ago, I was a young captain serving on the outskirts of a small village on the western front. It was our second winter against the Germans and we were being beaten. Not everywhere, mind you, just in my sector. I was fighting from the shelter of a dirt bunker dug beneath the snow, I and only three of my men left from our entire company. I was the only one not wounded. I had an older soldier for my first sergeant, a man who should never have had to fight a war. But we were there, and there was no way we could stop another advance. It was night and we decided we could make a run for it back to the village. We were not cowards. If we could have done any good, we would have stayed and fought to the death. But it was better to save our lives and rejoin the battle where our bullets would count. All except my old sergeant. He was too wounded to walk, much less make the precarious dash across the snow to the protection of the village houses, and if we tried to carry him we would be so slowed that we would not make it either. So I sent the other two on, out into the frigid dark, while I stayed for a few more minutes with the old man. I could not leave him to be captured by the Germans. They did terrible things to our troops, always ending in death, for they did not take Russian prisoners. Also, my sergeant was very familiar with our overall battle plan for the defense of our area and they would break him before taking his life.

"So, I gave him the last of my melted snow which I had in my drinking tin and the last of my biscuits. For over an hour I held the old man in my arms, reluctant to do what I knew I must. Finally, it was time for me to go. In a short while it would be light and I would have been trapped. He knew what I must do. He even leaned forward, grasped my hand, and touched his lips to my fingers as I put a bullet into his head."

"I understand, Father."

"Do you, Vladimir? Do you understand the agony of my choice? That old sergeant, who should have been spending his declining years soaking up the sun and sipping vodka while he and his comrades relived their youth in tall tales about adventure and women, was your grandfather. Just as I had to do with my father, Vladimir, you may have to do with your friend, Andrian, for the simple reason that there may not be any other way."

"I am sorry, Father. I will do what is necessary."

Koidunov grasped his son's hand. "This is for country, my son. Our land has sprung forth in a glorious mission to recover the earth for the workers of the world. We are the well of the revolution which will eventually be the drink of all who toil. If I sound idealistic, I am. Collectively, you and I and all of our comrades mean everything. But by ourselves, as individuals, we are subordinate to the needs of the State. That is the way it must be with soldiers. If we can sincerely lay down our lives for our Motherland, then we must be prepared to lay those of our friends on the same sacrificial stone."

"You are right, of course—if there is nothing else. I must go prepare. I would think that we can be ready to launch as you indicated."

"It is so ordered, Colonel."

The two men embraced and the younger left the room. The older remained standing in the door for a while, then returned to the dimly lit mission control room. The controllers were still at their positions but there was little activity. The spaceplane's red symbol was slowly crawling along its orbital path across the lighted map of the world on the far wall.

General Colonel Koidunov studied the battleground of the future. Limitless space, waiting for the first stain of blood that would forever end the eons of peace that had been its original purpose. The last frontier, the scientists liked to call it. Koidunov knew better; it was the last battleground. All the frontiers had been taken. It had been difficult to tell his son the details of his own father's death.

But he had been waiting years for the right time. Nevertheless, he knew it would not ease the pain that had been a part of him every day since he had squeezed that trigger and his father's hand at the same time.

Who was the American general who said that war was hell? Grant? Well, thought General Colonel Leon Koidunov, peace wasn't one hell of a lot better.

Chapter
15

Joe Dover stepped down from the white transport van, the custom fit of his sky blue flight gear bringing back that familiar feeling of impending adventure. He raised a hand to stifle a wide yawn, embarrassed. He really wasn't all that calm. This time, there was underlying urgency not all could see.

The soft floodlight erased the pre-dawn darkness around the 4,500,000-pound space shuttle assembly and bathed the winged centerpiece as if a giant flashlight had caught some huge winged insect crouched on its hindquarters, protecting its trio of silver elongated eggs. Not eggs of nature, full of potential embryos, but aluminum eggs of man filled with liquid and solid rocket propellants which in a few hours would explode in a masterfully controlled release of almost 6,500,000 pounds of thrust to start the *Valley Forge* on its journey toward the stars.

At its side, under threatening cloud-shrouded skies, stood the skeletal shadow of its launch gantry, its massive height even surpassing that of the waiting spacecraft and booster assembly. Once the eyes adjusted to the contrast of brilliant white and deep shadow, one could see two appendages reaching out to the nose and the left side of the *Valley Forge*. The top one provided stabilization to the 184-foot high shuttle assembly as it quivered in the first gusts of wind from an approaching but still seaward thunderstorm; the other was a covered boarding bridge and led to the open 40-inch diameter crew entry hatch in the nose of the spacecraft.

Occasional streaks of late summer lightning darted among the offshore cumulo-nimbus clouds, which rumbled in response to the sharp releases of electrical energy and dumped curtains of falling rain back into the Atlantic.

Macfay had ridden out in the same van and the two astronauts walked together in silence. It was a walk that each had taken before, many times.

"Lousy night," commented Macfay.

"IFR departure?" kidded Dover.

"We've done it before, partner." Macfay's remark turned Dover's thoughts back to other rainy nights when he had followed the dim signals of a young sailor's fluorescent wands across the wet deck of a heaving aircraft carrier a thousand miles at sea and positioned his heavy fighter atop the catapult shuttle. There was no blackness like that off the bow of such a ship on a stormy night. Then, the powerful launch of the steam catapult. After a few hundred of those, riding a rocket into the sky was a proverbial piece of cake.

They stood for a moment at the bottom of the gantry. The tall beamed tower seemed to reach all the way to the base of the low clouds, and along with the *Valley Forge* and its giant auxiliary fuel cylinder overpowered even the magnificence of the stormy night and filled him with pride and anticipation.

"Whatcha thinking, Joe?" asked Macfay.

"No matter how many times I've seen it before, Brian, or ridden it, it just gets to me."

"I know. All set?"

He joined Macfay and the other two crew members in the elevator and they rode up into the night. As they neared the top, he noticed several thought-provoking differences

241

in the exterior appearance of the military shuttle. The first was the replacement of the impressive NASA on the top of the right wing with a smaller, almost sinister USAF logo. The second was the absence of the familiar UNITED STATES block letters along the lower side of the fuselage and the substitution of UNITED STATES SPACE COMMAND. Forward of the bold designation, instead of the stars and stripes, was the red, white, and blue starred insignia of U.S. air and space forces. As proud as he had always been of his profession as a military officer, the shock of seeing the world's most advanced flying machine, from its inception a symbol of the hope for peace in space, in subtle war paint gave him a sobering there-goes-the-neighborhood feeling.

It disappeared with their arrival at the boarding bridge and he followed the others through the hatch onto the rear bulkhead of the crew compartment's mid-deck. Since the spacecraft sat nose up, the bulkhead was in effect the floor for boarding. From it they climbed onto the flight deck and used the various hand and foot holds to squirm into their seats, strapping themselves into their launch positions. The handover/egress team departed and Ortega, along with his pilot in the right seat, commenced the final phases of the pre-launch checks. The first raindrops were pinging against the skin of the spacecraft.

Dover watched the activities of the crew in silence, but somewhat concerned about the approaching storm. He felt useless as a passenger, while Ortega and the pilot took out their cue cards and made their initial communications calls to Launch Control and Mission Control. Everything proceeded smoothly and the entry hatch was secured by the departing gantry crew. Ortega pressurized the cabin.

About the time the main propulsion system helium was pressurized, the edge of the thunderstorm passed over the southern portion of the Space Center, the peripheral winds swaying the shuttle in an unscheduled test of the firm grip of the gantry. Dover knew that if this were a NASA launch, there would be a weather hold, but an operational military mission couldn't afford one unless the reason was life threatening. The countdown continued.

By T-minus-nine minutes, the winds had diminished and they received a GO for the launch. Dover felt the familiar flush of pre-launch adrenal flow. Ortega started the auxiliary power units, switched to internal power, and checked his hydraulic flight controls.

Right on schedule, the on-board computers started the three main engines and the *Valley Forge* strained at its leash, twanging against the couplings of the main fuel tank, actually moving upward and closer to it by 40 inches under the tremendous thrust of the roaring fires erupting from its tail. It was poised and cocked for liftoff. Three seconds later, the twin solid rocket boosters ignited and 2,225 tons of men and machine started upward into the wet dawn.

General Shyrr watched the *Valley Forge* clear its launch pad and roll into its 120-degree heads-down climb position, riding a thunderous column of white-hot flame and leaving in its wake a thick, twisting burble of white condensation. He remained standing before the bank of television monitors, following the shuttle's mind-boggling acceleration through the low scattered stratus as it began its long climbing arc into space.

Two minutes into its flight, the solid boosters winked out as the last of their fuel burned and they separated outward from their perches on the sides of the main fuel cell. Shyrr nodded in silent encouragement. The *Valley Forge* was searing the atmosphere at four-and-a-half times the speed of sound and already 28 miles above the earth.

A touch on his arm caused him to turn. His aide handed him a message which bore the red stamp, CONFIDENTIAL, and had originated at the Command and Control Center inside NORAD's subterranean spacewatch facility in Colorado:

ADVISE SOVIETS LAUNCHED KOSMOLYOT II SPACE VEHICLE FROM NORTHERN COSMODROME 250618 ZULU X PAYLOAD ENTERED CIRCULAR ORBIT 60 DEGREES INCLINATION 200 MILES ALTITUDE X SYSTEM TRACKING.

Shyrr checked his watch. The Soviets had a five-hour lead over the *Valley Forge*—if they were headed for the stricken Alpha Bug. But their orbital change problem was much more difficult and time consuming. There was still time.

"Shall I have Launch Control relay this to the *Valley Forge*?" asked the aide.

"No," quietly replied Shyrr, "not yet."

Chapter
16

"*Valley Forge*, this is Mission Control. Coming up on OMS-two. Over."

"Roger, OMS-two." The orbital-maneuvering-system engines roared into life for the second time since liftoff and pushed the *Valley Forge* into its circular orbit 200 miles above the earth.

Ortega gave Macfay and Dover a thumbs-up and reported to Mission Control, "OMS-two cut-off. We have achieved orbit. Over."

Dover unbuckled his seat harness and floated forward to peer out the window. The *Valley Forge* was upside down in the darkness over a slowly rotating earth, and below lay the shadowy terrain of southeast Asia, clusters of tiny lights blinking their betrayal of the larger cities.

Macfay made his way to the aft control panel on the rear bulkhead of the flight deck, and after checking with Ortega, opened the cargo bay doors. Their radiator lining would dissipate the heat created by the sun and the spacecraft's various power systems to prevent overheating of the crew compartment. Also, with the doors open, the windows at the aft crew station would provide additional visibility for their rendezvous with the Kosmolyot II.

"How's it feel, Joe?" asked Macfay.

"Just like I never left."

"You never do, you know."

Dover nodded. In the weightlessness of the cabin, he felt truly at home. Even his leg, still a bit stiff and strained when he walked, felt completely at ease with no demands on the muscle. Maybe there was a therapeutic use for space, he mused within himself. After initially checking the view outside and looking over Ortega's shoulder at the flight panels, he eased himself back to the rear of the flight deck and let his body assume an easy posture by the aft control panel. From there, he could wait for the dawn, casually observing the mild activity on the flight deck and the passing lights below, or above, depending on one's point of view.

Unlike his previous flights in the *Columbia*, when every minute was tightly scheduled for some sort of test, or evaluation, or experiment, the passing time of the *Valley Forge's* journey around the earth required little of its crew except the routine management and monitoring of its flight profile.

The time dripped by, seemingly minute by minute. Dover tried to keep busy by reviewing his plans for entering and checking out the Alpha Bug, but he could repeat himself only so much. He knew well what he planned to do; it only remained for him to carry it out. Bored and impatient, he even volunteered for mess duty and prepared their lunch meal. Still, the time hung like honey in winter.

Macfay noticed his impatience. "A watched pot never boils, Joe, to coin a phrase," he said as Dover checked his watch for the umpteenth time.

"I'm getting antsy."

"I know. The old hurry-up-and-wait syndrome; it's even going to be with us in space."

But, inevitably, the orbits passed one by one, and when the elapsed time indicated that they were two-and-a-half hours from rendezvous, Dover started his preparations for his extra-vehicular-activity. Before his EVA, he must purge the nitrogen out of his system absorbed from breathing the nitrogen-oxygen mix of the cabin's pressurized air. Otherwise, the 100% oxygen environment within his spacesuit would cause the nitrogen to bubble and collect in his joints, causing crippling pain or even death. He put on the face mask of the portable oxygen system but left it plugged into the spacecraft's oxygen system in order to conserve the walk-around bottle for later.

An hour-and-a-half passed. Ortega ignited his orbital maneuvering system engines once more and took the *Valley Forge* to its 250-mile intercept altitude. During the burn, they started their radar search for the Kosmolyot II, but were established in orbit before they picked up an intermittent target ahead at 23 miles.

"That looks like it," murmured Ortega.

"Piss-poor return," commented Macfay.

"It seems to be holding steady, now," said Dover. "I better get ready."

He put on his inner garment, a one piece, liquid cooled mesh underwear that enclosed his feet and left only his head and hands uncovered. A reinforced fabric tubing crisscrossed his back and reached out along each of his extremities, a flexible conduit for the cooling water which would circulate through it from the reservoir on the back of his spacesuit. He double checked to make sure that his urine collection device was properly fitted; he had no desire to repeat a slight mistake he'd made on his first flight, particularly in such an embarrassing area.

"I think I see it," exclaimed Ortega, looking ahead and pointing. Macfay and Dover sighted down his finger and soon saw an irregular light reflection. The green fluorescent blip on the radar scope confirmed an object at 18 miles. Macfay lifted his binoculars.

"That's it," he announced.

Ortega slowly closed and stationed the *Valley Forge* slightly below the Alpha Bug and only 40-50 yards away.

"No signs of life," observed Macfay. "He would have done something by now if he were aware of us."

"Let's watch him for a moment. He only has that top-side hatch to see out of. If his radar is on the blink, he wouldn't have any idea that we're here. It might be a good idea to move up over him, just in case he is conscious," suggested Dover.

Vladimir Koidunov completed his final change-plane burn. He was now in an identical orbit as the disabled Kosmolyot II. Soon, he would know the condition of his friend, Andrian, who should be approximately 70 kilometers ahead of him. His closure rate would eat that up in 15 minutes. He had his missile search radar on and could expect a target shortly. The spaceplane would give off very little return, much less than an ICBM which the radar had been designed to detect. He had other sensors which normally would augment his radar: heat sensors to detect the blast of rocket exhaust, and magnetic interference detectors. The former would be of no use since the target was a dead spaceplane but the magnetic detectors were quite sensitive and were already showing a slight indication.

Fortunately, he would be making his intercept during the daylight portion of their orbit. If he couldn't raise Andrian on the radio, he would have time to close and see if he could get a visual signal.

It was good to see again the black of space and the blue, green, brown, and deep purple of the earth below. The long curved cloud lines across its surface reached out to end in scattered clusters of white fluff. Far to the north, he could see the swirling masses of gray storm cells, punctuated by tall boiling columns of cumulo-nimbus as the low pressure masses of air left their arctic birthplace.

He could not help but feel a certain pride despite the discouraging nature of his mission. He was piloting the world's first spacefighter, not one in the sense of the American film, *Star Wars*, but one even more advanced than the "X" fighter that Luke Skywalker had driven in combat against the evil Death Star. He remembered the little boy thrill of adventure and fantasy he and his fellow cosmonauts had experienced as they watched a copy of the film which had been sent by one of Andrian's American friends. They had laughed quite a lot, it had been so ridiculous in spots. American films were so full of superheroes and filled with such obvious patriotic propaganda. Skywalker's fighter squadron was a transparent takeoff of the American Navy's aircraft carrier squadrons that were the central weapon of their battle groups in the Pacific and Indian Oceans. And Darth Vader with his thinly disguised role as sort of combination Nazi-Russian villain. The Americans could make interesting and absorbing films and were certainly masters of illusion with their complex special effects. But their space fleets were celluloid fleets, without substance. The spaceplane which fit so well around him at this moment was a real-world weapon, a triumph of Soviet technology. When the Kosmolyot II squadrons were deployed, all of the Americans' vast intercontinental weapons arsenal would be nothing more than a bad check, a needless expenditure which had been drawn on a voided account. Comrade Gorbachev would go to the next summit with nothing but aces in his hand. The world could very well be at last on the road to peace, a road where the political and economic superiority of the Soviet Union could come into its own and enable all the people to rise in struggles of national liberation, to throw off the oppressive yolk imposed on them by the capitalistic system of domination by wealth.

His thoughts were interrupted. For a moment, he thought his radar was picking up the first return of Andrian's spaceplane. There was a brief flicker of return but it was split as if there were two targets.

Major Ortega eased the *Valley Forge* to a position where it could be seen through the hatch of the Alpha Bug. If the cosmonaut were all right or at least conscious he could signal them. All four occupants of the shuttle became quiet in their anticipation, suspended in the weightlessness atmosphere within the *Valley Forge* and enraptured by the sinister beauty of the almost dreamlike Soviet spacecraft, a dull blue-green machine of death hanging far above the unsuspecting earth. Neither the laser mirror nor the six spidery legs were extended although the outlines of their housings could be clearly seen.

"Time to go to work, Joe," said Macfay.

Dover nodded and pulled himself down into the crew compartment's mid-deck. Macfay followed and they checked to insure that the airlock was pressurized. Dover entered the cylindrical enclosure and Macfay closed the hatch after him.

His spacesuit was mounted on a pipe frame which hung from the airlock wall. Dover gave it a final check for any rips or tears, then stepped into the trouser section of the bulky two-piece garment. Next, he wiggled into the upper torso section. Prior to sealing the unit by engaging the circular metal rings which joined the two halves, he connected the undergarment liquid-coolant hose to the umbilical from the life support pack on the back of the suit. He pulled on his communications cap, pushed the headset and mike plugs into the suit's communications jacks, and set the oxygen-control switch on his chest pack to PRESSURE. Finally, he slipped on his gloves, locking them at the wrist connections, and placed the Apollo-style plastic bubble helmet over his head. Just before disconnecting his life support umbilical from the *Valley Forge,* he reset his oxygen-control switch to EVA.

He depressurized the airlock and stepped out into the open cargo bay. Immediately, he felt the first heady thrill of being a space entity unto himself. He had left the aluminum womb of his mother ship and with just the slightest effort he could push away to drift forever through the universe. Deep within his primitive self, that subliminal suggestion struck him just as a feeling of wanting to jump occurs in the mind of a person staring down from a high structure. It was a normal but fascinating urge. Grabbing a handhold to insure that his whimsy did not become an irrevocable fact, he moved across the cargo bay to where his manned-maneuvering-unit hung. He lowered the arm rests, backed into it, clipped its two latches onto his backpack fittings, and gripped the control levers.

With his right hand he moved his yaw control, simultaneously using his left control to start an upward movement. He rose majestically out of the cargo bay, a self-contained human spacecraft.

His swing turned him toward the Alpha Bug and he activated the tiny nitrogen-thrust jets to carry him to it. As he neared, he adjusted his path to hover over the rectangular window in the upper fuselage entrance hatch.

The cosmonaut lay motionless in his G-couch, his sightless eyes fixed open. It was difficult to see the instruments in the shadow of the cockpit but after a moment he could detect the array of colored lights and flickering computer digital readouts that indicated the spacecraft was still powered. He took particular note that the Control Mode Selector switch was set to MANUAL OVERRIDE. There was the reason that the Soviet ground stations had not been able to recover the vehicle.

By shading the window with his head he could pick up most of the detail within the cabin. There was no evidence of any damage and the instruments all seemed to have normal readings. Dover reported to the *Valley Forge*.

"Brian, everything appears normal with the spacecraft. It's still under power and all of the readings check out, at least the ones I can see. But I think the pilot's dead. He's not moving and his eyes are open."

"How's the cabin pressure?"

"One hundred kilopascals—14 psi," replied Dover, interpreting the metric reading of the pressure gauge.

"Can you get to him?"

"Standby."

Dover adjusted the position of his faceplate against the window of the Alpha Bug's top entrance hatch. There had been a slight change in the angle of the sun and some of the distracting reflections had moved off to the side of the window. For the first time, he could see the cosmonaut's face clearly. "Oh, my God! Andy!"

Macfay missed the words, so high pitched they were with shock. "What was that, Joe? Say again."

Dover lay prone against the top of the fuselage, his body

suddenly weak from despair. Those glazed eyes staring back at him belonged to the cosmonaut who had been his Soviet counterpart on the abandoned Spacelab 5 project.

"Brian! It's Andy! Andrian Bykovsky, from Spacelab 5."

"The hell you say."

"Yes, it's him all right. This is bad, Brian. We were friends."

"I know. I'm sorry, Joe. I knew him, too, but certainly not as well as you. One hell of a fine man. You sure he's dead?"

"He's dead."

"Okay, go ahead and see if you can get him out. We can at least take him back."

Dover found it difficult to take his eye off his friend. Perhaps, if he looked hard enough, he could generate some spark of life. Nothing. Regretfully, he realized he should not let the shock of finding Andrian interfere with the primary purpose of his mission. He and the Alpha Bug and the *Valley Forge* were still speeding toward another night in space and he would have to recover Andrian and get back into the Alpha Bug before the short dusk ended his light. He could mourn later.

He attached the magnetic tethers of the MMU to the Alpha Bug and disconnected it from his backpack. Inexplicably, he rapped on the window, feeling silly, but it seemed the thing to do. Andrian's eyes neither blinked nor moved. Dover located the emergency depressurization handle under a small red plate beside the hatch and pulled it out. He could see the cabin pressure drop to zero. At the same time, his own eye widened with horror. He had not been able to tell that Andrian's spacesuit seal had been broken when in his last desperate moment he had tried to twist off his helmet. Too late, Dover realized that in evacuating the artificial atmosphere from within the spacecraft, he had also opened up his friend's body to the vacuum of space. The trapped air in the Soviet's lungs and the gases in his body literally exploded through his various body openings, ripping and tearing the flesh and taking with them the cadaver's fluids, a great portion of which spilled into the cosmonaut's helmet and coated the inside of his visor.

"Oh, God! Damn!" The words leaped from Dover's mouth, carrying with them the agony of his soul. He couldn't have killed his already-dead friend but the effect was there and it stimulated a release of bile into his throat that threatened to spill out into his helmet. He choked but forcibly swallowed until his throat cleared. There was an additional reason for his exclamation. It was just this kind of mental lapse that could cost him his own life. Perhaps he had been rushed into this task without rekindling the professional edge that he had kept so finely honed during his former astronaut days. Discovering Andrian's body hardly helped his concentration, either. Not that he could do anything about it now; he would just have to keep his head about him.

He twisted the manual release handle and opened the hatch. By leaning far in, he could unstrap the cosmonaut. Carefully, he extracted what was now just a high-priced body bag.

Holding Andrian's spacesuited remains against the skin of the Alpha Bug with one leg, he reattached the MMU to his backpack, then grabbed the cosmonaut and jetted back to the *Valley Forge*. He placed the remains in the air lock and raised his thumb to Macfay who had been watching through the aft crew station window. On his way back to the Alpha Bug, he heard Macfay's disgusted call.

"Holy Christ! What happened to him?"

"I inadvertently depressurized him."

"Well, if he wasn't dead before, he sure as shit is now— I didn't mean that the way it sounded, Joe."

"Just hang him on the wall, Brian, he won't hurt you." Dover instantly regretted the irritability betrayed by his inflection.

"Hey—I'm sorry. I'll keep him in the airlock for now."

"Whatever," replied Dover. He had his own problems. The retrieval of Andrian had taken longer than he had figured and the exertion as well as the mental strain had made him a bit testy. Once more he maneuvered over to the now abandoned spacecraft and tethered his MMU to the outside.

It was a tight squeeze to fit his inflated pressure suit through the hatch. The sight of the explosive decompression's effect upon Andrian's body made him acutely aware of what a tear in his own suit would do. After several minutes of careful wiggling and scooting, he succeeded in settling into the G-couch and locked the overhead hatch. His suit umbilical adapter didn't fit the panel connection but with the cabin repressurized he could remove his helmet and conserve his suit oxygen supply. Also, the release of the pressure in his suit deflated it and he better fit the depression in the couch. He adjusted and fastened the restraint harness. That felt better. A true pilot always felt more confident once his machine was firmly strapped to his bottom-side.

"I'm inside and pressurized," he reported.

"Roger, Joe. I'll tell Mission Control," responded Macfay.

Dover made a general visual sweep of the cockpit. After all the time he had spent with the eye-camera blow-ups, he at least had a slight feeling for his surroundings. There was no purpose in studying the computer panels to his right. They were programmed beyond his comprehension. Besides, in the MANUAL OVERRIDE mode, they were reduced to a standby status as far as flight control went. The monitoring bank would continue to feed the necessary data to his display screens for manual control. Tentatively, he placed his hand on the control grip and tried moving the spacecraft around its various axes. Response was encouragingly positive and smooth, even better than the *Columbia*. He would have no problem maneuvering the Alpha Bug in space. How it would fly once he reentered the earth's atmosphere remained to be seen.

"How's it look?" Now it was Macfay who was impatient.

"So far, so good. I found the cue cards for the manual reentry."

"Great! Any problems understanding them?"

"I don't think so."

"Enjoy."

Koidunov was having difficulty understanding the reason for two targets on his radar scope, one giving off a large return. He adjusted the gain manually and tried several filter settings. The stranger remained, glowing brightly beside the dim return of the disabled spaceplane. There was something else there and it took him only a moment to realize what it was: an American space shuttle. It had to be. Surely, the people back at the Northern Cosmodrome had detected the launch of the U.S. spacecraft. Why had they not informed him? He was still 50 kilometers away and he doubted that he had been detected by the shuttle. His electronic countermeasures equipment was showing no incoming radar signals. The logical thing to do at this point would be to try and see if he could raise Andrian on the radio. Even the weakest of signals might make it across the short distance.

"Andrian? Do you hear me? Andrian, this is Vladimir. Reply."

The background noise in his headset did not change. He tried three more times. Still no indication that Andrian was even squeezing his microphone button. He and the other spacecraft were rapidly approaching sunset. He would close slightly, inform Mission Control of the situation, and wait for daylight.

"Mission Control, this is Koidunov. Do you have me?"

"Go ahead."

"I have radar with Andrian. There is another target. I am sure it must be an American shuttle. Do you have any information for me?"

"Wait."

Fools. He could understand his father's irritability with incompetence. He should not have been allowed to approach without being informed of the shuttle's presence. The situation had taken on a new seriousness. He called again. "I am waiting."

255

"We are checking."

Vladimir could not wait for verification. It was obviously a shuttle. He must make his own decisions. "I will hold this position until daylight when I can make a positive identification without getting too close. Then, I will attempt radio contact."

For the next hour, Dover familiarized himself with the controls and instruments. Even as he passed around the dark side of the earth, he found the cockpit lighting more than adequate to continue his familiarization. Every minute he had spent with the photos back at the Cape had given him an excellent start in feeling at home in the spacecraft. By the time he was passing into the next day, he was ready to advise Macfay of his decision.

"*Valley Forge*, I think we've got a GO for the operation."

Macfay's reply was surprisingly calm. Dover knew that he was about to bust with excitement. "Understand we have a GO. Ready for a time check?"

"Whenever."

"At the mark, it'll be 143225 zulu . . . standby . . . mark."

The Alpha Bug's chronometer was accurate to the second. "Roger, mark," replied Dover. "We're right on."

"We show two hours, thirty-three minutes to de-orbit burn."

"I concur," responded Dover.

He checked his suit oxygen supply. The digital gauge on his chest pack showed four-and-a-half hours remaining, more than enough, even if he went back on the system now.

On board the *Valley Forge*, Major Ortega studied his radar picture. The low signal return of the Alpha Bug fascinated him. Whatever else the Soviets had done, they'd come up with a machine which literally absorbed much of the radar energy or presented such a curved surface that the beam was reflected at an obtuse angle rather than back at the sending antenna. He had backed off eight miles to give Dover some maneuvering room, but even at that close range the Alpha Bug's return was much smaller than normal. He mentioned it to Macfay. "You know, when we were approaching that thing, it sure didn't give off a good return. I wonder if our gear could be part of the problem."

"No, I don't think so," commented Macfay. "We noticed on the original telescopic pictures that they have apparently copied some of our Stealth technology. Remember how weak it was when we first picked it up? And we were only 23 miles away then."

"What say we back off and see at what range we lose it?" suggested Ortega.

"Okay, but stay within 25 miles or so in case Joe needs us for something." Macfay triggered his UHF circuit, "Joe, we're going to slip back a ways and check on the radar picture. Okay?"

"Roger—I'm doing fine in here. Give me a call every ten minutes just to be on the safe side. If no answer, close back up."

"Will do."

Ortega let the *Valley Forge* drift off opposite to their direction of orbit.

"Amazing, isn't it?" observed Macfay as they opened. The return was already weak and intermittent at 18 miles, probably due in part to the attitude of the Alpha Bug.

"Let's check a longer range on the scope. It shouldn't make any difference but it might be worth looking at," said Ortega, switching his range to 50 miles. The Soviet spacecraft still winked in and out at 18 miles although the picture on the scope now showed out to 50 miles at its edge.

"Looks the same to—what the shit is that?" Macfay pointed to a very faint but recurring blip at 26 miles.

Ortega switched to a 30-mile scale which put the new signal near the edge of the scope. He studied it as it closed. "Beats me, unless it's an echo or a piece of space junk."

"It's no echo," said a worried Macfay. "And I doubt if it's residue. The briefing people didn't mention anything, certainly not in this plane."

Ortega switched to the 20-mile scale; the blip was now inside that range. "Whatever it is, it's coming right at us."

Macfay retrieved his binoculars and searched along the indicated bearing. The radar mark was at 15 miles before he could finally make out a faint dark object. He followed it as it gradually grew fatter in the middle and sprouted short wings out to each side. As he studied it, a small shiny blob raised over it and six wirelike legs sprouted from under its buglike silhouette.

"Holy shit! It's another Alpha Bug! Get our asses back over to Dover.

Ortega started closing Dover's craft.

"Joe," called Macfay, "we got company. Read me?"

"Say again—"

"Company, Joe. You've got a twin brother twelve miles and closing."

"Another Alpha Bug?"

"You bet your sweet ass."

"That's exactly what I'm betting!" Dover yawed the spacecraft around to look back beyond the *Valley Forge*. His heart sank into his stomach as he picked up the wedge shape with the raised mirror, the downward curving wing, and spider legs. "Oh, shit!" he exclaimed, "I think we're about to get caught with our hands in the cookie jar."

Koidunov sat grim faced, head tilted upward as he watched the American space shuttle. He had followed its approach with a mixture of professional caution and anxiety. Once it had closed to within 20 kilometers he had deployed his weapon mirror and armed the system. The Americans had obviously spotted him, also. They had opened their range and were now back by the disabled Kosmolyot II.

He reported to Mission Control, "I am in visual contact with an American space shuttle."

"Vladimir," the voice was that of his father, "what is his position relative to Andrian?"

"He has closed to within 50 meters."

"Does it appear that he is taking pictures?"

"I suspect he has already done that. He has closed perhaps to use Andrian for protection."

"Can you talk to him?"

"I will try. Wait." Vladimir switched to the international emergency frequency. "American spacecraft, this is Soviet spaceplane holding position 500 meters up orbit. You must clear this area. You are in Soviet space and interfering with normal operations. Do you hear me?"

For emphasis, Vladimir swung his laser mirror from side to side before steadying it on the *Valley Forge*.

There was no answer.

"The American is not replying. What are my instructions?"

"Keep trying. If you cannot contact him, then insert yourself between him and the disabled spaceplane."

"Do I have permission to fire?"

"No! No! Not yet! You may defend yourself, but it is doubtful that the American shuttle has any weapons."

Vladimir decided he must be candid. His father was on the other end of the radio circuit and was certainly on top of the situation. "I am afraid the Kosmolyot II may be already compromised. The Americans undoubtedly have pictures by now. That action alone constitutes a mission of spying and justifies protective action."

"Is there any sign that they have visited the spaceplane?"

"No, I see no one outside. Andrian is probably undisturbed although I have received no answer from him."

"You understand the delicacy of this situation, do you not, Vladimir?"

"Yes, but I suggest that our prime consideration must be the possible compromise of our spaceplane."

"I agree."

"I can not allow the shuttle to return with its information."

"I agree."

"Am I cleared to make my own decision in this matter. I am the on-scene commander."

"I have confidence in you, Vladimir. But only as a last

resort must you attack the shuttle. We are in contact with United States authorities at this time.''

What good would that do? Even if the Americans claimed they had the most innocent of purposes in closing the spaceplane, they would be lying. They were spying and they had pictures, pictures which could be used by intelligence specialists and scientists to unravel the classified features of the Kosmolyot II. He would call them again on the radio since he realized that the situation was now both politically and militarily explosive. But he could see no other way out than the first operational use of his weapons system.

Macfay frantically reviewed his options and mentally searched desperately for new ones. He had heard the Soviet's call and deliberately refrained from answering. He needed to buy some time.

''Brian, what's happening?''

Of course. Dover had only their U.S. tactical frequency in his spacesuit radio and could not utilize any of the Alpha Bug's radio gear. He had no way of hearing the Soviet's transmissions.

''He's calling us on international distress, Joe. I'll keep you informed.''

''Does he know I'm in here?''

''No, he has no way of knowing that.''

''Unless he's able to come up on this frequency. This thing has that capability, you know.''

''He doesn't even know we're talking to each other. He has no reason to search.''

''We'll know if he does, you can be sure of that. Play it cool, Brian.''

Macfay would have to reply to the Soviet spacecraft. A dialogue might even give them time back on earth to possibly find a way out of this. ''Soviet spacecraft, this is the *Valley Forge*. Do you read me?'' Thank heavens, the Soviet had used English in his call.

''Yes, *Valley Forge*. Clear this area. You are in Soviet space.''

Macfay was deeply concerned and not just a little frightened, but who in the hell did this guy think he was? "We do not recognize your sovereignty in space. It is open, like international waters."

"Not with you within unsafe distance to our space vehicle."

"We are an unarmed spacecraft. Our mission is to offer assistance in rescuing your cosmonaut. That is our purpose."

"We have capability and require no assistance. I insist you retire to 500-meter distance or I defend property of Soviet Union."

Macfay *had* to get Dover back into the shuttle. He couldn't mention to the Soviet that he had Major Bykovsky's body on board. That would only compromise Dover. The Soviet was no dummy. Major Ortega came up on the intercom.

"Mission Control says to try and stall. The President is on the hot line with Gorbachev. If possible, we are to try and wait until we enter the next darkness cycle and then get the Commander back on board."

"Whose decision was that?" asked Macfay.

"Falcon One," replied Ortega, giving General Shyrr's personal call sign.

Perhaps there would be a way. Macfay switched back over to Dover's suit frequency. "Joe, we're going to try and stall and get into position to get you out as soon as we enter the dark side again."

"That's another 20 minutes."

"Hang in there. I'll get back to you shortly." Macfay surveyed the relative positions of the three spacecraft. The *Valley Forge* was still between Dover and the second Kosmolyot II. If they could remain there, Dover just might be able to spacewalk back to the shuttle in the dark, shielded by the deep fuselage and delta wing of the shuttle. It was worth a try. He returned to the international frequency. "I am sorry about the delay. I will do as you say. I only have to inform my control that we are abandoning our attempt to rescue your cosmonaut at your request. It will only be

261

a few minutes. We have been informed that our President is talking to your General Secretary at this very moment and they are aware of the situation. Is that satisfactory? You know how it is when our superiors get into the act.''

"You have five minutes," tersely warned Koidunov the Younger.

"Listen, my name is Macfay. Captain Brian Macfay, United States Navy. You are a military man also, are you not?''

"Colonel Vladimir Koidunov, Soviet Air Force—and I do not see any oceans up here, Captain Macfay.''

Good. The Soviet had a sense of humor, slight though it might be.

"Colonel, you and I are caught in the middle of this. We don't want to do anything that may allow this situation to get out of control. I'm sure you agree with me on that.''

"You are right, Captain Macfay, that we are both military men. But our actions are governed by orders we are under. I have mine. You have yours. We may not wish to carry them out but we have solemn oath to consider, yes?''

"I recognize that, Colonel Koidunov. But if either of us acts hastily, or without authority, the consequences could go far beyond this tiny corner of space. We *are* brothers up here—you and I—and I know we share the same emotions about this environment. Only those of us, astronauts and cosmonauts, know this feeling. We have even worked together. Let's remain calm until I get my authority to withdraw. It should come anytime now.

"Captain, I know what you are trying to say. But on wing of your spacecraft is military insignia of United States Air Force and on wing of mine is Red Star. The time for the scientists is past. I suspect you regret that as I do. For that, I bear you and your crew no ill will. We *are* brothers but we are trapped by our loyalties to what we believe in and those beliefs are irreconcilable.''

Good! I have him talking! Thinking! The night was only 15 minutes away. *Keep him talking!*

"Colonel Koidunov, do you have the ability to leave your spacecraft?''

"Yes."

Macfay could feel the suspicion in the Soviet's single word reply. "We have a large crew compartment. Join us in it. We can turn this event into an historic occasion that will benefit the image of both our countries. Both of our controls know we are here together so there is no danger to you in this. Think of the impact such a gesture would have back on earth. It isn't too late for us, Colonel. Let us turn this confrontation into a testimonial."

"You would make good politician, Captain. Two minutes."

Macfay knew that he had been reaching but there had been that wild hope that the Soviet would respond. Every man that Macfay had ever known who had gone into space had come back with the deepest conviction that it should be available to all mankind in the spirit of peace and exploration. You left the earth with national ties but when you returned you were a citizen of the world.

"Captain Macfay, this will seem strange to you but I am with you in spirit. Still, there is no way that I can disregard my responsibilities. At least, during our brief time, you have understood. Goodbye, comrade. I would have liked it to be otherwise."

Goodbye?! The bastard was going to act! Macfay hurriedly switched back to Dover. "Get out, Joe! We can't wait! We have to—" He never finished his sentence.

An eye-shattering white beam shot out from the erect mirror atop the approaching *Kosmolyot II* and sliced into the forward section of the *Valley Forge*. The crew compartment disintegrated, bits of metal and flesh hurtling outward toward the endless reaches of deep space. The noseless shuttle remained off Dover's upper fuselage with a jagged hole where only an instant before three humans had stood within a pressurized cabin.

He lay too stunned to pray. Instead, he opened his lungs and cursed. "Bastard!" he yelled. "You goddamned fucking bastard!" The words rang and echoed inside the metal confines of the Alpha Bug, all the more bitter for not being heard outside. Dover ripped off his communications cap in a gesture of futile anger and slung it aside. It was worthless to him, now. He couldn't talk to the Soviet on his American tactical frequency nor would his adapter fit their radios. He couldn't talk to anyone. Two strikes. The first when he depressurized the Alpha Bug cabin too hastily; the second, when he evacuated Andrian without keeping his communications cap, bloodied though it had been. Three, and you're out. To make matters worse, his position readout on the instrument panel indicated an earth latitude and longitude under him where his line-of-sight spacesuit radio would have only marginal performance. Even if he talked to a controller, what could the man tell him? "Repeat after me: Our Father, who art—" An old joke, but it had lost none of its sting.

He considered activating his weapons system but the Soviet already had the drop on him. The moment the cosmonaut saw any threatening activity by the Alpha Bug, such as the raising of the weapons mirror, he would know that there was one American left—in *his* spacecraft! No, Dover would have to play his present hand. The cosmonaut did not know he was in the disabled Alpha Bug. That was the one advantage he had. But it wasn't much of an advantage. The Soviet had not hesitated to destroy the defenseless *Valley Forge,* and he most probably reasoned his countryman was either dead or beyond help. As a matter of cold fact, it seemed to Dover that he was in the classically hopeless situation of being between a rock and a hard place. If he tried to fight back, the Soviet would nail him before he could even unsheath his mirror; if he didn't, the cosmonaut was most probably under orders to destroy the crippled Alpha Bug for there was no way he could get both spacecraft back to earth.

Methodically, he probed the deepest memories and resources of his mind for a way out, at the same time fighting the wave of panic that had been building up inside. He knew he must remain calm. That had been his first lesson as a student pilot: when an emergency arises, think it out, then act. The worse enemy at such a time was panic—and he could taste it.

Surely, the Soviet would close and try and look inside the cockpit for his comrade before he destroyed it. Would he try and spacewalk and open the hatch as Dover had done? If he did that, one glance through the window and he would see a U.S. spacesuit and not a CCCP one. Perhaps, he *would* try and get a personal look inside. Dover could wait for that moment, activate his weapons system, and blast the unoccupied Alpha Bug! The thought excited him with the first real glimmer of hope. But suppose the Soviet went canopy to canopy for his inspection. Dover's mind raced. Why would the Soviet even bother to check? He couldn't rescue his friend. Yes, he could. He could open the hatch, put the spacecraft back on REMOTE and the Soviet ground controller could deorbit the Alpha Bug. No, wait, if he did that— Dover shook his head as if he could shake all of the thoughts into one orderly progression.

In the past, his ability to analyze and conclude had made the difference in several tight situations where a lesser man would have been lost. He racked his brain for an escape plan with higher odds. There was one thing he could do! It all depended on surprise and timing, and even if he carried it off, it would create other problems. But the current odds on his survival heavily favored the guy in the black hat. He would have to cut those odds a little.

It was his only hope.

Chapter
17

Dover mentally rehearsed what he must do. One thing in his favor might be that they were fast approaching the dark side of their orbit. Whether he would be able to wait until they entered it was doubtful, however. His biggest worry would be the other Alpha Bug's ability to detect what was happening fast enough to get off a shot of his laser. After seeing what the vicious weapon had done to the *Valley Forge*, Dover knew such an end could very well await him.

The Soviet craft was still within the viewing area of his window and he could see that it was drifting slowly around the shattered U.S. shuttle, an ominous coroner performing a visual autopsy on the metal cadaver. The tightness in Dover's chest increased. The Soviet was going to examine the crippled *Valley Forge* in detail, perhaps to insure that no one was left alive that might be able to get off a radio signal. Certainly, anyone who remained was doomed. *Jesus!* Even from his distance, Dover could see the bright reflection of Andrian's white spacesuit through the now exposed port in the airlock. Once the Soviet spotted his dead comrade he would realize that there could very well be an American astronaut aboard the Alpha Bug. That would be it, for sure.

Shit! The MMU! Things were falling apart fast. His manned-maneuvering unit was still tethered to the fuselage of the Alpha Bug! Its white color against the dark blue-green of the spacecraft would stand out like a wart on a nun's nose. The Soviet wouldn't have to see Andrian's body but would only have to close the Alpha Bug and have the MMU stare him in the eye. Fortunately, for the moment, it was on the far side of the fuselage and shielded from the Soviet's view.

The other Alpha Bug was holding its position under the bottomside of the *Valley Forge*. Why? From that position, the cosmonaut could only see the heat tiles. Maybe, he was talking to his controllers. Maybe he was taking pictures, although Dover couldn't imagine any reason other than curiosity. The construction of the *Valley Forge* was an open secret.

Perhaps, the Soviet had already caught a glimpse of Andrian or, worse, the reflection of the telltale MMU. In that case, he could very well be requesting permission to destroy the Alpha Bug, as if he really needed it. The top of the Soviet spacecraft was still turned away from Dover. Quickly, he retrieved his communications cap and slipped it back on. There might be a chance he would yet be able to reach someone after he came out of blackout.

Next, he replaced his space helmet and pressurized his suit, adjusting his seat harness to allow inflation. Blown up like a balloon, his movements would be restricted, but he could still reach the necessary controls, and if the Soviet did manage to get off a shot and he lost cabin pressure his suit protection could be the edge which might enable him to survive.

He followed the cue cards, meticulously setting his engine and electrical switches for reentry. After checking to insure that the other spacecraft was still turned away from him, he cautiously aligned his Alpha Bug opposite the direction of its orbit. As it yawed and pitched to the correct angle, he lost sight of the other vehicle. Now, time was of the essence, for as soon as the intruding Alpha Bug turned to once more view him, his movement would be immediately apparent. The computer display screens and panel instruments in front of him comfirmed that he was in position. He started his auxiliary power unit and armed the single orbital maneuvering engine. Abruptly, a red warning light flashed its glow repeatedly in front of him, warning that his rocket boost engine selector switch was improperly positioned. He hadn't touched it, but then he remembered that the late cosmonaut had died before he had been able to return it to its off position, and the rockets were not used for the simple de-orbit burn. He set the selector on ZERO and the light blinked out.

The cue card indicated that a 2.70-minute OMS engine burn would be required at his 250-mile altitude, but he reasoned that a normal de-orbit burn might give the Soviet enough time to use his laser. He needed to get out of range as fast as possible, and the only other adjustment he could use which might make a difference would be to increase his descent angle. That might complicate the Soviet weapon's acquisition problem as well as slow the Alpha Bug to allow it to decay from its orbit. He pitched the nose down five degrees and hoped the deviation from the normal position would not be too extreme and dangerously affect his reentry speed. Also, if he kept his head about him, he could adjust the angle with one more burn once he was out of the radar range of the Soviet spacecraft. What it would do to his overall maneuver, he could only guess, but his prime concern had to be avoiding getting zapped by the lethal energy beam.

He checked his watch. It was still over two hours before his scheduled burn time. By starting it now, he would be landing way short, somewhere, and a full orbit off his desired path over the earth's surface. But he couldn't wait. He had to act before the other Alpha Bug became suspicious, even if it did mean a touchdown thousands of miles from his pickup area. Where he would wind up, he had no idea at the moment, nor was he overly concerned with taking time to figure it out. Wherever it would be, it would be. He dared delay no longer.

He pushed the IGNITE button and the OMS engine exploded into life, the instant acceleration forcing him hard against the G-couch. It was as if he shot ahead at hundreds of miles per hour, but the sensation was an illusion. He was actually slowing his orbital speed by that amount.

He tensed his body and waited. If the other Alpha Bug detected his escape attempt before it lost radar contact, the sudden flash of light and instant oblivion would mean that its cosmonaut was as fast on his feet as he. The seconds passed as hours, then a jarring shock startled him and the Alpha Bug slued violently to one side. Instinctively, he corrected it with the maneuvering thrusters. With the shock, however, his warning light panel had lit up like the inside of an electronic game machine! He had an OVERHEAT light on his OMS engine and a malfunction in his booster rocket-firing sockets. He shut off the engine and activated the fire suppressant system, then pulled the electrical circuit breaker to deactivate the rocket-firing circuits. The two red lights went out, but there were still two others left, one flashing red, the other holding a steady amber.

The flashing red indicated a rupture in a rear fuel cell; why it hadn't blown was a mystery. He hit the purging button which should vent the highly volatile fuel mix into space and the light went out. Only the orange light remained. It indicated a partial loss of hydraulic pressure to his rudder. No problem for the moment, for he still had the back-up system, and he wouldn't need the rudder until he reentered the atmosphere.

He had taken a hit, but a lucky one, probably fired as the radar-attenuating design of the Alpha Bug caused its signal to fade off the scope of his opponent's fire-control system. The Soviet apparently had been unable to zero in on the vanishing blip and had fired at its last known position. Fortunately, in the interim, Dover had continued just far enough for the laser to strike somewhere on his tail rather than duplicating the deadly slice that had destroyed the *Valley Forge*. His cabin pressure remained intact.

He had to be grateful to the unknown Russian designer. Dover had been riding the fire of a vehicle which had been specifically designed to thwart a radar-directed attack, and since he was still alive, the designer had obviously done well. After all, the *Valley Forge* had not picked up a viable return until they had been only 23 miles away. He was well beyond that range now. The very design feature which helped make the Alpha Bug such a formidable weapon had saved his life.

His emergency action had cut off his OMS engine early, shorting his burn time, but at least his attitude thrusters were still operative and he resumed his precise reentry attitude by raising his nose to the prescribed 30 degree nose-up angle. Now that the OMS engine was inoperative, he would not be able to make any further adjustments on his descent path. But, one crisis at a time.

He checked his switches and systems for reentry and exercised his hydraulically powered aerodynamic flight controls to insure they were activated. The elevons checked out, but the rudder moved erratically. Continuing with the check list, he dumped the forward-reaction-control-system propellant to change his center of gravity, configuring the Alpha Bug for its glide through the atmosphere. He was at the point where he should have on a G-suit, but he wore none under his pressure garment. Perhaps the automatically positioning contour couch would serve the purpose.

He was falling toward the earth at an astonishing speed. His altimeter readout was already passing 450,000 feet. In a few seconds, he would be kissing the outer edge of the earth's air cover. He wanted to pray, but hadn't been very faithful about that endeavor when things had been rosy, so he wasn't sure that praying now would find a sympathetic ear. But then, God was a spirit and had no ears, so perhaps he would hear. Or she. Or whatever. He couldn't help himself. *Lord, if it is your will* . . . The rest of his spontaneous prayer sprang from an old Negro spiritual which pleaded to the Almighty that if he couldn't help the treed black hunter, ". . . please don't help dat bear!" It seemed appropriate at this time.

The G's began to build, and he knew the heat shield of the Alpha Bug was beginning to heat rapidly as it plunged on its downward slant at over 17,000 miles per hour, feeling its first warmth of friction. The rare molecules of air would rapidly become the few; then, the many; and, finally, the full density of the earth's gaseous envelope. He was forced deep within the G-couch.

The heat shield should be glowing about now, and indeed it must be, for as Dover watched in fascination, the night heavens outside his overhead window began to glow with the fireworks of reentry as millions of ionized particles bled off the skin of the spacecraft. Even within the insulated airtight cabin and the equally secure environment of his spacesuit, he could sense the increased warmth. The inside temperature gauge rose to 55 degrees, Celsius—130 degrees Fahrenheit. He monitored the outside atmospheric pressure gauge as the spacecraft plummeted toward the earth, and as the gauge reached the levels indicated on his cue card, he secured the maneuvering thrusters. From this point on, his attitude would be controlled by his aerodynamic surfaces.

He entered maximum heat, with 1,500 degrees Celsius temperatures tinting the nose and leading edge of the Alpha Bug a cherry red.

A slight tremor shook him in the couch, then became a steady vibration, and his nose attitude wanted to wander back and forth. The shake increased to the point where it took full throw of his rudder pedal to control it. Even so, his command of the spacecraft became marginal. The altimeter readout spun through 180,000 feet and the glow outside began to fade. He should be coming out of the communications blackout zone with a speed down in the 8,500-miles-per-hour range. Even though the atmosphere was becoming more dense, and his control should be improving, the vibrations continued to worsen, and the side-to-side oscillations became more pronounced. He couldn't seem to catch up with them, no matter how rapidly he walked his rudder controls. The laser strike must have also damaged the tall tail, perhaps shearing off a piece of the rudder or twisting a portion of it into a ragged edge which was jutting out into the slipstream. If so, it was probably flexing and giving him the changing control forces, even now so severe that he was dangerously close to a side swing so violent it could throw him out of control if not stopped. He continued to fight the escalating swing of the nose until finally he could limit it by coordinating his elevons with the rudder in a frantic imitation of a skier's giant slalom technique.

He set up a 2,000 kilometers per hour glide speed, gradually decreasing it as he fell nearer the earth. Suddenly, he felt a distinct snap of his rudder pedals and the oscillations stopped. He had more control and could modify his slalom maneuver into a series of long sweeping turns. Perhaps the trouble-causing rudder remnant had worked itself into metal fatigue and tore off. He steepened his bank, trying to see the surface which was still over 90,000 feet below. He was only minutes away from touchdown, but he could see nothing in the night. If there were land below him, it was obscured by a low cloud layer. He tried his radar, but it was designed for fire-control on moving targets and useless as a navigational aid. There was one other thing he could do. If he could reach anyone with his in-suit radio, perhaps he could get some idea of where he was.

What would he use for a call sign? Certainly not Alpha Bug or Kosmolyot II! There wasn't time to be picky. "Hello . . . hello . . . any station this net . . . this is Joe Dover . . . over."

Nothing.

"Hello, any station . . . this is Joe Dover of the *Valley Forge.* Over."

An answer!

"*Valley Forge,* this is Mission Control, over."

He had a ground station!

"Mission Control, this is Dover. Do you read?"

"Station calling, I read you faint and slightly garbled."

"Roger, this is Dover from the *Valley Forge*. I'm all that's left. What station am I talking to?"

"This is the Perth tracking station. What's your status?"

"Damned if I know . . ." As soon as he blurted the words out, he knew how silly they must sound. He should come up with something more professional. "I'm out of blackout from an unscheduled de-orbit, unsure of my position, passing 75,700 feet."

"Roger, we hold an unknown at that altitude, descending."

"That's me, goddammit! Where am I?"

"You're over central Australia, *Valley Forge* . . . I can't be of any assistance on your approach . . . you're over relatively flat terrain . . . I don't. . . ." The voice trailed off. Dover could hardly blame the poor bastard. For all the surprised communicator knew, he held a U.S. space shuttle which was dropping back to earth in some sort of an emergency descent and would shortly pass out of his radio and radar range. No wonder he sounded so helpless. The spacecraft would have no chance of a successful landing in the dark night of the Australian outback.

"I'm not the *Valley Forge*," repeated Dover. "Will explain on the ground. I do have landing capability. Request you track me as long as you can and send assistance."

Already at 57,000 feet, Dover manually activated the landing system. The automatic sequencing would take over from that point on.

"Roger," came back the voice of Mission Control, "we hold you passing 50,000 feet . . . you sure picked a choice spot . . . you're coming down in the outback, some 180 miles west of Alice Springs. Work east, if possible."

Jesus! If he remembered right, he was over desert country, but wasn't there a low mountain range between him and Alice Springs? At the rate he was descending, he couldn't reach any distance east, anyhow.

As if that weren't enough to concern him, he suddenly began experiencing sharp pains in his joints and a pronounced tightness in his chest. *Nitrogen!* He had pressurized his suit with 100% oxygen after several hours of breathing the cabin air of the Alpha Bug, which in all probability was a standard nitrogen-oxygen mix.

Painfully, he managed a "Roger," but didn't feel he could talk any further. The pain was building fast, and breathing was difficult. He felt the characteristic jolt of a drogue chute filling with air as he dropped through 30,000 feet, then a few seconds later the heavy tug as the two main chutes billowed over his head. He didn't try looking up due to the pain in his neck and shoulders; besides, in the dark they'd be invisible. The solid feel was enough.

He wanted to cry out, as if he could cut the pain with his voice, but forced himself to maintain control. But he had to do something, maybe return to the nitrogen-oxygen cabin air. He was able to reach up and remove his helmet, and depressurize his suit. There was no immediate effect, but there was the chance the decision would halt, or at least reduce, the bubbling of the nitrogen in his blood and tissue. All he knew for sure was that the severe pain was blotting out all other sensations except for the faint voice in his earphones.

". . . Perth . . . passing 18,000 fee . . . we will . . . losing you . . . read. . . ." He had dropped below the line-of-sight limit of their transmissions.

His breath kept catching inside his lungs and he had to grunt to move it out, and each following intake was a painful gasp as his body became a mass of shooting hot needles, all converging in his joints and heating his bones with the fires of hell. He knew one of the final symptoms would be convulsions, but he seemed to be holding himself in check. If he could just hang on. He desperately needed a decompression chamber; perhaps, if he cranked the cabin pressurization system up as high as it would go, it might serve the same purpose. He knew that on the *Columbia,* you could exceed by a small margin sea level pressures when you were low enough; maybe the same held true for the Alpha Bug. With his suit deflated, he could reach over to the right console and set the knob for full pressurization.

274

He forced his eye into a hazy focus at the blurred altimeter and believed he read 12,000 feet. The stabbing pain in his eye sockets closed it again, and an agony of time passed as he floated the final miles to earth. Just as he resigned himself to the thought that he would be in the air forever, he felt the welcome thump as the Alpha Bug squatted heavily on its ground cushion bags. He was down.

For an unknown period, he lay there, barely conscious, but determinedly fighting off the wave of nausea and squelching the almost irresistible urge to open the overhead hatch. The pain didn't worsen, but he could feel his strength waning under the physical stress. He also suspected that he was dehydrating for his body was perspiring heavily within the polyurethane pressure bladder of his spacesuit. Groggily, he realized that he would have to open the hatch while he was still conscious. At touchdown, the spacecraft's power had been automatically cut off. If he didn't get some air flow before daylight, as soon as his suit power supply was exhausted, the coolant circulation would stop and he'd cook within the Alpha Bug like a human roast.

The bends be damned. By bearing down with his teeth, he could force away enough of the pain to concentrate on lifting his right arm to reach over to the right control panel. He fumbled around until he found the safety cover over the hatch-release lever. He took a deep breath, then grunted it out to give himself the strength to pull up the safety cover and throw the small arm forward. The window over him swung open and he could see the stars and feel the brush of the cool night air.

Everything faded to black.

The cool, crisp air of the Colorado high country swept down from the snow-capped peaks of the Rockies around the ranch and spread across the valley floor, swaying the grass into graceful dry-land waves that rippled over Dover's pastureland.

He sat on the steps of the front porch of the main house and watched the cattle graze, not just in the back pasture but along the sides of the frame structure and in the front, all the way to the weaving dirt road that marked the western border of his property. There were scores of tight miniherds of fifty or so beasts in each, all shiny in their rich dark coats and deep chests, a veritable black sea of beef. As he watched, the snorting males passed from female to female, stopping only long enough to approach their hindquarters, there to hump over the cows and hold themselves in place for the mating by the aroused grip of their forelegs on the females' backs. As the bulls finished and left, the cows immediately dropped healthy, braying Black Angus calves.

With each birth, Dover pounded the keys on his porch computer and watched the dollar figures increase.

Off to his left, under the shade of a compact grove of aspen, Carl was furiously digging a deep foxhole, and his long frame bent almost double as he wielded a child's toy shovel. From time to time, he would stop and place his hands in the small of his back to stretch and work out the kinks. Then, he would adjust the tilt of his old World War I steel helmet, wipe the glistening perspiration from his forehead and neck, and look at Dover. "We're goin' t' war, ain't we?" he'd ask, then resume his frantic digging.

Suddenly, a cube-like red, white, and blue U.S. Mail jeep appeared on the horizon and came speeding down the dirt road, throwing up a roostertail of swirling dust as it neared Dover's roadside mailbox. The vehicle skidded to a precarious stop, and the man inside held up a long white envelope, waving it at Dover before tossing it in the hollow metal loaf on top the four-by-four cedar post.

"Marie!" Dover called, and from inside the house came his beautiful bronze wife.

Hand in hand, they jumped off the porch and started running down the front path toward the mailbox. With each stride, they would lift effortlessly into the air and soar across yards of green grass before touching down and pushing off again. But, despite their pace, the mailbox seemed even farther away with each leap, and the faster they ran the smaller it became.

"No! No! No!" cried Dover as the rectangular tin housing became just a dot, then disappeared altogether. He turned toward Marie for solace, but she was no longer there. He stopped, confused, and looked back toward the house. It was gone, also. So was Carl. And the cattle. There was nothing but sandy soil and scrub grass from horizon to horizon. His mouth dropped open in despair and he whirled around to search the barren terrain.

The wind whistled and grew in strength until it began to lift the sand and blow it across the valley, its velocity increasing until the sound of its force became an overpowering roar, as if from the flight of a billion angry locusts, and the driven sand flew horizontally across the surface of the valley. A myriad of tiny particles peppered Dover's body, eating away his clothes and stinging the exposed skin. The heavy dust filled his nose and clotted as it tried to enter his mouth, forcing him to close his eye to shut out the horrifying view of the summer dust storm, but he could not close his ears and the unrelenting roar of the wind filled his head with a deafening sound which resonated within him until he was conscious of nothing else.

He squirmed and opened his eye. The sound was still there, but he was protected by the coal black face of prehistoric Man, who returned his quizzical stare with a pair of yellowed dark brown eyes. The piercing orbs were set deep under a heavy brow ridge and wide on each side of a flattened nose with nostrils the size of train tunnels. The thin lips pulled back in a friendly grin, revealing two rows of stained and broken teeth.

The creature was a female, and held him in her lap, his head pressed against her elongated bare breasts. Black hair, tinted with the rich ocher of the desert dust, hung in thin strands down her wrinkled cheeks in an irregular pattern, accenting the deep creases which crisscrossed her weathered face.

She held him under a shelter of stretched kangaroo skin, precariously stretched across the top branches of two pitifully dwarfed desert trees. Someone had removed his pressure suit but the mesh undergarment still clung to him. Seeing that he was awake, the woman raised an inflated animal stomach to his lips and let the water within the dried membrane drip onto his face. With her fingertips she rubbed the cooling liquid over his parched lips, allowing only a few drops to enter his mouth. She was the most beautiful sight he had ever seen.

Most of the pain was gone from his body and the remainder dimmed under the tender ministering of the aborigine woman. If only the incessant noise would stop. He became aware of a cluster of small children around them, the snow-white hair of the youngest in stark contrast to the ebony of their naked bodies. They stood with bloated tummies and watched him with a mixture of curiosity and good humor. Beyond them he could see several lean males, some wearing tattered loin cloths, others leaning on pointed tree-branch spears. An older one had his back to the group and was happily waving his withered arms at the loud roar which was still blotting out all other sound.

Dover tried to sit, and the woman braced his back. Then, he saw it. Beyond the small band of black clones of primitive Man sat the Soviet death machine of the twentieth century with its blue-green skin shimmering in the full heat of the desert sun. It rested on collapsed rubber and fabric bags, and its topside hatch was open. The impact had sprung open several of the antenna housings and the long coiled-steel legs flopped on the sand like the motionless legs of a dead spider.

Beyond the Alpha Bug was the source of the ear-shattering noise: a huge, squatting, round fuselage, slung beneath wide drooped wings and creeping toward them under the steady pull of its four turboprop engines. It was a Lockheed C-130 Hercules, and the classic cargo and troop carrier was wobbling across the uneven surface with all the grace of a pregnant elephant several months overdue.

It taxied to within thirty yards of Dover and the little band before turning broadside and letting its propellers whine to a stop. The massive tail ramp lowered as if the big plane were preparing to give birth, and in a sense it did. A squad of khaki-clad men trotted down it and over to the Alpha Bug, where they spaced themselves around it in a protective circle, the upturned side of their jaunty Digger hats giving each a professional and confident air. A four-wheel-drive military truck emerged next, towing a canvas-covered trailer of provisions. Then another. They plowed over to the ring of troopers.

All of the emotion and tenseness of the past hours collapsed inside Dover and he sobbed shamelessly as he recognized the blue circle and enclosed red kangaroo insignia of the Royal Australian Air Force painted on the side of the fat-cigar fuselage.

The forward crew hatch dropped open and a litter-carrying pair of medics ran toward him.

"Well now, Mate, you look a bit up a gum tree."

Dover tried to focus on the Aussie's face. It was a kind face, ruddy and smiling, and 20th century modern.

"Here—take a drop o' this. You'll be fair dinkum in no time."

The whiskey tasted delicious but the water from the stomach bag had tasted better. The aborigine female was still holding him, her fractured grin of broken and missing teeth even wider than before, the most perfect expression of a human emotion Dover had ever enjoyed. She was really God's unaltered creation, so ugly she was beautiful beyond belief. What was happening to Man between the Garden of Eden and Armageddon? What a lousy journey it had been from the Tree of Life to the Machine of Death that sat out there, too hot to touch from its soaking in the outback sun.

He squinted at the Alpha Bug, its shape shimmering under the effect of the rising desert heat. He had brought it back—at the expense of Yuri, and Charlie Kiger, and the young Soviet boat crew, and the Marine Harrier pilot, and Macfay, and Ortega and his copilot whose name Dover didn't even know, and Andrian. And just probably, Marie. Perhaps, the piercing pain in his own joints was going to add his name to the list. It could be taking his own life as he lay partly in the sand and partly across the comforting lap of the aborigine woman.

The Aussie tipped another shot into Dover's mouth. He gagged and squirmed deeper into the hug of the female. He wanted to stay there, but the Aussie reached to help. As they helped him stand, he pressed his lips against her dirt-encrusted cheek before closing his eye in a futile attempt to stem the tears.